John Pearson is a well-know
His many other books inclu
Life of Ian Fleming, and hi
Timbuctoo. Pearson has ba
research; his novelization o
from 1884 to 1929 is a tellin
through an era of drastic change, bound tragically to a social structure that was crumbling.

John Pearson

The Bellamys of Eaton Place

Futura Publications Limited
A Contact Book

A Contact Book

First published in Great Britain in 1976
by Weidenfeld & Nicolson
First Futura Publications edition 1976
in association with Weidenfeld & Nicolson

ISBN 0 8600 7397 1
Printed in Great Britain by
Hazell Watson & Viney Ltd
Aylesbury, Bucks

Futura Publications Limited
110 Warner Road
Camberwell, London SE5

Contents

To C. K. P. with love

Author's Preface

In chronicling this saga of the Bellamy family I have been more fortunate than most family historians in the help I have been accorded by surviving relatives and by the heirs of those who knew them intimately. It would be impossible to list all who have helped in my researches. Several of those who gave most freely of their assistance and their time did so upon the express understanding that they remain anonymous. Such wishes I must naturally respect.

At the same time I feel that I must record here something of my gratitude to several people without whose active sympathy and help this book would never have been possible. My foremost thanks must go to the late Elizabeth Wallace, *née* Bellamy, of New York, and I would like to pay a personal tribute here to the memory of this most charming and civilised of friends.

Before her death in 1967, at the age of eighty, she had already foreseen something of the present widespread interest in her family. A very private person herself, she would undoubtedly have liked much about her family to remain private too. But she appreciated that this could not be. Rather than attempt to censor or distort the facts, she decided that the wisest course was to have the whole story of her family set down, as she put it, "warts and all and once and for all." It is only now that I realise just how much I owe to the intelligence and extraordinary memory of this remarkable old lady, the last survivor of the Bellamys who form the subject of my book.

During the time I knew her she would often talk about her childhood, the holidays she had at Southwold and the daily routine at 165 Eaton Place. Her memory was remarkable, and it is primarily to her that I owe much of the *inside* story of the family—the feuds and loves and disappointments that made up their lives. She also gave me access to her own invaluable collection of letters from members of her family, and in particular from her mother, the late Lady Marjorie Bellamy. Again she left it entirely to my discretion how much of their contents—often of a highly personal nature—I revealed. In a few cases, when living persons might still be caused distress, I have omitted certain details; but throughout the book I have tried to give as wide and full a picture as possible of the private life of this passionate and strong-willed human being.

I would also like to thank the late Lord Bellamy's stepson and heir, Mr. William Hamilton, for all the help he gave me, and for permission to consult Lord Bellamy's private papers, an invaluable source of information on his long and often complex political career. Similarly I must thank the curator of manuscripts in the British Museum for his help in granting me access to the Southwold Papers.

Finally I must express my gratitude to Mr. John Hawkesworth and his associates for allowing me to consult research material on the Bellamy and Southwold families which they discovered during their work on the *Upstairs, Downstairs* television series. It is rare that the historian can pay tribute to a television programme, but it is only fair to say that without Mr. Hawkesworth's efforts several key episodes in the saga of the Bellamys would have been lost to posterity.

Florence, 1975

1884

1. *Homecoming*

THERE HAD BEEN RAIN ALL MORNING, HEAVY AND UNREMITTING London rain (that natural London element), marking the end of summer and keeping all but the hardiest equestrians from their morning canter through the Park. No other city in the world is so transformed by rain as London. It becomes sodden, dour, bad-tempered—a fused mass of animals and vehicles and men jostling each other in its narrow streets—broughams, berlins and heavy carriages, smart landaus with their black hoods up, open drays and coster carts and hansom cabs, their drivers cursing at each other and the world in general.

But not in Belgravia. Somehow this one small area of London manages to keep its dignity in every sort of weather. Even on this September day with the autumn rain cascading now in torrents over Belgrave Square, the houses seemed to stand aloof from the discomforts of the rest of London. These proudly laid out squares and terraces, these regimented lines of porticos that march from Chester Street to Wilton Place, proudly proclaimed this area for what it was—an enclave carefully marked off from the rest of London, a privileged and splendid place where the new-rich (and the overflow of London's older rich) could live their London lives untainted by the cries and turbulence and suffering of the remainder of the city.

All these grand houses seemed so much part of God's own scheme of things in the eighteen-eighties that it was almost blasphemous to recall that, some sixty years before, they had been built as a speculation by a mere jobbing builder, Thomas Cubitt. Other parts of London could still boast lovelier houses—Islington's fine old brick-built terraces, Mayfair's still fashionable squares, Carlton House Terrace like some new St. Petersburg. But Belgravia's houses seemed to have something that the others lacked. Confidence? A touch of opulence? Or was it, as some critics claimed, a certain whiff of *parvenu* vulgarity? Maybe. But one thing is undeniable No other part of London offered so clear a symbol of the self-assurance and achievement of our Empire in the eighties as Belgravia—even in the rain. And in its way the same applied to the one particular house there which is the center of our story—165, Eaton Place.

On this September day the observant passer-by (sheltering, one hopes for his sake, from the rain) would have noticed something unusual about 165, something that made it stand out from its neighbours in the street. It might almost have been *new:* everything about it seemed so freshly done—the varnishing, the paintwork and the windows all so very clean—that it appeared in almost pristine state.

It was the same indoors—none of those stains and signs of scuff and wear which give a house a lived-in look: in fact, for the previous two months a small platoon of men had been at work producing this effect—plasterers and plumbers, joiners and painters and upholsterers, paper-hangers, carpet-layers. The result seemed to commend their ant-like labours. As well as newness, there was a certain solid opulence about the house. It lacked luxury but possessed something possibly more important—real comfort: bell pulls, brasswork, gas-lamp fittings all of the finest quality, an impressive burgundy-and-emerald-coloured Wilton on the stairs, dark green acanthus-patterned paper in the hall making the entrance seem a good deal grander than it really was.

Clearly, a lot of money had been spent on these renovations, but the house lacked that vital something that can come only from actual habitation. There was as yet no sense of its reflecting any single personality, although various hands had obviously tried to give it character.

Family portraits had already been hung in the drawing room—not very good ones, but dignified and dark and forbidding: an angry-looking eighteenth-century general with an extraordinary nose, a very *décolleté* shepherdess (school of Romney, Emma Hamilton period) with quite alarming auburn curls and the suspicion of a squint, a frowning baronet against a thunderous sky. There was a good chandelier (Waterford?), a trifle overlarge, and the furniture looked exactly what it was—various fine, old-fashioned family pieces taken from store and placed where they seemed to fit.

One would have enjoyed the chance of wandering at will throughout the house, seeing exactly how the kitchen was equipped (always revealing), inspecting the servants' quarters just beneath the roof, risking a quick peep into the bedrooms. But this wasn't possible. The pretty brass clock in the hall had just struck three, and like an alarm bell it had brought people scurrying through the house. A young man with a very fresh complexion clad in a beautifully pressed black town suit was shouting orders.

"Alice, where are you, girl? Here, this instant!" It was a very Scottish voice, the Highland accent hard as granite.

"Yes, Mr. 'Udson?" replied a white-faced, wide-eyed girl with the starched white cap and black ribbons of a parlourmaid.

"The fire, Alice, in the drawing room."

"Fire, Mr. 'Udson? What's on fire?"

"Nothing's on fire, you stupid girl. That's just the point. It should be, Alice. It *should* be. The coal fire in the grate. It's your responsibility. They will be here any minute, and yon fire's scarcely smouldering."

"But, Mr. 'Udson, who wants a blazing fire, 'ere in September? It'll make them poor things wilt, an' no mistake."

"Do as you're told, girl, and *don't argue with your betters*. They've been abroad and they will feel the cold. Besides, on a day like this it will make the house a shade more welcoming. Oh, and Alice—one last word with you, if you please."

"Mr. 'Udson?"

"I trust that from the moment the new master and mistress enter the house this afternoon, you'll be remembering your place. For I am counting on you to set an example to the remainder of the staff—particularly the younger females. Please make them understand that I will tolerate no nonsense. I will be just but firm. We will start as we intend to continue. I will have this residence functioning like clockwork."

The girl nodded and he continued more confidingly, "Southwold's a very different place from this, Alice. A different world. And each of us must make an effort to dismiss our memories of Southwold from our minds. Both of us know of things that happened there that are best forgotten. We must see that the young couple coming here today are free to live their lives exactly as they like. It won't be easy for them, but we must see that the troubles of the past don't worry them."

The girl nodded again, and, encouraged by these confidences about her betters, asked, "I know Lady Marjorie, *and* her mother. I should, 'aving lived at Southwold all my life. But what about 'im, Mr. 'Udson? What's 'e like?"

"Him, Alice! HIM! I take it you're refering to Mr. Richard Bellamy, M.P. He is the master. And whatever you may or may not have heard about him in the past, it is my clear intention that he gets *all* of the respect which he deserves. Is that plain, girl? No gossiping below stairs. No tittle-tattling among the younger girls. Anyone I catch at it will get her notice instantly. The master has a right to total loyalty from all who serve him. And that is what he'll get, no more, but certainly no less."

Alice disappeared, but a few minutes later she was back, this time with four other maids and two footmen, both in livery. They lined up facing the front door, waiting. They were soon joined by a determined little woman in her middle twenties wearing an impressive dress of brown bombazine. Her name was Kate Bridges, and despite her show of dignity she was not feeling quite as confident as she appeared. For this was her first day of her appointment as cook with the family. Indeed, talk of "appointment" was in itself still premature, for Kate Bridges was very much "on approval" and aware of it.

Another cook, old Mrs. Hemmings, had been all set to come, but her rheumatics made her decide at the last minute to stay in the country instead. In this crisis Mrs. Petifor at Southwold had suggested young Kate Bridges, who had already worked several years in the Southwold kitchens. Perhaps she lacked experience as a cook in charge of a kitchen of her own, but Mrs. Petifor thought she should have her chance. Kate had the makings of a first-class cook and was "a veritable treasure." The truth of this remained still to be seen, but she had managed to impress on everyone the importance of her calling. Her kitchen was already thoroughly in order—pans scoured, range reblacked, copper dishes gleaming—and she had had a word with Hudson, who had agreed, reluctantly at first, but wisely, that she would be addressed by one and all, not as "Kate" but as

"Mrs. Bridges." (Hudson realised quite well that no self-respecting cook could be called "Miss Bridges.")

For a while there was silence in the hall, the particular strained silence of servants on their best behaviour. Then Hudson walked solemnly down the stairs, nodded distantly to Mrs. Bridges (none of the others rated an acknowledgment), and took up his position at the far end of the line.

"Any minute now, Mrs. Bridges," he observed, and then, ignoring the hall clock, he took out his own half-hunter, opened it judiciously (as if it contained some esoteric source of time), consulted it, then shook his head.

"Twelve minutes late. I don't know what the boat train's coming to."

"That's what you get with *foreign* trains," sniffed Mrs. Bridges.

"Not so," said Hudson in the accents of a man who valued justice in such matters. "I took the liberty of personally inquiring of the station master at Victoria just before luncheon and he assured me then that the train from Biarritz was right on time. I can't think . . ."

But at this point there was a clatter of hooves from the street outside and the excited cry of Tom the boot-boy, who had been stationed at an upstairs window.

"They're 'ere, Mr. 'Udson!"

A Victoria had drawn up outside the house—perhaps not the *grandest* coach in which a gentleman of fashion could wish to travel with a lady, but certainly the most elegant: and this one was beautifully maintained, a perfect work of art, with its arching pair of greys, its glass-like harness and its coachwork gleaming. Two outriders, "Tigers," well-built fellows in brown livery, stood at the rear, and on the door there was the elaborate coat of arms—not often seen in London now—of the griffon and the eagle and the lion, the three heraldic beasts which the Southwold family have carried since the Norman Conquest.

The coachman, an aged giant of a man in chestnut-coloured greatcoat, had reined in the horses, but the coach remained rocking slightly on its springs. One of the Tigers steadied it whilst the other—large green umbrella held against the rain—opened the door.

A young man stepped out, tall, almost handsome in a fresh-faced way, but looking distinctly apprehensive under his beautifully brushed silk hat, as if such extreme stylishness, such old-world elegance, was not entirely for him. (Nevertheless, it would have been hard to fault the cut of his pale grey morning coat or the set of his cravat.)

Old Lady Dunamore, the frail, ancient, drunken Irish peeress in the house next door, had been waiting, birdlike, half the morning and now witnessed the arrival. She took a widow's interest in the young man's looks.

"Seems like a well-set-up young fellow," she said to her friend, old Lady Meikeljohn. "Lucky to get a man like that these days, if you ask me."

But Lady M. was more romantic. "It's the dear bride I want to see. Ah, here she comes, pretty as a picture."

"Pretty indeed! She's just like her mother, and I remember *her* when she was married. All the Southwold women are the same. She'll go the same way, mark my words. Poor young fellow—I don't envy him."

"Hush, Bridie," said the other great old lady. "Look, she's coming now!"

A small, neat shoe, a shimmering of champagne-coloured silk, and, sure enough, the bride appeared, pausing a moment in the rain to glance up at her new home from beneath her small confection of a hat. She must have known that half the street was watching her, but unlike her husband showed no sign of nervousness. She smiled at him (love, happiness, or triumph?), then took his arm and walked in state across the pavement, the green umbrella high above her.

As they reached the steps the front door opened. Hudson stood there to greet them. As he drew back there was some slight confusion over who should enter first. The young man faltered, like an actor who forgets his lines, then, recalling them, bent forward, put his arm around her, and a shade unsteadily, his silk hat tilted at a very rakish angle, carried his bride across the threshold.

This is, of course, the moment that the servants love and housemaids dream of. There was an audible "Ah!" from several of them, and for the next few minutes everybody in the hall was living a sort of fairytale—Hudson beaming, Mrs. Bridges smiling and repeating "Well I never," and the maids curtseying. The only person who seemed quite immune to all this sentiment was the small, sharp-faced woman in a black holland dress who had followed in the shadow of the bride. This was Roberts, her personal maid, and she had been up all night on the train from France. But her bad humour passed unnoticed as the introductions followed.

These were conducted by the bride and done with considerable charm and ease. Until six weeks before she had been Lady Marjorie Talbot-Cary, Lord Southwold's only daughter, and she undoubtedly possessed the true aristocrat's supposed ability to get on with the servants.

"Hudson, how *good* to see you and to have you as our butler"—this with a smile and such apparent warmth that the young Angus Hudson nearly passed away with loyal pleasure.

"And this is my husband, Mr. Richard Bellamy. I know that you'll look after him."

"Indeed I will, your ladyship."

Richard Bellamy seemed still rather less at ease than his wife, and shook hands somewhat formally with Hudson.

"I gather that you'll also be valeting for me, Hudson."

"Such is my honour, sir."

Richard could think of nothing suitable to say to this, but was saved by his wife, who had noticed a familiar face among the housemaids.

"Alice!" she exclaimed, as if her presence were a genuine surprise. "How lovely to have someone here from Southwold to prevent my getting homesick," and Alice blushed with happiness.

Then finally it was Mrs. Bridges' turn, and Hudson tactfully explained how she had come at such short notice and how well she was coping. Mrs. Bridges preened herself at this.

"I'll do my best, I'm sure, your ladyship. Good honest food's my motto. In my opinion a body can't have too much of it."

"I'm sure one can't," said Marjorie. And then, quite suddenly, the politenesses were over and, like some machine that starts to function, normal life began in 165.

"Hudson," said Marjorie, in the tone of voice that she would use with him for the remainder of her life, "we shall take tea in the drawing room at four. And afterwards perhaps we could discuss the arrangements for the day. I take it Mrs. Bridges has dinner satisfactorily in hand."

"Certainly, my lady."

"Oh, and Hudson."

"Yes, m'lady?"

"Was there any message from my mother?"

None, m'lady, I'm afraid. But Lord Southwold sent the flowers that are in the bedroom. Most anxious his lordship was that you'd have the tuberoses when you came. He also sent the champagne and the claret for this evening with his compliments to Mr. Bellamy."

And so the Bellamys began their life in 165. Few people witnessing this scene, or hearing these somewhat stilted but assured exchanges, could have suspected the extraordinary happenings that had brought them here. Theirs had been the stormiest courtship of the year, but their behaviour gave no hint of the battle it had been—or of the long wars that lay ahead.

1883

2. Scandal in a Champagne Glass

LIKE ALL THE BEST ROMANCES, THEIRS HAD BEGUN IN PARIS IN THE spring—the spring of 1883. It was a vintage year to fall in love: Gounod was still conducting at the Opéra, Offenbach had set the whole of Paris dancing to his music, whilst at the Bal Musette and all the other houses of Montmartre there was the *can-can* with its message that all that mattered now was love and youth and pleasure. Yet at the time their love seemed so improbable—and came so unexpectedly—that it caused something of a scandal, and turned Richard Bellamy into what he emphatically was not—a high romantic character.

For by nature he was a careful, rather prudent figure at the time, ambitious certainly, but with a strong hold on his emotions and a keen eye on his future—quite the last person anyone would choose to carry off the daughter of a belted earl and jettison his future in the process.

He was just twenty-seven, a career diplomat, and for the previous two years he had been second secretary with the British Embassy, thus enjoying the rare privilege of working in one of the loveliest buildings in the whole of Paris, the old Hôtel de Charost in the Rue du Faubourg St. Honoré, once owned by Pauline Bonaparte. And since the Revolution the home of the British Embassy. Richard enjoyed this touch of splendour in his life.

At this time there were still two sorts of diplomat—those with money (and generally a noble name) and those who did the work. Richard was in the second category. Among the former he had a reputation as a very bright young man indeed, but as someone scathingly remarked, "he was not otherwise too unpleasant."

This rather summed him up. He had a certain blandness in those days, a way of smiling condescendingly and appearing to agree with everyone he met. People thought him, quite correctly, something of an intellectual snob. Among his English colleagues he was also seen as something of an oddity, a sort of poor boy who had improbably made good, and it amused him to play up to this. In fact he was not all that poor, nor were his origins anything like as humble as they were later rumoured. (Nor, for that matter, was there any real mystery, as the rumour-mongers had it, to his family—certainly nothing in the least discreditable in his paternity to account for the swiftness of his rise in his profession.) Like Clive and Nelson, he was the product of a country rectory, and he had received his education at Rugby. He was on a scholarship and luckily the school was gentler than in Tom Brown's school days. He was never to inherit any money from his parents: his father, the Reverened James Bellamy—an unworldly man and a distinguished amateur Latin scholar in his way—had died just before his son went up to Oxford on a scholarship. What money was around naturally had to go on supporting the widow and the elder brother, Arthur, who was still at medical school.

But none of this had ever caused Richard what could honestly be described as hardship. At Rugby he had already been an outstanding scholar, and he had made his way by a sort of easy brilliance, entering Magdalen College, Oxford, on a classics scholarship in 1874 and then taking most of the University classics prizes.

Magdalen, the home of the fastest, richest set of idle and effete young men in Oxford, would hardly have appeared the place for somebody like Richard Bellamy, but this never worried him. He was a great adapter and the antics of his social betters never concerned him. Just a few years before, young Henry Chaplin, the richest undergraduate in England, had made a habit of coming into chapel in his hunting pink, and whilst Richard was still there most Oxford men who could afford it would maintain a hunter and a mistress in the town. Richard merely smiled. His time would come. He had already set his sights upon the Diplomatic Service, which had been opened to young men of talent by the reforms of the late sixties.

His inevitable double first strengthened his intellectual arrogance (which like most double firsts he never really lost) and he sailed through the competitive examination and into the Diplomatic with the same effortless superiority he had shown with everything he had done since childhood.

All this had earned him his uncomfortable reputation, but, strange as it may seem, he really was somewhat indolent and soft at heart.

Wasn't it Metternich who said that diplomacy was the ideal world for idle clever men? He would have appreciated the up-and-coming Richard Bellamy. Others did too, particularly Cartwright, our ambassador in Paris and Richard's chief; this was the famous old Lord Cartwright of the *Memoirs,* himself a near-contemporary of Talleyrand and Metternich, who had won his diplomatic spurs at the Congress of Vienna and who by now was known as "the Grand Old Fox of English Diplomacy." He was wise, worldly and had once been very wicked. Now he was old and merely self-indulgent. Paris was something of a sinecure for him and he enjoyed the pleasures of the city. But he also still enjoyed spotting talent, and he took to Richard Bellamy at once and maintained that he had one of the sharpest brains of any of the young men in his embassy. Also, like many idle men, Richard had learned the trick of picking on the work that really mattered and finishing it quickly. Cartwright was impressed by this, and, thanks to his backing, Richard had already reached the rank of second secretary by the early age of twenty-six—and great things were predicted for him.

Youthful promise—infallible recipe for tempting fate! Richard had shown it, and was now to reap the consequences: which began one April evening when the Ambassador summoned him to his office for an informal chat over a glass of very good champagne.

For a comparatively humble and self-made man, Richard had quite a taste for good champagne, as he also had for most of the good things of life. His excellency, noted gourmet and good liver, had found this out and enjoyed indulging him. For a while they chatted on about the business of the Embassy, but his excellency didn't really feel like business at this time of day. A shaggy giant of a man with a face like that of a battered Neptune, he leaned back in his gilt-and-plush armchair, lit a slim Martinique cheroot, and started on a story. His excellency's stories—like his indiscretions, which were frequently malicious but never accidental—were notorious.

"Richard, dear boy, I take it that you've heard about my cousin, the present—and for your ears only I would add, the quite appalling—Lady Southwold?" Richard replied that he had heard about the lady.

"Heard, Richard? More precision, please. *What* have you heard?"

"That she is very rich."

Cartwright nodded. He was having trouble with his cheroot now and seemed preoccupied. "Go on."

"And powerful."

Again Cartwright nodded.

"And that her husband, the Earl of Southwold, owns one of the oldest titles in the country and is one of the more colourful members of the House of Lords."

"You could call him that. I'd probably just say that he was mad, but that would be ungenerous, and Southwold is a clever fellow in his way. The only really silly thing he ever did was marry my outrageous cousin. You know, it wasn't all that long ago that they were tipping him to succeed Disraeli, and if it weren't for her it might have happened. The Party trusts him and the people love him, with his Derby winners and his mistresses. Horse-flesh and whores'-flesh, the soundest basis for success in English politics; but as I say, his wife has put a stop to that. You must have heard about the unfortunate business with our plump, pleasure-loving friend, the Prince of Wales?"

Richard had heard several versions of the famous Southwold *gaffe*, but he also knew his excellency would enjoy retelling it. He shook his head.

"You haven't? My dear boy, where do you spend your idle hours?"

By now his excellency had abandoned his first cheroot and, throwing it towards the waste-paper basket—and missing—paused to select another. This time he was luckier and he leaned back, grunting, in his huge armchair and blew smoke rings up towards the Boucher Venus on the ceiling.

"It must be—how time flies!—three years ago now. Bertie—His Royal Highness—was a great old friend of Southwold's. In the sixties they were both young swells and used to chase around the town together. Southwold was always in and out of Marlborough House and they were both involved in the Nellie Jordan business— but that's another story. Despite all this, H.R.H. had never been to stay at Southwold. He had clearly heard enough of Lady Southwold to steer clear—and anyhow, Southwold is rather off the beaten track. But this annoyed my cousin, naturally. She is a jealous woman at the best of times and felt out of things. All her grand friends were having Bertie as a weekend guest, so why wasn't she? She kept inviting him, and finally—since Bertie is the kindest man on earth when it comes to giving pleasure—he agreed to come. During Goodwood Week, what's more. Southwold's a fair old drive from Goodwood, so you can see the favour he was doing the good lady."

At this point his excellency paused to give himself some more champagne. He looked a happy man and the cheroot was slowly filling the big gold-and-white *salon* with a blue haze and the aroma of smouldering exotic vegetation.

"Sure you won't have one?" he said to Richard, who shook his head.

"Bismarck always said that no man should think of dying until he had smoked a hundred thousand good cigars—but to get back to the story: Bertie, as you may, but probably don't, recall, was very *engagé* about this time with pretty Emily FitzAlban and as usual the private secretary, Knollys, followed standing orders and arranged for *la FitzAlban* to be invited out to Southwold also for the weekend. Our Bertie, after all, could hardly be expected to endure the *longueurs* of a whole weekend at Southwold without a little of his favourite self-indulgence. Emily was naturally invited *sans mari,* but my precious cousin thought this arrangement rather odd. In her world nobody invites a married lady without a husband. Quite unthinkable. So off her own bat she proceeded to invite FitzAlban too.

"You can imagine the rest. Rather funny, when one thinks about it now, but at the time it did create the most almighty stink. Midnight strikes. Bridge is finishing and as usual all the servants have been safely packed off to bed. H.R.H. rises, bids the company goodnight, goes to his room, and then, after a decent interval, comes waddling along the corridor in dressing gown to find his lady-love. Opens bedroom door, gropes forward in the dark, and finds her there in bed—*plus husband!*"

At this point his excellency found the whole idea so funny that he all but choked with laughter and cigar smoke and champagne, and sat there wheezing for a while before continuing.

"My, what a row! A simply marvellous to-do! You can imagine it for yourself. Billie FitzAlban is threatening his future sovereign to a duel, and Bertie, bless his heart, is threatening to leave immediately.

Billie, of course, is soon persuaded to see sense. Didn't they make the dear chap governor of Canada? Or was it Singapore? Or both? He deserved them both, poor Billy, with that wife of his. But Lady Southwold! *That* was another thing altogether, I can tell you. No one could hush *her* up, and at one stage she was threatening to tell all to the press unless she received a full apology from H.R.H. in *writing*."

"Well, of course, in the end even she saw sense, but by then the damage had been done. She was completely out of smart society for good. And, most unfairly, Southwold too got blamed. That's when he withdrew from politics as well as from society."

The Ambassador shook his ancient head, sadly now.

"A dreadful woman, a real gorgon of a woman, a man-destroying woman."

He sipped consolingly at his champagne, then smiled his shaggy, sea-god's smile at Richard.

"You'll have your work cut out looking after her when she arrives next Tuesday. But at least I've warned you."

Midday, the Gare du Nord: the great new terminus still unfinished (trouble with O'Higgins, the Dublin contractor who had just succumbed to bankruptcy and drink and typhoid almost simultaneously) and builders' men and rubbish everywhere, ladders and barrows, hoists and great stacks of masonry making the place look more like a demolition site than Paris's great international terminal. At the same time, hideous confusion caused by the company's decision to use it as it is. The result, a sort of Piranesiesque Inferno, with milling, shouting crowds against a background of steam, smoke and trumpeting black locomotives. Fiacres jammed the courtyard, porters in blue jackets tried to bludgeon their barrows through the crowds, and somewhere in the midst of all this chaos, the train from Calais was due any moment.

Richard had done his best to cushion the distinguished guest's arrival. The Ambassador's own coach was waiting near the platform (the coachman and two hefty ostlers were attempting to restrain the frightened horses). At the discreet suggestion of the Ambassador, Richard was resplendent in full diplomatic dress—white gloves, gold-frogged black tunic, slim-braided trousers. He felt conspicuous and over-dressed and as he tried to hold on to his position in the jostling crowd he silently cursed his excellency and his confounded sense of humour.

"It will do you good to have a deal with the lady," he had said at the conclusion of the interview. "A real test of your diplomatic skill." And he had gone on to explain that Lady Southwold was coming out to Paris to arrange for the marriage of her daughter, Marjorie, to a French duke. For since the Southwold *gaffe,* and the family's virtual ostracism by polite society in England, no noble English bachelor would have dreamt of putting himself so totally out of favour with the Prince of Wales as to marry a Southwold.

"Which duke will have the honour?" Richard had asked.

"The Duke d'Amboise," his excellency had replied with a malicious smile.

"But that's impossible, sir. Amboise is one of the most notorious . . ."

"Precisely, my dear boy. Everybody knows about the Duke—except for Lady Southwold. Quite typical, of course. The Lady Southwolds of this world would not acknowledge that such men exist. She has made up her mind that her daughter will become the Duchess d'Amboise—and that, I'm afraid, is that."

"Poor girl," said Richard.

"Oh, I don't know," said the one-time friend of Talleyrand, grey eyes glinting under ancient eyebrows. "Presumably the Duke will have a go at fathering an heir upon her—unpleasant though this probably will be for both of them. And if he can't, then others will. So she'll have children then, as well as lovers, and the château, which is glorious, and there are big estates along the Loire and in the South. No, Richard, you can spare your tears for our little Duchess."

"Then how are we involved in all this?" Richard asked. It was his excellency's turn to groan.

"As my cousin and a distinguished lady in her own right, Lady Southwold naturally expects that she and her daughter should stay here in the Embassy. And, God help me, there isn't much that I can do about it. I'll even have to give a ball here in their honour. And just to make it worse, Southwold himself is wisely keeping out of it. He is in England, hunting. And you, my boy, will have to take his place. Consider yourself simply *in loco parentis* to the lovely Lady Marjorie. And just one word of warning. No incest, please; that would cause such a lot of trouble."

The sudden screeching of a locomotive whistle told Richard that the Calais train was coming. The horses bucked and whinnied. Steam hissed and billowed, porters shouted, and with a clang and shuddering of iron the soot-black engine grunted to a halt. Then the great rush started. Doors were flung open, hotel touts descended on the weary passengers, and friends and relatives were kissing and embracing.

Richard did his best to be aloof and very English. He had no idea how to find Lady Southwold in all this chaos, but he reasoned that, provided he stayed by the coach with its royal coat of arms, her ladyship would finally find him: which was exactly what occurred.

"Young man!"—this in the sort of voice normally employed on under-gardeners and errant office-boys. "Is the Ambassador not here in person?"

Richard turned to see one of the most fearsome faces he had ever witnessed. It was not ugly—rather the reverse. In her young days Lady Southwold had been one of the most celebrated beauties of her time, and much of the basis of her beauty still remained—the upright carriage (was that backbone made of steel?), the remorseless profile with its geometry scarcely touched by time, and the full bosom which in any other woman might have been called voluptuous. But all these elements of what had once been beauty had been transformed by a glaring wilfulness into a heartless parody of beauty. The eyes, which were extremely large and greenish-grey, had become just a shade protuberant and stared with a sort of self-indulgent fury; the mouth, once large and generous, had grown thin and wide with unsuppressed determination. She wore a purple dress, and from beneath a purple hat tumbled the abundant curls of a bright red wig.

Richard, not normally put out by anyone, could only try to stammer some excuse for the Ambassador. It was totally ignored.

"Disgraceful. Quite disgraceful. He should be here to do his duty. Still, he needn't think he'll get away with it. I shall inform Her Majesty. I shall make sure that she at any rate knows how her servants can behave to ladies when they need them."

"Mother," said a voice. "Perhaps this gentleman could be doing something about our luggage."

"Luggage, Marjorie! There are more important things than luggage at a time like this. There are principles at stake."

But principles or no, Richard had seen his chance to do something practical and escape her ladyship's iron tongue. With some efficiency he ordered off a footman to sort out the Southwold luggage. A frightened-looking lady's maid of Lady Southwold's went with them, and with arrangements made, Richard walked back towards his guests. Lady Southwold was already in the coach but behind her, still standing on the platform, was the most beautiful girl he'd ever seen.

There was a certain echo, in the face, of Lady Southwold—the same classic profile, the same colouring, and the same clear line across the brow. But whereas with Lady Southwold all these features had become grotesque, here they retained a sort of virginal perfection. She was extremely slim and appeared younger than she was. She wore a blue-and-white-silk dress, and there on the platform of the Gare du Nord, against the background of that shouting, vulgar, garlic-smelling crowd, she seemed a fairytale princess in miniature.

Richard bowed. At that moment and with all that noise there seemed little else that he could do. The princess smiled in return, a faint northern smile.

"I'm Marjorie Talbot-Cary," she said somewhat primly.

"And I am Richard Bellamy."

Years later Richard would always say that this was the moment—the one moment in his life—when he fell truly, utterly, and helplessly in love. But did he really? How can one ever tell with anything as strange and as mysterious as love, especially a love like his, which came to dominate his life and rule it totally? There is a clear temptation to proclaim, "At such-and-such a time I fell in love and that was that!" But if this really did occur with Richard on the platform of the Gare du Nord, it must have been a species of unconscious love, an almost fleeting recognition of desire or adoration, call it what you will, to which he could subsequently refer as an amorous point of reference.

For the quite simple truth is that during these crucial minutes of his life Richard had far too many worries on his mind to be able to devote himself to any luxury as single-minded as falling in love. There was the business of instructing the coachman how to battle safely through the crush of vehicles and bring his charges back to the Embassy without loss of dignity or comfort. There was the sheer discomfort of his uniform (the trousers in particular, which, like most diplomats' ceremonial trousers, were far too tight). And above all, of course, there was Lady Southwold. Richard sat opposite that lady as her elephantine ego continued to assert itself. In such pained circumstances he had no chance of more than an occasional glimpse a fleeting glance towards the overshadowed and demure young girl who sat beside him.

"Disgusting city," her ladyship proclaimed as they swept past the Pont Royale and entered the splendid concourse of the Rue de Rivoli. Before them was the great palace of the Louvre, gilded and gleaming and the fountains playing. The gardens of the Tuileries were coming into leaf; beyond them lay the Seine.

"I refuse to be impressed," she said patriotically. "Cheltenham's far nicer, don't you think, young man?"

Richard, good diplomat though he was, found this a little difficult to take. "The Palace of the Louvre is generally considered one of the finest things in Paris," he replied politely.

Lady Southwold sniffed. "Oh," she said. "Oh, I see. So you're infected too by all these foreign habits. You must watch out, young man. One simply cannot be too careful," she added darkly.

He did his best, despite this warning, to point out some of the sights of Paris as the Ambassador's fine carriage with its pair of greys bowled its way on towards the Champs Élysées. Marjorie appreciated her first sight of this city she would soon inhabit, and her excitement—simple, girlish as it was—reminded Richard of her fate; to his surprise he suddenly felt angry at the thought of her linked with that ageing pederast, the Duc d'Amboise. He also felt obscurely jealous of that platoon of future lovers whom Lord Cartwright had predicted for her. As he thought of this he wondered how the xenophobic Lady Southwold could possibly inflict a fate like this upon her daughter. From this moment dates his positive dislike of her.

The next few days became a time of heaven and hell for Richard Bellamy. Hell centered irresistibly around Lady Southwold, heaven around her daughter; and as might have been expected, there was far more of the former than the latter. Everything, or almost everything, was wrong where Lady Southwold was concerned—the suite of rooms which Cartwright had allotted her within the Embassy, the sanitary arrangements, even the food at dinner. Her powers of complaint rose to the dizzy heights of genius, and Richard was there to bear the brunt of them.

Within two minutes of entering her apartment she had summoned him and he found her pointing icily towards a painting on the wall.

"*What* is that doing here?" she asked.

Slightly puzzled, Richard looked at a painting of nymphs and shepherds languishing wistfully in a wooded clearing. It was from Cartwright's own considerable collection of French eighteenth-century paintings.

"It is a Fragonard, your ladyship," said Richard.

"It is an obscenity," said Lady Southwold. "Remove it instantly."

There was trouble too about the introductions she had. She was outraged that Amboise failed to appear that evening and made quite a scene of this at dinner. Luckily the Ambassador was there to deal with it.

"His grace requested me to give you his apologies, but he is hunting."

"At this time of night?"

"That, madame, is when he generally does," said Cartwright drily.

On only one occasion did her ladyship show just the faintest personal interest in Richard.

"And *which* of the Bellamys are *you?*" she asked him after dinner.

He replied that his father was a Norfolk rector.

"Oh," said Lady Southwold.

But like some alternating image of Virtue linked irresistibly to Vice, there was Lady Marjorie. She was cool, elegant and curiously untouched, both by her mother and by the fate that lay in store for her. As Richard watched her after dinner, sitting so prettily and laughing so unreservedly at one of Cartwright's jokes (even Lady Southwold smiled), Richard found himself wondering just how intelligent she really was. Was she so clever that she could discount everything around her, or so stupid that it did not matter? He went to bed that night without deciding.

Nor did he find the answer next day, although his duties meant that he had to spend some time with her. She seemed, if not devoted, at least dutiful and uncomplaining with her mother; and on the one occasion when he had a chance to sound her out upon her marriage she seemed as down-to-earth about it all as if he had asked her whether a pair of shoes would fit or a new dress suit her.

He asked her if she minded being promised to a man whom she had never met, and her reply had more than a touch of Lady Southwold in it.

"Mind, Mr. Bellamy? But why *should* I mind? My parents have arranged it for my own well-being. They have considerable experience of the world, so I see no earthly reason why it should not succeed."

Even Richard, who was becoming quite besotted by her beauty, could find no answer against that.

Perhaps it was her unattainability that attracted him. Certainly she was totally unlike any other woman he had known. Not that his experience of women was that limited. Priggish he may have been, but this had not stopped him from enjoying the delights of female company. There had been village girls in Norfolk, bored diplomatic wives in Paris, occasional ladies of the town, and at the moment there was Juliette. She was in many ways the ideal mistress for a man like him—understanding, skilled in love, and beautiful, undoubtedly quite beautiful in her own heavy, peasant way. There was a painter who employed her as a model—a funny, dark, excitable young man called Degas—although Richard didn't like his pictures, saying quite rightly that they never did her justice. He had occasional doubts about the fellow, wondering sometimes whether he should be concerned about those portraits of his mistress in the bath. But, as he told himself, France was France and Juliette was certainly devoted to her *beau diplomate,* as she called him. Until now he had always been delighted with her. She kept house for him in their apartment off the Rue Jacob, and she was warm and passionate and undemanding. But suddenly Richard found her—what did he find her? He asked himself this very question the first evening after meeting Lady Marjorie. Boring? How could this generous woman whom he lived with possibly be boring? Coarse? Perish the suggestion! Hardly ladylike enough for a rising second secretary? Come now, Richard Bellamy had faults, but snobbishness like this was not among them.

But in fact—although he could hardly acknowledge them—all these defects *did* quite suddenly appear in Juliette once he set eyes on Marjorie. And since he could not acknowledge them, he felt guilty and morose when in his mistress' company.

The ball Lord Cartwright had so dreaded giving duly took place some four days after the Southwolds' arrival. It was a ravishing affair, for Cartwright, much as he might protest his distaste for it all, actually enjoyed these glittering events, and such was his taste and wealth and reputation that everyone in Paris who was anyone—and many who were not—clamoured for invitations. There were the notorious

Princesse de Noailles (currently rumoured to be the mistress of *both* Dumas and the Prince de Galles) and her banker husband, the most famous dandy in the whole of Paris. Their being there together was in itself quite an event. There were countless Rothschilds and the President of France. There were the De Brantes, who owned half Normandy, and the Comte de Limousin, who was said to be a woman. The great actress Réjane made a brief but dramatic entry. Her rival, Bernhardt, made an equally dramatic absence. The champagne flowed, as it did in those days only in the British Embassy, and the orchestra was directed by the great Boieldieu of the Paris Opéra. And all of this in order that Lord Southwold's daughter should be suitably introduced to her future husband. She took it very well: indeed, Richard was amazed at just how well. She wore a ball dress of shimmering white silk which looked, as he said afterwards, "like a waterfall of stars." She seemed as young as ever, perhaps even younger tonight. Richard's sentimental heart was touched at the mere sight of her, for there was something so defenceless and so lonely in that fragile face against that cynical and worldly throng. She looked anxious and wide-eyed as she walked among them all, on Richard's arm (he had that honour), to meet her fate. At the same time she showed the strength and iron will of her Southwold ancestors. There was no cowardice, no flinching, even when she reached the man she was to marry and Richard said solemnly, "Your grace, I have the honour to present to you the Lady Marjorie, daughter of the Earl of Southwold."

The music stopped. A hush, then an excited murmur came from the crowd as Marjorie, ivory-pale, faltered, then made her curtsy before the Duke.

Well might she have faltered, for his grace was not a pretty sight. Generations of inbreeding, years of indelicate excess, had finally produced this over-honoured jelly of a man. He was immensely fat—a barrel, a balloon—and had the curiously expressionless face of a young Silenus. But at the same time there was a sort of gloating charm as he surveyed her. (Was it possible, Richard asked himself, that he desired her?) When he spoke his voice was high-pitched, like a eunuch's.

"The honour is entirely mine," he said, "to see such beauty and—ahem—such purity." He bowed, or rather wobbled in Marjorie's direction, then took her hand and raised it to his lips. In Richard's eyes, Marjorie had never been as lovely as she was then, at the moment she confronted her fate, her Beast.

After that evening Richard's relationship with Marjorie changed. She had her duty to perform, he had his, and their former closeness seemed forgotten. Richard was still her guardian—or "her stud-groom," as he ruefully described himself to Cartwright—in the days that followed, and he performed his duties scrupulously and well: he was on hand to take her to the grand ball in her honour at the Presidential Palace, he accompanied her to Maxim's and the Grand Véfour, and she was on his arm when she entered the reception at the Palais d'Amboise. This enormous mansion off the Champs Élysées was *en fête* that night, with great *flambeaux* blazing round the court-yard and footmen in eighteenth-century dress on every stair, and beneath a galaxy of chandeliers there was a banquet cooked by the finest chefs in Paris. The real purpose of the evening was to present Marjorie to Paris and the Amboise family as their future Duchess, and Amboise relatives had been dragged from the distant provinces, summoned from deathbeds and dower-houses especially to meet her.

What a collection they all were: old crones ablaze with diamonds, old generals dithering with drink, young matrons who were already exhibiting the inherited misfortunes of their line. Normally Richard would have been silently amused and enjoyed his dinner, but tonight he was in misery. To make matters worse, he had been seated next to Lady Southwold, who at this point of triumph and success was almost affable with him. She wore the Southwold diamonds and appeared thinner—and her wig redder—than before.

"Such a *good* couple I think they make, don't you, Bellamy," she said, nodding towards the Duke and future Duchess where they were sitting at the head of the table.

"A *mature* man is so much what Marjorie needs. She's a mere gel, you know, and he can take her in hand."

Richard looked towards the happy couple and to his horror saw that Lady Southwold might conceivably be right. Was that a smile of lechery he saw on the Duke's fat lips? Could it be true, as some had recently been whispering, that d'Amboise was turning to females as the ultimate perversion?

That evening Richard had to wait for hours before Marjorie was ready to leave. Lady Southwold had retired already, so he was alone with Marjorie as they drove back to the Embassy through the light spring rain. She was silent, glacial, as they drove down the river, past the slumbering Bois with the bobbing carriage lamps lighting the black and silver cobbles of the road.

For the first time since Marjorie arrived Richard felt angry—no longer sorry for her. If this was how the aristocracy behaved, let them get on with it. She was one of them by temperament and breeding. Let her enjoy it, and if she ended up like her mother, so much the better! In half an hour he would be back with warm, faithful—or unfaithful—Juliette. At least they could laugh together and enjoy making love together. She and her friends might be coarse and uncultivated and unfashionable, but they were worth the whole Palais d'Amboise and *le tout Paris* together. They were healthy, honest and, unlike their betters, weren't prepared to deny their appetites and their emotions for a title or a fortune. Thank God for them!

As he was thinking this, Richard had been staring morosely through the window. Now something made him turn and look at Marjorie. Tears were streaming down her face.

"You must help me, Richard Bellamy," she said. It had always been Mr. Bellamy before, and Richard hadn't realised she knew his Christian name.

"What do you mean, ma'am?" he asked coldly.

"My name is Marjorie and I am counting on your friendship. I have no one else. Help me as a friend. I know so little of the world, but I can't go through with this. I can't, can't, can't."

She was really sobbing now, despite herself: great silent tears which racked her body. And Richard—much as he would have denied it—secretly enjoyed her suffering, if only as a lover's revenge for all the secret suffering he had endured for her. And so, perversely, he steeled himself against sympathy and found himself calmly repeating most of Cartwright's arguments in favour of the marriage—the splendid château, the distinguished name.

"And be sensible. You can please yourself once you are married. You can have lovers if you want them, children, money. You will be free to do exactly as you please."

He sounded very cold and very calm. In fact his heart was beating and his mouth was dry.

"I thought you were my friend," said Marjorie in a stifled voice.

"Your ladyship, I am. And as a friend I'm telling you that you have certain obligations to your position and you can't be too soft and squeamish. It is quite natural to feel as you do, but it is also very unimportant. Titles, land, influence—these are what count for people of your class, and if you have to give a little in return it doesn't do to moan about the bargain."

By now the carriage had reached the high gates of the Embassy. Marjorie said nothing, but as she stepped down from the carriage she gave him a look that stabbed his heart.

The Ambassador, who had brought Lady Southwold back from the reception, was still up to greet them—tall, in a long black cloak, with the rain glistening on the grey eyebrows and moustache.

When he had said goodnight to Marjorie he turned to Richard and with a sardonic, faintly mocking smile said, "Richard, dear boy, so pleased that it has all turned out so well. My sincere congratulations. Lord knows quite how you've done it but you seem even to have impressed my cousin. She must be in love with you—on the way back tonight she quite sang your praises. You'd better watch your step, my boy."

He laughed and put his arm round Richard's shoulders.

"Seriously, though, I can't tell you how grateful I am at the way you've handled things. It's all arranged, largely thanks to you. The engagement will be announced within a day or two: there are a few formalities to be settled with the lawyers, and then, thank God, we're rid of them. The marriage will take place at Amboise. And you, my boy, will always have an ally in the Southwolds and the Duke. They could be useful. Well done, well done," and after patting Richard gently on his back, the old diplomat walked up the stairs to bed.

But the night was not yet over for Richard. Juliette was at a late-night party at the Café des Artistes, and when he went to fetch her he found that, despite all the Ambassador's congratulations, he was not in the best of humours. Even when Monsieur Zola tried to joke with him, he sat scowling at his table, refusing to join in the singing which he normally enjoyed.

"What is it, Richard, trouble with women? You should be grateful—excellent material to write about. Don't brood on it—write about it. Put it all in that novel of yours, then let me have a look at it."

Richard politely thanked the fussy little man with the pince-nez and short black beard. But what could anyone like Zola ever know about his troubles? How could he ever understand?

Juliette was drinking beer and with her round pink face suddenly appeared quite blowzy. The neck, the tops of the arms—those tide-marks of all women past a certain age—were showing the encroaching marks of time. When Monsieur Degas painted her it scarcely mattered, but tonight, and after the vision he had had of Marjorie . . . When they were back in bed Richard couldn't bring himself to make love to her. She was offended but he was too tired to care; he slept restlessly and dreamed—of Marjorie and her Duke, an obscene dream with d'Amboise as a gross Priapus and Marjorie enjoying his embraces. He had to watch as they made love. Cartwright was there as well, his hoary locks crowned with vine leaves, and with each fresh contortion of the lovers he would congratulate Richard. And Lady Southwold was there, to join in the congratulations, and Réjane and the President of France.

"Well done, well done, Bellamy, well done!" they chanted, and their shouts urged on the lovers.

It was not all that easy for Richard to obtain a meeting with the Duke, particularly as he had to insist on secrecy and d'Amboise not unnaturally wanted to know why. But Richard knew d'Argenson, the *chef de protocole,* and finally obtained an audience late the following afternoon. The Duke was dressing. As Richard entered, a good-looking footman was helping him into his pale-grey britches and Richard caught a glimpse of the huge hams and of blue-veined flesh.

"Just *cinq minutes,* Monsieur Bellamy," d'Amboise muttered. "At seven I must meet *Monsieur le Président* at the Élysée, and after that I shall be seeing my *fiancée.* Whatever you have to tell me, please to be swift."

Richard was suddenly aware of the man's shrewd black eyes buried in the midst of so much flesh. D'Amboise was a self-indulgent man, and possibly a wicked one, but certainly not stupid. One of the skills that Richard had acquired as a diplomat was the ability to tell a story rapidly and to the point. It didn't take him long to spell out the gist of what Lord Cartwright and others had told him of the scandal created by Lady Southwold, Lady FitzAlban and the Prince of Wales. To his relief, the Duke did not laugh, and when he spoke the affected, high-pitched drawl had gone. It was a sharp Parisian voice that said,

"And so, Monsieur Bellamy, to be precise, you're telling me that as a result of this His Royal Highness *le Prince de Galles* has totally excluded, not merely Lady Southwold but the entire *famille Southwold,* from polite society?"

Richard nodded. "I suggest your grace should make his own inquiries. I think they will confirm that the situation is as I describe it."

The Duke stood up, breathed in, and waited as the footman laced his corsets. Finally, in a strained and slightly worried voice he said, "What you have told us seems most disturbing, Monsieur Bellamy. If it turns out to be as you have said, we shall not be ungrateful to you."

It took less than twenty-four hours for Richard's tiny germ of gossip to incubate into the full-scale fever of scandal that he wanted. Just before midday of the following morning Hunter, the chief clerk of chancery, told him that something must have happened to the Duke d'Amboise. He had apparently been taken ill and so would not be at the President's reception that same evening, where his engagement was to be announced.

"Sounds just a wee bit fishy to me," said Hunter with a wink. Richard said nothing and went off to lunch. He had scarcely returned when the Ambassador summoned him. It was the only time Richard had ever seen him looking slightly ruffled.

"What's this about the Duke d'Amboise, Richard? We were all set to have the engagement announced at tonight's presidential reception. Now Hunter tells me he has suddenly left town. It's quite unheard-of, Richard—most extraordinary behaviour. Lord only knows how Lady Southwold's going to take it: and then there's poor, poor Marjorie. Really no way to treat a woman. Most extraordinary!" Grumbling to himself and shaking his distinguished head, the great man walked off.

By that evening speculation over what had happened had turned into a *fureur,* the sort of scandal in a champagne glass that Paris loves. And Lady Southwold, naturally, made it all infinitely worse, once she heard the news that d'Amboise had defected. Richard had the misfortune to be there and for a moment thought the lady would explode. When she had calmed a little she shouted out that she was going to horsewhip the Duke and demanded a carriage and a pair of footmen straight away to help her teach "that French swine" the lesson of his lifetime. "No filthy frog is going to treat a gel of mine like that and get away with it."

And more, much more in the same vein. Red wig awry, face taut and mottled with rage, she stood there in the courtyard shouting for the Ambassador, who, of course, never came. But it was the sort of scene that servants, and especially Parisian servants, thoroughly enjoy. Throughout this little *tableau* they stood there like deaf-mutes cast in wax: but by that evening the whole story was round Paris And rather to Richard's horror and alarm, it was the *whole* story.

That night at a café one of the Goncourts collared him, an eager smile on his intelligent consumptive face that Richard recognised as evidence that Edmond was in hot pursuit of a first-class piece of social gossip for his famous journal.

"A friend tells me, *cher Richard,* that the precipitate flight of *le gros lard* wasn't coincidence or a case of bashfulness by an intending bridegroom. He tells me that the story is far more romantic than it seems."

"Really, Edmond, what extraordinary fantasies the two of you get hold of. That imagination of your brother's will be landing you in far more trouble than you bargained for."

"And that cold, diplomatic English face of yours conceals a romantic heart that will get *you* into still more trouble, *mon copain.* But it's a heart-warming story. We applaud it thoroughly. It does you great credit as a man of sensibility if not of sense. Beauty saved from that very beastly beast, and you as St. George and Don Juan in one. You'll find yourself the most romantic *jeune homme* in Paris if you don't look out."

And so it was. Richard, despite himself, soon found that he had inadvertently achieved a fame, a sudden notoriety such as most men would envy and none but the luckiest attain. By next morning hostesses were clamouring to give him dinner, courtesans were courting him, and the moustached and smiling figure of Monsieur Degas nodded towards him in the Bois. Normally all this would have delighted him, but nothing was normal now. Now that success had come to Richard Bellamy, he had no chance to make the most of it.

His excellency was soon summoning him again—but this time there was no champagne, no Martinique cheroot, no sympathy. Instead there was the man of steel and marble who had made Metternich and Europe tremble.

"Your behaviour, Bellamy, is not merely inexcusable. Many things are that. But it was irrational, and that is something that I can't allow. If we permit our hearts to rule us in this way . . ." He raised his hands in a gesture of such eloquent contempt that lesser men than Richard might have followed it with suicide.

"There is no point in lecturing you now. You're old enough to know the penalties. If it were left to me there might be something we could do, but I'm afraid it's not. Her ladyship has been in touch already with the Foreign Minister, and he has demanded your dismissal from the Service. That's all there is that can be said. I'm sorry. And I'm very disappointed."

For Richard Bellamy, dismissal from the Diplomatic Service came as a real disaster. He had no private means, no other possible profession. All his education and his training had been towards diplomacy. His friends, hopes, life itself had been bound up with this one career he loved: now, thanks to one ridiculous error of the heart, he'd thrown it away. And all, as he kept saying to himself, for nothing. If he had won the girl it would have been more bearable, but there had been no chance of that. The very night the scandal broke Marjorie had been bustled out of Paris and back to the virgin shores of England. She would probably have been better off wedded to d'Amboise—and Richard would still have had his chance of one day becoming another Lord Cartwright.

Remorse, regret, those old men's vices—Richard was to feel their bitter touch early on in life. He trudged the *quais* and brooded on his future. It was bleak.

May was coming and a morning mist was rising from the river. Paris, beloved city, had never been lovelier. The chestnut trees were coming into bloom, a barge was floating on the lilac river. The bridges were deserted. Youth was going. So was Paris. For him this was the bitterest loss of all. How could he possibly stay on without career or private income? True, there was the novel he was writing, but Zola had not been too encouraging and the thought of starving in a garret in the cause of art was not for Richard Bellamy. There was no possible alternative to England, but Lord, those fogs, that food, those dreadful women! Still, if one had to go, one went in style, and Richard did.

That afternoon a great deal of champagne arrived with compliments of the Duke d'Amboise. (Not quite such good champagne as Cartwright's, but more than good enough for Richard and his friends.) And that night there was such a party as the little street off the Rue Jacob had not witnessed since the Revolution. In later years Richard was never absolutely sure who turned up and who did not: Zola, Goncourt, Degas certainly. They would go anywhere these days for free champagne. But whether Verlaine and Saint-Saëns came remains uncertain. They were living nearby so they may have done. Not that it really matters, for by the early hours Richard had drunk so much that he could hardly have distinguished Rimbaud from Racine, and he never did discover how Degas and Juliette got him aboard the early train to London.

1884

3. *A Mésalliance in the Family*

RICHARD STILL HAD A HANGOVER AS HIS TRAIN STEAMED PAINFULLY THROUGH Clapham Junction (already, as he told himself, with a limp attempt at pride, the largest and most complex junction in the world) and he prepared to face the future. It seemed as grey and as depressing as the view from his carriage window—acre on slate-grey acre of identical small dwellings recently built across the once green fields of Balham, fog in the nostrils, soot which had even penetrated the third-class carriage where he sat.

What hope had anyone in such a country, especially without friends or influence and after a disgrace like his? How could he even face his family? It was as well his father was no more. His mother would be easier to placate, for in every mother there is something that secretly applauds a son's failure if it brings him back weak and in need of maternal comfort. And so it proved with Richard.

Since his father's death the family had left the rectory where he had spent his boyhood, and his mother was living in a small cottage opposite the church. Every day the trim, straight-backed widow in bonnet and black shawl would make her way up past the church and through the churchyard to visit the simple tombstone of her husband. Richard, who went with her his first afternoon at home, found this touching but also saddening. His father wouldn't have wanted such a cult of mourning, and in the past his mother had always been down-to-earth and self-reliant.

She had been the one who urged him on through college, who read him passages from Samuel Smiles, and who always told him that in life's jungle it was the tough and self-reliant who survived. (Mrs. Bellamy had always been a great reader and in those days had been impressed by the recently published works of Mr. Darwin. After Mr. Smiles he was her favourite author.)

So it had been from her that Richard had originally picked up his keen sense of ambition.

But now all his mother's energy and toughness seemed to have left her. In spirit she already seemed to have joined her husband in the churchyard. Richard's disgrace and failure scarcely seemed to concern her.

The first evening of his return he sat with her over their frugal meal, the candlelight making her once lovely face appear ethereal and infinitely old. He talked of Paris. In the past she would have wanted to know everything about the city—the great men he had met, its politics, its scandals, even the meals he had eaten. In the old days not a single detail of her favourite son's career had been too small for this ambitious mother. But no longer.

"I feel that this is God's will," she said softly.

"God's will, Mother? How on earth?"

"Yes, His will. There you were in that sinful city, beset by temptation on every side, but He was not content to leave you in corruption."

"Corruption, Mother?"

His mother smiled a knowing but forgiving smile.

"Come, Richard," she said gently. "I know you better than you realise. I know that there are pleasures in this life that appeal to you more than to most men. But the Lord does not tempt His creatures more than their power to resist. My boy, I must tell you something."

She paused and once again there was that strange, sad smile. "Before he died, your father spoke of you. He was not happy with the path your life was taking."

"He never told me this," Richard said roughly.

"Of course not. That was not his way. But he said that the Lord would bring you back to us—and so He has. He also said his dearest wish was that one day you, his favourite son, would follow him into the ministry, even continuing his work here in this parish. It would be a wonderful thing, Richard, if it could happen. And since the Lord has brought you back like this I feel your duty is quite clear. Walk in your father's footsteps, Richard. Become a clergyman like him. There is no better way for any man to spend his life than that."

❧ ❧

At first the idea of following his mother's wishes struck Richard as absurd, impossible. A country clergyman indeed! After the life he had led in Paris, the glittering prizes that had been all but within his grasp, how could he possibly retire at twenty-nine and let the remainder of his life moulder away in a country parish? The boredom, the interminable round of preaching, parish visiting, and village fêtes! Besides, there was the question of one's faith. Richard was a believer—of a sort. "Pious without enthusiasm" was the celebrated epitaph placed on the tomb of one distinguished eighteenth-century divine. It could have been applied to Richard too. He had none of his parents' fervent belief. At Oxford, when asked to describe his form of Christianity, he had flippantly replied, "An Indifferentist," and this was more or less the state of his belief today.

But on the other hand there really was something to be said for entering the Church, especially for somebody in Richard's somewhat hopeless, penitential state of mind. He who had played the world's game and had lost might just as well withdraw in dignity, living the remainder of his life in absolute obscurity, doing some good for those who needed help. If he could not become another Cartwright, he could at least attempt to follow the example of his father. If he could not have Lady Marjorie . . .! This, of course, was really at the bottom of his thinking, although he would never have acknowledged it. It was too degrading, too ridiculous to admit the truth—that he had sacrificed career, ambitions, wealth for love, then had that love totally ignored. For since Lady Marjorie's precipitate departure from France he had heard nothing—not a note of thanks, a whisper of her sympathy for what had happened—nothing!

He was not bitter but deeply hurt, and the idea of burying himself in Norfolk for the remainder of his days appealed to his craving for a romantic answer to that haughty lady.

Besides, the slow balm of the gentle Norfolk countryside had now begun to heal his wounded spirit. He had forgotten how much he loved the village he was born in, how much at home he felt among its slow-speaking, taciturn inhabitants, and how he responded to the strange flat landscape rendered immortal by the painter Crome of Norwich. With his degree from Oxford and his distinguished academic record it would not be difficult for Richard to take holy orders; he would then try for preferment to his father's living; since his death it had been held by a succession of temporary incumbents.

Gradually, without committing himself entirely (as a true Libran, Richard was congenitally one for carefully weighing one course of action against another: his behaviour in Paris had been quite out of character), he began to make inquiries, visiting old Bishop Gough in Norwich (a close friend of his father's), talking to rural deans, and generally discovering how the ecclesiastical landscape lay. The results were quite encouraging. Men of his calibre were wanted by the Church. It would take a little time, but Richard got the firm impression that if his sights were set on God, God would be willing to provide the target.

Southwold that spring was at its most spectacular, excessive best. From afar one saw the great tower built in 1201 by Guy de Southwolde—banker, rebellious baron who became Chancellor to King John and lived to set his family in their place of firm pre-eminence here in this fertile stretch of Wiltshire. His portrait by an anonymous French painter of the period was hung in the long gallery and showed a thin ruthless face, pale eyes and that extraordinary nose which in succeeding generations was to prove as much of a genetic trade-mark to the Southwolds as the prognathous chin was to the Habsburgs.

Guy built the tower, organised the lands, and laid the foundation, which almost every subsequent head of the family would add to o. adorn: Henry Southwold, fourth Earl and friend of Richard Cromwell, who dropped the preliminary "de" and subsequent "e" from the name and used the stones and wealth of the nearby monastery to construct the wonderful great hall after the Reformation; the Elizabethan Hugo Southwold who sailed with Raleigh and built the orangery, and the mid-eighteenth-century Spencer Southwold who was bitten by the building bug and built and built and built—the Palladian west wing, the folly on the hill, the stable block which is a sort of palace in itself. Nothing but death could still Earl Spencer's plan-encumbered fingers, and the great house owes more to his constructional zeal and recklessness than to anything else.

Marjorie had lived with these ancestors of hers since childhood; their personalities and legends had been so intertwined in the fabric of the great building that she often felt as if she knew them better than the living members of her family. She certainly preferred them. They didn't shout at her or let her down or try to teach her manners, and now that she was home again and in disgrace it was to them she turned for consolation. There was no one else. Her brother, Hugo, was away in Scotland, reluctantly pursuing the Highland sports that were expected of him—"I would rather catch no salmon than shoot no grouse if it comes to it," he said to Marjorie before he left—whilst her father, the eleventh Earl, was in the final throes of attempting once again to win the Derby. This naturally took precedence over everything and was a perfect alibi for being far from Southwold when his wife returned. She, having done her best to sever diplomatic relations between France and Britain—and ruin Richard in the process—had now retired to bed. She complained of nerves, of headaches, of the vapours. Every morning faithful Doctor Cowley would drive over from the village in his trap to assess her symptoms and prescribe fresh drops, a change of tablets or a different medicine. For Lady Southwold was a restless patient.

Marjorie steered clear of her. She knew her all too well in her current mood and realised that everything would be blamed on her.

"I've done my best for you, ungrateful creature," Lady Southwold had shouted at her daughter as they left Paris. By mid-Channel, when her ladyship began to feel unwell, she had inevitably blamed Marjorie. By the time they reached Southwold she was moaning and telling Marjorie that since she'd thrown away the one chance she had of making a successful marriage, she would now have to face an old maid's future.

None of this worried Marjorie. She was in love, so painfully and totally in love that nothing else mattered—certainly not her mother—and she felt nothing but gratitude when she was told that the marriage stakes were over. If she could not have Richard, and it seemed clear that she could not, she would not have anyone.

It may seem strange that so strong-willed and determined a young woman should have accepted so calmly the fact that marriage to the man she loved was quite impossible. But Marjorie was an aristocrat, and although she suffered from her mother and often fought with her, she had never rejected any of the principles by which she lived. Southwolds were not like ordinary people. Southwolds had standards to preserve. Southwolds had clear-cut duties to their family and their position in Society. And, above all, Southwolds did not complain if things went wrong. (This last unwritten rule, though often broken by Lady Southwold, was nevertheless endlessly enunciated by her.)

And so Marjorie kept her sadness, like her love for Richard, firmly to herself. Had she heard of her mother's action and his dismissal from the Service, she might conceively have written to him, or tried to do something to correct the wrong, but even this is doubtful. Marjorie was a realist, and as a realist she knew that when one broke the rules one paid the penalty.

But nobody told her what had happened, and when May came to Southwold she was still sadly picturing Richard's existence in Paris and feeling faintly jealous, miserably resigned.

She had her pony, Castlereagh, to ride, but he was old (Marjorie had been given him for her sixth birthday) and blind in one eye and not exactly cheerful company. Nor was her Irish elk hound, Cromwell. Several years ago, he had lost a leg in one of the man traps still set—illegally but quite effectively—on the estate. It had been Lord Southwold's idea to have the old dog fitted with a wooden leg. Augustus Talbot-Cary, his lordship's battling great-uncle, had lost a leg with Wellington at Waterloo.

"If Uncle Gus could make do with a wooden leg I don't see why Cromwell shouldn't," he had said consolingly to Marjorie. And make do Cromwell had, although complainingly and with a look of terrible reproach on his great shaggy face.

During the days of early May this melancholy trio would amble through the park. The deer would flip their small white tails and huddle by the beech trees at their coming. The Wiltshire skies had never been so blue, and in the distance Southwold with its towers and turrets looked like some shimmering enchanted palace. Love-sick Marjorie, one-eyed Castlereagh, and three-legged Cromwell went on their silent way, keeping their sorrows to themselves.

Ten-thirty in the morning. Pigeons were cooing in the trees of Grosvenor Square. An old man with a bell was shouting his wares and a hansom cab had just collided with a costermonger's cart. The interchange between the drivers floated through the third-floor windows of the big house opposite, summoning John Henry Talbot-Cary eleventh Earl of Southwold, to the unwelcome presence of another day. He groaned. How odd it was that the human body never got used to getting up! How strange as well that half a lifetime of waking to headaches and hangovers never allowed one to adapt to them. Last night he had been with—who had he been with? He groaned again. The Duke of Devonshire, as far as he recalled. Louisa Manchester had been there too. She always was these days. He couldn't stand the woman. Really, she *was* becoming just a little blatant in the way she pursued the Duke. She had one duke already, a perfectly good one, if a little dull. Manchester was all right, a dear fellow. Why did the wretched woman want another?

"Matthews!" he shouted.

"My lord," a voice replied. "Coming, my lord, this instant."

"Matthews!" The door in the sparsely furnished bedroom opened· a pink and curiously optimistic face peered in.

"Tell me, Matthews, why are you such a miserable, dirty-minded, thoroughly disreputable rogue?"

"We're made as we're made, my lord."

"And why do I still put up with you although you fornicate beneath my roof and continually rob me?"

"Come, my lord, there are limits."

"Exactly, Matthews! Absolutely, Matthews! Entirely, Matthews! Limits, you mangey scoundrel you, you whoring blackguard. Limits! I've warned you, Matthews, but enough's enough. You're dismissed, Matthews, from this moment, and if my head didn't ache so much I'd beat you too. Chastisement's what a case like yours calls out for. Damme if I won't give it, too!"

At this the Earl stumbled from his bed, a tall, thin, grey-haired man with hollow cheeks and a two-day stubble on his chin. Long and sensitively arched feet protruded from beneath his blue-and-white-striped nightshirt.

Matthews, who evidently knew his master's early morning habits, prudently withdrew behind a chest of drawers, but his precautions were not necessary. The Earl clapped a hand to a dramatic forehead.

"What did they poison me with last night, Matthews?"

"Port wine, my lord. You know what Dr. Cowley says about port wine, but still you drink it. Ever the sufferer, my lord!"

Southwold groaned and sank back on his bed. But once again Matthews proved that he knew his master and his job. From outside the door he produced a tray with a long thin bottle of hock and a dark blue one of soda water.

"Hair of the dog, my lord."

Once more the Earl groaned, but less aggressively now. And while he drank his hock and seltzer, Matthews, dismissal totally forgotten now, was energetically stropping razors and mixing a lather from a great bowl of shaving soap by the window.

"Lovely day, my lord. Just a bit in need of grooming aren't we?"

The Earl lay back on the pillows, Matthews tied a towel round his neck and, humming softly, shaved him.

In fact, the bond between Lord Southwold and his "man," as Matthews was designated, was probably the strongest in his life (apart possibly from his feelings for Malatesta, the Arab three-year-old who had won the Derby for him three years earlier). Matthews looked after him, procured for him, settled his debts for him (he kept his master's cheque-book and managed the accounts), doctored and often cooked for him. He was intensely loyal, reasonably honest and surprisingly discreet.

He was also efficient in his own strange way, acting as a sort of private secretary to his lordship when there was business that required attention, and it was thanks to him that the name Richard Bellamy came up that morning. It was during a session of discussing bills that needed paying and correspondence that could hardly wait much longer for an answer. The two men sat at the enormous table in the dining room, with the remainder of the room covered in dust sheets. The indispensable Matthews had made two piles of the previous month's correspondence. One—the larger—consisted of matters that could safely be ignored a little longer, and the other of those that Lord Southwold had to deal with. This pile consisted in the main of bills from farriers, grain merchants, and veterinary surgeons, but there were other things too that occasionally required his lordship's close attention. It was one of these which Matthews suddenly picked out.

"And how long have you been such a close friend of Bishop Gough of Norwich, my lord? Hardly your line of country, I'd have thought. Seems to be something to do with a request for a church living. The usual thing, but this one's interesting. He is appealing on behalf of somebody called Bellamy—father apparently in the Church before him, no suitable livings in the Norwich diocese. But this is the interesting bit, my lord: he's writing to you because this Bellamy fellow was until recently with our embassy in Paris, where he performed some useful service to her ladyship."

"The deuce he did!"

"The devil he didn't!"

"It must be him—*the* Richard Bellamy! Matthews, I take back everything I said to you this morning. You're not a ruffian, at any rate. not much of one. You're quite a clever fellow really, Matthews. We must most certainly do something for this diplomatic clergyman-to-be. Summon him, Matthews. We must meet him."

Three days later Richard received a coroneted envelope. Inside he found a five-pound note "to cover fare and incidental expenses," and an invitation to present himself to meet the Earl of Southwold at 44 Grosvenor Square at noon exactly, one week hence.

Richard's first reaction was to ignore the letter. Bishop Gough, as absent-minded as he was well-intentioned, had told him nothing of his correspondence with the Earl. All Richard could think was that this was a further episode in the trouble there had been in Paris, and this really *was* too much! Hadn't he suffered quite enough for what he had done? It was outrageous of Lord Southwold to be still pursuing him. A sense of the injustice of it all still obsessed him—and it was this that finally decided him to take Lord Southwold at his word and clear the whole thing up forever. Finally, a most aggressive Richard Bellamy set off to London, ready to beard the Earl in Grosvenor Square.

But he was in for a surprise. First there was the extraordinary character, with a red face and looking like a race-course tout, who opened Lord Southwold's door.

" 'E's in the library," he announced, then indicated the direction and disappeared.

Richard walked down a corridor, knocked at a door and entered. A tall man with a white face, an enormous nose and pale grey, slightly hooded eyes was sitting at a desk. He wore a pair of muddy hunting boots, a red silk dressing gown, and a white stock round his neck. He rose lethargically to his feet.

"Bellamy," he said. "So you're the young man I've been hearing all about."

He struck Richard as remarkably good-looking in a curiously foreign way. (Southwold's mother, the old Countess, was in fact a Russian from Kiev.) When he smiled the skin around his eyes wrinkled engagingly, and his cheekbones were unusually high.

"And what have you been hearing, sir?" Richard asked somewhat sharply.

"About your meeting with my wife and daughter whilst you were with the Embassy in Paris."

The icy, distant tone in which these words were uttered made Richard bridle.

"Sir, I'd rather not discuss it. All that I did was try to help a young lady who appealed for my assistance. I've paid the penalty for my stupidity. I'd rather we left the matter there."

"But that's impossible, since my wife and daughter are involved. I insist on hearing just what happened."

Something about the way Southwold spoke made Richard realise that argument was useless; so he did as he was instructed, telling the whole story, haltingly at first and then with growing confidence.

As he spoke, Lord Southwold's manner changed as well. The haughty look soon went, the grey eyes twinkled, and when Richard hesitated for a moment in describing d'Amboise, Southwold slapped his thighs and shouted, "Go on, go on! You can't shock me. Tell the truth!"

So Richard did—including a description of exactly how her ladyship behaved when the story broke.

At this point Southwold stopped him. "Wait just a minute, my dear fellow. This is too extraordinary. Matthews must hear it too. Matthews!" he bellowed, and the speed with which the man appeared made Richard certain he had already been listening at the door.

Matthews enjoyed the story, and soon he and his master were both laughing as Richard told about the scandal that swept Paris.

When Bellamy described the way he was dismissed, Southwold looked pensive, and when the story was finished there was silence.

"Well," said Lord Southwold finally, "it is quite clear that our young friend has been most shabbily treated."

"A damnable disgrace, my lord," said Matthews loyally.

"And all because you did my daughter and my family a service for which we should be profoundly grateful."

"Something should be done about it," Matthews said.

"Exactly," said the Earl," but first I think it's time we had a little something. Matthews, a bottle of the Krug, and there must surely be some cold beef left."

"Beef, my lord? You're joking."

"No beef? In that case make it two bottles."

"Three glasses, my lord?"

"Insolent fellow! I suppose so, then. Now, Bellamy, let's get one thing straight. This business of the Church. I hear that you are a candidate for holy orders. Are you serious?"

"Well, sir . . ." said Richard doubtfully.

"You're not. Capital. We understand each other. I can't stand cant on matters of religion. I take it that what you're looking for is really some sort of comfortable niche, somewhere where you can lead a life of decent comfort without too much effort."

"Sir, I . . ."

"Capital, Bellamy. Capital. You're a man after my own heart. Can't stand people who aren't honest with themselves."

The Krug appeared. It was cool, sparkling, and the sight of it took Richard back to his days of happiness in Paris. He drank appreciatively. Southwold watched him closely.

"What d'you think of it?" he asked.

Something about the way he asked the question gave Richard courage to reply, "Do you want my opinion as your guest—or as a connoisseur?"

Southwold smiled. "The latter, naturally."

"Then I would say that, judged by the very highest standards, this really is too light to take too seriously: also a little too *frissonnant* for my taste, and obviously we're drinking it too soon. Ask me again about it in, say, five years' time and the story could be more encouraging."

A shocked silence greeted Richard's verdict—then Southwold roared with laughter.

"Your hand, Bellamy, your hand! It is an honour to know you. Did you ever hear such judgement on a bottle of champagne, Matthews?"

"Never, my lord."

"That decides it, then. Your future's settled, Bellamy my lad."

"Settled, my lord?"

"Yes, settled. There's only one place for a man who has such powers of judgement. In Parliament, my boy! In Parliament!"

❧ ❧

Until that moment Richard had never thought of politics as a career. To be quite honest, he had the usual civil servant's professional contempt for politicians as a breed. But there was no resisting the decision of Lord Southwold, now that he'd set his mind upon this course of action. His energy and his efficiency were phenomenal, and almost overnight Richard found himself swept up in a whirlwind of activity which was to carry him, shaken but triumphant, to Westminster.

What surprised him from the start was the apparent ease and confidence with which this great magnate seemed able to dispose of seats in Parliament almost as if they were tied cottages on his estate. Surely the days when the aristocracy had such power were over? But quite clearly they were not. There was a by-election pending in the market town of Sutton, twelve miles south of Hyde Park Corner, and before the week was out Richard discovered that his lordship, who was quite a power in the district, had obtained his nomination.

Everything, it seemed, was taken care of. Matthews had booked him into Brown's Hotel and settled such mundane matters as his clothes for the campaign (from his lordship's private tailor), his transport (a phaeton from his lordship's stables) and his expenses (a hundred guinea draft upon his lordship's bank.)

And it was his lordship who took charge of his protégé's *début* as a politician. He dined him in the House of Lords, then introduced him, almost casually, to several of the greatest in the land. A dizzying round of social life followed, as a somewhat baffled Richard Bellamy found himself the centre of attention. But he adapted quickly. He had looks; charm, and Lord Southwold in the background. After the drawing rooms of Paris this was child's play. A rejuvenated Richard, failure and disgrace receding rapidly, started to rediscover the mainspring of his life—ambition.

Lord Southwold seemed increasingly impressed and clearly liked him. One thing that worried Richard was the question of finance, but the Earl explained that once he was elected (the possibility of his defeat was not acknowledged) he would receive a monthly stipend from the family. Embarrassed, Richard inquired what would be expected in return. His lordship smiled but was as usual rather vague. As an M.P. he would be unofficially regarded as "a Southwold man," and "on certain issues," the Earl went on, "I would expect you to consider my advice and protect my interests." But when Richard asked him what those interests were, Southwold began to tap the heel of his boot with his riding crop (a sure sign of irritation) and mumbled something about following straightforward Tory principles.

Thinking about this later, Richard realised that he was none too certain of what Tory principles involved—and still less whether he believed in them. But this did little to impede his progress as an up-and-coming conservative politician. Rather the reverse. As his campaign gathered strength he was able to encourage his supporters and confound his enemies by what the local paper somewhat generously described as "Mr. Bellamy's open-mindedness." He professed himself "quite open-minded" on the question of the Balkans, whilst on Irish Union he was "fairly open-minded." On the reform of tariffs he was "utterly open-minded." Such lack of prejudice endeared him to the burgesses of Sutton, and by the eve of the hustings the combination of Bellamy charm and Southwold influence seemed to have won the day. But although old Pyecombe, the local Tory agent, was exultant—"It's in the bag, Mr. Bellamy sir, it's in the bloomin' bag!" —Lord Southwold was determined to take no chances. There had to be a full-scale rally of the faithful on the village green, and Southwold himself had promised to speak. There would be the mayor, the town band, and on top of that his lordship had told Richard to expect a personal surprise. Until he stepped up on the platform, Richard still had no idea what it could be.

❧ ☙

It was by purest chance that Marjorie had heard of Richard's meeting with her father. Matthews had had to visit Southwold to collect some harness and was in the stables just as she returned with Castlereagh. She hadn't seen her father for several weeks, and it was when she asked for news of him that Matthews slyly answered that his lordship was all right and that he'd taken quite a shine to her ladyship's friend from Paris.

"What friend?" she asked.

"That good-looking young chap Bellamy. The one as caused you all the trouble."

"Don't be impertinent," said Marjorie. "He did nothing of the kind. But what do you mean about my father being friendly with him? Father hasn't been to Paris?"

"No, Lady Marjorie. Bless your soul, didn't anyone tell you? Your young Bellamy's in London, and all set to stand for Parliament as well. You ought to go and see him."

Marjorie disliked her father's "man"—always abusing his position and indulging in this sort of forwardness—but just for once she felt like kissing him. Richard in London, and with her father!

"You might even help him with his campaign," Matthews continued. "Ladies are very popular with voters these days."

"Perhaps I will," said Marjorie thoughtfully.

When Richard caught sight of Marjorie on the platform, sitting with her father, his first reaction was that this must be some sort of joke, and a joke in the poorest taste. She had helped him ruin his career once, and since then not a word, and now suddenly she was back again, prettier and more desirable than ever. The sight of her revived the pain and disappointment of the days he had spent with her in Paris; his instinct was to turn his back on her. But how could he? The band was playing, the packed audience was cheering, and when the cheering stopped the chairman began introducing the guests of honour: "The Right Honourable the Earl of Southwold" (lusty cheers), "and to show that our Mr. Bellamy has beauty as well as brains and breeding on his side, the lovely Lady Marjorie Talbot-Cary." This time the cheers were deafening as Marjorie waved politely to the crowd, then smiled at Richard. It was a smile to melt the hardest heart, and Richard's (which was still extremely soft where Marjorie was concerned) melted instantly.

This did not keep him from speaking with unusual eloquence when his moment came. Earlier his speeches had been competent but somewhat tame. Now he was suddenly a man inspired, and when he finished the applause echoed and re-echoed. By now there was only one person whose applause concerned him, and she was clapping heartily as well.

Two days later Marjorie stood with her father when a triumphant

Richard Bellamy was declared the winner; and as she drove back to London in the Southwold carriage she said, "Father, there's a favour that I want."

"What's that, my dear?" Southwold replied somewhat absent-mindedly. Now that the by-election had been won, it was time to get back to the stables. The Derby was only weeks away.

"I want to marry Richard Bellamy," she said.

"You *what*?" he shouted.

"Richard. Richard Bellamy. I want to marry him."

"But what about your mother? She'd explode if you told her."

"I know, Father dear," she said, and placed her hand gently on her father's.

"That, I'm afraid, is why I need your help."

Lord Southwold didn't win the Derby. His horse Matignon, at three to one, threw his jockey early in the race and his disgruntled owner went back to Southwold for whatever solace could be found in the bosom of his family.

Richard meanwhile had been enjoying some of the most satisfying weeks of his career as the Mother of All Parliaments took him to her bosom. Barely a few weeks ago he had been hopeless and unemployed and in disgrace. Now he was suddenly a member of the most exclusive club in London, a legislator and an up-and-coming man.

He met the Party whips and then was formally introduced to Mr. Speaker. He had a brief and somewhat distant interview with the Party leader, the immense and very bearded Lord Salisbury.

"Well done, my boy! . . . Great things . . . expected of . . ." The great Lord Salisbury's somewhat meagre voice trailed away as he turned his gaze from Richard to the Thames, where a sailing barge was manoeuvring on the tide.

Once this ordeal was over Richard was free to start his personal apprenticeship, attending the debates, preparing for his maiden speech, and settling into his new-found lodgings in Lord North Street, three minutes' walk away from Parliament. It was here, on Thursday afternoon, that he came back to find a letter waiting from Lord Southwold.

"Dear Bellamy," it read. "Now you've had time to settle in, why not come down to Southwold for the weekend? Marjorie would love to see you. So would I."

❧ ☙

Despite his firm resolution *not* to be over-impressed by Southwold, it was hard not to be, especially on the summer morning when Richard found himself being driven down the mile-long avenue of limes and glimpsed the long battlements and towers ahead of him. This was no ordinary house. It was a private town, a principality. There was a drawbridge, and the Southwold standard, gold and lilac, fluttered on the lime-scented air.

Richard came warily. After his previous experience with the lady of the house, his first reaction to the invitation had been that nothing on earth would make him offer himself again as a victim to her tongue. But then he wavered.

"Marjorie would love to see you," Southwold had written. Would she? But for that matter, what if she did enjoy his company? There was no future in it, not for either of them. Why give himself more pain by seeing her?

But once again the thought of seeing Marjorie made him change his mind. There in his lonely chambers he remembered her as she had been at Lord Cartwright's ball in Paris, and driving through the Bois with tears welling in her enormous eyes. Futile or not, the chance of seeing her again was more than he could resist. If Lady Southwold was the price he had to pay, so be it.

But as it happened, he need not have worried. Lord Southwold was soon explaining. "Her ladyship unfortunately has had to go to visit her poor sister, Helena, in Kent."

"Nothing serious, I hope," said Richard.

"Good gracious, no," Lord Southwold said, then added, "Marvellous to see you, Bellamy my boy. I trust that you'll excuse me this weekend. I am a little occupied, you know—the stables and the horses, dreadful chore, especially with my idle son Hugo away as well. I hope you won't mind if I leave you to the tender mercies of my daughter.

Richard thought he detected just the faintest suspicion of a smile.

❧ ☙

"Ah, Mr. Bellamy, M.P. And how, pray, is Westminster?"

Marjorie was sitting in the window seat of the library. It was a place she'd chosen carefully. The window looked out on the moat, and the light, she thought, was flattering. Equally, the books should certainly provide a background that would appeal to a literary young man like Richard Bellamy.

For months she had thought of very little else but Richard. Now he was before her, she could think of nothing in the world to say. And nor could he, except how much he loved her.

"Quite fascinating, Lady Marjorie," he replied. "Of course one needs to learn the ropes, but in a month or two . . . a month or two . . ."

"Yes, Mr. Bellamy?"

He stared at her. The light reflecting from the water outside danced on her forehead. Her hair was golden as the sun. Her eyes were even larger and a deeper shade of violet than he remembered.

"In a month or two . . . one might be thinking of one's maiden speech," he said.

He paused, and suddenly she started laughing. It was his face, that serious, respectful look of his, and that pompous nonsense he was talking.

"Richard," she said. "I've missed you dreadfully."

They spent a magical weekend. Lord Southwold would materialise at mealtimes like some very hungry, well-born ghost and would keep them laughing with his stories. Marjorie clearly loved him very much, but he was a curious, inaccessible man. Sometimes, as in his rare appearances this weekend, he could relax and be delightful company. But Richard had already learned that he could withdraw quite abruptly and leave people wondering how they had offended. With Marjorie, however, he was completely at his ease, talking about the bird life and the Downs and the customs of the villagers like the true countryman he was.

Apart from these conversations, Richard and Marjorie had Southwold briefly to themselves. They walked together through the park to see the deer, then through the Tudor garden (reputedly planted by Anne Boleyn) and up into the great house, which Marjorie showed him as if it were her private, almost secret domain. For years this had been her personal world because she had lived a strangely solitary life. To Richard she was like some princess showing him her palace.

And it was in the heart of this enchanted palace, in the great deserted long gallery under the disapproving gaze of fifty of her ancestors, that Richard kissed her—very chastely—and asked her to marry him. She—very coolly—said she would, and for a few idyllic moments their life seemed full of happiness—and very simple.

◆§ §◆

Simple it was not to be. In years to come, when Marjorie and Richard looked back on the months that followed, they often wondered how they had endured them. As they said, they had to have been really in love to have won through. The first tornado hit them on the Sunday of that first weekend, just before luncheon, when Lady Southwold came back earlier than expected. She was tired, barely civil, and obviously outraged to discover Richard Bellamy, of all people, in her house. Luckily Lord Southwold was able to explain that he and Bellamy had various political matters to discuss since Bellamy—did she know?—had just been elected M.P. for Sutton.

"An M.P.!" she replied. "Good heavens!" And then again, "Good heavens!" With which she sniffed, turned on her heel, and swept from the room. From the distance Richard could hear her shouting at her husband that she insisted that this upstart leave the house at once. Richard required no second bidding. Empty of food, but full of hope and love—Marjorie had whispered words of everlasting love as his carriage drew away—he returned to London.

The next few months were months of frustration for the lovers. But even frustration has its own particular delight when you are young and very much in love. A secret letter, a brief meeting in the park, a few words exchanged when Richard called, apparently by chance, at Southwold's house in Grosvenor Square—these were all the contacts they had, but they were quite enough to feed their passion. Richard was busy, and for him the days slipped by. But for Marjorie, at Southwold most of the time with only Cromwell as a confidant, life became intolerable. There were long battles with her mother. She declined her food and rarely bothered to ride Castlereagh. By Christmastime even her father had begun to realise that she was ill and pining and that something must be done.

◆§ §◆

Normally it is the intending bridegroom's task to broach the subject to the lady's father, but in this case roles were oddly reversed, and it was actually Lord Southwold who broke the stalemate by inviting him to dine. He was in such a sombre mood that at first Richard wondered in what way he had offended him. There was no champagne and the first course went by virtually in silence. Finally Lord Southwold spoke.

"Bellamy," he said, "are you in love with my daughter?"

Richard's cautious nature made him wary of replying.

"Come now, man, don't beat about the bush," said Southwold angrily. "Are you or aren't you?"

Richard nodded. "Very much in love," he said.

"And I presume you want to marry her?"

"If I have your permission, sir."

"My permission's neither here nor there. The point is, Marjorie's pining. Frankly, I'm worried for her. I've tried to make her give you up but of course she won't. She says she'd rather die. And quite honestly, I think she might."

"My God!" said Richard.

"Yes. My God indeed! Something must be done. Either you must leave her, absolutely—write to her at once to give up hope—"

"I'll not do that," said Richard.

"Then there is only one thing to be done," said Southwold gravely.

"What's that?" said Richard.

"You must elope. Lady Southwold would never, never acquiesce in your marrying my daughter. She'd rather see her dead. I must admit that there are other men than you that I'd prefer to see her marry, but since she's made her choice, I'll help you both."

And so the plans were laid. Several more months passed during which Richard and Marjorie still met rarely, but their letters now were full of hope. Somehow their secret was kept from Lady Southwold, but his lordship now became increasingly involved in it. It appealed to his romantic nature and to his love of plotting. (Perhaps it also appealed to him because of the pain he knew it would cause his wife.)

Quite early on he promised Marjorie that after she was married she could have the house in Eaton Place. It had stood empty since his mother died in it some five years earlier, and Matthews proceeded to engage workmen and, ultimately, servants for the house.

But it was Richard and no one else who decided when and where they would be married. Since they had met in Paris they would marry there as well, and where better than in the British Embassy? Cartwright demurred at first, but when Richard in a long and tactful letter carefully explained the circumstances, even he gave in. A special licence was prepared and Cartwright himself agreed to give the bride away.

On an August morning, in the great *salon* with Boucher's Venus smiling at them from the ceiling, Richard Bellamy, M.P., and Lady Marjorie Talbot-Cary were safely and irrevocably made man and wife.

1884

4. *Happy Families*

WITHIN A FEW DAYS OF MOVING INTO 165, RICHARD WAS DISCOVERING, somewhat to his surprise, that the whole tempo of this quiet married state was suiting him. And as for Marjorie, she had never been so happy in her life. There were a few weeks still before Parliament was due to reassemble, so she had her husband to herself. During this period she was everything that an experienced woman of the world would say a young wife shouldn't be—demanding, difficult, possessive and devoted. And once again, to his surprise, Richard discovered that this sort of total adoration suited him.

Apart from old Castlereagh and Cromwell (both left behind with tears at Southwold), he was the first living creature she had ever had entirely for her own. As a result, Marjorie could not bear to leave him for a moment. When he was in his study, theoretically working on his novel, she would continually be coming in with tea and a loving plateful of thin arrowroot biscuits—or else with problems or requests.

"Darling, my necklace is entangled in my hair—it's *agony!*" And Richard would untangle it and kiss her pretty neck as a reward.

Or "Dearest Richard, Mrs. Bridges is so *obstinate* I fear she'll have to go. Without so much as bothering to consult me, she has decided that we're having apple pie tonight instead of the delicious *meringue glacé* I ordered specially for you." And once again Richard would get up from his desk and take her in his arms and tell her that apple pie, especially Mrs. Bridges' apple pie, was the one thing he had wanted all of his life.

"But I thought I was that," she said, pouting happily.

"Whoever told you so?" he would reply, and not surprisingly his famous novel (he had recently found it in a trunk where it had lain since Paris, liked it, and decided to start work on it again) remained exactly as it was—unfinished.

But love gained what literature lost. Richard's affection for his young wife grew with every day that passed. However, it was still very different from the devouring love she felt for him. Her love was passionate, romantic and demanding.

"I'll kill you, Richard Bellamy, if ever you're unfaithful," she told him their first night in bed in Eaton Place—and meant it.

"Make love to me *here!*" she ordered him the very next afternoon as they were finishing their tea in the drawing room.

"*Here,* Marjorie?" Richard replied, suddenly apprehensive. Even in Paris, with the very fastest set, he had never been asked such a thing by the most outrageous courtesan. Embarrassed, he tried to escape.

"The servants, Marjorie dear! Just think what Hudson will say when he comes in for the tea things."

But Marjorie was determined and was already carrying the tea tray to the door. She placed it quietly outside, then closed the door, locked it, and lay back invitingly on the sofa.

"What sort of husband *are* you, Richard?" she said softly. "Why don't you show me? Or are you afraid?"

Richard enjoyed these games with his young wife, whose eagerness more than made up for her innocence. Besides, her innocence was tempting in itself, and it flattered him to play the experienced older man to this eager pupil in the art of love.

"Show me exactly *everything* that *la Beccucci* did when you slept with her," she ordered.

"I never slept with her," said Richard.

"How very disappointing. I thought that everyone in Paris did. Still, do your best to show me just the same."

Amused at first, and then excited, Richard would do as he was told.

This sort of passionate devotion, this combination of lubricity and licit love, was something he had never known before. Nor had he known the luxury of so much time to spend on love. Even with Juliette love had been essentially a partial pleasure, something to be enjoyed amidst or after the various demands of a most busy day. As a result, in Paris Richard had never lost himself entirely to love, never acquired the dangerous habit of forgetting time and place and work and immersing himself in pleasure. Now that he had the chance, he discovered quite a taste for it. With this discovery his love for Marjorie began to change.

During those first weeks of their honeymoon he had still been very much in charge, the knowledgeable, sophisticated man of the world Marjorie first fell in love with. He had loved her, but not with that passion which she felt for him. He had been—faintly but unmistakeably—condescending in his love. Now it was different. He was becoming the dependent one, and Marjorie's stronger, more single-minded character was starting to assert itself—and not only in the bedroom. For the truth was that without a regular routine, without the discipline and ambition of his former very busy life, Richard was the sort of man who could rapidly become soft. He half realised this himself. It worried him but there was not a great deal he could do about it on his own. The pattern of a marriage is a subtle thing. His was forming. At this crucial stage he might have lost out almost totally but for the presence of one key person in the household—Hudson.

In many ways, some of them obvious already, Marjorie was the antithesis of Richard. Partly through breeding, partly through the influence of many generations of nobility who had had their way in almost everything, she was a natural authoritarian. (Indeed, old Lady Dunamore's remark about her similarity to her mother hadn't been all that wide of the mark.) She was also selfish, self-assertive, and at heart, entirely self-confident.

Richard was quite different. Like many sensitive, intelligent men, he lacked self-confidence and was over-diffident. He couldn't bear a real argument (when it came to it, Marjorie thrived on them); he disliked rudeness (Marjorie was rarely aware of it when she behaved badly); his instinct in all unpleasant situations was always to give in, accommodate, or else use tact to bring about a compromise (Marjorie would fight).

In light of these differences it would have been quite likely for Marjorie to have soon become the virtual tyrant of the house and

Richard little more than an amiable ghost about the place (as happened with so many noble households one could name).

But Hudson, from the start, seems to have realised the danger and to have worked quietly to avert it. It was always hard to know quite how consciously he did this, whether his behaviour was the reaction of the perfect servant who always managed to do what was required by a curious sort of sixth sense, or whether an astute and slightly cynical intelligence lurked behind that rocklike sense of precedence and order.

Whatever the answer, one thing is certain. From the beginning of the marriage it was Hudson, and no one else, who built up the respectful myth of Richard Bellamy's supremacy within the walls of 165. Richard was the master, and, with a fine Calvinist inflexibility, it was to him and him alone that ultimate loyalty was due, above stairs and below.

With Hudson this was a subtle process, often no more than a glance, an intonation, or a way of asking "Does the master know?" or "Would the master approve?" But it was enough. In his quiet way, Hudson was a match for anyone—including Marjorie. Sometimes they clashed. Sometimes she felt like screaming at him. (Sometimes she did.) But Hudson was like some old past master in this strange game of domestic chess. He knew all the rules, the pieces and their places. Nobody—and this included Marjorie—ever truly managed to checkmate him.

Of course, this was Hudson's great strength from the start. When he told the servants that he would have the house run like clockwork, he had meant it. He had a massive sense of order: everyone in 165, from lowliest kitchen maid to Richard Bellamy himself, found themselves living by it. Each new servant would discover on the day he joined the household a daily list of duties pinned to the wall beside his bed and written out in Hudson's own strong, spiky hand. Hudson also possessed a quite uncanny nose for the slightest item that had been forgotten. And if it had been—a grate unblacked, a floor inadequately scrubbed, a cabinet unpolished—he would convey to the offender, not merely threats or admonitions but a deep sense of shame that one of the laws of nature had been broken.

Even Richard found that he was soon being ruled by Hudson's sense of what was "fitting." True, he was "the master"—but on Hudson's own very rigid terms. Several times that autumn Richard tried varying meal times: twice he was late for luncheon. Without a word being spoken, Hudson managed to convey to him the sense that such behaviour simply was not fitting: finally Richard took care not to offend again.

Similarly with all questions affecting Richard's wardrobe (and here, as Richard's valet, Hudson was in an even stronger position to enforce what he thought was suitable). Richard was still something of a dandy by inclination, and in Paris had quietly enjoyed indulging in the coloured waistcoats and elaborately frilled shirts (most of them purchased from Manessier in Rue de Rivoli) that were considered very chic. Paris was still behind London in imposing a drab uniformity of dress upon its males, and Marjorie romantically approved of Richard's finery. Hudson did not. Once again nothing was ever said, but Richard sensed, without a shadow of a doubt, that Hudson felt his clothing inappropriate—and once again quietly conformed.

When Marjorie chided him about this he could become quite irritable.

"Dearest," she'd say, "you're scared of Hudson and his steely eye."

"Nonsense. Sheerest nonsense, Marjorie. Nothing of the sort. It's just that—dash it—well, London isn't Paris."

Inexorably and rather to Marjorie's regret, Richard's appearance sobered perceptibly as the first months of marriage passed.

There was another faint but gradual change in Richard Bellamy's appearance at this time—and here not Hudson but Mrs. Bridges was responsible. Thanks to her increasing success in the kitchen (whatever Marjorie said, Mrs. Bridges was becoming one of the best family cooks in Belgravia), Richard had started to put on weight. This was not serious—yet. As a young diplomat, living on his nerves and eating when he could, he had been what Marjorie called "the Embassy bean-pole," all brains and bones. Since then, regular hours and three good solid meals a day (plus Mrs. Bridges' irresistible scone and fruitcake teas and plates of delicately cut bedtime sandwiches in case of that dread ailment, night starvation) were starting to flesh him out a little.

There was a long way still to go before he could be thought fat, or even flabby. Marjorie thought his body was becoming "manlier" and thoroughly approved. But Richard wasn't sure, especially when he reached that first disturbing point of male disquiet when trousers become a little tight and jackets call for letting out. Occasionally he'd try eating less, but once again the house defeated him. Much of the life of 165 centred on the ritual of good food: how could he possibly turn away the game pie or the partridge *en culotte*, or—pride and joy of Mrs. Bridges' repertoire—her *bécasse dorée Duc d'Aosta*? How could he refuse a second helping of her wonderful jam roll which she cooked especially for him (in an unguarded moment he had once told her it was his favourite pudding as a boy)? It was a problem but a pleasant one, and the truth is that Richard never made a serious attempt to solve it.

⁂

What was surprising about 165 was the way it imposed certain clear routines on those who lived there. It was a friendly house. Richard could never quite work out why, but as he said, it had a calming atmosphere that was all its own: within a few days of moving in he had the comfortable feeling that he had always lived there.

He was surprised too that the fact that legally it was not *his* house soon ceased to trouble him. He never did care for the Southwold portraits in the drawing room, and soon persuaded Marjorie that they should move the painting of her great-great aunt, which bore a frightening resemblance to his mother-in-law. Once this was done, he felt instinctively as if the house were *his*—in its way a considerable tribute, this, to Marjorie's tact.

But both of them loved the house, and after the turmoil that had led up to their marriage their first reaction was to withdraw entirely into it from the world outside.

"What do we want with people?" Marjorie asked. "They'll only cause us trouble. We've each other. Isn't that enough?"

And Richard would laughingly agree, even when the visiting cards left by inquisitive (or friendly) neighbours threatened to swamp the table in the hall.

"What shall we do with these?" he asked.

"Burn them!" she cried.

"And offend half the dowagers in Mayfair?"

"Certainly. Just think how peaceful it will be. No one will visit us, and we'll make love all day and be happy ever after."

⁂

For that brief splendid autumn it seemed as if they would. Apart from their pleasure in each other, and in their fine new house, they now also had a chance to enjoy London on their own like two young lovers.

The London season (as the *Times* remarked in a weighty editorial) was no longer confined to the once traditional three months from May through July when all its main events occurred. Now for the whole year round London had suddenly become "the pleasure city of the world." Perhaps this was pitching London's claims a shade too high, but certainly enough was happening early that September to keep the two Bellamys happy.

Neither of them had had a chance to know London well: now they discovered it and for the first time became real Londoners. Richter was conducting at St. James's Hall and Ellen Terry was at Drury Lane; the Italian Opera had begun at Covent Garden and there were evening concerts in Hyde Park.

In later years they never quite recaptured—or forgot—the magic of that first London autumn they spent together. Perhaps this was simply because there were just the two of them: children, friends, social success are great dividers in a marriage. Together they heard Brahms in an autumn evening, then walked back through the Park as the lights went twinkling on along the Mall and the excitement of the London night began. Sometimes they dined *à deux* at Scott's or at Romano's and jolted back romantically to Eaton Place in a Hansom cab. And sometimes they just walked for miles arm in arm around the city, talking continually (they never knew of what) and simply indulging in that rare lovers' pleasure of each other's presence. London had never seemed more beautiful (and never did again for either of them) than it did that autumn while it was still their bridal city.

This golden isolation could not last. They enjoyed nearly three weeks of dodging friends and seeing the servants at rare intervals, and then the outside world closed in on them. The friends came first. One of the earliest was a tall, gawky, inconsequential-seeming girl with cornflower-blue eyes, lank fair hair and a determined manner. She had already called twice in person before she found the Bellamys at home.

Marjorie was still in bed—it was nine-thirty in the morning—and Hudson summoned Richard to meet the lady in the hall.

"I'm Prudence," she announced before the faintly stunned Hudson could announce her. "*What* have you done with our Marjorie? I demand to know. Some of our friends are saying that you must have eaten her. Have you?"

"Now really, Miss . . ."

"*Lady* Prudence Fairfax—but you can call me Prudence. Please not Pru. And, of course, provided you haven't really eaten our dear Marjorie. That would be *too* bad."

"And I would have to call you Lady Fairfax then."

"And I'd have to call the police. Cannibalism in Eaton Place. Think of the headlines in the evening papers. Seriously, Mr. . . ."

"Richard."

"Seriously, Richard, I think you must produce her straight away."

And of course he did. Or rather, at the sound of voices Marjorie produced herself, and Richard was secretly disappointed at how glad she was to see her friend.

"Prudence, how lovely!" Kisses, invitations followed. "What's been happening. How simply marvellous to see you again. Richard, you know Prudence is my oldest friend!"

The first carefree stage of the Bellamy marriage was over.

Then politics. Whenever Parliament reassembled after the long summer recess Richard would always feel that it was like going back to school. There was the same excitement of finding out what had happened after the holidays—who had been promoted, who had left or died or been disgraced. There was also the same sense of challenge in the new session as there had once been in the autumn term at school—the chance of suddenly distinguishing oneself, of being picked for some new job that had fallen vacant. In short, there was a curious promise and excitement at returning to Westminster. But just as with school there was also the dread of going back to work, of pleasure being over and the long grind starting. Particularly, of course, this first year. For both Marjorie and Richard knew that once he took up his role as Richard Bellamy, M.P., their days as carefree lovers were behind them.

So both of them were dreading that last week of September when, by Royal Decree, the Lords and Commons would reassemble in Westminster Palace and the widowed Queen would arrive in her state carriage and formally start up the political roundabout again.

But when the day came, both of them enjoyed it hugely. One of the simplest pleasures (common to Hottentots and cardinals alike) is the childish but irresistible one of feeling *somebody*. By the standards of the vain, rather silly world in which they lived, neither Marjorie nor Richard could be accused of snobbish ostentation—rather the reverse. Especially at this time of their lives they weren't essentially concerned with how the world saw them. But when the chance came—as come it did that grey September Tuesday morning—of taking their superior positions in the crammed social pantomime of the State Opening of Parliament, they did it with a certain style (and, one must add, a certain relish).

As an earl's daughter Marjorie was entitled to her own place in the gallery of the House of Lords, and had taken as much care and thought for her appearance as if she were invited to a full state ball. Her gown of ivory silk had been concocted for the occasion by Madame Desoutter's establishment in Hanover Square (which on more than one occasion recently had sewed for the Princess of Wales herself). Her ostrich feather hat was very *à la mode* (Richard said it would block everybody else's view of the proceedings but admired it immensely).

And Richard was resplendent in full morning dress, the lavender silk cravat which Marjorie had bought him from Messrs. Swan and Edgar held in position by the heart-shaped diamond and ruby pin which was *her* wedding present. He was, of course, a very junior backbench M.P., but he managed to find himself a place in the crammed chamber of the Lords while the royal speech was being read. It was an impressive sight in its strange, unreal-seeming way, a blending of the ludicrous and the legendary. Great, centuries-old traditions—the reverence and pomp around the throne, the massive and historic power of the Lords themselves in scarlet robes and ermine—blended with the reality of power and change and opportunism, represented by the men who really mattered: the craggy face of Gladstone, the Prime Minister, looking as if carved from granite; the bearded, ambitious face of Dilke; young Randolph Churchill, all rolling eyes and beetling moustache; and the monocled round face of Chamberlain, the dangerous Birmingham radical. But the ones who really held Richard's attention were the small group of recently elected Irish members led by Charles Stuart Parnell. Parnell was still an enigma to Richard. He looked like what he was—a stiff, withdrawn, upper-class Englishman—as he sat there unsmiling and aloof at the end of the opposition benches. But how much of a fanatic was the man? Would he, as many rumoured, finally lead Ireland into rebellion if he could not get Home Rule? Was he a true fanatic?

The sight of all these men of power set Richard wondering about his own political beliefs. He disapproved of people like Parnell. He thought he disapproved of the sort of violent change and uneducated populist politics championed by Chamberlain. But apart from this—and from the fact that he was, nominally at least, a Tory, what were his true political beliefs?

He tried enumerating them to himself. He believed in decency and honesty in government. He was against extremists of all sorts. He believed, with Jeremy Bentham, that government should aim to secure "the greatest happiness of the greatest numbers"—but how? This was the question he still had to settle for himself.

Marjorie, of course, had no such political uncertainties. That night at dinner, when she had finished giving her views on Mrs. Gladstone's hat, the length of Lord Salisbury's eyebrows, and "how desperately miserable the old Queen looked—she can't *still* be missing Albert!" she told Richard that she had heard the Duchess of Manchester ask "Who is that good-looking young M.P.?"

"You can imagine how I felt when I realised she was talking about *you*. I suddenly realised how famous you are going to be, and I was so proud of you, my love. Dearest, I'm glad that you're a politician, really glad, for there's so much you can do. You can fight those beastly radicals and Liberals and Irish, and defend the things that we believe in."

But were those things as similar as Marjorie imagined? He wasn't sure. One thing he did know, though. He was not in Parliament simply to keep the world safe for people like the Southwolds.

Since he and Marjorie moved into 165 there had been an ominous silence from that quarter; not a letter or a word since their return from honeymoon. Richard could hardly have been more delighted, but Marjorie began to worry, particularly when she failed to see her father at the State Opening. She had called twice at Grosvenor Square but the house was closed up and deserted. Richard knew that Marjorie was uneasy and would have liked to help, but by tacit agreement neither said anything about it.

Richard was beginning to wonder if the Southwolds had just vanished or disowned them totally—with somebody like Lady Southwold anything was possible—when a letter turned up in the morning post from one Geoffrey Dillon suggesting that Mr. Bellamy, M.P., might care to call in at his chambers in Lincoln's Inn. "The Rt. Hon. the Earl of Southwold has suggested that there are certain matters which concern you and the Lady Marjorie and which need to be arranged."

"Do you know anyone called Dillon?" he asked Marjorie. Since Parliament had started they had begun breakfasting together in the breakfast room. Marjorie was now immersed in toast and Cooper's marmalade and the personals column of the *Times*.

"Mmm?" she replied.

"Dillon. Geoffrey Dillon."

"Of course I do. He's Mother's lawyer. I can't stand him. Does he say anything about the parents?"

"No, not a word, but he wants to see me."

He handed her the letter and she read it thoughtfully.

"Don't like the sound of it, dearest. Do you have to go?"

"If there are things that really do concern me, then I suppose I'd better."

Dillon's office turned out to be a strange mixture of impressiveness and squalor. "Rather like the Law itself," said Richard to himself as he waited in the outer office after a skeletal old clerk with rheumy eyes had taken his message that Richard Bellamy, M.P., would like to see Mr. Dillon.

Cobwebs festooned the windows, piles of old law reports rose like strange vegetables from floor to ceiling, a portrait of an anonymous Lord Chancellor leered down at Richard, whilst the office cat picked at a chicken carcass left on a side table littered with dirty plates and porter bottles. There was a small bell with a note beside it saying, "Ring for attention." After five minutes, Richard took its advice. Nothing happened, except that the cat began choking on a bone and was quietly sick in the middle of the room. Disgusted, Richard watched, and so failed to notice the arrival of the tall, thin individual who entered the office from behind him.

"Bellamy? Dillon's the name. Extremely kind of you to come at such short notice."

Richard turned.

Like his voice—dry, high-pitched, faintly inquisitorial—Dillon's appearance seemed to match that sunless office. There was undoubtedly distinction in the man, yet also something faintly squalid and, yes, a little frightening. One could not be quite sure of what a man like this might do behind one's back. Perhaps it was simply the way in which he seemed to hide his real thoughts behind his large-lensed spectacles. Even seeing him for the first time, Richard could understand Marjorie's dislike.

Yet he seemed affability itself—respectful, grateful, almost servile to Richard for coming. It was Richard who had to bring him down to business by asking what Lord Southwold wanted them to settle.

"Ah, certainly, certainly. I am afraid that we must talk about something I'd almost rather not." He shrugged apologetically.

"And what is that?"

"Money, Bellamy. Money. There is the question of the settlement which Lord Southwold has agreed to make from the estate, to assist Lady Marjorie—uhum, and of course yourself—to continue the way of life to which she, both of you, have naturally become accustomed."

"I am most grateful to Lord Southwold, naturally, but surely there is no difficulty? Since I was elected, Lord Southwold has very kindly honoured his promise and made me a handsome stipend to allow me to perform my duties. Since my marriage he has, with still greater generosity, made over to us the lease of 165, Eaton Place. The stipend—plus what I earn from my literary work, and Lady Marjorie's own income—means that we are quite adequately taken care of."

"Ah, yes," said Dillon, staring vacantly towards the anonymous Lord Chancellor.

"Yes, indeed. That will naturally continue."

He paused as if searching for the words he needed. Richard tried to fix his eye, but he evaded him.

"Well, man," said Richard, suddenly impatient, "what's all the fuss about?"

"Now, now Bellamy, a little patience. Just a little patience. This isn't particularly agreeable for me."

He leaned back in his chair and continued staring at the portrait, so that when he spoke his words took on a cold impersonality, as if he were delivering an opinion to the old gentleman in the full-bottom wig.

"Bellamy, you talked about your 'stipend.' There is no stipend. That was a purely temporary *ex gratia* payment made by his lordship to assist you at the time."

Richard exploded. "Rubbish! It was nothing of the kind. Lord Southwold gave me his explicit word that as long as I was in the House of Commons, I could count on the support of the Southwolds. He . . ."

"Please!" Dillon raised a long grey hand as if to halt a flow of hostile traffic through the room.

"Support. You talk about support. You can count on that—and not merely for your time in Parliament."

Richard was puzzled. "So?"

"Since you have married Lady Marjorie it has been decided that the right and proper means of continuing this support is through the whole marriage settlement."

"That sounds quite reasonable," said Richard.

Dillon nodded. He had now turned his gaze from the Lord Chancellor to his shirt cuffs. "But I must, with respect, point out that the marriage settlement is naturally in your wife's name, not yours. A year or two ago this would have made no difference. A wife's property and chattels automatically belonged to the man she was married to. But since the Married Women's Property Act—of which as an M.P., you, I take it, are not unaware—money vested in the wife remains *her* private property."

Dillon stopped, and returned his gaze to the Lord Chancellor. For a moment there was silence, save for the sound of the office cat who was now scratching herself.

"There must be some mistake," said Richard finally. "I must speak to Lord Southwold."

"There is no mistake. And Lord Southwold is not available, now or at any other time, to discuss this matter."

"But it is monstrous!"

"Monstrous, Bellamy? Come, come! You have the woman that you love, a seat in Parliament, a house most men would envy—and you call it 'monstrous.'"

"But I was promised."

"Can you prove it?"

"There are certain things no gentleman should have to prove."

"Unfortunately, an income of eight thousand pounds a year isn't one of them."

"Then I suddenly find that I am placed in the position of being my wife's pensioner for life."

"Oh, come, come, Bellamy! That's no way to talk about what is by any standards a piece of great generosity. Besides, it's scarcely flattering to Lady Marjorie."

"I'll ask you not to be impertinent about my wife."

"Impertinent, Bellamy?" For the first time Geoffrey Dillon faced him, but the big magnifying lenses of his spectacles had made his eyes vanish into a sort of elusive nothingness.

Richard rose, mastering his desire to strike the man. "You'll be hearing from me later. For the present there is nothing else to talk about."

"Evidently not," said Dillon.

Richard missed lunch. He was so angry and upset that he could not bring himself to eat. At two the House was due to continue the debate on the Ecclesiastical Causes Bill. This concerned the power of the government to regulate church livings in the interests of greater fairness and equality among the clergy. Consciences including Mr. Gladstone's, but not including Richard's, were much aroused. Should the Church of England be established or disestablished? Should it remain a branch of the state or continue freely on its own? As a rector's son and one-time potential candidate for ordination, Richard intuitively felt that the whole system, which had worked in its own strange way for more than 350 years, should be permitted to continue. But as with most things in the House, where the lawyers felt their right to have their say, the whole subject seemed to lose touch with all reality. And how tedious, how infinitely, wearyingly dull the speakers seemed. He tried to concentrate on the debate in an attempt to take his mind off Geoffrey Dillon. But instead, the House suddenly seemed full of Dillons with their "with respect" and "on a point of order."

By three o'clock he'd had enough. But as he strolled through the main lobby someone stopped him.

"Bellamy, isn't it?"

"Quite right, and you are . . ?"

"Dangerfield. Dick Dangerfield. I was at Balliol when you were at Magdalen. Huddersfield North."

"Oh?" said Richard.

"My constituency. I got in three years ago with the swing to the Liberals. I must say you were confounded lucky to take Sutton as you did. I meant to write congratulating you at the time."

"From a Liberal that's very generous."

Dangerfield smiled. It was a winning, conspiratorial sort of smile, and Richard now remembered him as one of the wildest undergraduates of his day.

"Come, come. You don't honestly believe all that old nonsense about Liberals and bloody revolution? Some of us really are quite human. Come and have a drink."

Perhaps it was the contrast with Geoffrey Dillon and the ecclesiastical lawyers, but Richard rather took to Dangerfield from the beginning. He was a short, vital man with black curly hair, dark eyes, and a spectacularly broken nose. He had a habit of putting his head on one side and watching you so quizzically as you talked that in the end it was always hard not to burst out laughing. He told Richard that since he left Oxford he had married a rich wife, left her, and was now working at the Bar.

"Another lawyer!" Richard said and groaned.

"What's wrong with lawyers?" asked Dangerfield, and Richard told him the whole story of his marriage, of Lord Southwold's promise, and finally of that morning's interview with Dillon. It was good to find someone intelligent to talk to and to get the whole thing off his chest. When he had finished, Dangerfield whistled—rather commonly—between his teeth.

"Tricky position, Dick my boy!" (He had called Richard "Dick" automatically. Normally Richard resented it.)

"Pity you didn't see me, or someone else in my disreputable profession, *before* you plunged. Not a leg to stand on now, I'd say. I may be wrong. It may just be worth a learned counsel's fee to make sure how you stand. But I don't think there's much chance, and Dillon's quite well known as the sort of tricky lawyer who doesn't make mistakes."

"So what advice *can* you give me?" said Richard miserably.

"Advice? You laymen always want advice. Well, speaking as something of a man of the world, I'd say, 'Hold tight to Marjorie.'"

The Southwold settlement hung over Richard, as it presumably was meant to. It was designed to cause him days of agony and nights of sleeplessness, to make him moody and morose. It also upset things seriously between him and Marjorie. He could think of no honest way of telling her that her parents had, as he saw it, tricked him. And she for her part could think of no way of discovering what was on Richard's mind.

She suspected, with a woman's intuition, that it had something to do with Geoffrey Dillon. But when she asked Richard what Dillon had wanted he replied, "Nothing serious, my love. Just a few details on the lease here that required seeing to. Nothing important."

Marjorie knew he was lying, but there was not a great deal she could do.

Since Parliament had reassembled Marjorie had reluctantly begun to do what she knew to be her social duty as a rising M.P.'s wife. In fact she was good at it, and really enjoyed the role of political hostess on the minor scale of a back-bencher's wife. She told herself that it was "good for Richard's career" and as if this weren't enough, added that "the servants so enjoy having a few celebrities to dinner," which wasn't strictly true.

But Mrs. Bridges did excel on these occasions; already, in certain knowing, not uninfluential quarters of the Commons, 165, Eaton Place was becoming known as "the sort of place where you can always be sure of the food—if not of the conversation."

This particular evening, Mrs. B. surpassed herself, with her cucumber soup and a splendid *cassoulet* made to a complicated recipe of Baron Brisse. (Richard had recently been trying to introduce a more cosmopolitan note into the menu at 165, and surprisingly Mrs. Bridges quite took to it.)

This was as well, for Richard had invited Dangerfield, and young George Wyndham and another young Conservative M.P. named Brooking were guests. Brooking had brought his wife, a frilly little thing related to the Macclesfields, but as Dangerfield was currently without a presentable lady he could bring to dinner, Marjorie had asked Prudence Fairfax to make up the numbers. Marjorie was none too pleased at the idea of having a Liberal M.P. to dinner in her house.

"You'd better tell Hudson to count the silver," Richard said, laughing. "With Liberals you can never be too careful!"

But from the moment he appeared, Dangerfield's rather rakish charm won Marjorie over, and that evening the after-dinner talk was far more animated than was usually the case at 165. As it was a small party, the gentlemen soon joined the ladies and the talk got onto the subject which was obsessing London—the fate of General Gordon, who had exceeded the admittedly extremely vague instructions given him by Gladstone's government and who was now face to face with the forces of the Mahdi at Khartoum.

When the talk got onto the subject of Gladstone's slowness in despatching a relief expedition, Marjorie became extremely heated.

"How can that criminal old man hesitate a moment when the fate of that gallant soldier hangs in the balance?"

But Richard, who had the politician's inborn mistrust of generals who attempt to force their views, however justified, upon a government, refused to let this pass.

"Majorie, dearest, you've simply no idea," he said irritably. "And I won't allow you to call a great man like Gladstone criminal. You can disagree with him, but that's another matter. Besides, the General from the start has known the risks that he's been taking."

Marjorie controlled her temper at this show of male superiority, although she *was* tempted to tell her husband that she would call old Gladstone whatever she felt like. Instead she said softly, "Richard, darling, why aren't you a Liberal yourself?"

"I'm not a Liberal—but I should hope I'm fair," replied Richard somewhat pompously.

"Fiddlesticks!" said Marjorie. "And what do you think, Mr. Dangerfield?"

Until this point Dangerfield had prudently abstained from the discussion.

"I think that General Gordon is a great hero who now wants to become an even greater martyr. And I believe he's going to succeed."

"You mean you think he'll die in Khartoum?"

"Certainly."

"And what will happen then?"

"I think that the country will rise and rend the Old Man limb from limb."

❧ ❧

The whole discussion had upset Richard. Apart from the question of General Gordon, this was the first time he and Marjorie had clashed on a point of politics. Until this moment he had not thought it possible. Also, the way that Marjorie had flared at him revealed a facet of her personality he had not suspected. Marjorie for her part was quite contrite, realising that just for once she had gone too far.

"I'm sorry, darling," she said as they were getting into bed. "I'm sure that I was wrong about General Gordon and you were right. I'm just an ignorant young woman. You know best."

But this apology, which normally would have brought Richard straight into her arms, failed completely. Instead he sat gloomily beside her on the bed, his face a study in male misery. Marjorie was alarmed.

"Dearest, what *is* it?"

"Nothing," said Richard, gloomier than ever.

"But I know it's *something*. Ever since you saw that wretched Geoffrey Dillon you've been different."

And so the whole story finally came out—Lord Southwold's promise, Dillon's attempt to change the arrangement, and the new settlement that placed all their money in Marjorie's name.

"And that's all it was?" said Marjorie tenderly. "All that upset and worry over something so simple and so unimportant? Shame on you, Richard Bellamy. When the money arrives each month I'll simply have it transferred straight into your account. Then we'll have nothing at all to worry about."

"But that's not the point," said Richard lamely, reluctant as he was to abandon a matter of principle.

"Oh, darling, I'm so sleepy. Come to bed," said Marjorie softly and turned out the light.

❧ ❧

But Richard knew that much more was at stake now than mere names in a bank account. For one thing, his pride was much involved: something within his puritan soul made him hate the idea of being, as he bitterly described it to himself, "the kept man of a rich wife." And there was something else. Previously, when he had received his stipend straight from Lord Southwold, there had been no strings attached. Southwold was far too big a man—and far too vague—to have tried to use the money to bring any sort of pressure on him. But now that Dillon was involved he wasn't sure. Nothing had been said, but he had an uneasy feeling about that gentleman.

The only answer, Richard realised, was to earn money for himself, preferably so much money that he could politely tell the Southwolds what they could do with their wretched settlement. But that was a luxury which for the moment he could not hope to afford. Eight thousand pounds per annum is a lot of money: the opportunities for an unknown back-bench M.P. to earn so much were limited.

He lacked connections in the City, and although there were undoubtedly opportunities for less scrupulous politicians to sell their influence to business interests in return for a discreet appointment to a directorial board or two, this practice struck Richard as dishonest. He had strong views on the independence and integrity of M.P.s, views which he put forward with some sharpness in an article he wrote about this time that was published in the November issue of the *Political Quarterly*.

"The Member of Parliament," he wrote, "has a sacred obligation to preserve himself from the blandishments and pressures of the businessman. And Parliament itself must recognise the insidious dangers of the newest form of corruption in its midst."

Brave words, even reckless words, from someone in Richard's vulnerable position, and they caused quite a stir. Ironically, it was barely a week after they were published that Richard received a visit from Geoffrey Dillon at the House of Commons. Richard was distant but polite. Dillon looked strangely out of place in the Strangers' Lobby of the House: away from his chambers in the Temple he seemed to lose that slightly chilling sense of power. Suddenly there was something servile about the man.

It took him some time to come to the point—a request that Richard sponsor a private member's bill on behalf of a company called "Imperial Holdings Ltd."

"Before you refuse," said Dillon quickly, "I feel I must say that this is a perfectly straightforward legal document, a sale of land for which, because of some bureaucratic nonsense, the form of a parliamentary bill is needed. And also Southwold interests are involved.

As you have benefited not inconsiderably from them in the past, I should have thought . . ."

Richard cut him short. "I don't need you to tell me what I owe the Southwolds. Leave the bill with me. When I've considered it I'll let you know my decision."

The next few days were crowded ones, as Parliament prepared for the Christmas recess and he and Marjorie prepared for their first Christmas together. There had still been no contact with Southwold, and Richard was secretly delighted at the prospect of Christmas at 165. Christmas in his own home—something that he had not experienced for years. Perhaps his mother could come up from Norfolk, and they would have a few close friends for a party on Christmas Eve. Then on Christmas Day there would be himself and Marjorie and the servants—presents around the tree, carols, a quiet dinner. It was a pleasant dream, and like most of his dreams these days it was abruptly shattered, in this case by Marjorie herself.

He had been Christmas shopping—a gold bracelet for Marjorie, cuff links for Hudson, embroidered handkerchiefs for his mother—and had then gone on to the tail end of the debate in the Commons. It was the second reading of the Armed Forces Bill, a governmental attempt to deal with some of the traditional abuses in the army. Richard was more or less in favour of it, as he was with any obvious reform—and certainly the army needed it, especially with the old die-hard Duke of Cambridge still its C-in-C. But the debate was flat. As usual, Richard admired the fire and penetration of Randolph Churchill. How he could dominate the House! But once he had spoken, everyone lost interest. Richard included. No real Englishman *cared* about the army—the navy was what mattered. Perhaps there was even something to be said for keeping the army weak and inefficient; at least it would be no threat to English liberty.

When he got home he found a delighted Marjorie.

"Guess what's happened?" she said, arms around his neck as he came through the door.

"Great-Aunt Flo's died and left us a fortune."

"No, be serious."

"I've no idea."

"I've heard from Father, and he wants us to go down to Southwold for Christmas. Oh, Richard darling, I'm so happy. Say that we'll go!"

Richard succeeded in not showing his deep disappointment. How could he possibly refuse when Marjorie was suddenly more thrilled than she had been for weeks?

"It will be lovely, dearest. You've no idea how marvellous Christmas at Southwold can be. I can't wait to share it with you!"

So Richard's private dream of a quiet Christmas at 165 was forgotten, and preparations went forward for the trip to Southwold. The house would be closed up for several weeks. Hudson would go up to Aberdeen to spend Hogmanay with his family, Mrs. Bridges would go down to Broadstairs to her sister, whilst Miss Roberts and two of the housemaids would accompany the Bellamys to Southwold.

The arrangements were extremely complicated, and Marjorie took charge of them with great efficiency—so much so that when Richard had his next encounter with Geoffrey Dillon he was not really in a position to say afterwards to Marjorie, "Cancel the visit! We spend Christmas here!"

He should have done, but then, the situation was not easy, and he was not the sort of man who cares to make his wife unhappy.

He had had more difficulty with the legal terminology of the Imperial Holdings Bill. Dillon had phrased it in the usual mumbo-jumbo favoured by lawyers, and Richard had shown it to the only lawyer friend he had—Dangerfield. He, in turn, asked for a few days to consider it and finally gave Richard unequivocal advice.

"Don't touch it with a barge-pole. All very shady, I'm afraid. Dillon's the front man for Imperial Holdings, but I've found out the list of shareholders. The major one is your mother-in-law, Lady Southwold, and your bill would legalise their buying up of common land in Wiltshire at rock-bottom rates."

"You mean it's criminal?"

"Not criminal, but very sharp. And after what you've written about M.P.s and their business interests, it could have an unfortunate effect on your political reputation."

Richard thanked him. When he called at the Temple to tell Geoffrey Dillon that he would not be presenting his private member's bill, there was an icy silence.

Finally the lawyer said. "Thank you, at least, for your frankness, Bellamy. I will make sure that your words are suitably conveyed to Lady Southwold. Perhaps I should warn you that I hardly think her ladyship is likely to be best pleased when she hears that the Member she supports in Parliament is behaving in this way. Like most generous people, Lady Southwold appreciates a little gratitude from those she helps."

Snow transformed Southwold from a great country house into some legendary northern city. As the coach crested the hill by Bordon village, Richard and Marjorie could see its windows glittering in the distance in the setting sun. The park looked like a huge white lake and the house seemed to float above it with its walls and battlements, its roofs and towers gilded against the wintry sky.

"I'd forgotten just how beautiful it was," said Richard.

"I hadn't," Marjorie replied, and when Richard saw the way her face lit up as they drove into the avenue of yews behind the courtyard and she saw old Cromwell standing on the steps, he was glad that he had let her come. Southwold was a part of her. It was pointless to try to fight the fact.

She was soon hugging the old dog, and the dog was licking her face and making mournful noises welcoming her back. Then one by one the servants all appeared—Widgery the butler, Mrs. Petifor the cook, Charnock the gamekeeper in his anchovy-red tweeds, and pretty, excited little Rose Buck, the lodge-keeper's daughter, who was jumping up and down and shouting, "Welcome home, my lady, welcome home!"

"Marjorie, how marvellous, you've really come!"—and Hugo, his jacket off, had rushed out and was hugging her.

"Hugo, my dear old thing. And a very happy Christmas!" There were tears in Marjorie's eyes. "Where's Father?" she asked quickly.

"Still up at Newmarket, but he's due back tonight. Mother's not been too well, but she'll be down for dinner."

"Oh!" said Marjorie, then put her arm through her brother's and led him in towards the house. Richard heard them laughing and suddenly felt lonely.

The house seemed even grander, vaster, more elaborate than he remembered. It was also rather cold, despite the log fires that were burning in the hall and in every available fireplace in the house. His breath condensed in Southwold's Arctic atmosphere, and the cold seemed intensified by the sheer mass of stone and marble all around

—acres of black-and-white-marble floors in all directions, hillsides of blood-red marble billowing up the stairs, grey stone buttresses which bore the ceilings and the great cage-like chandeliers. The fact that it was Christmas scacely impinged on this inhuman quarry of a place.

He and Marjorie had been allocated an apartment in the Gothic wing, where the décor reminded him of parts of the Palace of Westminster. There was a lot of red and gold, a gilt four-poster hung with crimson curtains, and an elaborate brass chandelier ablaze with candles. More to the point, the rooms were warm and water was steaming in the bath. Marjorie had had the sense to pour him a man-sized tumbler-full of whisky. Soon he was feeling more attuned to Southwold and its splendours.

His only worry now was Lady Southwold. Not even Marjorie had seen her mother yet, and according to Hugo (usually the pillar of discretion), "the mater has been rather playing up of late." As Richard struggled with his evening tie, he found his hands shaking very slightly.

"Nonsense," he told himself. "Pull yourself together!" All the same he wondered just how much the loathsome Dillon could have told her ladyship.

"Don't worry about Mother," said Marjorie, cheerfully echoing his thoughts. "It's Christmas. She'll be delighted to see us all"

To start with it seemed as if she were. When she swept into the anteroom (next to the silver dining room) just before dinner she seemed unusually affable and animated—a flashing smile for Richard, the offer of a cheek to kiss, and a seductive "How *are* you, son-in-law? A very happy Christmas to you."

Apart from the Bellamys and Hugo, there was Aunt Emily (the legendary "Bolter," now looking very flushed and fiftyish), Cousin Alec (Lord Lindsay Banting Browne, a chinless captain from the Grenadiers), and Mr. Prothero, the vicar. (Lady Southwold apologised for him before he came in words that were all too accurate—"rather a vulgar little man, but old and fairly harmless.") After a jug-full of mulled claret and apologies from Lady Southwold for her husband's non-appearance, Widgery announced dinner.

It was a nervous meal from the start. One of the footmen dropped a plate of vegetables which seemed to explode like a grenade on the marble floor. And when Cousin Alec started on an interminable anecdote about the use of elephants in the Afghanistan Campaign (in which he had fought with some distinction), Lady Southwold abruptly shut him up with an unanswerable "I disapprove of elephants *on principle*—always have, always will!"

By this time they were into the third course, a succulent haunch of venison superbly cooked by Mrs. Petifor and carved by Widgery. But Richard noticed, rather to his alarm, that Lady Southwold was not eating: on the other hand her glass had been frequently replenished. There were now tell-tale spots of colour on her cheeks and the glint of battle in her eyes. For a while she was silent, and as the other diners munched their venison the Reverend Mr. Prothero regaled them at length with memories of other Christmases he had enjoyed in the mission field. ("Dear Uganda and those sweltering Christmas Eves! Adorable Assam!") Cousin Alec nodded sagely, and Richard was wondering what he could add to the desultory conversation when he felt Lady Southwold's eye fixed, like a sighted rifle, on him.

"You're very quiet, Bellamy," she said.

He mumbled something about not wishing to interrupt such interesting talk.

"But you're not always quite so silent are you, Bellamy? You're a great one for lecturing others on their duties, aren't you, Bellamy?"

"I have my views, your ladyship, and as an M.P. naturally expound them."

"Expound. I like that word *expound*. So tell me, what do you expound on the subject of loyalty?"

Richard had fortunately drunk little and was quite clear-headed as he replied.

"One can have several loyalties, Lady Southwold. Sometimes they clash. When they do, one must rely upon one's conscience."

Lady Southwold nodded. There was a strained silence in that icy room. Then with a curious effort she said, "Doesn't your conscience tell you of your duty to the family that picked you from the gutter, that pays for the food you eat, the very clothes you wear? Isn't that where your precious loyalty should lie?"

Richard had risen, white-faced, from the table.

"Mother!" said Marjorie, aghast.

"Marjorie," said Richard softly, in a voice that she would not forget, "please to go to your room and pack. We're leaving instantly!"

Marjorie rose. She was in tears now. Richard took her arm and with considerable dignity led her towards the door. He bowed silently to the other guests, but no one spoke. The only sound was the nervous drumming of Lady Southwold's great amethyst-and-diamond ring upon the table.

Richard discovered that he was relieved at Lady Southwold's outburst. At least it cleared the air, and he would be justified in ending all relations with his wife's hateful family. It was good to know exactly where one stood.

As for Marjorie, she was still stunned—and ashamed of her mother. She was also slightly cowed by Richard, for this was a side of her husband she had never seen before—firm and furious and cold.

"Call Roberts and get her to help you pack immediately. Also to please order us a carriage. We'll spend the night in Bordon at the Southwold Arms, and tomorrow we'll go back to Eaton Place."

"But Richard, dearest, it's Christmas Eve; 165's closed up. We'll have no fires, no food, no servants."

"Blame your mother."

Marjorie was sobbing now. "But think of the gossip, dearest. Everyone will know. Richard, you can't do this to me."

But Richard appeared inflexible. He knew that this was a crucial moment in his marriage, one of those points on which the entire future hinges.

"Marjorie, please ring for Roberts."

But Marjorie, weeping quietly now, refused to move. "Dearest, we can't go," she said.

"Can't, Marjorie? I'm afraid we can, and will."

"Then if you go, you go alone. I'm as hurt as you are by what happened downstairs. I'm humiliated by my mother. And I love you, Richard. But I'm not leaving this house tonight."

"Why not? For God's sake why not, Marjorie?"

Marjorie looked at him with great tear-filled eyes, then almost whispered, "Because I can't risk our baby."

"Our *what?*" shouted Richard.

"Dearest, I thought you knew."

"Knew? Knew what?"

And then it was Richard's turn for tears as she gently told him she was four months pregnant. It was a strange switch of emotion for him—Lady Southwold suddenly forgotten in a new wave of unaccustomed happiness. He begged Marjorie's forgiveness. She said there was nothing to forgive; and when midnight struck from the clock above the stables, the flickering of the log fire in their bedroom showed them sleeping gently in each other's arms under the gold and crimson canopy of their enormous bed.

They awoke, late, to Christmas Day. The storm was past, the sun was shining on the snow, and Southwold once again appeared a place of magic. At breakfast Widgery told them that Lord Southwold had arrived during the night, but there was no sign of him—nor of his wife—until the whole household had assembled in the great hall at eleven-thirty before Christmas service in the Southwold chapel. It was a feudal gathering—more than two hundred souls, house servants, retainers from the estate, all with their families and all in their Sunday best—and Lord Southwold too was there, distinguished-looking, very tall and lean, almost a parody, thought Richard, of the English aristocrat. After the service he wished each member of the household a happy Christmas and gave everyone a present which had been carefully prepared and labelled. Each gift was handed to him reverently by Widgery as he called out the recipient's name.

Lady Southwold stood beside him throughout the ceremony, paler, if anything, than usual; but anybody seeing the Earl of Southwold and his wife there for the first time would have said what a splendid couple they made.

As they went in to Christmas luncheon, Lady Southwold passed by Richard.

"So you stayed, Bellamy, I see. Extremely sensible. A happy Christmas to you."

"And to you, your ladyship."

And this was all that passed between them.

Lord Southwold, however, was extremely affable. He was delighted to have Marjorie back with him—a delight that she shared—and throughout the whole luncheon kept the party laughing with his anecdotes about his friends, his jockeys and his horses, particularly the three year-old *Myrmidon* which he was hoping would prove one more Derby winner.

Later that afternoon he and Richard had some time together and for a while they talked of politics. Then Southwold said, "I gather there was just a spot of bother last night, Bellamy. Sorry about it. Try to forget it. Damnably difficult woman, as I ought to know. Don't let it come between you and Marjorie."

"Nothing could do that now," said Richard.

1885

5. *The Firstborn*

RICHARD HAD SET HIS HEART ON HAVING HIS FIRST SON BORN IN EATON Place (with all the confidence of expectant fatherhood, he never doubted Marjorie would have a boy), and during those first weeks of the new year the idea of this son-to-be virtually ruled his life. It gave a great boost to his morale and quite offset the bitterness he felt against the Southwolds. This would be *his* son and bear *his* name. Not even Lady Southwold could alter that.

The idea also increased his love for Marjorie. She was no longer the naïve young girl he had married, always so eager to throw herself into his arms. Almost overnight she had ceased to be his "wild Marjorie," as he had somewhat condescendingly called her after they married. She was a dignified young matron and her pregnancy was so important that he felt it was almost an act of loyalty to him against her mother. So he was grateful, and with his gatitude his love for Marjorie grew. He was more tender, more solicitous than he had ever been before, bringing her presents, worrying over her, trying to spoil her. It marked a further shift in their relations. He was no longer the dominating partner of the marriage, the omniscient man of the world Marjorie had once regarded with such awe. Nor was she the one who loved much more than she was loved.

Instead, in many ways it seemed as if *he* was now becoming the dependent one. She was the one who had to reassure him (he seemed so anxious, so unnerved by the processes of procreation), particularly once Herr Professor Dr. von Bülow came on the scene. He was a fashionable women's specialist, recommended to Richard as "quite the best man in London." He had apparently studied under the famous Hoche in Munich, and Richard took every word he said as gospel. Generally the fat Prussian doctor merely made Marjorie laugh.

"There is absolutely no cause for *alarrrm,* Herr Bellamy," he said in a voice of thunder after his first examination of his patient. "But she is delicate. She is highly strung. She is not what we would call a brood mare. She is, I think, anaemic, and she needs rest and fortifying foods, Herr Bellamy."

So rest and fortifying foods she had, despite her strong objections. Mrs. Bridges proved a virtuoso of beef tea and calf's-foot jelly.

"You'll make me too gross to move," cried Marjorie. "That's what old Herr Dr. von Bülow wants. He's only happy when his women are as fat as he is."

And she *was* starting to get big, but Richard liked it. The larger Marjorie got, the more certain he became that she would have a boy.

To make sure she had the rest she needed, he insisted that she have breakfast in bed each morning. She would agree to this only if he was there, and so the habit began of Richard, once he was dressed and shaved, bringing in her breakfast himself. Hudson would take the double tray up to the landing. Richard would carry it in, then eat his breakfast with her on the edge of the bed. Afterwards they'd read the *Times* together. Marjorie had recently started to enjoy the agony column, and as Richard struggled with the leader page, she would read out items to make him laugh.

"Darling, we must send a contribution to the Royal Sea Bathing Infirmary at Margate for the treatment of scrofula. It says that scrofula's our national disease."

"Perhaps they would take your mother."

"And perhaps you should apply to the Rupture Society. It says here it was founded in 1804 'for supplying trusses to the necessitous classes.' I'm sure you're necessitous, my love. Oh, and guess who it says the patron is?"

"The Archbishop of Canterbury."

"Silly—try again."

"Queen Victoria."

"Warmer."

"His Royal Highness . . ."

". . . the Prince of Wales. Well done!"

Richard's happiness affected his whole life. It was as if he'd reached one of those magic periods when nothing can go wrong—the equivalent of the gambler's golden run of luck—and for these months he began to lead a charmed existence. As always happens, people began to recognise his luck, and at Westminster he was pointed out as "one of the coming men."

It was a good moment for a young politician to be "promising." Gladstone's government was obviously doomed. Gordon was speared to death that January in Khartoum, and Gladstone's unpopularity was almost as serious as Dangerfield had predicted. Richard was in the House for the great debate when the censure motion against the government failed by a mere fourteen votes.

From that moment the whole opposition sensed the exciting tang of blood—Gladstone's blood, his whole ministry's blood. Carnage was in the air, and Richard knew that once the quarry fell, the pickings would go to those with the confidence and the strength to take them. It was a rare occasion, one of those crucial moments that come perhaps twice in a century, when the whole field of politics is open, when the old are sacrificed and the young and resolute grasp at their opportunities.

Richard was more than ready. Gordon's death had finally convinced him (not that he needed much convincing) of the "incompetence and moral bankruptcy" (as he put it) of the Liberals. And the outcry in the House had also finally given him a leader, someone whose cause he could believe in and whose personality he could entirely admire.

Even today it is impossible to read the tirades of Randolph Churchill against the Gladstone government without feeling something of the excitement of the time. For Richard the immediate effect of these passionately lucid speeches was electrifying. Richard had no time for Salisbury nor that oligarchy of rich landowners around him who still ruled the Party. (When Joseph Chamberlain the year before had accused great Salisbury of "constituting himself spokesman of a class who toil not, neither do they spin," Richard had secretly applauded.) But in Randolph there seemed the hope of a different tradition, conservatism that was not simply a rich man's club but had its roots in

Disraeli's dream of uniting Britain's "two nations," the rich and the poor. And under Randolph's spell, Richard was rapidly becoming one of the new phenomena of English politics—a Tory Democrat.

In many ways it was a shrewd move, for it gave Richard a decisive chance to use his talents. Men of his abilities are rare in any party at the best of times: among the Tories that spring of 1885 he ranked as something of a potential prodigy. He could write. Perhaps he was no Zola, but his political journalism of this period gave him a standing well ahead of his rank as an unknown, and still untried, backbench M.P.

It also gave him money. Not a lot. Certainly nothing like that target of eight thousand pounds a year which he had set himself to gain his independence from the Southwolds. But he had started writing regularly for those influential literary-*cum*-political journals that abounded at the time—*The New Age, The Political Gazette,* even *The Economist.* And since he had a good brain and spoke his mind, he began to be respected.

It was a new and quite intoxicating experience for Richard. He began to be invited out and Marjorie with him. She, whilst suspicious of his views, enjoyed his new success, She also enjoyed the sort of political gossip that became their conversational life's blood. He in his turn was very proud of her. Pregnancy seemed to suit her. She had lost that slightly waif-like air which she had had before her marriage, and in its place was a stately sort of beauty that naturally attracted attention. In Richard's eyes she never had been lovelier than now.

He was glad that she made no attempt to hide her pregnancy (it would have been difficult). Instead she seemed to glory in it, wearing loose-fitting long silk dresses and having her hair unfashionably long. Richard called her his "earth mother" and his "fertility goddess," and there was something goddess-like about her now. Together they made a rather splendid couple. Men made a fuss of her and envied him. Success became them.

One night at Manchester House she found herself talking to Lord Randolph Churchill. He was extremely flattering, as he could be when he wanted to. Then he spoke of Richard just as gracefully. "We are all waiting, Lady Marjorie, for your husband's maiden speech."

"And so am I," she said.

And so was Richard. He knew that it was overdue and that if he was ever to achieve his real ambition as a politician he would need to make his name in debate. His journalism on its own would never be enough. But the idea of speaking secretly appalled him. He felt he was no orator, and the prospect of rising in the House of Commons and risking everything before that critical assembly was a nightmare. He told himself that there was nothing in it to be afraid of, that the standard of debate was lamentably low, that he was cleverer, brighter, better educated than three quarters of the House, but it was still no use. The fearful duty of his maiden speech hung over him like a suspended sentence.

March came, and with it, life at 165 began to change. Marjorie was now beginning her eighth month and Herr Dr. von Bülow ruled that she must stop her social life. This did not worry Richard, who was delighted to spend more evenings with his wife at home. But then something did upset him. Southwold again impinged upon the private world he shared with Marjorie, and in a way that he could not do much about.

The first he knew of it was when he returned one Wednesday evening from the House to find an irate Mrs. Bridges puffing up the stairs with a tray. He asked her why.

"It's her," said Mrs. Bridges darkly.

"Who?"

"Her. Nanny Whatsername. She came this afternoon, and not a word or a by-your-leave. The girls all have their half-day, Alice is sick, but Nanny Whatsername demands her supper. I tell you, sir, some people!" and with a flurry of her outraged rump, the good Mrs. Bridges went on up the stairs. Richard followed her, to be met outside the bedroom door by Marjorie.

"Dearest," she said a little awkwardly, "I've something to confess."

Richard looked puzzled.

"Nanny's arrived."

"Who is this Nanny creature?" he said testily. "Already she seems to have brought our Mrs. Bridges to the brink of mutiny. It really is too much!"

"She's Nanny Webster. My old nanny. She looked after me and after Hugo, so naturally I want her here for our baby too."

"You mean she's come from Southwold?

"But of course."

"And by arrangement with your mother?"

"Richard, be reasonable!"

And, of course, he was. But he could hardly help feeling resentful of the way the influence of hated Southwold seemed to be infiltrating the most private places in his marriage. And Nanny Webster didn't help. She was a gaunt, dark-eyed woman with a dominating manner. Since she had nursed and loved Marjorie from babyhood, she still acted just as if she owned her. Like so many of her kind, she seemed to think that fathers were some alien, unfeeling, barely necessary class who were best kept out of things at times like this. From the day that she appeared at 165, Marjorie was firmly taken over.

"Now, Mr. Bellamy, her ladyship must have her rest"—this when he was settling for the after-lunch chat he often had with Marjorie, only to have her hustled off to bed. Or "Surely you realise her ladyship should never drink champagne in her condition."

It was her manner that annoyed him—as it did the servants, all of whom loathed her. But Nanny Webster knew her rights and used them ruthlessly. Richard could do no more than grumble impotently to Hudson.

"But, sir, just a few weeks, then you can send her packing," Hudson would say encouragingly.

"That's just the hell of it—I can't. Once the baby's born, she's here forever."

"Patience, sir," Hudson would reply. "Things have a way of working out."

"Usually for the worse," Richard said gloomily.

What Richard hated most about the situation was that it cut him off from Marjorie. Just when he'd felt so close to her, so proud of her, so very much in love with her, this dreadful harridan from Southwold had come and thrust herself between them. And there was nothing he could do.

Inevitably he began to stay later at the House. And inevitably too, the question of his maiden speech began pursuing him again. How effortless it seemed, this business of making a speech in a debate! Most of the members could apparently rattle off their speeches in their sleep (and many of them sounded like it too). Yet for him it was a paralysing chore. Part of his trouble was that he felt so much was now expected of him. It had been a mistake to wait so long, and the perfectionist in him made it more difficult still. What should he speak on? Foreign affairs? Finance? The Suez policy? They were all subjects he had views on, and he prepared himself before each big debate. (Dangerfield advised him to learn his first speech off by heart, then practice it before his mirror. This he had done, to Marjorie's great amusement.) But when the big debates occurred, he either lost his nerve or was not called. Once he had sat on till nearly midnight with his word-perfect speech on Gladstone's Balkans policy ticking in his head, only to hear Herbert Wilson, the government chief whip, move the adjournment of the house "owing to the lateness of the hour." Never again!

Then on the twenty-third of March came the big debate on Gladstone's Irish policy, and the opposition planned a full attack upon the government. Richard had written several pieces recently criticising Gladstone—for his weakness, for the way he seemed to abdicate to force, for his lack of a coherent policy. And on the day before, a note arrived at 165 for Richard Bellamy, M.P.

"Perhaps you would care to speak on the motion for the adjournment?"

It was signed by Elkins, one of the opposition whips. For a backbencher it was a rare honour—and a challenge—to be singled out in this way for a maiden speech. Richard was terrified, but there was no evading this time, and he spent many of the following twenty-four hours polishing, perfecting, memorising what he intended as the great speech of his career.

Perhaps wisely he said nothing now to Marjorie, except to warn her that with the big debate he'd probably be late. It was a great, full-dress occasion. Gladstone spoke magnificently. What an extraordinary performer the old man was! Here he was, harried and reviled by the press and the opposition, just on the edge of losing power, and yet for nearly two hours he held the House of Commons in the palm of his strong old hand. No one could match him—with Disraeli dead—for his combination of lucidity and feeling; not even Randolph Churchill, who spoke after him. Randolph could attack—and did—with sarcasm and wit and extraordinary passion. Richard was reminded of some violent swordsman, lunging again and yet again at the body of the government. Yet somehow Gladstone stayed aloof, untouched by the intensity of feeling, and did so through the rest of the debate. Parnell, O'Donovan and several of the Irish members had their say. So did the opposition's stars—Chamberlain (distinctly pompous), Bright (restrained), Hatherfield (too legalistic). It was, as

Richard realised, a great set-piece of parliamentary history, the like of which he'd never see again, and yet he had the feeling that none of these fine phrases, none of this eloquence would change that rain-swept, bitter island where the ricks were burning and the people starving.

Richard had the dreadful task too of attempting to hold on to his own speech as one by one his favourite points got swept away by other speakers. There was no question of his being called to speak until towards the end of the debate, and he stayed gamely on until seven-thirty, when the House began to empty. Then finally he rose, trying to catch the Speaker's eye. But so did someone else, just ahead of him, a tall, thin, rather languid-looking man recently elected to the House. Richard had not met him but knew him as young Arthur Balfour, Salisbury's nephew. He and not Richard was called to speak.

The next fifteen minutes were among the most excruciating in Richard's life, as one by one young Arthur Balfour made the points that Richard had prepared. It was uncanny, like some exercise in thought transference: the need for firmness and for justice, Ireland's economic ills, the doubts he had about the Irish members. And to make it worse, Balfour spoke with an extraordinary elegance and ease, which Richard knew quite well he could not hope to equal.

So he sat listening—hopeless and rather envious—as this gilded youth spoke on, then sat to a chorus of "hear-hears." There was silence then, as more members anxious for their dinner left the chamber. And then, to his alarm, Richard saw that the Speaker was looking straight at him and nodding. Flustered, Richard half rose as he heard the Speaker calling the name of his constituency. The moment he had dreaded and dreamed about had come, and with a vacuum in his head, he was on his feet.

He never forgot those next few seconds as he stood mute and mindless in the House of Commons, trying to find the words he needed. That telling opening and those Gibbonesque phrases he had labouriously prepared had gone, and he stood tongue-tied, horribly aware of members watching and of the Speaker's eye (like a brown glass marble) fixed on him from beneath the long grey wig.

He faltered. Then suddenly, just ahead of him, he caught sight of the small fiery figure with the bulging eyes and enormous black moustache. Randolph Churchill was watching him and nodding towards him.

Somehow this was all Richard needed. Somewhere in the recesses of his brain he found a phrase that he had written recently on the Sinn Fein terrorists—"these murderous men who feel that they can make their way with bomb and bludgeon . . ." It was enough, the opening he needed, and the remainder of his speech came almost automatically. It was not a polished speech like Arthur Balfour's but it somehow caught the mood of ordinary people who were appalled and sickened by the Irish violence. Once he had started, Richard had the feeling that the House was with him: no one else left for dinner and he enjoyed the silence that a speaker gets only when everyone is waiting for each succeeding phrase. He didn't speak for long, but when he sat the "hear-hears" were as loud as Balfour's.

There is a tradition in the House of indulgence and politeness for a maiden speech. Richard enjoyed it, and stayed long enough to hear the next speaker praise the "wisdom and sagacity, unusual in a maiden speech" of "the honourable member who preceded me." It was all he wanted, and he left the chamber.

As he passed the opposition lobby, somebody stopped him.

"Well done, Bellamy, well done! You've finally pulled it off! Feeling better? We'll be hearing more from you."

There was a nod, a smile from those strange protuberant eyes, and the black moustache was gone before Richard could so much as stammer out his thanks.

This was a moment of pure triumph which Richard remembered all his life. It was a fine spring night, and as he walked out into Palace Yard the sky was clear, the moon above the river.

"Cab, Mr. Bellamy?" inquired the policeman at the gate.

For just that moment Richard felt like telling the policeman that he had made his maiden speech and been praised by Randolph Churchill. Instead he said, "No thank you, officer. I'll walk."

In fact he felt like bounding across Parliament Square. Big Ben was striking ten. He was much later than he'd thought, and had eaten nothing. Almost light-headed with euphoria and hunger, he set off past the Abbey and up by St. James's Park to Hyde Park Corner, swinging his walking stick and humming to himself. He hadn't felt like this since he was at school and heard he'd won his scholarship to Oxford.

He was still in this state of pure excitement when he reached Eaton Place. The downstairs lights were on, and although he let himself in with his latch-key, Hudson was waiting for him in the hall. Richard failed to notice the look of strain upon his butler's face.

"God, I'm starving, Hudson! Is there a cold bird in the house—and some champagne? Perhaps a bottle of the 1860 Krug?"

Normally a request for a bottle of the best champagne would have elicited from Hudson a tactful "Something to celebrate then, sir?" and Richard would happily have told him the cause of his excitement. He might even have suggested that Hudson join him in a glass (Hudson, like Richard, had a taste for good champagne).

But tonight it was a very wary Hudson who replied, "The *best* champagne, sir?"

"Certainly," said Richard. "Oh, and Hudson—is Lady Marjorie still awake?"

"To the best of my knowledge, sir. But if I might suggest . . ."

"Capital, Hudson. And bring up the champagne. Blow Nanny Webster! I'll take it up to her and she can have a glass!"

By night Marjorie's boudoir was a pretty sight, with its gilt mirrors, flowered curtains, and the twin gold cherubs holding the draperies above the big rococo bed. The room was lit by gas-lights with pink silk shades. It was the one room in the house that really breathed her presence, and Richard very often felt just faintly uneasy there with so much total femininity. But not tonight. After his maiden speech, his triumph in the House, and with the champagne on a silver tray, he felt that he had more than justified himself.

Marjorie was sitting up in bed, her hair unpinned, her skin just tinged with rose from the lamps, her eyes mysterious with deep shadows round them. This was the sort of sudden beauty which she could always summon up and which took his breath away. So near her time, she was enormous, and her size gave her a sort of majesty as she sat enthroned on her silvery pillows. The room was heavy with her scent of lilies of the valley.

He kissed her and she smiled indulgently. His hair was rumpled, his cravat askew. This was a side of him she loved—the mischievous schoolboy she enjoyed detecting in her sophisticated husband.

"Are you training as a waiter, dearest?" she said, laughing at his tray.

"Not a bad idea. It looks as if the government will soon collapse and I might need a job after the election."

He uncorked the champagne, filled the two glasses, and began telling her about his maiden speech. But there was something on her mind and he soon realised that she was not listening to him.

"Marjorie, what is it?" he asked, rather more sharply than he intended.

"Nothing," she said, "nothing at all. Please go on. You were saying?"

"Marjorie, what is it? I refuse to say another word until I know."

And then, emotionally and tearfully, the story of her afternoon emerged. How Nanny Webster had been getting worried about her, how she had summoned Dr. Cowley up from Southwold.

"*That* old quack!" exploded Richard.

"Dearest!" said Marjorie, shocked as people always tend to be when doctors, priests and other childhood pundits are referred to disrespectfully. Then she went on to say that Dr. Cowley gave it as his opinion . . . Here she was overcome with tears and for a while would not continue. Finally Richard calmed her.

"What did he say?" he asked anxiously. Marjorie all but whispered her reply.

"He said that for my well-being and the safety of the baby I should be in the country."

"Say it. At Southwold!"

Majorie nodded. "Dearest," she said, "do please try to understand."

"I understand too well!"

"But for the baby, Richard. Surely it's not much to ask."

She was sobbing now, great tears that seemed to rack her body, but Richard was stony in his anger and said nothing, in case bitterness might make him give vent to something he would regret. How typical it was of the whole pattern of his marriage. Even at a time like this, a moment that should have been a happiness to be enjoyed alone with Marjorie, the Southwolds still insisted on intruding. And they spoiled everything. If he allowed them to continue they would destroy his marriage, possibly his life.

"There's no question of it," he said finally. "The house is more than adequate, and everything's prepared. Just because your mother wants to rule you—and spite me—she will use any trick she can, even her old doctor, to attain her ends. No, Marjorie. I wish you to stay here and have our baby in the house."

He kissed her goodnight and left the champagne on the dressing table—where Miss Roberts found it next morning when she came to wake her mistress.

"It's disgusting how these people waste the good things of life," she said as she carried it away.

Richard was resolute—but of course his resolution could not last. What mere man's could in such a situation? Marjorie had quietly made up her mind that her first child was to be born in Southwold, and as well might Richard have attempted to resist the march of time or the power of an earthquake. Not that she nagged him (she was too smart for that), nor did she resort to further argument (again she realised her weakness against Richard in straightforward argument). She just relied upon the female power of silence, of refusing to discuss the matter when Richard brought it up again next morning.

"I'm sure that you know best, my love"—which made him wonder whether he really did.

She also secretly enlisted Prudence Fairfax in her cause.

This was a canny move, for Prudence was the only one of Marjorie's friends whom Richard respected. She was intelligent and could make him laugh. And so, that selfsame afternoon, when Prudence called on Richard in the Commons and then had tea with him, she was able to convince him without too much trouble.

"Richard," she said, "I think you've been—forgive me if I say it but I must—just a little selfish with poor Marjorie. Don't you realise how lonely she has been in London, and how much she misses Southwold? She's very loyal, but this feud between you and her mother naturally distresses her."

"Well, Prudence dear . . ." said Richard, trying to be reasonable.

"And besides, don't you realise that every male Southwold has been born there in the house since fourteen hundred?"

"I never realised," said Richard.

"Well," said Prudence, big blue eyes wide open with surprise, "I think perhaps you should."

So Marjorie went to Southwold two days later, with Miss Roberts and the embattled Nanny Webster. The baby was due in ten days or so. Richard was needed in Westminster for at least another week, until Parliament adjourned for Easter. He would then go down to Southwold for those last few days when the birth was due.

It was a tense week in the Commons, with the whole opposition pressing hard and the government still managing to hang on to its majority. Richard spoke again, this time on foreign policy, with which he felt at home, and this time he was at ease and in command from the start. Within a matter of two weeks it seemed as if he'd passed from parliamentary innocent into the role of hardened old debater.

Finally, in that first week of April, just before Easter, Parliament adjourned, and Richard was free at last to join Marjorie. He had mixed feelings about going. On the one hand he was longing to see her again and genuinely missed her. But on the other, all the talk about the Southwolds and the way he felt the family had exploited her fears about the birth seemed to have robbed the whole event of its original excitement. He also dreaded seeing Lady Southwold. He hated scenes and arguments. Christmas had upset him dreadfully and one simply never knew what she would pick on next.

So it was a wary—as well as weary—Richard Bellamy who caught the evening train to Salisbury and found himself struggling through the crowd of passengers to see who had come to meet him. It was drizzling, and in the dark it took some time for him to find the carriage they had sent: not the phaeton, nor even the victoria, but the small hacking coach they used for carrying the servants. Old Mandible, the half-retired coachman, touched his derby with his whip when he saw Richard and smiled his knowing, toothless smile, looking as if the tip of his nose would touch his chin.

"Evenin', Mr. Bellamy," he said. "Great news from Southwold!"

"News? What news?" said Richard.

"Why, of 'er ladyship, of Lady Marjorie. A fine boy, born this afternoon. A great day for Southwold now and no mistake."

He laughed and cracked his whip, and the old cob broke into an uneasy trot. Richard shivered and buttoned his coat against the rain.

So this, he reflected bitterly, was how he got the news that his son was born—from an old drunken coachman. Typical, he thought. Just one more insult from the family. Throughout the drive his anger quite outweighed all sense of the excitement of the moment. He could not even think with tenderness of Marjorie.

As they drove down the long avenue of limes leading to Southwold he could see the lights gleaming through the rain. They passed the giant figures of Gog and Magog by the courtyard entrance, and then Mandible reined in by the back door before clambering off the box like an old crab in livery. Nobody greeted them and the coachman opened the door. Richard entered.

As he did so there was a smell of woodsmoke from the fire in the hall, and Cromwell rose barking angrily at the intruder: then he recognised Richard and came hobbling over, his peg-leg thumping on the floor, his great rope of tail swinging with pleasure. Richard patted him.

"Good dog, Cromwell," he said. "Good old boy. Where's everybody?"

Cromwell barked mournfully but no one came.

So Richard walked across the hall and up the great Southwold staircase to the Prince's Landing, the long, galleried landing that runs the length of the first floor of the house. And there he saw Hugo. He was rather drunk.

"Richard! Good Lord, how most appropriate!"

"Hugo, where are they?"

"Who?"

"My wife and my son!"

"Oh, they're in Lord Henry's Room. Why don't you come and see them? You really should, you know, old boy."

Lord Henry's Room was one of the great historic apartments overlooking the formal garden at the back of the house, and it was there, in the huge four-poster where generations of Southwolds had been born, that Marjorie lay. The whole family was there—Lord and Lady Southwold, Great-Aunt Helena, Cousin Alec of the Grenadiers, and several of the household servants. Even Geoffrey Dillon had been summoned, and they were all busy (as Hugo put it) "wetting the baby's head."

But Richard barely noticed. Once he saw Marjorie, all the bitterness and anger of the past few weeks completely vanished.

"Dearest," she said, and held out her arms to him.

"My love," he said, and held her very tight.

"Richard," she whispered, "you're forgetting somebody." And then Richard saw his son. He was beside her on the pillow—monkey-faced and tinged with yellow, with sharp tufts of darkish hair (slightly premature, the baby weighed a mere six pounds at birth).

"He's yours," she said, and held him up for Richard, who took him warily.

"Funny-looking little devil," said Lord Southwold. "Still, they all are. Marjorie was just the same."

"Marjorie was beautiful," said Lady Southwold.

"What are you calling him?" asked Lord Southwold.

"I hadn't really thought," said Richard.

"I have," said Marjorie. "I want to call him James, after Richard's father."

"But we've never had a James in the family before," said Lady Southwold.

"Then it's time we did," said Marjorie.

1885-87

6. *Setbacks and Successes*

There are certain absolute realities great families acknowledge: property, of course, is one, money another, power yet another. And so is birth, legitimate birth, for birth and pedigree establish certain rights to the whole jealously acquired and guarded mass of rights and wealth and land which a great family like the Southwolds represents. Because of this, the birth of James did far more to establish Richard's status in the family than his marriage to Marjorie.

It would still be a slow and sometimes painful process as the Southwolds gradually accepted him. But it effectively began now with the birth of sickly and undersized James Francis Bellamy. Even that weekend Richard felt the difference as the family began those feudal celebrations which for generations had been held at Southwold when a male was born. The fact that the infant's father was not a Southwold did not matter. The Southwolds no longer had their ancient right of descent through the female line if the male one failed. But this scarcely lessened James's importance. Until Hugo married and produced an heir, little James Francis was the effective heir of all that wealth and splendour that surrounded him. He seemed supremely unaware of his importance as he lay with his mother in that great four-poster. (She still felt weak, but quietly triumphant. James cried a lot, but Dr. Cowley had pronounced him healthy: already he was proving quite a greedy baby. Marjorie fed him and enjoyed it.)

So in the absence of his wife and son it fell to Richard to have the place of honour in that Sunday's celebrations. He stood beside Lord Southwold in the Southwold pew as the Reverend Prothero, in a shaky, old-man's voice, gave "heartfelt thanks to our Creator, Jesus Christ, the source of all life, for the happy delivery of our beloved Lady Marjorie." He also joined the prayers for his son—"May he be upright, just, and fearless in the Lord!"—a strange sensation.

"Now comes the moment everyone's been waiting for," said Lord Southwold as they left the church.

On the green beyond the church the ox had been roasting on its spit all day and Groundsel the bailiff had set up a great barrel of the strongest Southwold ale, brewed for the occasion. There were two fiddlers from Bordon and already the green was crammed with villagers, several hundred of them, yokels and wood-men, labourers and craftsmen from the estate. Richard saw old Dan Hegarty, who claimed to have been a drummer-boy at Waterloo. He had his grandchildren and his great-grandchildren round him. Like all the villagers, they were dependent on the Southwolds for their living, and his lordship was something more to them than the rich man in the big house up the road. He was their lord, employer, benefactor. He settled their disputes, knew them by name, punished them for poaching and gave them a guinea when they married. Their grandfathers had served his grandfather. Whether their grandsons would continue the tradition was another matter, but in that year 1885, in a changing world and with the aristocracy threatened by death duties and the Liberal Party, Lord Southwold still continued much as the feudal Earls of Southwold had for centuries.

He was extremely popular (her ladyship, "a regular tartar" to the villagers, less so), and as he stepped onto the green there was a loyal cheer from everyone. There was also a cheer for Richard and a short loyal speech from Foat, the Southwold carpenter, thanking his lordship for the party and congratulating one and all on "this happiest event." Then Groundsel tapped the cask, the cooks began slicing at the ox and the fiddlers struck up. That night, in celebration of the birth, the village ate and drank, and the traditional bonfire blazed on Bordon Hill.

The Southwolds celebrated too, with slightly more sophistication than the villagers. James's birth seemed to have induced a new touch of family feeling in the egocentric Southwold clan. Southwold himself appeared much moved by the villagers.

"This is the world that matters," he said several times to Richard. "Not London, nor that claptrap about the Empire, but the real heart of England."

Even Lady Southwold seemed mellowed by her new role as grandmother. For the first time in her life she addressed her son-in-law as "Richard," and she spoke quite sentimentally about the baby. Hugo, jovially drunk, repeated several times that he would have to start thinking seriously about making heirs himself.

"Best to get married first," said Richard cheerfully. And Hugo, whose long-drawn-out attempt to land an American heiress was rather a sore subject, winced.

Marjorie came down to dinner. The unhappiness and jealousy that had marred the end of her confinement still lay uncomfortably between them. Despite himself, Richard still resented the way she had made him let her have the child at Southwold. Also, he always found it hard to feel happy with her in this unhappy house. (Only in Eaton Place, in their own home, was he completely at ease with her.) But he was very proud of her that night, and she too made an effort to offset the bitterness against Richard in the past.

So the evening turned out to be the happiest one that Richard ever spent at Southwold. He felt himself accepted there at last (a premature assumption, as events would prove) and even managed to enjoy the stormy personalities of both of his wife's parents.

Much of the credit for this happy state of things must go to Widgery, the butler: he knew Lord Southwold well enough to understand that on a night like this he would demand the very best champagne. And very good it was—three bottles of the legendary Château Jubloteau of 1848.

"The year of revolutions," Southwold murmured gloomily. "The year the rot began. The world has never been the same again. But it was a great year for champagne."

It was indeed. As Richard savoured the caress of that mysterious, flat, wonderful champagne, he felt that he was tasting the last sad flavour of a world forever lost. It was Southwold's world, not his, but as he drank, toasting his son and the latest heir to Southwold, he could understand his lordship's passion for the past, for that *vraie douceur de la vie* which old aristocrats remembered.

Richard was worried about James. Not for his health—that soon improved. Within a fortnight all the yellowness had gone, the wrinkles disappeared, and young James Francis, improving on his weight at birth, was on the road to bonny babyhood. He still kept Nanny Webster up all night ("Good for him," thought Richard), but he was much admired and made a fuss of, particularly by Marjorie, who adored him.

What disturbed Richard was his own lack of feeling for his son. He who had so looked forward to him, who had been so thrilled at the *idea* of fatherhood, was sadly disappointed by the reality.

Part of the trouble was that he never seemed to see him. Old Nanny Webster seemed to have taken entire charge of him, just as she had originally taken charge of Marjorie. As far as Richard was concerned, he wasn't "James," nor was he his son. He was a forbidding character called "Baby"; Baby was not allowed to be excited or picked up, Baby was not allowed to be disturbed. Baby was bathed, wrapped up and changed by Nanny Webster; and that, as far as Richard was concerned, was that.

He also felt that Baby, in some obscure way, belonged to Southwold, not to him. The fact that he was born there, and not at 165, made him seem one of "them" to Richard. Also, there was all the business of the inheritance, which Richard found disturbing. He knew it was illogical, but he could not help resenting the way that whilst he was still officially dependent on his wife for everything, this son that he had fathered was already heir to all the Southwold riches. This seemed obscurely wrong and made it hard for him to treat the infant as an ordinary baby. As he told Marjorie, he really could not wait for Hugo to sort out his marriage problems, get himself an heir, and so relieve *his* family of its hideous responsibility.

Hardly surprisingly, Marjorie found all this difficult to grasp. She was delighted at the idea that her son was heir to Southwold and she could still not understand (she never really had) the true extent of Richard's resentment of her family. To her it was, as she confided now to Prudence, "really very tiresome and silly of him," and she would never fathom quite how much Richard's attitude to Southwold was bound up with his own self-respect, and to that strong vein of disappointment in his life.

For her it was inconceivable that Richard could still be worried over money and the whole business of his wretched stipend. Her attitude, inherited from centuries of plenty and largesse, was that money was something one took for granted like the air one breathed. When she arranged for her whole allowance to be paid into the Coutts account in Richard's name, she felt that the affair was settled—but it wasn't. Richard never ceased now to be conscious of the fact that he lived, as he bitterly reflected, "almost entirely off a rich wife."

The bitterness was not alleviated by the pleasure that the money gave him: unlike Marjorie, he had inherited a bourgeois attitude to money. He was a puritan in this, as in much else, and he believed, deep down, that a man should earn his living and support his wife and family. The fact that Marjorie and now his own baby son were both potentially so much richer than he could ever be seemed not just wrong but curiously unnatural. He would have been hard put to it to explain his attitude on this. It was not strictly logical—as he would have been the first to admit—but just the same it troubled him. And since he never risked discussing it with Marjorie, she never even had a chance of understanding what was perhaps the deepest source of trouble in her marriage.

Nor did she ever really grasp the differences between them over politics. These too were fundamental and very much bound up with Southwold. She was so much her father's daughter that she took it for granted that politics, including Richard's politics, had one essential aim: to preserve, assist, and encourage a society like Southwold. For her this was self-evident. For Richard not. And during this crucial summer of their marriage she was to find herself baffled—and quite often pained—by her husband's behaviour.

When young James Francis was only a few weks old, history intruded into the new, nanny-dominated life of 165. Embattled old Mr. Gladstone's long-lived Liberal administration finally collapsed, and both the Bellamys found themselves thrown into the rough and tumble of the hustings.

It was a tough contest. Richard, with so much recently acquired political ambition, was determined to win. His opponent was equally determined. Since the last election the local Liberals had taken on a new man, a wine merchant called Tatham. He was bucolic, lively and energetic, a great enthusiast for lost causes, and he was popular. Unlike Richard, he possessed the common touch. His meetings were much livelier—and more crammed—than Richard's, and whilst in theory the Conservatives should have been able to expect a landslide, Richard began to worry.

True, he had a great deal in his favour: respectability (which his opponent lacked), a reputation as a concerned constituency man, and the name he had earned from his journalism. But the fact was that little of this cut much ice against the bounding tactics of the outrageous Tatham. Tatham kissed babies by the pram-load. (Richard insisted that this wasn't quite his line.) Tatham imported droves of glamorous Liberal ladies for his canvassing. ("*Ladies?*" said Richard. "Surely not!") Worst of all, Tatham made fun of him as "Dithering Dick" and "Bumbling Bellamy." ("The man's clearly a cad," said Richard when he heard.)

But cad or not, the Liberal was having an effect and Richard was not. After the first week of the campaign he was beginning to get worried. So was his agent, Pyecombe, a hardened old professional who knew a loser when he saw one.

"Dodgy, extremely dodgy, Mr. Bellamy," he said, puffing at a large cigar. "We must find something big to pull out of the bag, and no mistake. And quick's the word, Mr. Bellamy. Quick's the word!"

Easier said than done. Richard knew himself and knew he couldn't hope to rival Tatham in sheer popular appeal. He was no demagogue, no natural democrat. (To be honest, he disliked elections, and disliked the brute necessity of "meeting the people.") But if he failed now, his whole career was finished, and with it his last shreds of self-respect. How could he ever face the Southwolds, let alone his wife and servants, if he failed? A hideous prospect, and he spent that first weekend (in those godly days there was no electioneering on the Sabbath) sunk in forboding and the deepest gloom.

It was Marjorie's turn to help. She had made two brief visits to the constituency: Richard insisted that it was too soon after the baby for her to do much more. But these two visits had been enough for her to see quite clearly what was happening. She said nothing at the time, but on that Sunday, when she saw Richard's crumbling morale she spoke.

"It's no use pretending, is it, Richard?"

"Pretending?" he said angrily. "Who's pretending, Marjorie?"

"Dearest, for heaven's sake talk to me. I can't bear to see you giving in like this."

"Marjorie, I am *not* giving in. It's simply that for me this isn't politics. It's a bear-garden, and it isn't me."

"You know," she said softly, "there is one man who could save you."

"One man? Who on earth?"

"Father. He's in London. I think we ought to see him."

"For God's sake, Marjorie, talk sense!" said Richard.

But that night there were dinner guests at 165, Lord Southwold and his man, Matthews. They talked long and stayed extremely late.

With the intervention of Lord Southwold into the Bellamy campaign, Tatham had met his match.

"Everybody loves a lord"—the burgesses of Sutton did at any rate, and Southwold played the part to perfection. That Monday evening Richard had a rally of the faithful at the Constitutional Hall, and had prepared an earnest speech upon the virtues of "the New Conservatism." His lordship changed all that.

There was the rumble of a coach and four. A post horn sounded in the High Street, and Lord Southwold, clad in top boots, riding coat and fine silk hat, strode into the meeting. He paused to wave his whip at the crowd which his arrival had attracted in the street. They cheered. He raised his hat to them and the fun started.

His was an extraordinary speech—the very last thing Richard would have imagined to appeal to the working voters of this very ordinary constituency, and also the last thing that Richard would have put his name to. It was reactionary and sentimental. It poured scorn on "that common fellow the common man." It said quite baldly that this had traditionally been a Southwold seat—and long may it continue. (At this everybody cheered.) When the chairman asked for questions someone asked, "Will Lord Southwold win the Derby this year?"

"As long as you vote for Bellamy, I'll do my best!" he said. To Richard's puzzlement this brought the house down.

And so the remainder of the campaign went on. Tatham did his best, but the presence of Lord Southwold *and* the blunders of Mr. Gladstone were too much. The initiative had swung decisively to the Conservatives. But somehow not to Richard. Increasingly he felt that this was no longer his campaign, but he gamely did his best to tell the voters what he believed and what he would do for them when he was elected. None of them showed much enthusiasm, but they voted for him in the end by a majority of over three thousand. Marjorie could never understand why Richard was not more excited, nor why he disliked the way the news appeared in the local paper.

"Victory for Southwold Interest," proclaimed the headline.

As far as the country was concerned, the general election brought a baffling result. The Liberals were out, that much was clear. But who was in? That was anything but certain. The old party lines had broken, and there was no clear grouping now to form a government. The Tories were a motley crew, an *ad hoc* alliance ranging from feudal landowners like Manchester and Devonshire and Southwold to their avowed opponents, Empire-toting businessmen and radicals like Dilke and the hated Joseph Chamberlain. Richard was somewhere in between both groups, with his star hitched firmly now to Randolph Churchill. But the big question which would have to be decided was the question of the leader. Who was powerful enough and tough enough to unite the Tories and so lead the country? It was by no means clear, and Richard found himself disastrously involved in the negotiations that ensued.

It was just two days after his re-election that Richard was invited by Lord Southwold to have dinner with him at the Carlton Club. Here in the hallowed sanctum of high toryism, his lordship cut a very different figure from the rumbustious, gallivanting Southwold of the hustings. It was another facet of this very complex man that Richard saw that night—Southwold the statesman, who, as Cartwright said, had once been tipped to step into Beaconsfield's shoes as leader of the Party; Southwold the involved grandee who suddenly seemed ready to do battle for his class and for that threatened antique view of the England he loved.

He was immensely dignified and Richard found himself suddenly in awe of him. He tried to thank him for his help in the election.

"Help, Richard? Come, you flatter me. That was just slapstick comedy, but it's what the people like. Still, I must say that the result encouraged me. A majority like yours shows what can be done. Reform has had its day. The Liberals are totally played out. The time has come for men like us to stand up clearly for the things that matter."

He leaned back, sipped his port, and stared at Richard with his pale grey eyes. "I have been sounding out my colleagues in the Lords. Most of them are with me."

"And Salisbury?" said Richard.

"Who can trust a man like that? He tries to be all things to all men—Churchill and even Chamberlain. If he succeeds there's not much hope for us."

"And so you'll challenge him for leadership?"

"Someone must. Whom else do you suggest?"

Richard was shaken by the calm and the assurance with which his father-in-law told him his decision.

"Why do you tell *me* this?" he asked.

Southwold eyed him shrewdly. "Because, Richard, I must know if you are for me or against me."

❧ ☙

Lord Southwold's bid to lead the Tories was kept out of the press (the Party still possessed a knack for keeping its squabbles to itself), but during the next few days it came to be the one great point of speculation in the clubs and lobbies of Westminster. The rumours also reached Belgravia (as rumours inevitably do).

Marjorie was thrilled. "Dearest," she said to Richard, "it's what we've longed for. With Father as Prime Minister, think of the boost that it will mean for you. Besides, it will be wonderful for him."

Richard agreed. What was less certain was whether a Southwold government would be so wonderful for the country—or the Party—but he judiciously kept such doubts to himself.

Certainly the pace of Southwold's movement was astounding: he had not underestimated the strength of feeling in the Party against the mood of change that had recently been so fashionable. Rumour had it that he could already count on a firm majority within the Lords and that a number of the old Whig families were tempted to his side. Rumour also had it that the Queen was contemplating whether to call on him to try to form a government. But there were other rumours too—more disturbing ones. In Birmingham, Chamberlain was already said to be threatening to join the left wing of the Liberals if there was any question of a Southwold government. Lord Randolph and the Tory Democrats were up in arms. Only Lord Salisbury, impenetrable as ever, was keeping what was known as "all his options open."

Richard did not enjoy the sudden prominence this development thrust upon him. A silence fell in his club the moment he entered. Informed journalists tried to talk to him. Elkins, the opposition whip, tried to tap him over Lord Southwold's policy. He avoided all of them. Indeed, his inclination was to avoid all involvement in the squabble, but, unfortunately for him, this was impossible. Two days after dining with Lord Southwold, Richard received a summons he could not refuse.

"So, my dear Bellamy," Lord Randolph said, stroking his great moustache and speaking with that strange intensity he had, "the ties of marriage are proving stronger than the ties of principle."

"I'd not say that," Richard replied uncomfortably.

"What would you say, then?"

"That it's a matter for the Party to choose whom they will for leader. As a loyal member I shall accept . . ."

"As a loyal member, poppycock, Bellamy! Forgive me speaking plainly, but I must. As a loyal member who is not entirely bereft of all intelligence, you must know that the choice of your father-in-law—fine man although in some ways I acknowledge that he is—would prove an unmitigated and unprecedented disaster to your party. It would split it down from top to tail. It would put everything you and I believe in back a hundred years. If, that is, it did not bring a bloody revolution to our streets."

Richard smiled. He was finding the Churchillian eloquence excessive.

"Really, Lord Randolph . . ." he began.

"And really, Bellamy, it's no smiling matter. Salisbury's the only one who can possibly unite us. You know it, just as well as I. Admit it, Bellamy."

"If I admit it, what then?"

"Then, Bellamy, I think you must do something about it."

It was a painful interview that Richard had later that night with Southwold—and an historic one as well (although its true importance lies in the secret history of our times, which rarely finds its way into the history books).

Southwold was cock-a-hoop at the support he was gathering, and it took Richard some time to convince him he meant business.

"The other day you asked me if I was for you or against you. I have to tell you now that I'm against: firmly, irrevocably against."

Southwold look puzzled. "Richard, my dear boy—just as we're winning . . ."

"That's just the point. You can't win. I realise that now. If you win the leadership, you split the Party, and the country. It will be the end, not only of the Party, but of the things that you and I believe in."

Southwold was angry then, but Richard was implacable. Point by threatened point he spelled out what would happen if Lord Southwold took the leadership; and finally his lordship listened.

When Lord Salisbury stitched together his administration a few days later he performed one of the greatest feats of his career. As Lord Randolph had predicted, "Old Dead-Weight" had succeeded in keeping his jumble of a party somehow united. And although of course no one knew it at the time, it was to be this Salisbury administration that would rule the country for virtually the rest of the century.

But although Salisbury kept his party together, his list of ministers had some notable omissions, Southwold among them. When he was offered the position of Home Secretary, he didn't bother to reply. As a gesture this was totally in character, but it sealed his fate as a real contender for the power he longed for. He would continue as a symbol of an eighteenth-century England—increasingly eccentric and increasingly beloved—but his real chance was over.

Paradoxically, Richard's political career was badly damaged too. Lord Randolph, who was to become Salisbury's Chancellor of the Exchequer, saw to it that Richard was rewarded by the offer of an Under-secretaryship at the Treasury. It was a key position. Given Richard's undoubted talents at the time, plus Churchill's patronage, it could have led him to great things. But as he wrote to Churchill in his private letter of refusal, how could he possibly accept political reward for the destruction of Lord Southwold? Perhaps a more ruthless politician could have done it, but not Richard Bellamy.

One has no way of knowing whether Lord Salisbury ever knew how much he and his party owed to Richard; and anyhow, what great men can afford the luxury of gratitude in politics? By refusing office, Richard sealed his fate. Salisbury would not offer it again, and Richard would now be saddled with the reputation of Lord Southwold's creature. It would take him years to live this down; yet Southwold never quite forgave him for betraying him.

Marjorie never learned the truth of what had happened. It was probably as well, for it is hard to see how she could have forgiven Richard either. Instead, for her, those hectic early summer days always remained a mystery. She never understood quite why her father shied away from power when he appeared to have it in his grasp. Still less could she understand Richard's refusal of Lord Salisbury's offer.

In years to come, she would secretly despise him for it, since it seemed to prove that Richard had never possessed the will to win, and that he had never been much more than that conscientious, slightly uninspired back-bencher that she knew. But at the time this hardly mattered, and she actually felt relieved when all the jockeying for power was over. She had her husband to herself again, and suddenly he turned from his ambition to his home and family. He was relaxed and easier to live with, more like that loving Richard she had known before James was born. Now for the first time he seemed to take an interest in his son—he came to love him dearly—and he had time to spend with her. That summer young Rose Buck, the lodge-keeper's daughter from Scotland, came to help look after James, and it was Richard's idea that he and Marjorie should go off to Italy for a romantic holiday together—Venice, the Lakes, then down to Florence, where they spent most of August. It was an idyllic time, with politics and Southwold far behind them. They were young lovers once again, and it was there on a summer night, with the whole of Florence lit by moonlight, that their second child was conceived.

1887

7. *Jubilee*

There are a few great tribal celebrations which remain like landmarks in the memories of families as well as nations: the 1887 Jubilee of Queen Victoria was one of these. Mention the Jubilee to an historian and he will tell you that it marked the high point of a period of unexampled human progress and prosperity. Speak of it to Richard Bellamy and you would spark off memories of an uncomfortably eventful summer marked by the memory of that frail, bobbing figure driving to the Abbey with her black state landau ringed with potentates and princes.

This was the year when Hudson married and Randolph Churchill suddenly resigned. It was the year when young James nearly died, and without question it was also Hugo's year.

Richard's uncomfortable concern about his brother-in-law, Hugo Talbot-Cary, really began one breakfast time in early January when Marjorie suddenly exclaimed, *à propos* of nothing in particular, "Oh, poor Hugo!"

"And why *poor* Hugo, pray?" Richard replied quite testily. He was not in the best of humours. On top of his political frustrations, he had just heard from Hudson that the customary kidneys and bacon, which he loved for breakfast, were "just a shade suspect, sir, after the weekend," and that Mrs. Bridges had seen fit to send up boiled eggs instead. Richard detested boiled eggs. For him the British boiled egg summed up almost everything he hated on a Monday morning. Hudson and Mrs. Bridges should have known his feelings about eggs. So should Marjorie. How could a household be so damnably insensitive to a man's inner needs?

Richard felt suddenly hard done by (he often did these days), but rather than complain outright and make a fuss, he tried to make a martyr of himself (which was also typical). He merely grunted back at Hudson, then as ostentatiously as possible made do with porridge, Melba toast (as part of his attempt to bant) and tea. (Marjorie naturally had coffee.) At such a moment the chance of venting just a little of his ill humour on the perennial subject of his ineffectual brother-in-law was irresistible.

"I really *don't* see, Marjorie, why everybody's quite so sorry for him—even you! He's idle, he's extravagant, he drinks too much and even then he's deadly dull. Simply because he's too soft to stand up against your sainted mother, I don't see why that entitles him to pity."

"Richard, you're getting pompous," Marjorie replied. "*And* middle-aged." She cracked another egg before expertly decapitating it. She was looking very pretty in her grey-and-white-silk dress (she would be meeting Prudence at ten-thirty for a shopping expedition down the road to Swan and Edgar's).

"Everybody knows that poor Hugo . . ."

"There you go again," said Richard, grinning now.

". . . that *poor* Hugo never had a chance against my mother. He's really very sweet. He's always very nice to you, and Jumbo adores him. I think we ought to help him gain self-confidence. He's still so very shy with women, and totally incapable of standing on his own two legs in politics. We should help him, Richard."

Richard had his own ideas on the subject of Hugo and the fairer sex. As for his brother-in-law's relations with young James (recently nicknamed "Jumbo" for no reason anybody knew), this was secretly a distinctly sore point. Hugo was James's godfather and the child obviously adored him. When James was still quite tiny, before he could even talk, Hugo had always gone up to see him in the nursery whenever he happened to be in town. Richard always felt that as a Southwold he was permitted privileges by Nanny Webster which he was not allowed himself. Hugo spent hours there, charming that sour-faced old baggage and playing the strange games babies love.

Richard, who found it hard to deal with babies (and who anyhow had nothing like the time to spare that Hugo had), was really rather jealous, especially when James's first spoken word was an unmistakeable "Oo-go!"

Since then the bond between young Jumbo and his Uncle Hugo had become closer still, especially after Elizabeth was born in May of 1886.

From the beginning she had been the perfect baby—Marjorie said she had inherited her father's looks and placid temperament. She was bonny, rather plump, and rarely any trouble. She was more affectionate than James, and whilst Richard did his best to have no favourites, he secretly worshipped her. James was a complicated infant, passionate and moody and distinctly delicate. Elizabeth was just the opposite. When they succumbled to the usual childish illnesses, James always suffered badly. Elizabeth would shrug them off. Richard always felt some barrier between himself and James, whilst with Elizabeth there was passionate devotion on both sides.

Marjorie had for some time felt this lack of closeness between Richard and his son and was always trying to do something to repair it.

James's fourth birthday was approaching, so she said suddenly, "Why don't we make up a party for the circus as a birthday treat for Jumbo? He'll adore it and Hugo can come for the weekend. Perhaps we could ask Prudence too. She doesn't get much fun these days." (Major Fairfax's drinking had been getting worse, and once again Marjorie was intent on helping.)

"Marvellous idea," said Richard, and then added as Marjorie knew he would, "Why don't you arrange it?"

James's birthday treat was to be far more memorable than anyone expected or desired. From the beginning the idea appeared distinctly fraught. Richard was none too anxious to have Hugo. (Marjorie won that one on the grounds that "After all poor Hugo *is* his godfather and his uncle.") Nanny Webster thought it wrong to keep young Master James up so long past his bedtime. (Again Marjorie won with the self-evident and virtually unanswerable argument that "birthdays come but once a year.") And finally Richard learned that his son's birthday would inevitably coincide with a big debate on Ireland for which it was rumoured there would be a three-line whip. ("Well, dearest," Marjorie said quite philosophically, "just do your best.")

But as it turned out, much the most interesting complications came, not from Parliament, but from Hugo. Originally Marjorie had planned the party solely for her family and the two godparents, Hugo and Prudence. The circus would start at seven and end by nine. Afterwards James would be taken home to bed and the four adults would go on to celebrate his birthday at Romano's.

At the last minute Hugo wrote, begging her not to let a word out to the family but explaining in that schoolboy way he had that he was in "something of a fix. This friend of mine happens to be in town that week and is expecting me, but I couldn't bear to disappoint young Jumbo. Could you be a brick and invite my friend as well? Her name is Lilianne Spinkhill-Greye. She lives in Onslow Gardens, number 53."

Even if Marjorie had not been fond of Hugo, it's still hard to imagine her refusing such an irresistible request. Hugo was still officially in passionate pursuit of the financially and physically well-endowed Miss Stuyvesant from Baltimore. She was not one of *the* Stuyvesants but she was extremely rich, and Lady Southwold had long set her heart on having a dollar heiress in the family. (Ever since Lord Randolph married Miss Jerome they had been quite the thing.) And Hugo had always seemed quite willing. True, the courtship had been a trifle long—"Such a good thing to let them get to know each other," Lady Southwold said—but he had never given any hint of being anything but eager for this strapping beauty.

So who on earth *was* Miss Spinkhill-Greye (supposing it was "Miss")? Neither Debrett nor Burke's gave any hint of her resounding surname, nor could Marjorie discover anyone who'd heard of her. The only way to satisfy her curiosity was to write back, "Of course, do bring her," and send a separate invitation off to Onslow Gardens.

The birthday itself was a great success, although the cult of children's birthdays hadn't yet become anything like the sentimental business that began a few years later. There was a cake, of course, with four small candles, and Mrs. Bridges made a special nursery tea; but there were no conjurers, no party for the other well-born children of the neighborhood, and few of those expensive toys which children would soon start expecting as their birthright. Richard and Marjorie gave James a large red model fire engine. Richard had chosen it. Marjorie considered it "rather too old for such a little boy," but James was thrilled with it and rang its bell all afternoon, to the confusion of the staff. Had any other child done this, there might have been complaints, but somehow Master James was not the sort of small boy who got blamed for anything. With his enormous brown eyes, velvet party suit and page-boy haircut, he looked angelic.

Richard occasionally complained that "everybody spoils him and he gets away with murder," but the fact was that little James could twist everyone in 165—Richard included—around his elegant little finger. He could get anything he wanted out of Mrs. Bridges. Hudson would tell him stories by the hour, and Marjorie coddled him, indulged him, spoiled him on the ground that he was "delicate."

But on his birthday, the one person he kept asking for was Uncle Hugo. When he was told that he would meet them at the circus, he couldn't wait for six o'clock to come.

Richard meanwhile was luckier than he expected, thanks to his one-time rival, Arthur Balfour. During the past two years that smooth young politician's star had risen as inexorably as Richard's had declined, and the surprise resignation of Lord Randolph from the government earlier that year had sealed his success. With Randolph off the scene there was no one in the House to rival Balfour's eloquence. For Richard, on the other hand, the Chancellor's resignation had removed his one potential patron in the government.

Balfour had just been appointed Secretary for Ireland, a post his enemies said would finish him. In fact it was to establish him as what the *Morning Post* described, a trifle fulsomely, as "the great new star in the Tory firmament," and that afternoon it was Balfour's speech, a passionate defence of firmness and legality, which saved the government from a division—and allowed Richard, feeling a little like a truant cutting school, to escape in good time for the circus.

As he was hurrying through the Central Lobby he passed Lord Randolph. He seemed thinner and his face was more lined and yellow than when Richard had seen him four months earlier. He appeared to shuffle slightly as he walked. Just for a moment those extremely angry, bulbous eyes met his. There was the faintest nod of recognition: then Lord Randolph shuffled on his way. That was the last Richard ever saw of him.

The circus was extremely fashionable that year, and the Bellamys' evening coincided with the visit of the Prince of Wales and Princess Alexandra with their two youngest children, the Princesses Victoria and Maud. So there was a great excitement from the start. The Bellamys were sitting in the front row, just below the Royal Box, where they enjoyed a fine view of the portly Prince and stately Alexandra. (James kept asking Richard where their crowns were.)

The presence of Royalty turned the performance into something of a gala night: the show started with the national anthem, followed by the Prince's special tune, "God Bless Victoria's Son." The elephants were lined up to attention and the seals and clowns and chimpanzees joined in as the top-hatted ringmaster led the loyal applause. James was oblivious of most of this patriotic splendour. He wanted one thing only—"When will Uncle Hugo come?" But the two seats beside his parents remained cruelly and obstinately empty.

Nothing made up for that: neither the dazzling high-wire *artistes* from the Cirque Médrano, nor statesque Madame Albuquerque with her performing lions, nor even the three Fratini Brothers from Milan. These clowns made the Prince of Wales slap his fat thighs with laughter, but James sat on, almost tearful now for Hugo. There was an interval, with boys selling toffee apples and black, snakelike strips of licorice. James wanted nothing. Only the dimming of the lights as the show began again could hide his tears.

Then suddenly Hugo was there. There was a flurry of "excuse me, please" and "sorry," and Uncle Hugo, tall and god-like Uncle Hugo, had arrived.

"Happy birthday, dear old chap!" he whispered, pressing a large brown-paper parcel into James's lap. "Sorry I'm late."

But Uncle Hugo was not alone. There was a lady with him. James couldn't see her properly in the darkness, but he had smelt her dress as she pushed past his seat and hadn't liked it. Not that she mattered very much: with Uncle Hugo there beside him, nothing mattered and the remainder of the show passed in a daze of happiness. There were the Shetland ponies and the seals and the six jugglers who stood on each other's shoulders. He never did forget them, and when the lights went up and the band was once more playing "God Save the Queen" he was able to slip the brown paper off his parcel. It was a large toy elephant with a long trunk, glass button eyes and the saddest face that James had ever seen.

There was a label round its neck which Richard read for him: "Jumbo for Jumbo—Happy Birthday from your Uncle Hugo."

After the circus there was some confusion. It had begun to rain and the road beside the park was jammed with cabs and private coaches. For nearly twenty minutes the Bellamys had to stand huddled in the rain before their coach arrived.

Nanny Webster was outraged when they finally got back to Eaton Place. "Really, your ladyship, young James is soaked through to the skin, and it's hours past bedtime!"

So James, still hugging a large, damp elephant, was bustled off to bed without the birthday story he had been promised. Whilst adults changed he was popped into a steaming bath before the nursery fire, wrapped in a large, warm towel and then tucked into bed without even being made to say his prayers.

"I can't imagine what his mother thinks she's up to," grumbled Nanny Webster to the nursery maid.

Marjorie did have other things on her mind just then. There was the problem of finding dry clothes for her guests—fortunately, both ladies were her size and Roberts was a gem in such emergencies. Similarly, Hudson soon found Hugo one of Richard's jackets. After some whisky and ten minutes by the fire in the drawing room, the party was quite ready to go on to dinner. But there was still one thing that worried Marjorie—Hugo's latest friend, Miss Spinkhill-Greye. She was quite presentable—what Richard would have called "a fluffy little thing"—with bright blue eyes, blond, finely curling hair, and a manner which was best described as kittenish. She called Hugo "dear," which Marjorie found irritating.

But there was something else that worried her about the lady (something beyond the fact that Richard seemed to find her rather too attractive). Marjorie was sure she'd met her somewhere but couldn't for the life of her remember where.

Romano's was quite packed that night. It was, said Richard, really becoming far too fashionable, but Marjorie enjoyed the famous faces. Irving was there, and several actresses, and somebody that Marjorie thought was the comedian Dan Leno (but was in fact Lord Queensbury). The food was good—whitebait, spring lamb, *profiteroles* and a good burgundy—and even Richard had to admit that it was months since he had had such an enjoyable evening out. Hugo had improved enormously and he told some very funny stories. Prudence was on excellent form, and as for Hugo's pretty little friend, she really did seem rather good for him. Mark you, she clearly had him taped and Richard sensed that Hugo's bachelor days were numbered. But lucky Hugo!

As they were leaving there was a strange incident. There was a loud, drunken fellow in the doorway, and as Hugo's friend walked past he raised his hat to her. Richard admired the calm way that she ignored him.

"Spinkhill-Greye," Prudence said thoughtfully. "I must admit it rings no bell, but I agree she certainly *appears* familiar. And you had best watch out, my love, or you'll be finding yourself with a new sister-in-law, unless I mistake that cold gleam in the lady's eyes. What did you say her first name was?"

"Lilianne."

"It would be, somehow. Poor dear Hugo. But what about that terrible American?"

"Miss Stuyvesant?"

"Exactly. What's become of her?"

"I think officially they're still engaged and Mother's set her heart upon the marriage."

"I'd back Miss Spinkhill-Whatsername against your mother any day."

"You would? Good Heavens!" Marjorie said, thoroughly alarmed.

But she had other things to worry about than Hugo and the mysterious Miss Spinkhill-Greye. James, for instance. The morning after his night at the circus, Nanny Webster said he had a chill. Marjorie was inclined to see this as a well-known nanny's tactic of "I-told-you-so" and was not as worried as she might have been. All the same, she said that James must stay in bed.

Then there was trouble once again with Hudson. He had been very difficult of late. Marjorie admitted she was sometimes tactless with him, but Richard really was absurdly lenient and would never hear a word against him. As a result he was, in Marjorie's mind at any rate, becoming guilty of that most difficult of all domestic sins known as "getting above himself." It was hard to put a finger on a clear example (which was why it was also hard to make Richard understand), but she always felt that he was really running 165 and that all the rest of them, including Richard and herself, were little more than puppets managed by this maddeningly perfect butler.

If only the man drank or swore or attempted an occasional something with the maids (as all the butlers she had ever known invariably did) she would have felt much easier with him. Instead there was always that soft, knowing Scottish voice with its "Surely, m'lady?" or its "Wouldn't the master prefer, m'lady?" And to make it ten times worse, Hudson was always, always right.

He had been right that morning too when he suggested that "perhaps young Master James should see a doctor with that cough of his?" And she had been in the wrong—she admitted it now freely to herself—when she jumped at him and shouted to him to mind his own beastly business. She had apologised to him later in the morning, and he had said, "But, m'lady, you have nothing to apologise for. Of course you were in the right."

That too was typical of Hudson.

Marjorie was certain she would remember where she had seen Lilianne before. So was Prudence. But as it turned out, it was Richard (that staunch enemy and critic of all female scandalmongering) who solved the mystery. When he came home for dinner, he was clearly longing to tell Marjorie his news, but he restrained himself. Finally, at dinner, he said, "Do you remember a man called Pinkerton? He was in the House. A Liberal, I'm glad to say?"

Marjorie shook her head. "Why do you ask?"

"Because you met him once. He gave a party two or three years ago at the house he had at South Street. Tall man, pink face, orange whiskers. Dreadful ruffian."

"Heavens!" Marjorie almost shouted. "*That* was it. That was where I saw her. Dearest, you're a genius. She was with him. Lilianne. What ever happened to him?"

"Absconded to South America with all his company's money . . ."

"And leaving Lilianne. Richard, do you realise what this means? Poor Hugo's in the hands of an adventuress."

"You make it sound as if he were entwined by a boa constrictor."

"And so he is, a female boa constrictor. Dearest, we really *must* do something to save the poor lamb."

Richard's inclination, as with most human problems, was to stay clear and let it sort out on its own; and particularly so in this case, as he felt no responsibility for Hugo, and knew that Lilianne's success would infuriate Lady Southwold. But Marjorie wouldn't hear of this. Moral rectitude and sisterly concern alike dictated action. Hugo *must* be saved. And Richard would have to be his saviour. There was no one else.

But before he could bend his mind to this delicate affair, he had other problems. Hudson was the first. After dinner he asked Richard if he might have "a few words on a somewhat delicate personal topic." Richard said, "Of course, Hudson," and took him to his study. It was there, seated nervously in Richard's easy chair (Richard sat judiciously behind his desk), that Hudson, the perfect butler, the paragon of deference and duty, stammered out his own all too human story.

He was in love. Her name was Annie Ferguson. She lived outside Aberdeen, where her father was bailiff on Lord Rayleigh's place. They had been corresponding now for several years.

"And you wish to marry her?' said Richard wearily.

"Naturally, sir."

There was an awkward silence: both men realised exactly what this meant. There was no place at 165 for a married butler.

"What will you do?" said Richard finally.

"I plan to return to Scotland. The young person's father is retiring, and is willing to recommend me for the post he holds. I take it I could count on a satisfactory reference from you, sir."

"Oh, for goodness' sake, Hudson! What do you take me for?"

"You are most kind, sir. In these circumstances, not all employers would be anxious to provide a reference."

"Listen," said Richard. "You've been the loyalest of servants and of friends. I will always be grateful for what you have done for me and for my family. I wish you every happiness. The only thing I do ask is that you give us time to find a suitable successor and stay long enough to see him in."

"Of course, sir. You are very kind. I'm sorry, sir, but . . ."

Had Hudson not been on the edge of tears he would have tried to explain the problems and frustrations of a celibate butler's life—and Richard would have been most embarrassed.

Richard decided not to break the news to Marjorie at once, for on top of her worries about Hugo, there was James. That night his cough was worse, Nannie Webster was muttering darkly about bronchitis, and at 2:00 A.M. there was a knocking on the bedroom door. Marjorie rose. It was Nanny Webster.

"It's young James, m'lady. I'm most worried. He keeps calling for you."

Marjorie was used to James's illnesses but they always frightened her. This was worse than anything that she had seen before. He had thrown back his blankets and was lying very still. There was a night light burning: this made his small, pale face seem paler still, with vast shadows round his big bright eyes. When Marjorie took him in her arms, his boney little body seemed unnaturally hot. His nightshirt was quite damp with sweat.

"What is his temperature?" asked Marjorie.

"I've not taken it, m'lady."

Marjorie said nothing, but took the thermometer from its silver case, shook it, and inserted it beneath his tongue.

"There," she said, "there, my darling boy. Mummy will make you better."

The child lay and stared at her with his mournful elephant beside him on the pillow. When Marjorie read the thermometer, it showed 104 degrees.

"Shall we call Doctor?" Nanny Webster asked.

"Of course," said Marjorie. "Kindly wake Hudson. He can fetch him."

Dr. Bingley lived in Chester Street, just round the corner, but the ten minutes that he took to come were quite the longest Marjorie ever lived through. He was a plump, bustling young man with a pompous manner. He insisted on taking the patient's temperature again, sounded his chest, tut-tutted, then listened to his heart with his stethoscope. Even when the cold ivory of the instrument touched the child's chest, he did not move, but simply lay there, staring at his elephant.

"No call for great alarm," the doctor said finally. "Just keep him warm. A light diet. Inhalations for the chest. I shall return in the morning, and we'll see then about medicines. In the meantime, Lady Marjorie, I would suggest some sleep."

But neither Marjorie nor Richard slept again that night. Richard, in dressing gown and slippers, saw the doctor out. With him, the doctor's reassuring manner abruptly disappeared.

"I didn't wish to alarm Lady Marjorie at this time of night, but I must warn you that it could be serious."

"Serious, Doctor?"

"One cannot take pneumonia lightly in a child of four."

It seemed as if life at 165 was suddenly ruled by the sickroom. The house was hushed. The servants spoke in whispers. Marjorie was distraught and spent her days and nights in the nursery. When she slept (which she did rarely) it was for an hour or two on the camp bed put up near her son's.

Part of the trouble was that she blamed herself for what had happened. As she sobbed out to Richard, "He was far too young to be kept up so late. I should have had more sense. If anything should happen . . ."

"Nonsense, Marjorie. Nothing will. He's a sturdy little boy, and you've nothing to reproach yourself about—nothing at all."

But Marjorie *did* reproach herself, inevitably, and by the second day it was impossible to pretend that this was some childish illness that James would soon shrug off. He still lay there in his narrow little bed and still said nothing, and it was frightening to see how wasted he had become in so short a time. His temperature remained as high as ever, and by the second night, Dr. Bingley was prescribing cold, wet towels to keep his temperature as low as possible. And it was that night too that he became delirious.

Marjorie called Richard and they sat, anxiously holding hands, as their son, face flushed and big eyes bright with fever, rambled on in the darkened nursery. Most of the time the pathetic little voice talked nonsense. Then he became frightened. There were foxes after him, "wicked, horrid foxes," and he was shrieking out for somebody to save him.

Marjorie clutched him, but he lay there whimpering. "Uncle Hugo," he was saying, "Uncle Hugo, kill the wicked foxes!"

Marjorie and Richard both agreed that Hugo must be summoned. Between fitful bouts of sleep, James kept calling for him for the remainder of the night and through the next morning. But nobody seemed to know where Hugo was. In London he usually stayed at

Brown's Hotel, but the hotel said they had no news of him, and a telegram to Southwold brought no reply. James was weakening visibly now, and Dr. Bingley said there was nothing further he could do.

"The fever must take its course, Lady Marjorie."

And still the weak, frightened little voice called out for Hugo. It was Richard who finally suggested trying the address in Onslow Gardens.

He went himself. It was not far and it gave him something positive to do. Number 53 turned out to be a large grey house let out in apartments. There was a blear-eyed woman downstairs. No, there was no Lord Ashby living there. Perhaps he should try the House of Lords. Richard now had the patience of desperation. Was there a Miss Spinkhill-Greye?

"Mrs., she calls herself. Second floor. Knock hard—she's usually in bed. I wouldn't know who with."

Richard thanked her and ran up the stairs. The old drab was right. Richard had to knock and knock to get an answer, and when Lillianne appeared she wore a flimsy wrapper and her hair was round her shoulders.

"For God's sake," she shouted, and then, recognising Richard, said, "Oh, excuse me, Mr. Bellamy, I didn't know that it was you."

At first she insisted she had not seen Hugo, "not for a week at least." But when Richard told her it was a matter of life and death, she said, "All right. Come in. I'll fetch him."

Hugo must still have been in bed. He came out in his underpants and shirt, rubbing his eyes and muttering, "What in Hell's name, Lillie?"

Then, seeing Richard, he said angrily, "So that's your game, Richard. Spying on me, eh? Well, tell my mother what you like. This is the woman I intend to marry."

"Your private life's your own affair," said Richard stiffly. "I'm asking you to come and see my son. He's dying and he's calling for you."

Hugo, to do him justice, came at once, but he appeared to be too late. James was in a coma when he arrived, and the doctor was there.

Although Hugo whispered, "Jumbo, old chap, hullo. It's Uncle Hugo!" there was no sign of recognition in the unfocussed eyes. The only sign of life was the child's rapid breathing.

"This is the crisis of the illness," said the doctor. "He's in God's hands."

"How long will the crisis last?' whispered Marjorie.

"A few hours. Maybe longer. One never knows. The longer it goes on, the better chance he has."

The bedside vigil went on through the remainder of that day and through the night. Hugo took turns with Marjorie and Richard as they tried to rest. But no one slept. From time to time, Hudson would tiptoe in with sandwiches and pots of tea, but no one ate much either.

Marjorie no longer wept, but she said once to Richard, "If we lose him, I won't be able to go on."

Richard kissed her gently.

"Thank God, I've still got you," she said.

They sat together, hand in hand, for what seemed an eternity. Hugo was sitting on James's bed and the three of them saw the grey light of dawn creep through the curtains. There had been no sound or movement from the child for hours.

Then suddenly there *was* a noise, faint, like a small voice speaking from far away, in the dim shadows of the nursery.

"Uncle Hugo. Did you kill those foxes?"

James was awake and—miraculously, it seemed—alive.

"Yes, old chap," said Hugo very gently. "We got them all. They won't bother you again."

"Thank you," said James, "I knew you'd kill them. They were horrid."

He tried to smile, then floated off to sleep.

It was a slow recovery, through April and most of May, and everyone agreed that Hugo was wonderful. He all but lived at 165 throughout the period, playing with James and telling him endless stories. On the few occasions when he was away, James would pine for him. Under the circumstances, it was inevitable that Lilianne as well should become part of the daily life at 165.

She was extremely tactful, making herself liked by the servants—particularly by Nanny Webster, which surprised Richard—and was most helpful and polite to Marjorie. James liked her; so, despite herself, did Marjorie.

"Maybe her past *is* questionable," she remarked to Richard, "but she does have a great deal in her favour. She's very kind and certainly makes Hugo happy."

"Perhaps he really ought to marry her, then?"

"And have Lilianne as the next Lady Southwold? Now, Richard, that would never do."

But whether it would do or not, the idea was becoming more of a possibility each day, and neither Marjorie nor Richard had the heart to do anything against it.

As something of a realist, Richard began to wonder how long it would be before somebody from Southwold learned what was going on and tried to come between the lovers. And as something of a realist, he did not give much for their chances once this happened. But for some while they seemed to be enjoying a sort of charmed immunity from the world outside, and quite inevitably the Bellamys abetted them.

The first hint that their immunity was ending came towards the end of May. By then James was totally recovered—a little thinner than before, but just as lively as (and a touch more spoiled than) before his illness. Naturally, the boy's illness had changed Richard's attitude to Hugo. He was immensely grateful to him. As for Marjorie, she looked on her brother as her son's saviour.

Because of this, they both expreseed concern one night at dinner when Hugo suddenly exclaimed, "I don't know what to do. The mater's on the warpath once again."

"You mean she's found out about Lilianne?" said Marjorie.

"Good Lord, no! That would be the end of everything. But Connie Stuyvesant is back in England—especially to see this wretched Jubilee affair—and Mother, bless her heart, has asked her down to Southwold. I am expected there as well and, as Mama puts it in her letter, 'it will be a good opportunity to pop the question.' Marjorie, my love, what on earth am I to do?"

"What do you want to do?" asked Richard.

"I've told you. I want to marry Lillie."

"But you're scared of Mother," Marjorie added.

"Aren't we all," he said.

Richard and Marjorie that night had the sort of long discussion married couples love. What was to be done? They owed a debt to Hugo and clearly ought to do their best to make him happy. They also saw his situation as a romantic one and not unlike their own. But here their agreement ended. Marjorie was all for doing something positive to help her brother. Richard was warier.

"It's usually disastrous if one interferes in affairs like this."

"But if one doesn't interfere, poor Hugo will simply be bullied into marrying this rich American. If I let that happen after the way that he saved Jumbo's life, I never would forgive myself."

Marjorie had made her mind up and there was not much anybody—Richard least of all—could do about it. Miss Stuyvesant was no great problem. Marjorie discovered she was still in London, met her and told her plainly that her brother was not in love with her.

"Since I'm not in love with him, that makes two of us," the lady answered with some spirit.

Lady Southwold was as usual rather more difficult, but once again Marjorie thought the straightest course was best.

"Poor, dear Hugo," she told her mother, "I've heard that he's been jilted by that terrible American. And after so long. It really is too bad."

"It's criminal," said Lady Southwold. "What does the hussy think she's up to?"

"What else can one expect with somebody from Baltimore?" said Marjorie snobbishly. "But he really should get married."

"If he doesn't soon he'll die a bachelor."

"Luckily there *is* somebody else—a girl named Lilianne. Buckinghamshire family. Rather pretty."

"Rich?"

"Extremely."

"I must invite her down. Would Hugo come with her?"

"He might," said Marjorie.

And so that muddled, all but tragic season of the Jubilee seemed to end happily, and on a perfect June day the two Bellamys and their small son James watched the old Queen drive down Whitehall towards the Abbey. Hugo Lord Ashby was in the Abbey with his *fiancée,* Lilianne; so were his parents. Hugo and Lilianne were as happy as they should have been; so were the Southwolds. Their son was marrying at last. It was a great weight off their minds, and Lady Southwold, perverse as ever, thoroughly approved his choice.

And so as the fanfare sounded and the bells rang out and the small black figure of the Empress Queen progressed up the aisle, it was a celebration for the Bellamys and for the Southwolds too. It was a memorable year.

1888

8. Marjorie and the Prince

"Ortolans," thought Richard to himself. "Birds no bigger than a sparrow, caught in the South of France, sent at great expense to London, bought by the Prince of Wales's chef, trussed, cooked, fussed over, and then turned out as the highlight of the meal." He found something symbolic and depressing about ortolans: to him they tasted exactly as he imagined roast sparrows would taste, but because of the name, because of the expense and rarity they represented, they were considered *de rigueur* at this sort of banquet and everybody gobbled them.

Thinking these slightly sour thoughts, he silently surveyed the big, distinctly over-heavy dining room at Marlborough House. It was crammed with people eating. Flunkeys were dashing to and fro, everybody else was chattering noisily, and at the far end of the table, fat, gross and cheerful, sat his future sovereign, Albert Edward, Prince of Wales. He at any rate liked ortolans. During the past three minutes Richard had counted as he ate fourteen of them, this after celery soup and a slice of turbot; and there would be more to come, much more, roast beef and *poire hélène* and devilled kidneys and then Stilton and cigars. Where did His Royal Highness put it all? It was not as if he were a big man like the majority of his courtiers—tall, gloomy-looking Sykes or the enormous Henry Chaplin. Yet he out-ate them all. Richard refused to find the thought attractive.

He pushed the ortolans away and leaned back to enjoy his claret —Beychevelle '68. Good, but not all *that* good. Albert Edward, he reflected, was an undoubted connoisseur of food, cigars and women, not of wine.

"Don't you think, Mr. Bellamy, that this dreadful man Parnell should be on trial for treason?"

This interruption of Richard's seditious thoughts came from a red-nosed little woman dressed like a bright green cockatoo. Her name was Lady Orrery, and Richard had not met her before. Already she was starting to annoy him.

"Why do you say that?" he replied. "Treason's a very serious affair."

"And so are these letters from Parnell the *Times* is publishing. Clearly the man's a traitor—and a dangerous one at that."

Normally Richard might have assented politely. He had no liking for Parnell or what he stood for. But tonight he had other things on his mind. Instead of answering he twirled the pale red liquid in his glass and sniffed the odour of baked earth and ancient sunlight.

"Don't you agree, though, Mr. Bellamy?" the cockatoo went pecking on. "These letters in the *Times* leave no doubt as to this dreadful man's intentions, and as a member of the House you have a duty to do something."

"Parnell claims they're forgeries."

"Oh, but he would. Obviously he would."

"And so does Mr. Gladstone."

"Now, Mr. Bellamy, I ask you, *would* the *Times* publish letters of this sort if they were forgeries? It's inconceivable. As an M.P. you must do your duty. See that Parnell is placed behind bars, then given his deserts."

She chattered on, angry and birdlike, whilst Richard nodded, drank his wine and vacantly looked on. At any other time he would probably have answered that the Piggot letters fascinated him and that at heart he was inclined to agree with Lady Orrery. But at the moment he was too preoccupied, and finally the indefatigable little woman gave up on politics.

"His Royal Highness seems on particularly good form tonight, don't you think, Mr. Bellamy? Who is that very pretty woman he's flirting with? It seems only yesterday that he was still pursuing Mrs. Langtry. This one must be his latest, I'll be bound. Look at her now, look at that knowing look she has. I wonder who on earth she is?"

"That, Lady Orrery," said Richard drily, "is my wife. And now with your permission we will change the subject."

⁂

The Bellamys' rise to favour in the eyes of the Prince of Wales had happened quite recently—and most unexpectedly.

It had been barely a month before that Richard and Marjorie were invited out to Hatfield for a long weekend. Someone had told Lord Salisbury that he ought to have more contact with back-benchers in the Party, and recently he had started inviting them to visit him at home. Richard's turn had duly come.

He was not keen to go. Politically he still disapproved of Salisbury as much as ever, and he found the "Great Dead-Weight" personally formidable, very large and distant and aloof.

But at 165 Richard found himself a minority of one. Marjorie was excited at the prospect of weekending out at Hatfield and instantly ordered a new dress from Madame Alberoni (of Hanover Place, much patronised by Royalty). Richard was press-ganged into ordering a new tweed country suit. (His old one, Marjorie said, would get him arrested as a poacher if he went on wearing it.) Miss Roberts had been told that she would be going too as Marjorie's maid, and the new butler, an Irishman named O'Donovan, would be valeting for Richard.

This was another reason Richard had for not being over-keen to go. He missed Hudson's presence on occasions such as these, and the new butler, for all his eager blarney, was no substitute. A tall, good-looking man from County Wicklow, O'Donovan was always polite and seemed efficient, but there was something wrong about him. Richard could not decide quite what it was, but the straight fact was that 165 without Angus Hudson as its butler had become a wilderness. The other servants had got out of hand, service was erratic, and even Mrs. Bridges' cooking had declined.

O'Donovan also had an extraordinary knack for getting on Richard's nerves. One of his first remarks when he heard about the trip to Hatfield was, "I take it that his lordship will be expecting you to shoot."

Hudson, who knew Richard's dislike of the sport, would never have said this, but Richard checked himself and said, "Good heavens, no! I'd end up shooting him."

And to the other servants O'Donovan let drop such little snobbisms as, "I hear the service out at Hatfield has been falling off of late. It will be interesting to observe how Lord Salisbury's butler runs things."

Then, just a day of two before they were due to go, O'Donovan produced his bombshell. As he was stropping Richard's razors he remarked, "I hear, sir, that there's an excellent chance that His Royal Highness will be gracing the weekend with his royal presence."

"Nonsense, man," Richard said quickly. "The Prince is still at Homburg, and from there he always goes to Biarritz. No, mercifully, there's no chance of that at all."

But next day O'Donovan triumphantly showed Mrs. Bridges an item in the court circular in that day's *Morning Post:* "Today H.R.H. the Prince of Wales returned unexpectedly from Homburg, where he has been staying for the last three weeks."

The real reasons Richard dreaded the weekend were far more profound than he would probably have admitted. He would simply have said that he enjoyed his home and was an idle fellow. But it was more complicated than that: the fact was that despite his time in Parliament and his marriage to Marjorie, he still felt uncomfortably aware of his disadvantages when he went into the top Tory world of wealthy landowners who, under Salisbury, formed the nucleus of government. There was his lack of a noble name, his lack of interest in hunting or shooting, and, worst of all, there was his crippling lack of money.

These condescending plutocrats alone could make him feel his place. Perhaps he was over-sensitive, but when he met them they seemed to be implying (in the discreetest way imaginable) that he was only there among them because he had had the great good fortune, or good sense, to marry Southwold's daughter.

As it turned out, none of this treatment occurred, and the weekend was most pleasurable. Richard could hardly fail to respond to Hatfield—that enormous house, those splendid gardens, and the Cecil standard fluttering on the battlements. But to his surprise the part of the weekend that he most enjoyed was Salisbury himself. Here on his home ground the great statesman was quite different from the forbidding figure Richard knew at Westminster. Here he seemed simply a large, bumbling man with a black jacket shiny at the elbows, who for some reason seemed to make an effort to be genial to Richard.

"D'you ride, Bellamy?"

"No, my lord."

"No more do I. I have always regarded riding as at best a mode of transportation of which the horse is an inconvenient adjunct."

Richard agreed.

"Come and see my tricycle," his lordship said. And the great Lord Salisbury led Richard to the back of the house, where a whole series of paths were laid out across the lawns and between the orchards. Lord Salisbury had a big black tricycle.

"Unbeatable exercise," he said, and mounted, and with a footman on the step behind him went pedalling away, his coat-tails flying. When he returned ten minutes later, red-faced and puffing, one of the servants came running out of the house and handed him a note. Salisbury read it, frowning.

"Forgive me, Bellamy," he said, "but it seems we have an unexpected guest. This very evening too. His Royal Highness will be coming here for dinner. I invited him some months ago but never thought he'd come. To be honest, I have always thought I bored him. Oh Lord, Bellamy, oh Lord, oh Lord! The whims of princes, Bellamy! What was it Disraeli used to say about our gracious Prince? That he could deal with the Balkans but not with Bertie?" And he began to laugh with a rumbling noise that shook his big grey beard.

Lord Salisbury need not have worried. The Prince turned out to be no trouble—rather the reverse. During his time at Homburg he had been massaged, dieted and purged of at least twenty pounds of the Prince Regal girth. His breath was purer and his liver in good shape, so there was not much danger of the sort of outburst that could upset an unsuspecting gathering in his honour. The Prince, that afternoon, was at his genial and charming best.

Richard had never met the Prince before and so was grateful for the opportunity to examine him. He found him more extraordinary than he had expected; very dapper, very fat, and very foreign with his guttural voice and heavily rolled Rs. But the strangest thing about him was that one so small—he was little more than five feet two or three—could simultaneously appear so very much larger than life. He had extraordinary assurance and awareness of his royal role and dignity: it was this that saved him from absurdity. Even so, Richard was amused by the strange sight of towering Lord Salisbury with this portly little man.

The Prince talked to everyone with great good humour. He seemed to know that Richard had once served in Paris; Cartwright had recently died and he spoke of him with some affection. To Marjorie the Prince was warmer still, chatting about her father—"It has been far too long since I have seen him. Tell him that he must see me when he is next in London"—and tactfully avoiding any reference to her mother. But it was after dinner that Marjorie was confirmed in the princely favour. His Royal Highness was showing signs of some impatience for his customary game of bridge (there was no other way of filling in the time between his rising from the table and his going off to bed). But who would complete the four? There were luckily Lord Hardwicke and the good-natured Mrs. Jenkinson, a wealthy widow who could always be relied upon the keep the Prince happy and contented. But, typically, Lord Salisbury had overlooked the need for a final partner. Who would oblige? Worried inquiries ensued, and H.R.H. was waiting.

"Would Lady Marjorie be able to fill in?" Salisbury asked anxiously.

"I'm sorry," Richard said, "but my wife . . ."

"As long as the Prince will make allowance for my lack of practice," Marjorie said, and rose. "Richard, excuse me. Lord Salisbury, I will do my best."

The first invitation to a Marlborough House reception duly arrived at 165 three days later. The servants were thrilled. So, to be fair, was Richard. Marjorie was somewhat cooler. But they went, and it was all a great success. The Princess was beautiful—even more beautiful, Richard thought, than in her photographs—and very gracious. The Prince was affability itself. There was champagne, a band was playing on the lawn, and H.R.H. spent nearly twenty minutes chatting to Richard—about Paris, about Parliament, and about the committee, on which the Prince was sitting, to provide dwellings for the poor. Richard had always prided himself on being far too rational to be, as he put it, "seduced by this royal mumbo-jumbo," but seduced he was.

"Extraordinarily intelligent man, the Prince," he said to Marjorie as they drove back to Eaton Place. Marjorie nodded pensively.

The Bellamys' success did not stop there. After the reception further invitations followed almost as if by magic: to a ball at Manchester House, to another given by the Beresfords, then to a weekend three days later up at Hardwicke Hall. And everywhere they went the Prince was there. It was as if a touch of the Prince's popularity had rubbed off on them. They were mysteriously "in," and for the first time in his life Richard enjoyed the strange, rather dizzying sensation of being sought after by Society.

Again this was something he would previously have said he despised, but there is something irresistible about a dinner invitation from a duchess or a weekend with a Rothschild. Above all there is something few men can resist in the confidence of princes—and Richard really felt that Albert Edward liked him. How else explain the trouble he took to put Richard and Marjorie at ease? How else explain those confidential chats that H.R.H. so obviously enjoyed? He really had an extraordinary grasp of what was happening in Europe, and he knew absolutely everybody—from presidents and kings to courtesans, especially courtesans. Richard was even given the great honour of playing billiards with him on several occasions, although as Marjorie said, this was possibly because Richard was an indifferent player and the Prince always liked to win.

Throughout the early summer the Bellamys basked in the princely favour. Then suddenly, for Richard, everything went wrong. They were at Goodwood, members inevitably now of the exclusive party invited down to watch the racing and enjoy the splendours of that lovely house for the few days the Prince was staying there.

Richard was bored by racing. He was also bored by the Prince's horsier friends (rather a ruffianly lot, he thought them) and by the fact that he saw so little there of Marjorie. On the second day he was standing on the edge of the enclosure, trying to concentrate upon the splendid view across the downs as an antidote to the view of the horses, when he overheard two loud gentlemen in loud check suits talking about the Prince. The Prince himself had at that moment just arrived with several of his friends—the Duke of Richmond, Hardwicke, Carrington—and Marjorie was with them. Richard was pleased to see that she had just said something that made Bertie laugh.

"So that's what Bertie's up to," one of the loud gentlemen said.

"She looks very happy," said the other.

"Naturally. They all are. Must be exciting to submit to the future King of England."

"Rather beautiful, but older than Langtry. Interesting how his taste changes. Any idea who she is?"

"They say she's married to a dull dog of an M.P. called Bellamy."

"Poor dog."

"Oh, I don't know. He'll be all right. Rather an honour to be married to a royal mistress when you think of it—and Bertie always does the decent thing by the husband anyhow. Nobody ever loses out by being cuckolded by H.R.H."

Richard was shattered. Unfaithful? Marjorie? And with the Prince of Wales? It was unthinkable. But was it? Everyone knew the Prince's reputation, and mightn't this explain why the Bellamys were suddenly so popular? The idea tormented him, and for the remainder of that afternoon Richard did his best to settle the matter and to decide what he could do. Neither was easy. There is—fortunately, perhaps—no way of proving absolutely any wife's fidelity. And if—perish the thought—she really *had* been intimate with the Prince, what could he do? Make a fuss? Antagonise the Prince and all Society? Another jealous husband, Sir William Mordaunt, had done just that: he had even had the Prince in court, and today Mordaunt was a broken man. Not for nothing was His Royal Highness known discreetly as "the Bismarck of Society."

But if Marjorie *were* deceiving him, the whole idea of playing the complacent husband sickened him, especially if it meant this sort of social life with everybody laughing quietly behind his back.

Fortunately for Richard, they were due back from Goodwood that same evening, and it was reassuring to be home again in 165 with the children there to greet them. Four-year-old James could hardly wait to hear about the Prince and what uniform he was wearing. Elizabeth jumped up and down with excitement at having her parents back again. The servants were naturally agog for any crumbs of royal gossip. For Richard it was suddenly a huge relief to be out of that whole hothouse world of kings and courtiers. Never had Eaton Place appeared more welcoming. Marjorie was different too—far more at ease, more natural, more loving—and by the time they went to bed Richard had made up his mind. His suspicions were unworthy. Marjorie could not possibly have been unfaithful. But on the other hand this elevated social life of theirs was over. It had been enjoyable while it lasted, but he had had enough. The risks were far too great, and Bertie's world was not for him.

But how to convince his wife? That was the real problem, especially now that Marjorie was enjoying life more than she had for years. The truth was that as Southwold's daughter she was by nature and inheritance fitted to take her place around the Prince. Richard was not, and for the first time in the marriage she was sampling just the sort of life she would undoubtedly have enjoyed had she married a husband of her own rank and class.

These bitter and uncomfortable thoughts pursued poor Richard for the ensuing fortnight. It was a hateful fortnight, for him at any rate. For Marjorie it simply marked the continuation of a time of glittering success.

Richard did his best to reduce their social life, but how could he, short of confronting Marjorie with his hideous suspicions? The invitations had all been accepted and the arrangements made. Richard was not the man to put his foot down and, without giving any reason, tell his wife they were not going to the Warwick Castle Ball or for dinner with the Londonderrys or for the weekend with the Rothschilds out at Tring. (Nor, for that matter, would Marjorie have accepted it if he had.)

And so he went to all these fabulous affairs and hated every minute of them. Gone was his own naïve enjoyment of the social whirl, gone too his pleasure in a *tête à tête* with Bertie or a chat with Soveral or Cassels. Several of the regulars in the Prince's circle remarked knowingly on "the sour look of the Bellamy fellow—I suppose the usual trouble." Even Marjorie chided him for his ill humour, but there was nothing he could do.

The role of jealous husband is surely the most uncomfortable affliction of the married male. Richard bore it badly. His straightforward nature found it hard to cope with the degrading turns and twists of jealousy; nor was he tough enough or dishonourable enough to stoop to those machinations which alone might have told him the truth and brought the whole hateful issue to a head.

Instead he did his best to act as if nothing had gone wrong, and he acted badly. All he did was alienate Marjorie. ("Richard has suddenly become so boring," she confided to Prudence. "I just can't think why.") He knew this too, and to make it worse discovered—as most jealous husbands do—that Marjorie had never seemed so lovely or desirable before.

Finally he decided that the one sane course was to have a few days apart. Hugo and Lilianne had invited them for a few days to their new country place at Oakthorpe, not far from Ashby de la Zouch. Using the excuse of the big Irish debate due that week, Richard suggested that Marjorie go alone—and was pained by the alacrity with which she agreed.

Richard hated being alone. It was bad enough with Hudson gone. Without Marjorie, Eaton Place was not home at all. He breakfasted alone and dined alone. He also slept alone. (The thought of seeking consolation did occur to him, but he was too miserable by now to do anything about it.) Trouble still rumbled between O'Donovan and Mrs. Bridges; his stomach suffered as a result. He found he was edgy with the children: they missed their mother too, whatever Nanny Webster might say to the contrary.

The only alleviation of his troubles lay in the House of Commons. He had his friends there and for these few days attended the debates more conscientiously than he had done for years. He also made a speech on Ireland. It was rather out of character—a bitter, angry speech in which he named Parnell as "the source of all that wretched nation's troubles"—but for Richard it worked off a little of the anger that had been building up for several weeks. It also brought him jeers and fury from the opposition—and made the headlines in the evening papers.

Two days later, just after breakfast, O'Donovan brought him a message. There were two gentlemen downstairs to see him.

"Gentlemen?" said Richard. "What sort of gentlemen, and what do they want?"

"Just gentlemen," O'Donovan replied. "They didn't say."

"They must say," Richard answered testily. "Good heavens, man, I can't have strangers coming in my house without even announcing what they want. You will please go and either find out or send them packing."

Two minutes later O'Donovan was back. "Mr. Bellamy, your honour, they still won't say. I think you'd better see them."

"Really, O'Donovan, what *is* going on?" and still clutching his copy of that morning's *Times*, Richard strode from the dining room and out across the hall. As he did so there was a flash and an explosion and something knocked him to the ground. People were running. Someone shouted, "Death to Ireland's enemies!" and the front door slammed.

Richard lay by the stairs. There was a great pain in his chest and his head was bursting, but he had not lost consciousness. Someone else ran past him, then he heard Mrs. Bridges' reassuringly familiar voice calling him from what seemed miles away.

"Mr. Bellamy. Mr. Bellamy, sir!" Then, "Alice, don't just stand there. Fetch Dr. Bingley instantly! Boy, off to the police. Tell them they've tried to murder Mr. Bellamy!"

He must have lost consciousness then, for the next thing Richard remembered was coming to in St. George's Hospital. The pain across his chest was so intense that he groaned, then fainted again.

His next memory was of Dr. Bingley's plump face peering down at him and asking rather pointlessly, "Feeling better, Bellamy?" It was a question Richard felt too ill to answer, but despite the pain, he remained conscious then. Luckily, the doctors had already seen to his injuries, dressed his wound, and made him as comfortable as possible.

"How bad is it?" Richard whispered.

"Not as bad as it might have been," said Dr. Bingley cheerfully. "The bullet missed your heart and came out just below your shoulder. You've lost a lot of blood, but no vital organs are damaged as far as I can tell. Lucky that cook of yours kept her head and fetched me as quickly as she did. Probably saved your life."

The attempt on his life turned Richard from an obscure M.P. into the nearest he ever came to being a public hero. The news swiftly reached Westminster, and by lunchtime he had been visited by Lord Salisbury in person. (His lordship said, "Dastardly, dastardly!" Richard smiled weakly. Salisbury said, "Dastardly!" again and departed shaking his big grey beard as if in disapproval of the dreadful times they lived in.)

There were further visitors. A police superintendent from New

Scotland Yard took a statement (not that there was much that Richard could tell him) and informed him that "the assailants have made their getaway"; Mrs. Bridges arrived with beef tea and a knuckle of boiled veal and the news that O'Donovan the butler had disappeared; and finally an equerry from the Palace brought a message from the Queen wishing her loyal M.P. God's blessing and the royal hopes for a swift recovery. By early afternoon he had had enough. A doctor offered him a sleeping draught and he floated off gratefully into a dreamless slumber.

When he awoke it was nighttime. There was a faint lamp burning in the middle of the ward and somebody was with him. He felt a hand take his, and Marjorie's voice was saying very softly, "Richard, my dearest one, I'm here."

He looked at her and smiled. She was more beautiful than he had ever seen her.

"I'm never leaving you again," she said, and kissed him tenderly.

The attempted murder remained a mystery, though it was put down to a pair of Irish terrorists. Descriptions were issued by the police and the investigation dragged on, but no one was ever caught. Paradoxically, this unsolved crime solved some other problems in Richard's life, including the future of his marriage. The high-flying social life was over for both him and Marjorie. She nursed him through his convalescence and afterwards took him to the South of France, where for a month they had a sort of second honeymoon.

When they got back they found that the unknown gunmen had helped them with another problem. O'Donovan had never reappeared and was therefore assumed to have been involved with the terrorists, and an apologetic letter had arrived from Hudson expressing deep concern and asking to be taken back. There was no mention of his wife. Richard telegraphed immediately telling him to come.

With Hudson back, alone, life finally returned to normal. Richard never liked to ask him what had happened with his marriage. (Years afterwards he heard that they had not got on, had parted, and the wife had died.) Nor did he find out if there was any truth to his suspicions about Marjorie and the Prince. With wives as with butlers certain mysteries are best left as they are.

1895

9. Richard Resurgent

MOST MORNINGS IN THE AUTUMN OF 1894 AT AROUND NINE O'CLOCK Richard Bellamy could be seen standing by himself on the black-and-gold-painted iron bridge in St. James's Park watching the ducks. During the past few years his figure had filled out, his face had lost that faint hollowness of youth, his hair had started to turn grey. At forty-one he had now reached the one-way doors of middle age, but he was one of those fortunate few who mature physically quite early in life, then never seem to change; and certainly the last few years had not done much to age him.

These had been years—as he in his own apologetic way would have been the first to admit—of quiet self-indulgence. After the year of Victoria's first jubilee—his year of incidents—life had mysteriously slowed down: no crises and no great excitements either. The children had started to grow up; James was eleven now and Elizabeth was nine. Marjorie had changed from the girl he married into a woman in her prime: their love, rather like their life itself, had now become more placid and, Richard would have said, far more profound. (Marjorie, although a little restless and occasionally a little bored, would probably have agreed.) The keynote of these years had been contentment. Even that gloomy day more than a year ago, when Richard lost his seat in Parliament (in the big Liberal landslide which brought eighty-seven-year-old Gladstone back for his fourth and final ministry) had really done little to upset his equanimity. Rather the reverse. He told himself that he had had enough of politics. It was a thankless, dirty business and he consoled himself philosophically with the thought that his sort of personality simply was not made for active politics. Nor was his background. He was not tough enough, nor arrogant enough, nor rich enough to reach the parliamentary heights. Gilded young men like Arthur Balfour might (especially if, like Balfour, they happened to have Lord Salisbury for an uncle), but Richard hadn't been prepared to settle for much less. If he lacked the qualities to take him to the top, he also lacked the resignation to plod on as a perpetual back-bencher.

And so, like many ambitious men before him, he had bowed out of politics swearing he had done with it forever. His natural indolence had done the rest. He had slowed down a lot. Increasingly his life revolved round Eaton Place. He loved its comfort, its security, its warm and reassuringly set routines. Since Hudson had come back it was once more the perfect household, and life there could flow peacefully and comfortably by.

Indeed, it was hard to think of any way of life quite as agreeable as Richard's now. He had no worries. (The children were still too young to be a nuisance, and since Hugo married the Southwolds had left the Bellamys alone.) There was sufficient money. (Richard had finally stopped fussing over living off his wife.) And 165 was everything a house should be. It had a modern bathroom now, with piped hot water from the boiler in the basement, and just that year electricity had been installed for lighting the first two storeys. At the same time 165 remained as solid and as civilised as when it was first built. Once inside it, Richard felt unassailable.

Durng his period out of politics, Richard had been occupied. He still wrote occasional journalism, though less than in the past. His real work had been his novel. He had been writing it for years, but now for the first time he could take it seriously. He had a title for it—"The Melting Pot"—and it had grown out of all recognition from the manuscript Zola had once rejected. What was fascinating about it was that the story was so similar to Richard's own—a good-looking, bright young man comes up to London from the provinces, woos and then marries a rich politician's daughter, then pits his wits against the hostile world of the metropolis. Where it differed from Richard's real life was that his hero seemed to have all the qualities he lacked.

He was ruthless, eloquent, and something of a bounder, unscrupulous with women and indomitable with men. He treated his wife dreadfully, had a series of affairs, made himself a fortune, and died cynically deriding the great "melting pot" of London for the unsatisfying sham it was.

It is hard to know how much of a conscious daydream this strange tale became. Perhaps it did not at all. Certainly Richard worked conscientiously at his book each morning, and started to see himself as something of a literary figure. He took endless trouble, *à la Zola,* getting the details and the background right. (He even re-visited the Commons twice and sat in the gallery with his notebook for his chapter on a great political debate.) Where he was all too conscious of his weakness as a novelist was in his portrayal of women. The virtuous ones all sounded like Marjorie and the unpleasant ones like Lady Southwold, but as he said to Marjorie (who read the book page by page each evening), "It's so dashed difficult to be a good husband *and* a good novelist!"

When the book was finally finished and submitted to a publisher, Richard, like many a greater author, felt lost without his morning grind. It was then that he began his morning constitutional through the park, and as he watched the ducks, and felt the first sharp chill of autumn rising from the lake, he began to suffer the dangerous discontents of middle age. Perhaps the book would be a great success and make his name. Perhaps he had found his *métier* at last. But if not, what could he do? This perfect life he led could not go on without a purpose, and what purpose had his life except his book? He would stare thoughtfully across the lake at the crisp elegance of Horseguards' Parade and wonder, as middle-aged men in early autumn often do, just what he wanted from his life.

"Mr. Bellamy," said a voice. "How are you, Mr. Bellamy, sir? They said I'd find you here."

Richard turned and saw a fat man with a purple nose, a familiar bowler hat and an unmistakeable large cigar.

"Good heavens, Pyecombe, my dear chap! How very good to see you! And how's the world of politics been treating you?"

Richard's one-time agent shook his head.

"Dodgy, extremely dodgy, Mr. Bellamy. Ever since you lost the seat and then resigned as candidate nothing's been quite the same. That Liberal, that Tatham fellow. Too big for his bloomin' boots if you ask me, Mr. Bellamy. We've not much chance against a man like that."

"But you've a candidate—rather a good one."

Pyecombe shook his head and spat mournfully into the lake. "*Had* one. Past tense, Mr. Bellamy. Robinson the banker—just gone bankrupt. Never did like the man. No class, no breeding. Only money, and now not even that. A tragedy for us Conservatives and no mistake."

"How very difficult," said Richard lamely.

"You could say that—especially at a time like this, what with that old Gladstone cracking up and his government on the way out any day. We've got a seat now going begging if the right man comes along."

"And nobody's been after it?"

"Several, naturally."

Pyecombe puffed at his cigar and looked away across the lake. "Several, including someone you know rather well. I won't say who. But I will say this, Mr. Bellamy—and this is why I'm here. If you'll take up the seat again I'll guarantee you'll get it. And I for one will be a very happy man to have you as our Member. Think on it, Mr. Bellamy. There's no great hurry, but we have to know by the New Year at the latest. Now if you'll excuse me . . ." Bowler conspiratorially around his ears, Pyecombe walked away.

"Well," said Marjorie, "will you or won't you?"

"Will I what?"

"Accept their offer?"

"What offer?"

"My love, I wasn't born yesterday. Just two days ago, Pyecombe lost his candidate, and this morning he turns up all hot and bothered saying he must see you. There's only one thing he could want. I think you should accept. Politics is still your life. It's what you're good at. I want to see you back in Parliament."

But Richard pointedly refused to give an answer straight away. One side of him agreed with Marjorie and he was flattered to be asked to stand again. But against this stood the years of thwarted hopes and wasted effort from his time in Parliament. He had few illusions now about his old ambitions. He knew that he was second-rate, but still, but still . . . It *was* extremely tempting, and he *had* missed the strange excitements of the House. He weighed the pros and cons—and found it impossible to decide. Finally he wrote to Pyecombe, thanking him for his support and promising a firm decision by the first of January.

❧ ❧

Christmas loomed, and once again the Bellamys prepared to spend it *en famille* at Southwold. Richard had given up objecting to this practice, which had become traditional. Marjorie assumed that they were going, and so did the children—and against the assumptions of his family, Richard was powerless.

These last few weeks before the Christmas holidays were a disturbing period for him. As usual at this time of year he felt guilty about his mother. She was in her seventies and although he knew that she would have adored to spend Christmas with them, it was impossible. Not that she complained. She never did. But just the same Richard felt guilty at the thought of her spending Christmas by herself in Norfolk.

Then there was the news about his novel. The publisher had not rejected it. (Would that he had; it would have saved a lot of trouble.) Instead he sent it back with several pages of suggestions and a vague promise that if they were followed he might see his way to publishing it in the spring. Marjorie was loyally indignant, Richard secretly aggrieved. How could he face that manuscript again, how possibly endure the tedium of yet again rewriting it?

Finally there was the big decision about Parliament. Somehow the rumour had slipped out and several of his friends had asked him what he was up to. But how he hated having to make decisions! Perhaps he should simply do as Dangerfield suggested, and let Marjorie decide everything for him. She had a far clearer, much more masculine mind than his. But there was less than two weeks now before he decided what could well be his entire future. How could one ever do it?

With so much on his mind, it was a great relief when the bags were packed, the servants organised, and the whole Bellamy *ménage* was finally *en route* for Southwold. The children's sheer excitement was infectious. So was Marjorie's never failing pleasure at the prospect of seeing her old home again. And in fact Richard's own attitude to

Southwold had mellowed. It was no longer quite that "hostile principality" which it had been for Richard in the past. It could no longer threaten him or make him feel the *parvenu* intruder he had been so conscious of appearing after his marriage. Instead he could appreciate it now for what it was—a miraculous relic from the past, a piece of English history which could hardly last much longer.

The last time he was there he had seen the telltale signs of imminent decay: some of the lime trees in the great avenue that led up to the house had rotted and been felled, fences were broken, and he noticed that the roof needed mending. Lord Southwold had complained about the dreadful harvests and the failure of his tenants to pay their rents, but what could be done?

"Evict them all, you fool," his wife had muttered savagely.

"No, my dear, no. That's simply not the way one behaves. Most have been there for generations. One can't get rid of them like that."

As the old coach that met them all at Salisbury station crested the hill by Bordon village, and both the children shouted with excitement at the sight of Southwold in the valley, Richard wondered whether Lord Southwold or his wife had won, and how the fortunes of the great house had fared in his absence.

Miraculously, the house appeared to have revived. The fine clock tower on the stable block had been repaired, the whole west wing had been repainted, and young trees had been replanted in the unsightly gaps along the avenue. And the welcome in the house made the whole place seem happier—there was a great fire burning in the hall, the chandeliers were lit, and an enormous Christmas tree was ablaze with candles.

As it was Christmas Eve the choir came from the village to sing carols. Everyone joined in, including Richard and the children. Old Widgery the butler brought out great trays of gingerbread and hot spiced ale, and for a moment Richard had the strange feeling that Southwold House was his, that he had lived here as a child and that he loved it as passionately as Marjorie did.

But when the singing stopped and the villagers departed, Richard could see the reality of Southwold for what it had become. There was Lord Southwold, gouty now and barely able to walk since a fall out hunting in September. Lady Southwold seemed to have deteriorated too. She had a dreadful twitch—"Something wrong with this confounded eye"—and she had started to repeat herself. She was still forceful, but the frightening aspect had now become a shade pathetic. Despite himself and despite the trouble she had caused him in the past, Richard felt sorry for her. Like the fallen lime trees in the park, there were some fresh gaps in the family. Aunt Emily, the famous "Bolter" of the sixties, was no more and Cromwell the Great Dane had gone. Marjorie and the children insisted on visiting his grave—a very large one by the scullery—and all returned solemnly tearful.

There were some new arrivals too. Hugo had brought Lilianne and five-year-old Martin, their son and heir (and heir to Southwold). He was small, white-faced and inclined to cry. Unfortunately, the poor child had inherited Lilianne's most disagreeable qualities. The Bellamy children both despised him (one of the few things on which they managed to agree) and Richard and Marjorie suspected Hugo did as well. But now, since it was Christmas Eve, there was a great show of family feeling. Martin in sailor suit was blowing a toy trumpet, Elizabeth was looking after him, and Lady Southwold was pretending to be amused.

"Grandchildren make this place," Lord Southwold said, and Richard wondered what the grandchildren would make of Southwold in the years to come. James might have made an effort to preserve it, for as Richard realised, he loved it fiercely. But whining little whey-faced Martin—what would he do when he became Lord Southwold? It was sad to think that the future of this extraordinary house would ultimately rest with him. Perhaps it was a pity after all that it wouldn't come to James. Perhaps that would be his son's tragedy, and Southwold's too.

Dinner that night turned out to be a sad affair. There was a lot of talk of death, despite the fact that it was Christmas Eve. Lord Southwold went on incessantly about "that hideous new tax on rank and property," the death duties which for him at least spelled the extinction of the landed interest.

"When I go it's going to be a struggle for you, Hugo, to maintain the place. God knows quite how you'll manage. I must tell you I've been selling land simply to pay our way."

"Terrible, just terrible," Lady Southwold muttered.

But it was Hugo's wife who answered then. In the years since her marriage she had become extremely grand—more Southwold than the Southwolds. (Marjorie had grown to detest her.)

"Surely there's no earthly reason for us aristocrats to feel defeatist," she remarked. "We've simply given in too easily. People who should have spoken up for us in Parliament have let us down."

"Quite right," said Lady Southwold, "so they have," and stared at Richard.

"So what do you intend to do?" he asked.

"We," said Lilianne, putting an almost regal force upon the pronoun, "intend to enter politics."

"Both of you?" said Richard mildly.

"Hugo intends to stand for Parliament. I shall be behind him."

"Which constituency?" Marjorie asked.

An embarrassed silence followed, which Hugo broke with an awkward little laugh.

"Richard, my dear old thing, I've decided it's my duty to take on the old seat in the next election."

"Which seat?" said Richard coldly.

"Why, your old seat, the Southwold seat. Since you lost it, we can't let that bounder Tatham walk in again."

"I should just think not," said Lady Southwold.

"I quite agree," said Richard.

Richard woke on Christmas morning to the sound of battle from the room next door. Elizabeth was screaming; James was demanding back his roller skates and pulling his sister's hair; the room was in chaos.

After the tensions of the night before (the prodigies of self-control required to avoid telling Lilianne exactly what he thought), Richard's first instinct was to beat his son. But this was something that he never did. He liked to think that he had sufficient understanding of the boy to control him without violence, and on the few occasions when Marjorie said, "That boy needs discipline," Richard would urge patience and sweet reason—virtues which it was easy for a gentle, somewhat distant soul like Richard to adopt when his day was spent working in his study or discussing literature and politics with editors.

To be woken in this way on Christmas morning was different. Nevertheless, as a man of principle, Richard controlled himself, pulled the two savages apart and warned them both, with unaccustomed venom, that any more of this behaviour and there *would* be trouble.

"I just can't think what's come over James," he said to Marjorie as he climbed back into bed (it was very cold outside). "As soon as he gets to Southwold he becomes quite uncontrollable. It's extraordinary."

"Are you sure it was not Elizabeth? She's a frightful little minx, and knows you'll always take her part."

"Now, Marjorie, really. James had her by the hair. One simply can't allow a boy to treat a girl like that, even if she is his sister."

But despite Richard's warning and his show of anger, James did not behave. Richard was right. At Southwold something did get into him, particularly with his Uncle Hugo there. Hugo was still his hero and in some strange, unconscious way Hugo would always egg him on to some sort of devilment. When Richard mentioned this to Marjorie, she would just laugh and say, "You really can't blame Hugo. He's a boy himself at heart." Richard had other theories.

They were confirmed at breakfast time when Hugo—fresh-faced, bright-eyed as ever—said to James, "Here, Jumbo. Happy Christmas!" and took from his pocket a small velvet bag. Something inside it moved. James undid the string and two minute black eyes glared back at him.

"Hold him; take care he doesn't bite," said Hugo.

"What is it?" James asked a little nervously.

"Why, a ferret. Every boy should have one. We'll go rabbiting with him."

"On Christmas Day?" said Richard.

"Oh, we'll find something," Hugo replied airily.

James meanwhile had taken the small red furry creature from the bag and held it on his lap. "It's the most beautiful animal I've ever seen," the boy exclaimed. "I think I'll call him Jesus."

And so Jesus the ferret entered the family. He was an endless source of trouble. He nipped Elizabeth, climbed the curtains, got into Lady Southwold's bath. But James always rescued him, loved him, and slept with him. Richard disliked the whole idea, particularly when Hugo took them rabbiting,

"It's cruel," he said to Marjorie, "and a bad example for the boy."

"Oh, nonsense, Richard," she replied. "There's no use being squeamish in this life, no use at all."

The truth was that he objected to far more than this. In some obscure way he still felt jealous—of Hugo and of Southwold. Both were attempting to steal James away and it was this that Richard hated.

After the tedium of school and Eaton Place, Southwold was a paradise to James. He loved it, and he knew every corridor and hidden corner of that enormous ancient building. He knew the land as well, and the people on it. Charnock the gamekeeper would take him through the woods to show him the young pheasants being bred for next year's shooting. Foat, the estate carpenter, would show him forbidden places in the attics and the six-hundred-year-old roof with is Norman timbers, and the spot where James's Catholic Southwold ancestors had hidden their priests in the persecutions. And there was always Uncle Hugo to make life exciting when he was bored.

For the last day of the Christmas holidays Uncle Hugo had promised James a special treat. Together with Charnock they would go ratting by the old barn on the edge of the estate. They had a pair of terriers and as a special privilege James was allowed a gun, a six-bore Hugo himself had used to shoot pigeons as a boy.

It was unfortunate that Marjorie and Richard should have been walking in the park when the shooting started—still more unfortunate that they should have gone to investigate just as the terriers had caught a rat and were tearing it to pieces. It was not a pretty sight. Charnock was shouting at the dogs, Hugo was beating more rats from the barn, and an excited young James Bellamy was waiting with his gun to shoot the next one that emerged.

Marjorie was naturally distressed at the sight of blood. Richard was furious. He had been told nothing of the escapade, and if he had been told would have instantly forbidden it.

"Charnock!" he shouted. "Stop this right away! James, leave that gun alone and come with me!"

There was a sudden silence. The rat had finished squealing, and both the terriers stopped their yelping at the sight of this angry, white-faced stranger in their midst.

"Sorry, Mr. Bellamy, no harm meant," said Charnock quietly. "And, Master James, you'd best leave the gun with me."

But James was not giving in that easily. Still clutching his precious gun he faced his father.

"Why, Father, why? The rats need killing. Uncle Hugo said it was the best thing we could do."

The gamekeeper stared at his feet, and Hugo, a faint smile on his lips, was standing by the barn.

"James," said Richard softly, "I have told you to come. I won't tell you again."

The child paused, then suddenly stamped his foot and shouted, "Father, I won't, I won't! You're just a pig, a dirty pig! I won't, won't, won't!'

Had it not been for Hugo, James might still have got away with a stiff reprimand from Richard and the remainder of the day in bed. But at that moment Richard saw Hugo laugh, and Richard's self-control was ended. The expression on his father's face was something James would never forget.

Gone was the gentle advocate of reason, gone the sophisticated literary man. Instead he was suddenly enraged by Hugo's supercilious face and goaded beyond endurance by his son's rebellion, which suddenly appeared the ultimate humiliation Southwold could heap on him. He had endured so much—but there were limits. After twelve years of marriage he had reached them.

The speed with which he grabbed the child startled everyone, Hugo included. But this was nothing to the sudden fury with which he began to beat him. Richard had never beaten anyone before, never really lost his temper, so he had no idea how strong he was. Nor had James, until that moment. Nothing could stop him, neither Marjorie's cries nor the child's muffled screaming, and it was not until he felt Hugo's hand on his shoulder and heard him saying, "Stop it, Richard, or you'll kill the boy!" that he desisted.

He felt curiously clear-headed then.

James was whimpering at his feet, then, seeing Marjorie, ran towards her crying, "Mummy, Mummy!"

Hugo was no longer smiling.

"Get the boy to bed," said Richard curtly. "And, Hugo, I'd be grateful if you'd keep away from my son. You've your own child now."

The Bellamys were back at Eaton Place that night, subdued but grateful to be home. And after dinner Richard wrote a letter. It was to Pyecombe, thanking him for his support and accepting the Conservative nomination for the next election.

1899

10. *Peace in the Family*

Eton, the fourth of June, was an occasion Richard attended but never relished, not even this year, when his son was captaining the eleven and one of the heroes of the school. For 364 days of the year the fact that he, plain Richard Bellamy, was the son of a Norfolk rector lacking both family and fortune never troubled him. He was quite proud of it. He would, if pressed, have boasted of the fact to anyone.

But on this one day, when his own son's school saw fit to commemorate their royal founder, Richard always felt obscurely inferior.

It was a strange sensation, for he felt this nowhere else—not when he visited the House of Lords, or Marlborough House, nor even when he chatted with Lord Salisbury. But here, on these Windsor meadows with these overdressed rich parents all around him, he felt excluded and distinctly *gauche:* once more, as in the first years of his marriage, he felt that he was being judged as "that bounder Bellamy who married Southwold's daughter." The fact that he could never possibly explain all this to Marjorie made it worse, and also made him irritable.

How beautiful it all was—how absurdly beautiful: the distant view of Windsor, the gentle river and the chapel with its pinnacles there on the skyline, just as when Canaletto painted it! And yet how stupid all these so-called aristocrats around him seemed, how futile and how arrogant.

"And who's that splendid-lookin' fellah battin' now?" he had just heard one of them ask.

"Oh, that's the captain. Boy called Bellamy."

"Bellamy? Bellamy?"

"Yes, Southwold's grandson."

"Oh, *that's* who he is. One of the Southwolds. You should have told me."

This infuriated him. The fact that Richard Bellamy had served his country in the Commons now for fifteen years and knew half of the most powerful men in Britain by their Christian names barely counted. As far as Eton was concerned, the Bellamys did not exist and James was not his son, simply Lord Southwold's grandson.

In one thing at least the idiot spectator was quite right. James *was* a splendid-looking fellow, and a most graceful cricketer—one of those naturals who instinctively know how to play any game with a sort of inspired virtuosity. He had been batting scarcely half an hour, yet already had a score of thirty-six, including three fours and an effortlessly placed boundary. It was the same with every game he touched—rowing, tennis, even billiards and backgammon—always that same effortless and elegant success.

Richard was proud of him and rather envious (as nonathletic fathers usually are of successful games-playing sons) but at the same time something about this virtuosity at games worried him. It was a shade too effortless. He never got the feeling that James had to fight to win. At a result he always seemed just faintly bored, even by success. And then, of course, he was still more bored by anything to do with school work.

"Poor James," Marjorie would say. "If only he'd inherited your brains instead of mine." But this wasn't strictly true. James was no fool. Occasionally, when something captured his imagination—as rock collecting and zoology had briefly done the year before—he could produce the same sort of sudden brilliance he showed with his games. But this was rare. Boredom was becoming James's way of life. He lived with it, accepted it and even made a sort of cult of it, which earned him considerable kudos from the young sophisticates at school, for whom he was the embodiment of the Etonian tradition of "effortless excellence."

Still, he was more admired than popular. He had extraordinary good looks but no close friends, and Richard himself complained that he could not "get through to him." This was a source of sadness and of worry. Richard often put it down to that time at Southwold when he had lost his temper with his son and given him his celebrated thrashing. Their relationship had never been the same again, but Marjorie would have none of this.

"All boys are beaten by their fathers. James has been far more mollycoddled than any boy I know. That's been his trouble."

It was subtler than that. James was his mother's son, and as a Southwold had inherited most of the vices and the virtues of that long and noble line. By breeding he was naturally fitted to have taken over Southwold, to have ruled the county, managed his estates and lived his life out in the one true paradise he knew—beloved Southwold. But this could never happen: he could still remember the shock that hit him when he was barely seven and heard that his cousin Martin had been born. That was the dreadful moment when he knew he had lost Southwold for good. Ever since that moment nothing had really been worth while. What point had anything against that legendary world he had lost? How could he possibly explain this to his father, or to anyone—except to Uncle Hugo, and what use was that? Success at games amused him for a while. So did the admiration of the other boys. But it was all quite futile, really. Without Southwold, James had lost out on life before he even started.

He faced the bowling once again. The whole Southwold clan was watching him—his adoring mother, radiant in white summer silk and picture hat beside his father; next to her his Uncle Hugo, stylish and ever youthful in an Eton Ramblers' blazer; Aunt Lilianne trying to imitate the Princess of Wales; fifteen-year-old Elizabeth, enormously self-conscious and extraordinarily pretty; and beside her sat his grandfather. For the first time since James had known him, Lord Southwold was starting to show his age. The white hair was as thick as ever, the back as ramrod straight, but there was now a look of fragility in those fine patrician features. In the past he had always looked as if carved in marble; now the face could have been cast in porcelain.

James was glad the old man had come (for he was secretly immensely proud of him) and grateful too that Grandmother Southwold had been left at home. She was becoming something of an apparition, and he was upset by her drinking, which was becoming more of a problem to the family. Even his mother talked about it now, wondering what could possibly be done.

James hit another four and stood back, watching the fielder scuttle to retrieve the ball and showing no sign of hearing the faint murmur of applause from the spectators.

"Ripping!" said Hugo, clapping raucously and nodding towards Richard. "Absolutely ripping, eh, old boy? You must be very proud of him."

Hugo was being heartier than usual, mainly from nervousness. It was only recently that the feud between him and Richard had been healed. (Not that anything could ever make Hugo *like* the man again—too much had been said and done for that: all that ridiculous jealousy about his son, and then the underhanded way he had grabbed back the Southwold seat in Parliament. It hadn't done the wretched man much good. Wise old Salisbury had still excluded him from any office in the government—*and quite right too!* Ingratitude, ambition, lack of breeding. Marjorie should never in a thousand years have married him. But since she had, one made the best of things. One could at any rate *pretend* and be quite amiable.)

"I wish he'd show as much promise with his studies," Richard replied.

"What does the boy intend to do?" Lord Southwold asked. "Oxford? Same college as his father?"

Richard shook his head. "Not even Oxford would take him, I'm afraid. Unless he pulls his socks up pretty fast, there'll only be one thing for him."

"What do you mean, Richard?" Marjorie asked a little briskly. She disliked the way he criticised their son in public. Brains, as she kept on telling him, weren't everything.

"I've told you, dearest one, the army."

"That's ridiculous," said Marjorie.

"Oh, I don't know," said Hugo. "Dashed fine fellows in the Brigade these days. He'd fit in very well. Make a man of him. He'd show those Boers a thing or two."

"Think how that uniform would suit him," added Lilianne. "Darling James, so very handsome. Look at him now. Quite the young Greek god!"

At that moment the young god had just hooked the ball, which sailed right up against the bluest of blue skies and then descended, as if looped to some invisible string, straight into the welcoming cupped hands of an anonymous fielder on the boundary.

Somebody cried, "Owzat!" There was a moment's pause, as if the catch might still miraculously prove in doubt. Then James's inning, like a life cut short, was over and he was walking off the field to the leisurely applause of those elegant spectators.

"Poor James," said Marjorie. "Two short of his fifty."

"Mummy," Elizabeth said in a loud whisper. "There's something wrong with Grandpapa!"

Lord Southwold's heart attack put something of a damper on the game and on the celebrations. Both continued in the best English manner, which abhors any sort of fuss because of human frailty. But for the family there was inevitably a panic—a doctor summoned, his recumbent lordship carried on a stretcher to a nearby house, everybody waiting for the doctor's verdict. It was the sort of moment when Richard always appeared at his best. Unlike Hugo, who was suddenly quite useless, Richard was very calm—consoling Marjorie, sending Elizabeth off to fetch some brandy, then talking discreetly with the doctor to decide what should be done.

"Difficult to tell at this stage," said the doctor, a small, bouncy man more used to curing schoolboys than ancient members of the House of Lords. "I can't pretend it's not extremely serious. He's still unconscious at the moment, but provided there's not another attack, he could still be all right. One will have to see the damage this one's caused. After that, all will depend upon his constitution."

❧ ❧

The family stayed on at Windsor for the night (Elizabeth was secretly and guiltily delighted, since it meant she could see the fireworks), and all that night Lord Southwold remained in a coma. Marjorie insisted on seeing him. He was still lying in the little downstairs schoolhouse room where they had brought him. The doctor had insisted he must not be moved, and he lay like an effigy upon his own tomb, hands by his sides and scarcely breathing. His face was quite calm and deathly white.

Marjorie whispered, "Father! Father!" very softly, but there was no response, no sign of life at all, save for that shallow breathing.

Suddenly she was overcome with weeping. It was strange. Unlike Richard, who was easily and often moved to tears, Marjorie rarely wept at anything, but something about this proud, eccentric man she had never really known moved her uncannily. He who had always claimed so much from life was now so near to death. He who was so unlike mere ordinary mortals was now assailed by ordinary mortality. Never until that moment had she realised how much he meant to her or what a loss his death would be.

It was the same for everyone who knew him. For years now Southwold had been living out his life on his estates and had become accepted as an institution, taken for granted, frequently ignored. But now that the institution was at risk, everyone seemed desperate to preserve it. News of the illness must have travelled swiftly, for the sickroom gradually became the focus of this wide concern. The Provost of Eton called in person, then the college chaplain, a thin fussy man with High Church tendencies who upset Marjorie by hinting that "some form of last rite might be acceptable." Richard told him firmly it would not. Soon afterwards a reporter cycled over from his newspaper in Windsor. Again it was Richard who dealt with him, telling him the little there was to know. And Richard was still there, fortunately, when around nine o'clock Geoffrey Dillon arrived.

For that most lawyer-like of lawyers was clearly determined to take over everything, and his uncomfortably mournful presence magnified the gloom. He took it for granted, from the start, that Lord Southwold was dying, and spent some time talking deferentially to Hugo. Then Marjorie heard him calling Lilianne "Lady Southwold."

"Dillon!" she cried. "My father isn't dead."

"Indeed not, Lady Marjorie," he replied. "Forgive me. My emotions got the better of me."

"Take care that mine don't do the same," she said.

Another doctor called a specialist from Windsor, who confirmed that there was nothing to be done except wait. And wait they did. James returned to his house. Elizabeth, Lilianne and Marjorie were found beds for the night. But Richard, Hugo and the lawyer kept a vigil all that night by the recumbent body of the eleventh Earl of Southwold.

As he sat there Richard could not help wondering what effect Lord Southwold's death would have. An era would be over. One of the very last of the old grandees would vanish. And his successor? As Richard looked across at Hugo, nodding in his chair, he was struck more than ever by the contrast with his father. It was as if the incipient decay of Southwold power had started to affect the Southwold stock. Lord Southwold had maintained the power and the position of the family by what? Faith in himself and strength of character. And now poor Hugo (Marjorie was right, he *was* "poor" Hugo) would be unable to perform those miracles which had preserved the Southwold lands so long. Richard knew all about his debts—and Lilianne's. Friends in the City had warned him of what his brother-in-law was doing—borrowing on expectation, mortgaging his whole inheritance. Hugo knew nothing, only how to spend and to indulge that scatter-brained wife of his. (And to think that he and Marjorie had actually encouraged their romance!)

Once the life ebbed from the silent body lying there, and Hugo became Lord Southwold, the Southwolds would be finished. True, the title would continue, and the name, but names and titles scarcely mattered any more. There were enough of those. The house would go, the land would go, the power would go. The Southwolds would become a name in history and nothing more.

Did it really matter? Richard pondered deeply but found it hard to answer honestly. He was too involved. A few years back and he would still have answered bitterly that they deserved to vanish, that their usefulness was over, that their arrogance and privilege unfitted them for any role in the new society that was emerging. He still believed this in his heart of hearts, but now with age he also realised it was not so simple. He and his wife and son—especially his son—all had a stake in Southwold. His house, his income, all depended on the Southwold fortunes. But more than this would be at risk if Southwold House were sold. A cold wind would blow down Eaton Place.

There was a faint groan. It was still dark outside; the oil lamp cast deep shadows on the room and nothing moved. Richard could see the lamplight twinkling on Dillon's spectacles. He was asleep as well. The noise must have come from him. It came again then, stronger this time, and Richard realised the truth. It was not Geoffrey Dillon but Lord Southwold. He was still alive—and conscious!

Richard tiptoed across the room. The sick man lay so still and looked so deathly pale that Richard thought he must be mistaken.

"Are you awake?" he whispered. "Can you hear me?"

There was no reply, no movement from that fine, waxlike mask of a face; but then with a shock he realised that the eyes were open and were staring at him.

"How do you feel?" he whispered urgently.

Still no reply, no sign of life. But then, suddenly and unmistakeably, Lord Southwold winked at him.

❧

Southwold's survival through the night seemed to produce a certain sense of anticlimax from all who were set to mourn him, Hugo and Lilianne in particular. However much they loved him—and who could say they did not?—the fact was that his continued presence on this planet must have come as a keen disappointment. The Southwold lands, the Southwold title and the Southwold fortune (what was left of it) last night had all seemed finally and irrevocably theirs. And now this morning there was nothing but uncertainty, that maddening uncertainty when everything depends upon the heartbeat of an ailing man.

"How typical of Father," Hugo thought. "Even in dying he must cause the greatest inconvenience to the greatest number."

In fact, Lord Southwold had not the faintest intention of dying if he could help it. Old pagan that he was, he had no faith in anything beyond life's pleasures; and since Providence had given him so much more than ordinary mortals, he felt he had more reason to hold on to what he had. As he lay, so feeble and so wan, the thoughts of this sick, grand old gentleman would have appalled those loved ones who, with bland solicitude, came to his bedside. Whatever drowning men may really see of their past life, Southwold was being lulled by hazy recollections of plump bosoms, splendid fetlocks, fabled vintages—and it was these, far more than the prayers of his children and the care of his doctors, that kept his life flickering on that morning. What Southwold had had, his lordship intended still to hold.

❧

After two days—two days in which the bedside vigil of those with the most to gain and the most to lose from Southwold's death went on—it became clear that he would not die, not yet at any rate. The doctors started to congratulate themselves and calculate their bills. Dillon talked loyally about "his lordship's courage, an example to us all." Marjorie did her best to stop her mother coming to Windsor. "If anything would bring on a relapse, it would be dear Mama," she said to Richard. And Lilianne, quite stony-faced with anger, had a perpetual migraine and gave Hugo hell.

But, without being over-cynical, the truth was that Lord Southwold still alive was much more of a problem than he would have been stone-dead.

Who could look after him? He needed London specialists, and there was no question of his going back to Southwold with Lady Southwold in her present state. Nor could he possibly be nursed in his half-furnished house in Grosvenor Square (his man Matthews was now old and ill himself). Hugo half suggested that maybe he and Lilianne should take him in. "Quite impossible," that lady said decisively. "You must be mad. Anyhow, it's Marjorie's duty, and it's the least that she can do."

So Lord Southwold, still extremely ill but perceptibly improving with every day that passed, came and stayed at 165.

Richard was wary of the whole idea. He knew how difficult his father-in-law could be. He had never been particularly close to him (Richard's "betrayal" back in 1885, when Southwold might have been Prime Minister, still rankled) and he hated anything that might disturb the orderly routine of Eaton Place. More than ever Richard cherished the calm and order of his home; more than ever it appeared the one sure guarantee of happiness; and he knew Lord Southwold well enough to understand how much the demanding old man could stand his household on its head.

In fact the reverse occurred. Lord Southwold always reminded (Richard's "betrayal" back in 1885, when Southwold might have been rude unintentionally," and whatever faults he had, his manners were impeccable. He was given the large back bedroom on the second floor, and in no time at all had charmed everyone from Richard to the boot boy. He had to stay in bed—and Marjorie was very fierce making sure he did—but before long his room became a sort of clubroom. He would sit regally propped up on a pile of pillows, wearing a stylish dressing gown and frilled silk nightshirt, and discoursing, chatting, telling stories through the day. Mrs. Bridges managed to excel herself cooking the old gourmet dishes that he liked (often to his own direction) and Richard would complain that he never saw anything so delicious on *his* table. Hudson would visit him—in theory to "make sure everything is to your lordship's satisfaction" but in fact to discuss horses, discreetly cadge any tips Lord Southwold cared to give for the day's races, and place his lordship's bets with a bookmaker he knew. (Hudson never quite worked out why Lord Southwold always seemed to win.) As for the housemaids, it was never too much trouble to take Lord Southwold up his tray or shaving water in the morning. In short, his lordship rapidly became universally admired and loved.

Elizabeth became a particular favourite of his. She was intelligent (a little too intelligent for her own good, according to her mother), but it was precisely this that endeared her to Lord Southwold. "There's no virtue in stupidity," he'd say to Marjorie. "No virtue at all, although it seems to be the fashion with young women now. When I was young, great ladies still spoke French and knew their classics. Nowadays they're just as empty-headed as their maids."

Marjorie would reply that all a well-brought-up young lady needed was "good looks, good manners, and finally a good husband." Her father strongly disagreed, and he would talk to Elizabeth for hours about the classics and philosophy, which he still read for relaxation. She was a natural bluestocking (here she really had inherited Richard's early academic cleverness) and all her adolescent battles with her mother seemed to revolve round her refusal to be "ladylike" in one way or another. She was untidy, absent-minded, unconventional. She refused to believe that she was pretty. So-called polite society—what she saw of it—bored her intensely, and whatever interest she may secretly have had in boys she dismissed as "silly." The older servants disapproved of her at heart, especially Mrs. Bridges, who thought her a "ragamuffin" and objected to her "finicky manners" with her food. "I can't think what her ladyship will do with her—although I know what *I* would do if she was my daughter," she would say darkly to Hudson.

"Oh, she'll turn out all right," he would loyally reply. "She's at an awkward age. A trifle headstrong. But she has character. Give it a year or two and she'll be as lovely a young lady as ever her mother was."

But none of this seemed to concern Lord Southwold. That extraordinary old gentleman had found a fellow spirit in his granddaughter.

He taught her whist and gin rummy and they would play when she came home from school. (Somehow she usually seemed to beat him, and as they played for halfpennies, this was a source of useful income.)

But in a way by far the most unlikely friendship that developed during this time of Southwold's convalescence was between him and Richard. In the past there had been so many disagreements and misunderstandings that there had been no possibility of closeness between the two of them. Richard had looked upon his father-in-law as an outrageous old reactionary and naturally had blamed him for the indignities he had endured from his connection with the Southwolds. (True to human nature, he had not offset his resentment by much gratitude for the benefits he'd also had.)

And Southwold, similarly, had always considered Richard fundamentally "disloyal" and "undependable," although for Marjorie's sake he'd always kept these particular opinions to himself.

Now for the first time they discovered how much they had in common. Richard's famous novel had finally appeared. Partridge the publisher had been optimistic up to the point of publication (as publishers invariably are) and particularly enthusiastic at the changes he believed Richard had made at his suggestion. (In fact, all that Richard had done had been to shorten one offending chapter, then have the manuscript expensively recopied by a "lady typewriter" from the Pitman Institute.) Since then the splash which Partridge had predicted had proved the gentlest of ripples. There was a lukewarm notice in the *Pall Mall Gazette,* and Richard drew a certain fearful pleasure from the appearance of his book, along with twenty others, in Messrs. Hatchards' window. But that was almost all. Instead of the fortune he had dreamed of, Richard's novel made him barely thirty pounds, then sank without a trace in the broad seas of literary oblivion.

But Lord Southwold read it during these days in bed—and liked it. Richard was flattered; more than flattered, he was secretly delighted. No one since Zola had paid his literary efforts serious attention, but Lord Southwold questioned him on this and that, frequently discussed his hero's character, and showed in various ways just how much he had appreciated Richard's theme.

Elizabeth quite naturally proved another link. Both men agreed upon the need to educate the girl. Both men adored her, and before long the three of them began to form a sort of intellectual trio from which Marjorie began to feel excluded.

But, strangely, it was politics which finally cemented this belated friendship between Richard and Lord Southwold. Success in politics invariably comes early or comes not at all, and Richard, after nearly eighteen years of loyal back-benching, was more or less resigned to staying there. Others evidently felt (and if they felt it, who was he to disagree?) that he was no longer ministerial material. Earlier in life this would have upset him terribly; now he was philosophical. He enjoyed politics quite simply as a way of life. He loved the drama and the gossip and the strange addictive sense of being at the centre of affairs. He valued his membership in "the finest club in London," and with middle age he was becoming quietly popular among the other members.

In every Parliament there is a handful of experienced, unassertive, essentially *decent* men on both sides of the House, men who speak rarely and who play no part in policy or great decisions, but who are generally accepted as the collective conscience of the House. Richard was one of these and as such had his importance. Ministers would make a point of informally discussing things with him when they felt the need to know "what the ordinary back-bencher thinks," and in this way he did not merely make his mark on the ever shifting map of politics but also got to know most of the major politicians rather well.

As a result, he was able to enliven Southwold's convalescence with exactly the sort of gossip the old man loved. More than that, the two talked of politics and before long Lord Southwold had begun to reminisce about the past—the great politicians he had known, the parliamentary battles he had fought, the hopes and pleasures of his youth.

Years later, when Richard was appointed Southwold's official biographer, he would draw on these anecdotes. But at the time they simply served to bring the two men closer. Every evening after dinner Richard would take his brandy to Lord Southwold's room, and while the fire burned low, the talk went on and on.

Lord Southwold stayed a month at Eaton Place, and when he left, it was Richard and Elizabeth, far more than Marjorie, who missed him. Shortly before his departure, he summoned Dillon to his bedside and then called Richard.

"Richard," he said, "I realise that we've not always seen quite eye to eye, but recently I've been feeling guilty."

"Guilty, sir?" said Richard. "I'm sure you've no need for that."

"I said guilty, and I mean guilty," he said crustily.

"Dillon," he went on, "as you know just as well as I, Richard has suffered some injustices at my hands over that wretched stipend. I promised it to him and he should have had it."

"Really, sir," Richard said. "That was long ago. It scarcely matters now."

"To me it matters. You've been extremely good to me over these last few weeks, and I can see now that you've made Marjorie happy. I've no intention of being in your debt a moment longer than I can help. What do you suggest we might do, Dillon?"

The lawyer sniffed, then in his dusty voice said, "Under the present circumstances there seems to be no way in which the Southwold estates could possibly incur more expense."

"Expense, expense. That's all you ever think of, Dillon. And anyhow, who said that I was thinking of paying Richard any money? If he's the man I think he is, he wouldn't accept it, would you, Richard?"

"No," he replied uncertainly.

"There. You see, Dillon. Not everybody thinks like you. No, what I propose is this. At present this house is leased to you in Marjorie's name. I want that altered. I think that you should have it, Richard. As a gift when I die. I know Marjorie agrees. I've talked to her about it. So, Dillon, would you please arrange a special codicil to my will ensuring that it happens. I take it you know how to do it, Dillon?"

"I think I ought to," said Dillon blandly.

1903

II. *A Junior Minister*

WHATEVER THE GALSWORTHYS OF THIS WORLD IMPLY ABOUT THE UPPER middle classes, Richard Bellamy really was not much concerned with money. On the contrary, he was quite other-worldly, almost to a fault. Nor was he much impressed by money for its own unpleasant sake. True, he had known and mixed with quite a lot of rich men in his time. His father-in-law, Lord Southwold, had been very rich (and still, despite his illness and his losses, managed to act as if he were). Some of the politicians he knew—men like Devonshire and Rosebery and Manchester—were undeniably immensely wealthy. Then there were other rich men with whom he happened to get on, men like Sir Ernest Cassels (for years banker and crony of the Prince of Wales) and Baron Ferdinand de Rothschild. But with all the Edwardian millionaires Richard Bellamy maintained a splendid unawareness of their wealth. He enjoyed Cassels' company because they shared a taste for salmon fishing: he was genuinely surprised when that latter-day Maecenas suddenly invited him and Marjorie to spend part of August at his distinctly sumptuous villa outside Biarritz. Similarly, his friendship with the Rothschilds really started more from his desire to show his dislike of the fashionable anti-Semitism of the time than from any passion for the Rothschild millions.

Marjorie, one must admit, was different. Aristocrat though she was, in this one respect she could almost have been a *parvenue*. A true

Edwardian in this, she never could resist the magnetism of a fortune —and it was for Marjorie's sake that Richard reluctantly accepted the invitation that arrived from Alex Steiner.

Who *was* Alex Steiner? Nobody knew for sure—which of course made him appear even more exciting than your run-of-the-mill millionaire. Not that there was any lack of theories on this intriguing gentleman and his origins. One had it that he was an illegitimate son of the Emperor of Austria and had resourcefully gained his capital by blackmailing his august father. Another story was he owned a string of brothels and had tied up that tender trade from Beirut to the Bosphorus. Others hinted—but who cares what others hinted? Steiner was not alone in the rumours he attracted, for this was a period when high financiers were still regarded (generally with reason) as a romantic species of the international adventure. But Alex Steiner also looked the part, with his strange, twisted face and heavy-lidded eyes. The Marqués de Soveral had christened him "the money lizard," which was no bad name for him, with his reptilian manner and his sharp, thrusting nose for wealth.

Where he was different from other grand financiers of his time was in his ostentation. Men like the Rothschilds, and the Hirsches, Casselses and Barings of this world tended to be discreet. Steiner was a showman. It was Steiner who sent a pair of cheetahs to Sarah Bernhardt's dressing room when she appeared in London, and it was Steiner whose enormous Park Lane mansion had become a meeting place for almost anybody in the news. The receptions there were brash, extravagant and vulgar, but on an ordinary night of any ordinary week you could be sure of seeing several members of the government, a royal mistress or two, the latest fashionable *divorcée,* writers and journalists and portrait painters, actors and editors and visiting or exiled foreign royalty. The only qualification Steiner demanded of his guests was that they be *somebody*—and even Richard understood that this invitation meant that he had finally *arrived.*

As it happened, Steiner was for once a little late. Richard had "arrived" some nine months earlier. During the government reshuffle which had followed Salisbury's departure from the premiership, Balfour had appointed him one of his few new junior ministers. On the face of it, his appointment as Parliamentary Undersecretary at the

Admiralty was no great recompense for sixteen years of devoted service on the Conservative back benches. Marjorie was disappointed. "I thought Arthur Balfour was your friend," she sniffed. "Fine friend, I must say." Lord Southwold even went so far as to advise Richard to refuse. But for once Richard didn't pay too much attention to his family, and for once he was right.

Someone has said that the real division in the House of Commons isn't between the parties but between the members of the government and the rest. Richard discovered this now for himself. There were the small perquisites of power: the extra deference it won him in the Commons, the contact with the other ministers, the sense of being in the know. But there was more to it than that. The Admiralty was what Balfour called "a working ministry," the nerve centre of the new Prime Minister's own ambitious plans for imperial defence. The Dreadnought Plan, to keep the British fleet ahead of all competitors, Germany included, had just begun. And Richard, from his small office in the old Admiralty building, found himself, as he described it, "in at the deep end from the start."

It was unusual for an untried minister of his rank to have quite the responsibility (and quite the work) which Richard faced. There were the dockyards to be visited, the secret sea trials to attend, the vital decisions (about such fascinating things as turbines, guns and armour plating) to be made. Not that he did this on his own account. There was a horde of civil servants, admirals, advisers—all of whom had ideas and most of whom could put them very forcefully. Richard was generally the man to whom they put them, and he acted as the link between them and the politicians, both in Parliament and in the influential Committee for Imperial Defence. In the committee he was sitting with the small group of generals and admirals and cabinet ministers who had the real responsibility for rearming Britain and the Empire. Balfour was usually the chairman. Lugubrious General Kitchener attended for the army, and the small, squeaky-voiced Admiral of the Fleet, Lord "Jackie" Fisher, for the navy. In any argument this formidable little sailor had, as Richard said one night to Marjorie, "the power and tact of one of his own eighteen-pounders." More often than was good for his own comfort, Richard found himself having to stand up against him.

Fisher would put the case for yet more and better fighting ships. Balfour would tug at his moustache and say that in theory he agreed, but there were practical arguments against. Then he would call on Richard to provide them. Richard was good at this. Not that he enjoyed having to damp down Fisher's enthusiasm all the time. He admired him and frequently agreed with him, especially on the need for naval power. But he was also an experienced politician. He was practical, and by nature he was an excellent committee man. He knew his facts. His reputation grew.

It was an exciting time for Richard. Now for the first time since he had left the Foreign Service he was employing his intelligence and ability to the full. Balfour relied on him increasingly and made it clear that when the time came he would be promoted.

There was some irony in this, for at the moment Richard's very real success was by its nature secret. He remained one of the unknown men of the administration, and all his promise still lay in the future.

It was ironic too that Marjorie, who had always coveted success for him, always longed for him to be a man of power, could not appreciate this power when it came. She had no way of knowing how important Richard really was. To her a junior minister was simply a junior minister, almost two-a-penny. There could be no reflected glamour for her here: on the contrary, Richard seemed always tied up with his dreary dockyards and depressing naval estimates.

She and Richard formally attended a couple of court *levées*. It was strange to see their one-time friend the Prince of Wales transformed into that forbidding monarch Edward VII. He looked extremely grand of course, but rather pompous, in a way his mother never was. And rather disappointingly for Marjorie, there was no sign of recognition in that once too ready royal eye.

Apart from these visits to the Palace, the Bellamys' social life had actually declined since Richard's elevation—chiefly because Richard never had the time. True, there *had* been dinner several times at Number Ten, but Marjorie didn't care for Mr. Balfour—far too much abstract conversation for her taste, and she suspected that she bored him. (Just to make it worse, Balfour and her husband seemed to get on like a house afire, with all their talk of books, philosophy and, of course, the wretched naval estimates.)

Marjorie was frankly bored with life, and that summer there were several things to make her boredom worse. James was away at Sandhurst, so that she never seemed to see him now: when she did his talk was so full of parties, balls and hunts that he just added to her discontent. And young Elizabeth had left for Germany. This had of course been Richard's bright idea. There were some distant Southwold cousins, the Von Eckensdorffs, living near Dresden. Richard for some time now had been concerned for Elizabeth's education and Lord Southwold had suggested she might spend a year or two living with her cousins "and getting the sort of education that is impossible for well-brought-up young ladies in this country." Marjorie had of course objected. What the girl needed was a good finishing school simply to give her what she lacked—a little charm and a few of the necessary social graces—then possibly six months in Florence. But philosophy, and German philosophy at that? Who ever heard of such nonsense? It would only lead to trouble.

But Elizabeth and Richard were a strong combination when they got together (particularly with Lord Southwold in the background), and despite Marjorie's objections Elizabeth had gone, and the house seemed very empty without her.

"Steiner?" said Prudence Fairfax. "Not *the* Alex Steiner? My, we are becoming grand!"

Marjorie had told her of the invitation, and just for once Prudence had been agreeably impressed. Marjorie's best friend knew everyone these days. Once it had been a different story, but a year ago a lifetime's drinking and debauch had finally caught up with red-haired Major "Sandy" Fairfax, and Prudence had been left a rich and very merry widow.

During the major's drunken and depressing lifetime Richard and Marjorie often wondered at Prudence's loyalty. As far as anybody knew, she had been faithful to him, and certainly she never criticised him or complained of the way he treated her. But now that the major had consumed his final brandy-soda this side of Eternity, Prudence was making up for lost time and opportunities. She had a house in Thurloe Place, a mansion down in Sussex, and she had suddenly—and somewhat late in life—begun to bloom.

"But is this Steiner creature really quite as rich as everybody says?" asked Marjorie.

"As rich as Croesus, whoever Croesus was, or is," said Prudence knowingly. "Come to think of it, my dear, he's just the man we want to back St. Mildred's Ball. Millionaires are just a little scarce this season."

The Bellamys' appearance at the big affair which Alex Steiner gave a few days later was more than a success—it was an overnight sensation. Marjorie had dressed to kill, and after Prudence's advice was quite determined to be as charming as she knew to Alex Steiner. Richard too, for Marjorie's sake, was quite prepared to be as affable as possible. But this was nothing to the treatment they received from Steiner.

There were various celebrities for dinner at that big resplendent house—d'Alembert, the French ambassador, Marie Corelli, Lord Lansdowne, both the Keppels and Miss Ellen Terry. But in some strange way Steiner managed to imply that it was the Bellamys who were the unofficial guests of honour. He was a foreigner, of course, and foreigners, as Marjorie knew, *do* tend to be effusive, but even so there was no denying the extraordinary fuss he made over them. Marjorie was seated on his right, and during dinner she was subjected to such charm and flattery that, as she said to Prudence later, "had I been ten years younger, I'd not have been responsible for what occurred." For Alex Steiner was one of those very ugly little men who, like d'Annunzio, possess such magic that ten minutes is enough for them to captivate any woman they choose. But Steiner's conversation was not mere idle flattery. Clearly he knew a lot about the Bellamys. He asked about Lord Southwold's health ("delighted he is so much better"), James's recent posting to the Life Guards ("you must be proud of such a handsome son") and how Elizabeth was faring out in Germany ("I have some friends that she must visit").

But there was one small area where he appeared to know even more about the Bellamys than Marjorie, and this was Richard's work.

"What I admire about your husband is his modesty," the little man exclaimed. "Look at him now, so very English and so self-effacing. Who would guess, who didn't know the truth, how much that man was doing for his country? What do you call such people—unsung heroes? What a good job that just a few of us know what he is and so can honour him as he deserves."

Steiner did back St. Mildred's Ball, and far more lavishly than even Prudence hoped. His presence that night at Londonderry House served as a guarantee of its success. The Queen was there—looking, as usual, younger and lovelier than anyone imagined. And all polite society danced and drank champagne and paid their guineas (some of which finally did find their way to Prudence's pet charity, the St. Mildred's Homes for the Unfortunate Daughters of the Gently Born).

But once again the whole event seemed to glorify the Bellamys. Steiner paid graceful tribute to "the lovely Lady Marjorie" in his short speech announcing he was doubling the take. He was quite effusive when Marjorie introduced him to Lilianne and Hugo, and he talked amiably to James, self-conscious and resplendent in his new uniform as ensign in the Life Guards.

"Take care," said Prudence later. "Your tame little millionaire has got his eye on you."

And so Marjorie thought herself. But although Alex Steiner would probably not have found the lady too unwilling for a discreet flirtation (those afternoons and evenings on her own were hideously boring), the pass—as Prudence would have called it—never came. There were orchids from him, certainly, and scent and a little something set with diamonds from Cartier which arrived at 165 on the day after the ball. But there were also brandy and cigars for Richard and some expensive tickets for Drury Lane for James.

Indeed, it soon looked as if the millionaire was not in love with Marjorie but with the Bellamys, every one of them.

Richard was far too busy to take much notice for some time. He quite enjoyed Steiner's company and even suggested to Marjorie that he should come to dinner.

"We seem to owe him rather a lot of hospitality, my dear."

But once Alex Steiner entered 165 he never seemed to leave it. There was something strangely inescapable about him now. Marjorie was quite a regular at his receptions and, with Richard, spent a brief weekend at the big house near Ryde which Steiner had taken during Cowes Week. James too was frequently invited to the Park Lane House. Even Hugo—spendthrift, footloose Hugo—felt the spell of Steiner's curious benevolence: it was around this time that he accepted Steiner's offer of a directorship of one of his financial subsidiaries. (Hugo was never sure quite what the firm did or what the job involved, but since it paid three thousand pounds a year he cheerfully allowed his name to go on the company's official writing paper.)

◂§ §▸

That summer Richard and Marjorie were forced to delay their usual summer holiday. There were the sea trials up at Scapa Flow of the *Royal George,* the very latest, very costly, very secret eighty-thousand-ton addition to the Royal Navy. Richard was the member of the government deputed to attend, and for a week he braved the elements —and Admiral of the Fleet Lord Fisher's tongue—as the great ironclad ploughed its way through the summer storms of the Atlantic. He was unusually impressed. The ship responded wonderfully, the men's morale was quite magnificent, and the gunnery trials, on an abandoned coaster off the West of Ireland, were a great success. Richard agreed with Fisher that the *Royal George* could "lick the pants off anything the Kaiser cares to throw at us." And he reported back, in words to this effect, to a meeting of the Cabinet on his return to London.

There was still powerful opposition in the Cabinet, and in the Party as a whole, to the expanded dreadnought policy. Balfour, as usual, seemed to vacillate. But Richard and his favourable report appeared to influence him. What remained uncertain was whether he would back the plan for the four more versions of the *Royal George* that Fisher wanted.

Richard had returned intending to take Marjorie up to Norfolk for a few days on the Broads. It would have been a good chance for him to see his mother. It was six months since he had seen her now, and he knew that she had had some sort of fall. As usual, he was feeling guilty at his failure to visit her, especially as he knew the pleasure his visits gave the frail old lady.

At the same time Lord Selbourne, his new chief at the Admiralty, had invited him and Marjorie to his place outside Kings Lynn for a few days' holiday, making the trip an opportunity to combine business with some days of quiet pleasure.

Marjorie was not enthusiastic. "Norfolk, how very boring at this time of year, and I suppose that I'll be stuck all day with Lady Selbourne while you discuss your precious naval programme with his lordship."

"What would you suggest instead?" he said, trying to be tactful and realising that Marjorie's life *was* becoming somewhat tedious.

"Well, dearest," Marjorie said, putting on her most appealing look. "Alex has invited both of us to his place near Deauville for the summer. Couldn't we forget Lord Selbourne and just slip across? I always win at the casino, and there's that little restaurant that you love outside Étaples."

France, gambling and food—normally the three combined would have proved quite irresistible to Richard. But to Marjorie's surprise and disappointment, he grunted, "Not if it means enduring that Steiner fellow."

"What's wrong with him?" she said.

Richard shrugged his shoulders. "I don't know, but he seems a little too damned rich. And he hasn't bought us—yet."

Norfolk in fact was beautiful. Old Mrs. Bellamy was so thrilled to see them that Marjorie was glad she went, and the Selbournes were delightful. When they got back to London, Richard took Marjorie on to Paris for a fortnight, which they both enjoyed. It was romantic to be back in the city where they met and they spent days revisiting the places they remembered all too well—the Gare du Nord, Maxim's, the town house of the Duke d'Amboise. (The Duke was dead and a distant cousin had inherited the place. "To think," said Richard, "if it had not been for me, this would have been all yours." "I prefer Eaton Place," said Marjorie loyally.)

For Marjorie it was wonderful to have Richard to herself again and be able to forget the Admiralty. For Richard it was marvellous to rediscover the passionate and tender woman he was married to and not hear about Alex Steiner and his money.

But Steiner hadn't done with them. No sooner were they back in Eaton Place than the invitations started once again. Richard was cool and Marjorie was forced to refuse them. Steiner became more pressing, and finally, for Marjorie's sake, Richard agreed that they would dine with him. Apparently quite unaffected by Richard's recent coolness, he was as welcoming and brash and the food as sumptuous as ever.

He flattered Marjorie in his usual way, sang Richard's praises, and after dinner, over the vintage port and very fine cigars, he suddenly said to Richard, "Bellamy, I feel I should be doing something for you."

"How very kind," said Richard. "What do you suggest?"

Steiner smiled his funny twisted smile and said, "I am a rich man; you are relatively poor. I know something of the work and the responsibility you have to bear. It would be my privilege to make things easier, financially, for you."

"How delightful," said Richard drily. "How could you do that?"

Steiner laughed. "Don't be offended. There'd be no charity involved, simply a few straightforward business deals and share transactions. They would be in your name, but I'd suggest you let your lawyer handle them. I'd tell them what to buy and sell and I could guarantee you, shall we say, a useful profit."

"But I'm in no position to buy anything. I'm not just 'relatively poor.' I have no capital whatsoever."

"You don't need it. It will all be done on credit, and I will willingly stand guarantee for you. I know your lawyer, Geoffrey Dillon, and the directors of your bank are friends of mine. Take my advice, Bellamy. Let those who like and admire you help you."

Richard was very much tempted. His lack of capital had always been a source of concern. It was not that he wanted for anything. A new suit or two, perhaps, more books, more vintage wines would be pleasant to acquire, of course, but there was no pressing need for them. As a rule, any extra cash he had he spent on Marjorie or the children, for he had learned from sheer necessity the virtues of frugality. Throughout his marriage he never had had much to spend upon himself—and now at forty-nine he did not want it.

But capital was something different. He knew full well the uncertainties of politics as a career. He also knew Lord Southwold would not last forever. Once the old man went, Richard and Marjorie would have no assurance about their income. A plump portfolio of shares and a few thousand on deposit in the bank would make their future much rosier.

And Geoffrey Dillon added to the temptation. Over the past few years that slippery gentleman had been advancing his career. An astute marriage to a Birmingham paint manufacturer's only daughter and some risk-free dabbling on the Stock Exchange had assured *his* fortune. He had recently been working for the Treasury Solicitor, and thanks to his old Southwold connections had made his mark as something of an unofficial legal adviser to the Party. His knighthood was expected in the New Year's Honours. He had worked hard for it—even Richard conceded that—for these days Geoffrey Dillon knew a lot of politicians, and Richard was amused by the unaccustomed deference with which Lord Southwold's lawyer treated him.

It was a most judicious and respectful Geoffrey Dillon who called at 165 a few days later to discuss Steiner's offer. He was all in favour of it. "A great man, Alex Steiner," he murmured solemnly. "You're very fortunate to have him as a friend. Between us, he and I are sure that we can guarantee your future and that of Lady Marjorie and the children. For your sake, for the family's sake, I am delighted."

"I'm still a little worried, though," said Richard. "You're the lawyer. You must know these things, but surely as a member of the government I must be rather careful."

"Careful, Richard?" Dillon smiled his old, familiar fish-like smile. "Surely you don't imagine I'd advise you to embark on anything at all improper."

The way Dillon spoke the word "improper" made Richard laugh. "Good heavens, no! It's simply that I'm not sure that I trust friend Steiner."

"Don't trust him, Richard? But he's a millionaire! You've always been *too* cautious, Richard. These things are done. You'd be surprised at what is done these days."

"I'm sure I would," said Richard.

In the end, Richard thanked the lawyer, promised to consider Steiner's offer, and said he would give him a decision in a day or two. In fact the Admiralty took up all his time for the next ten days, for the battle still went on within the Cabinet over the dangers and expense of the dreadnought programme. Richard, now a convinced supporter of Admiral Fisher, was at the heart of it, and this left him little time to spare for Steiner or for Dillon. Then something happened which made up his mind for him.

James was now stationed down at Windsor. This meant that he and Marjorie saw rather less of him, but on that Sunday morning, whilst the whole household was still in bed, there was a honking from the street outside.

"What on earth is that?" said Marjorie.

"Ought to be arrested, whoever it is, making such a filthy noise at this time on a Sunday!" said Richard.

But the noise went on. Still grumbling, Richard climbed out of bed, pulled back the curtains, and peered out.

"Good God," he said, "it's James!"

"Don't be ridiculous," Marjorie said sleeply. "How could it be?"

"I tell you that it's James. He's got a motor car."

There was naturally great excitement. Apart from the eccentric Lord John Prizeman several doors away, who had recently bought a thundering Daimler-Benz from Germany, no one in Eaton Place had been so daring or extravagant as to own a car. Hudson and the servants were all most impressed, and over breakfast James was quite lyrical about the new machine. It was a six-horse-power De Dion, and it had made the journey up from Windsor in an hour. One or two officers had motor cars, but James was insistent that his was the best.

"Incredible the speed it does! On the road from Brentford I was going thirty-five!"

"How dangerous, my dear," said Marjorie. "Do take care!"

But it was not the speed of James's car that worried Richard, it was the price. Three hundred pounds.

"How could you possibly afford it?" he asked finally.

James tried to look mysterious.

"Ah, that's a secret, Father," he replied, and grinned cheerfully towards his mother. Marjorie smiled back, and Richard sensed that something had gone on behind his back.

"James," he said angrily. "I insist on knowing!"

James still smiled boyishly. "I tell you, it's a secret, Father. It was a friend who paid, and I've promised not to say . . ."

"And I tell you that I insist!" said Richard, who was now thoroughly alarmed at the thought of someone spending all that money on his son.

"Really, Father, when an officer and a gentleman gives his word, how could you possibly try to make him break it?"

"James, for the last time," said Richard, struggling to keep his temper, "I demand to know."

Marjorie prevented what would certainly have been an uproar between her husband and her son. "It's quite all right, Richard," she said calmly. "The man who paid could easily afford it. It was Alex Steiner."

It was the De Dion that ultimately saved Richard Bellamy, for it was the shining gold-and-scarlet car that finally aroused his slumbering suspicions.

"I'm sorry, old chap," he said to James. "It's going back."

"Going back, Father? What d'you mean?"

"I mean exactly what I say. The motor car is going back immediately to the garage where you bought it—and I will see that Mr. Steiner is repaid in full."

It was a great deal to expect of somebody like James to accept this ultimatum. But something in Richard's manner told his son that this was not the time to argue. Nor did Marjorie argue when Richard said that any gifts she'd had from Steiner were to go back too. That same morning he sent a telegram to Geoffrey Dillon.

"On no account, repeat no account, agree to Steiner offer."

"Interesting," said the small man with the round, rubicund face. "Extremely interesting. We had an idea this was happening, but it is clearly on a larger scale than we imagined. I must compliment you, sir, on the way you've handled it. I can see it must have been embarrassing for you, but that's nothing to the trouble it could have caused you in the end."

"You really think Steiner has been up to something, then?" Richard asked.

"Up to something? Admiral Sir Adam Hall, the head of Naval Intelligence, began to laugh and his jolly face became still redder. "Well, yes, you could say he was up to something. Up to a very great deal, to tell the truth. We've a dossier on him as thick as my arm. You were a natural target for him from the start."

"But why? I still don't really understand."

The Admiral paused to light a stubby sailor's pipe. "I take it you don't know how Mr. Steiner makes his money?"

"Some sort of banking business, I suppose," Richard said vaguely.

"Banking? Oh, dear me, no! Banking's too tame a business for the Steiners of this world. Not enough profit either, for his taste. No, Steiner's in armaments. He doesn't advertise the fact, of course, but all his real investments are in Germany—Essen, Hamburg—Hamburg in particular. He has a lot of money tied up in their naval programme and I suspect that's where his real loyalties lie."

"So he was hoping he could pick up information from me? Not much hope of that."

"Information? Oh, God bless you, no! Steiner was no common-or-garden spy."

"What *did* he want then?"

"He was out to break you, sir! And a lot of other people too, if he'd had the chance. He can't have cared much for the way that you've been championing our Admiral Fisher in the Cabinet. The expanded dreadnought programme doesn't suit the Germans, not a bit. He knows how delicate the matter is in Parliament, and he also must have known the scandal there'd have been if the news leaked out that the Undersecretary at the Admiralty and his whole family had been receiving bribes."

"Bribes?" said Richard. "Come now, Admiral!"

"Oh, I know, sir, that it was all quite innocent. And thanks to your action now no harm's been done. But you have no idea what some of Steiner's cronies in the British press would have made of it all when he decided that the time was ripe: expensive gifts and holidays for your lady wife, a brand new motor car for your son, and then a mass of carefully rigged shares for you. No, Mr. Bellamy, you'd have been mincemeat by the time the press and Mr. Steiner had had done with you!"

This set the Admiral off again, and for some moments he sat laughing jovially at the idea. Richard, however, didn't laugh, and when the merriment subsided he asked the Admiral what would happen now.

"Nothing," the little man said briskly. "Fortunately nothing. And if we keep our fingers crossed—and Mr. Balfour's sums come out—Jackie will get his battleships."

"And Steiner?"

"The man's committed no crime, and he has a lot of powerful friends. But I've an idea that—thanks to you, sir—we'll soon be able to take care of him."

Steiner's departure two months later caused considerable regret, not least in 165. The servants missed his lavish tips, and Marjorie knew that the next St. Mildred's Ball would never find so generous a backer. Neither Marjorie nor James ever really understood why Richard had suddenly become so scrupulous, and for years to come James would regret that superb De Dion. Dillon missed Steiner too, and when he became Sir Geoffrey Dillon, he never knew how much he owed Richard for his title.

1905

12. A Lady and Her Lover

THERE ARE ESSENTIALLY TWO SORTS OF HUSBAND: THOSE WHO BLAME their wives when they discover they have been unfaithful, and those who blame themselves. Fortunately for Marjorie, and for the peace of 165, Richard was among the latter. Not that it wasn't a grave shock to him when he realised, without the shadow of a doubt, that the woman he had been married to for twenty-seven years had wantonly deceived him.

For without being over-subtle on the precise meaning of the verb "to love," Richard undoubtedly still loved his wife. For twenty-seven years he had been technically faithful to her. He depended on her for his emotional security and physical release. He admired her, looked up to her, and in his way was still extraordinarily sentimental about her. Small things she did—the way she organized her dressing table or addressed a letter or arranged a vase of flowers—never failed to move him. And he still found her beautiful—as indeed she was—so that the discovery that she was having an affair with one of his son's brother officers caused him considerable pain. It was not simply jealousy. He was no longer anything like as jealous as he had been ten years earlier. (Does jealousy in some merciful manner subside in time with a man's virility?) What really caused the pain was the natural feeling that the one person he had thought he could trust completely had suddenly betrayed him; and without Marjorie, everything was lost.

"But why?" he asked himself. "Why did she have to do it?" And since he was the sort of husband that he was, he spent some days of agony and doubt trying to decide just where and how he'd failed.

◆§ §◆

When a good-looking, wealthy, middle-aged woman finds herself suddenly in bed with someone other than her husband, there can be several explanations for her conduct. In Marjorie's case the obvious reason was the best: her lover, Captain Charles Hammond of the Indian Army, was six foot two, lean, bronzed and eager, and she found him irresistible. James had brought him to visit at Eaton Square. An uneventful evening at the opera followed, and then purely by chance Marjorie met him in the book department of the Army and Navy Stores. From then on, innocence was over. When he invited her back to his lodgings in the Ebury Road to read some poetry, she knew exactly what would happen, and when it did she thoroughly enjoyed herself. The captain was a skilful lover. Marjorie, who had read this phrase in novels, had always wondered what it meant. Now she discovered. Richard, for all his youthful indiscretions years ago in Paris, was not particularly imaginative. Politics and age and years of familiarity had rather sapped his energies as well. The contrast between him and the captain startled her. Not for nothing had Captain Hammond served in India, home of the *Kama Sutra* and the temple prostitutes of Kerala. Unlike your decent Englishman who had been taught that sex hadn't much to do with female pleasure, he was an uninhibited young sensualist who taught Marjorie things that Richard would have said were too depraved for honest women. Had she been younger she might have felt the same, for a while at least. But she was of an age now where she was grateful to be discovering pleasures rather than losing them, and at forty-seven she was more passionate and more frustrated than ever in her life.

A lover barely half her age? How Prudence would have laughed. But when she was in his arms and felt his firm young flesh, what did it matter? It was all something of a game, of course, although she would never have admitted it. There were the tender declarations and the avowals of undying love—the captain was romantic to a fault. There were tears, red roses, lines of Keats and Shelley. Marjorie found them all delightful. At her age it was marvellous to be called "My goddess" by an eager young man as he slipped your dress from your shoulders and admired you by the flickering firelight in his darkened room. It was thrilling too when he rhapsodised about your naked body when you were lying on his bed. But best of all was the moment when the pretence of all romance was over and he was hungry, dominating, cruel—the sort of lover she had longed for since she was a girl.

At first she was shy of showing him her body, not from prudery but from concern that he would find it old and ugly. This was one thing she need not have feared. She was more desirable than at twenty-five. Then she had been slim, undeveloped, unawakened; now she was in her prime, mature, full-bosomed and desperately eager to experience anything her lover wanted.

After the first few hesitant experiments she was soon taking the initiative. She was so reckless and so hungry that even the ardent captain showed signs of tiring. Marjorie told herself that she must be a little more discreet and restrained if she wished to keep him, but discretion and restraint were not in her nature. Always headstrong, she had always taken what she wanted. She had had enough of restraint with Richard, and now there was little she could do. Now that she had finally abandoned herself to passion, she was completely in its grasp. Sense, conscience, even self-respect meant nothing, as did other people. For those few autumn weeks of 1905, Marjorie existed on a sort of island: its centre was the large brass bed in Ebury Street, its sole inhabitants herself and Captain Hammond.

The gallant captain was in love as well, although in his case "love" was something very different from the emotion felt by Marjorie and Richard. For all his sexual expertise, he was the most romantic of the three. Like many hardened lechers he was a simple man at heart. Bored wives in Poona, courtesans in Kashmir had not given him the sort of social sophistication he would have picked up in London, and when he fervently addressed his naked mistress as his "goddess" he meant it.

Previously, the nearest he had ever come to rank and glamour in a woman had been a sad flirtation with the wife of a colonel of the Punjab Horse, and he was still a firm believer in the gulf between a "woman" and a "lady." Women were fair game for anything, but ladies were so elevated, so romantic and refined that the thought of having an affair with one was almost inconceivable—and very thrilling. Particularly with Lady Marjorie Bellamy. She wasn't just a lady, she was the daughter of an earl, the wife of a minister in a Conservative government, the mother of a brother officer. The taboos surrounding her were so intense that poor Hammond—experienced and hardened though he was—was actually trembling when he took the, to him at least, appalling risk of asking her to his apartment.

For those first few ardent weeks of the affair his sense of awe continued, and it was this that fueled his romantic love for her. Even at those moments of quite perfect fleshly ecstasy, even when Marjorie was giving him abundant proof of her instincts as a very normal woman, Hammond was still whispering to himself that this was a lady, not a woman, in his bed.

But with every time that they made love this odd distinction became harder to maintain. "Surely," another small insistent voice began to whisper in the captain's ear, "surely no *real* lady can behave like this." And since he knew he was in love, the small voice troubled him.

Marjorie, of course, had no such doubts. She enjoyed the blissful unconcern of all single-minded women. She had no qualms about her love, no sense of guilt, and precious little thought for anyone except her lover, so she was not much use to Richard just as that moment when he needed her. She barely noticed what he was going through.

Even before he learned the truth about Marjorie, things had been perversely going wrong for Richard that fall. He was concerned about Elizabeth. The few recent letters she had written from Germany had been extremely odd. She seemed to have changed, and he was not sure he liked what she was changing into. James worried him as well—he had heard rumours of extravagance and heavy drinking in the mess. He looked unwell and tended to flare up at anything.

Worse still, for Richard, all his great hopes of political preferment had been swept away in that year's disastrous elections. Balfour had thought it might be "good for the country to experience a short sharp dose of the Liberals' medicine," but not even the pessimistic Balfour had expected anything quite like the great Liberal landslide that had occurred. Nearly two hundred Tory seats were lost. Richard's majority fell to a bleak three hundred votes, and when he returned to Parliament the former Undersecretary at the Admiralty found himself a mere back-bencher in a demoralised and muted Tory opposition.

Loss of power can have an extraordinary effect on politicians. Overnight Richard lost the dominating role that had consumed his energy and enthusiasm. Overnight he lost his chance of shaping history. And overnight he was reduced from a somebody, with propects of the highest office in the land, to a virtual nobody. Time hung heavy on his hands.

This was when he needed Marjorie, but she had little time for him. He was depressed and lonely, but she complained of feeling tired in the mornings and was also mysteriously tired at night. He suggested that they go to Southwold for a few days by themselves. (Lady Southwold was in hospital and his reinvigorated lordship had gone off to France.) Normally Marjorie would have loved to: now she replied impatiently that it was quite impossible. There was some charity affair with Prudence that took all her time.

"A pity," Richard said. "It would have done you good. Lately you've been looking pale, my love."

"Do you think I'm looking pale?" she asked her lover later that afternoon.

"Pale, dearest one?" He eyed her thoughtfully. She *did* look pale—and slightly haggard too. He always found the same thing with his women. In the first flush of passion they were flawless, but then, like fading roses, they began to show their faults.

"Pale as ivory," he murmured as he leant forward, cushioning his slightly weary head between her breasts. Long experience had taught him that this was a useful way of ending a discussion.

"You still love me?" Her voice seemed to come from miles away.

"Mmmm!" he replied. The warmth and comfort of her body welcomed him. He sighed.

"Charles," she said softly; then more urgently, "Charles!"

But her lover was asleep.

It is an ancient truism, but none the less accurate for that, that the last people to hear about a love affair are those who are having it. One by one everybody round the Bellamys picked up the gossip, but Marjorie and her captain stayed on their amorous island sublimely unaware of how much interest and excitement they were providing.

The servants learned about it first. Words of love read off a blotter by an inquisitive lady's maid, are one of the clichés of the period. (Not even Albert Edward was immune to this strange source of aggravation.) But when Miss Roberts held up Lady Marjorie's blotting paper to the mirror and read her ardent words to Captain Hammond, it merely offered confirmation of the telltale signs that everyone at 165 had been noticing for weeks.

If it is true that no one is a hero to his valet, it is still more true that no one can keep a secret long from a houseful of servants. Upstairs life is so exciting—and downstairs life so tedious—that servants naturally cherish any piece of gossip they can find about their betters. This provides the only touch of glamour and excitement in their lives, so one should not be too censorious about the habit. On the other hand, one ought to be aware of it. Lady Marjorie, like so many of her kind, was not. She had grown up to think that the lower orders were as discreet and limited and stupid as they seemed. She who was always wary of revealing anything about her private life before her friends was strangely careless in her own house. One pair of eyes would notice those afternoon excursions off to Ebury Street. Another pair would see the private notes that were addressed to Lady Marjorie in the captain's firm, round hand. And yet another would observe the state her dress was in before she changed for Mr. Bellamy's return.

Hudson was fairly loyal in the discussions that inevitably ensued in the servants' hall. All the servants knew that there were limits beyond which it was unsafe to go. Theoretically at least they had to maintain the fiction of "respect" for Lady Marjorie. But even Hudson could not disguise the shock he felt at her ladyship's behaviour or his staunch sympathy for the master of the house. On the other hand, the female servants—Rose and Mrs. Bridges in particular—tended to side with Lady Marjorie (except when she was irritable with them). Her ladyship seemed so romantic. She was by turns so radiant and then so desperately sad that their female hearts went out to her. For once they could share her feelings, and the captain, it was generally agreed, was enough to turn the head of any woman, even her ladyship. So 165, above stairs and below, was soon agog with interest in the love affair; and the interest inevitably spread.

For once again one ought to understand that servants talk to other servants and that they in turn quite often gossip to their mistresses.

They oughtn't to, of course. One ought to offer a severe reproof and close one's ears to anything they say. But human nature being merely human nature, self-restraint of such an elevated order cannot be counted on. Every Wednesday afternoon Miss Roberts took tea with Prudence Fairfax's maid, Miss Farquhar; and by evening Lady P. would be *au fait* with what was going on.

And similarly throughout Belgravia (and beyond its borders into Mayfair and across the social canyon of the Park) the news would spread. Marjorie Bellamy, that ice-cold paragon of virtue, had succumbed at last. According to the rumours, Richard knew and the Bellamys were on the edge of breaking up.

Fortunately for everybody's sake—especially his own—Richard did not catch the lovers *in flagrante*. All that happened was that his growing suspicions were finally confirmed when he realised that Marjorie's panic, when she read about an accident to an unnamed officer at Henley, could not possibly have been on behalf of James as she had said, for she had known quite well that James was safe and sound in London all the time. The only officer she knew who fitted the bill was Captain Hammond. And of course he too—damn the man—had turned up safe and sound next day at 165, and there was no disguising Marjorie's relief when she saw him.

But what *could* Richard do—aside from masochistically blaming himself for what had happened? His misery apart—and that was really quite considerable—he obviously needed to make up his mind, but this was difficult. He felt he couldn't talk to Marjorie. He knew her well enough to realise just how much in love she really was and feared the bitter things that he might say to her. All he wanted, he told himself, was Marjorie's happiness. If he had failed her—as he realised he had—by far the best thing would be for him to offer her her freedom. Then she could marry Captain Hammond—and he would have to try as best he might to find whatever solace life could offer him.

Full of these noble, slightly maudlin sentiments, Richard sought out the only really sympathetic woman he knew to ask her what *she* thought.

Prudence had never really been in love with Richard Bellamy, not physically in love. But she had always had what she called "rather a soft spot for the dear old thing." Therefore when Richard called on her and blurted out the not entirely surprising news that Marjorie was having an affair, she had a slight temptation to exploit the situation. It says much for her that she resisted it.

Instead she listened sympathetically as he poured out his sorrows, and expressed nothing but admiration for his decision to allow his wife her freedom.

"How very noble of you, Richard dear," she said at last. "I'm sure that no other husband in London would show such real self-sacrifice."

"You think not?" Richard answered, surprised. "Surely any decent chap would do the same."

Prudence, remembering her own departed spouse, raised her blue eyes to heaven.

"Oh, certainly some husbands would let their wives divorce them in this situation, but that's not what I mean. You will be losing everything, of course—your home, your income, your political career. That's what I call *real* self-sacrifice."

"Will I?" said Richard, who in the midst of his romantic misery had not paid any heed to the economic—still less the social—facts of life.

"But of course, my dear. Now don't pretend you've forgotten that all the money is in Marjorie's name, and the house as well, nor that the divorce will mean that you'll be giving up your seat in Parliament. Marjorie should feel very flattered that her happiness means so much to you."

❧ ❧

Two days later, when Marjorie took tea with Prudence, she was astonished at the way her friend immediately guessed her secret, and Prudence's explanation—"you look so radiant, my dear"—made her a shade uneasy. Was it as obvious as that?

She was still more surprised at Prudence's enthusiasm when she confided more of the affair to her.

"But how wonderful, my love! And young and handsome. I think it's so unfair the way some people make fun of women of our age who fall in love with younger men. As if age matters, or money either. I suppose he's penniless?"

Marjorie nodded.

"That makes it so much more romantic. It must be wonderful for you after all those years with dreary old Richard. Frankly, Marjorie, I just don't know how you've put up with him for so long."

Marjorie nearly said, "How dare you speak about Richard like that—he's nothing of the sort!" But then she realised that in the circumstances this might sound hypocritical, and also something at the back of Marjorie's mind was asking just *why* Prudence Fairfax was so anxious to see her marriage broken up. Hadn't she always been a little interested in Richard herself? That evening after dinner Marjorie found herself wondering just what was happening.

⁂

The afternoons in Ebury Street continued. They were still wonderful. Charles was as passionate and as ingenious as ever. He still recited poetry, bought her roses and called her by the embarrassing but touching pet name he had given her their first afternoon together. But at the same time she began to notice that he no longer talked about the time when they would finally elope; nor for that matter did she mention any more the little house just outside Cannes which Lillie Ankaster had said they might use for a winter holiday together.

The Christmas holidays were looming now. Elizabeth would soon be home from Germany and James would be expecting a dinner party in the house for some of his brother officers. What would Hudson say? Best to leave it to James to ask him personally, and of course Mrs. Bridges too, since she'd have to do most of the work. Then they'd be off to Southwold. During the last few days Richard had suddenly begun to talk about it quite enthusiastically—and as she thought of Christmastime at Southwold Marjorie discovered she was looking forward to it, whereas a week or two before the idea of even a day apart from her beloved Charles would have appeared impossible.

⁂

Prudence didn't see the Bellamys over Christmas, although she often found herself wondering about them both. Rather a pity about Richard; he might have been the answer she was looking for, and possibly she really was a little more in love with him than she had suspected. But it would have been no use, of course. She'd had enough experience of married men who were still in love with their wives.

And Marjorie, silly goose though she might be, was her best friend. Much the best thing to have acted as she had.

She finally saw them both the second week of January at the big ball at Londonderry House. They looked happier than she'd seen them for years, and Richard, she thought, was handsomer than she remembered. Later she learned that Captain Hammond had been ordered to return to India just before Christmas. After all Marjorie had said about him, Prudence felt sorry that she had not met him.

1910

13. Money and Other Troubles

"CHILDREN," RICHARD THOUGHT GLOOMILY, "WHY DOES ONE EVER HAVE them in the first place? Of course they were adorable when they were very young. Elizabeth, plump little button-eyed Elizabeth, was angelic, and young James . . ." He smiled to himself as he remembered James in short trousers, all skinny legs and wilfulness and the long-vanished charm of eight years old. Now he was surly, often drunk, and all set to make a thorough shambles of his life. As for Elizabeth! He sighed.

"Marjorie, dearest?" he began thoughtfully.

"Mm?" she replied from the depths of births, marriages and deaths in the morning *Times*. "Yes, Richard, what is it?"

"I was just wondering—where did we go wrong?"

"Wrong?" She put down the newspaper and stared at him as if he had just gone slightly mad. "I was not aware that we had."

"No, I mean with the children."

Lately the worry of his offspring had been eating into him. Marjorie, however, seemed immune, unchanging and unchangeable. How he envied her!

"Richard," she said, "now pull yourself together. The children are both of an age now and are their own responsibility, no one else's. They have their lives to lead and *we* have ours."

Marjorie was quite right. She generally was when it came to a crisis, and God knew there'd been enough of them this year. First there was all the trouble with Elizabeth—his beloved, intelligent Elizabeth. My, what a lesson she had been on how not to educate a daughter. Marjorie was right (again he found himself admitting it). Elizabeth should never have been allowed to go to Germany. All that education: the lectures in philosophy and art and politics—especially politics. He winced as he remembered how impossible Elizabeth had been that winter, just two years ago, when she returned to Eaton Place.

That in itself had been a sort of nightmare, for the trouble was that she had taken everything that *he* believed in—literature and art and pure philosophy—*and tried to live by them*. Hideous mistake! He'd done his best, of course, to tell the girl that life is not a matter of ideals. He tried explaining how even he had had to come to terms with people like Lady Southwold and Lord Salisbury. All that she had said was that she was sorry for him, and she had gone her own sweet way with her socialism and her suffragettes and her art-for-art's-sake.

It was embarrassing, of course, especially for Marjorie. He didn't mind too much when other members in the House raised their eyebrows when they heard that Bellamy's daughter, of all people, had been working in a soup kitchen in Whitechapel or, worse still, was mixed up with those confounded Fabians. But it really was too bad when she ducked her presentation to the King and Queen! Marjorie had had a dreadful time with her during her season as a débutante, the spring following her German period. She had been quite unmanageable and had scared away any potential husbands, so that her last-minute absence from the presentation had not come as a complete surprise. But it could have caused a scandal. His late Majesty had been very difficult on points of protocol. His son, young George V, was different, but Elizabeth had spent her season enhancing her reputation as a "difficult" young lady.

During the past two years neither he nor Marjorie had had much influence on her. "Wilful and obtuse" was what Marjorie had called her and she was right again. That was why it had been such a great relief when she announced her wish to marry the young poet Lawrence Kirbridge.

Again one could be wise after the event, but at the time it had seemed the lesser of two evils. Richard had had his doubts about the boy from the beginning. One can't be totally naïve after twenty years in politics, and from the start he'd sensed something effeminate and weak about the wretched fellow. Even his verses gave the game away. No, as a responsible and common-sense man of the world, he, Richard Bellamy, ought to have realised that Kirbridge never could be a husband for his daughter and he should have spoken out. Then at least something of this present ghastly muddle might have been avoided.

But since it had not, it was no use feeling sorry for himself now. He'd better try to do something to clear up the mess. That was presumably what fathers were for.

"Elizabeth," he said, knocking a second time on the nursery door. "Elizabeth, I'd like a word."

To his relief it was his daughter who opened the door, not Nanny Webster. (Despite all his objections that all-too-faithful and unpleasant old family nanny had been resurrected from the depths of Southwold and duly sent up to nurse the next generation of the Southwolds, Miss Elizabeth's new baby daughter, Lucy.)

Luckily, Elizabeth and Lucy were by themselves. Elizabeth was in her dressing gown. She looked pale and lethargic and there were deep shadows under her eyes. Despite her mother's exhortations to "pull yourself together," Elizabeth still felt terribly apart—from her parents, her baby, even life itself.

"Elizabeth, dearest." Richard kissed her and tried not to show the anxiety he felt. "And how is Lucy?"

Elizabeth shrugged. Richard peered into the cot. His granddaughter seemed minute (he had forgotten just how tiny babies were), with strands of thin black hair. She was asleep. Even to Richard she seemed beautiful, and he continued looking at her as he tried to decide how he could possibly broach the subject that had to be discussed.

"Elizabeth," he said at last, "something extremely painful and distasteful has occurred. I wish we could avoid it but we can't. It's about Lucy."

"Lucy?" his daughter echoed flatly. "What about Lucy?"

"Last night Sir Geoffrey Dillon called and told me some incredible story about Lawrence not being her father. It isn't true, is it, Elizabeth?"

The girl had no expression as he spoke, but she shrugged again and murmured, "Absolutely true."

"And the father? Dillon said . . ."

"Henry Partridge. Lawrence's publisher. Yes, I'm afraid that's true as well."

There was a silence broken only by the ticking of the nursery clock. Richard wiped a hand across his forehead and wearily shook his head.

"I just don't understand," he said slowly. "Partridge is older than I am. He's fat, he's vulgar, and for that matter he's my publisher as well. Elizabeth, how could you?"

His daughter stared at him, then smiled. What an extremely nice, extremely stupid man her father was! And how embarrassed the poor love got at anything which shocked that touchingly conventional old mind of his. Her mother had been so much more sensible when she had told her. "Not a word to anyone," was her advice, "and least of all to your father. It'll blow over. These things do."

But thanks to that dirty-minded, dry-as-dust old lawyer, it looked as though nothing could be allowed to be that simple.

As Richard tried to explain to Marjorie that evening, surprised at how calmly she reacted to the news, the whole question of the child's paternity was crucial to the divorce that Elizabeth was claiming from her husband.

"Provided that no hint of the truth slips out, and provided too that Kirbridge sticks to his part of the bargain to give Elizabeth grounds to sue him for adultery, we'll still be all right. But if these rumours get around—and you know how people talk—things could be difficult."

"Difficult, Richard? How?"

"Dillon was most worked up about it last night. If the divorce judge heard that Elizabeth had already been unfaithful to her husband it could torpedo the divorce—*and* lay Elizabeth open to a charge of perjury. It seems that the courts are now becoming very strict about these things."

"But how ridiculous! It must be obvious to anyone that the whole marriage was a terrible mistake, and that the sooner it's ended and forgotten the better it will be for everyone."

"That's not the point," said Richard. He was beginning to get exasperated now, and Marjorie knew how terribly upset he was by the whole unpleasant business.

"There," she said, smiling gently. "I'm sure that everything will be all right."

❧ ☙

But Richard wasn't. Dillon had always been able to upset him, and on top of that there were other worries too, most of which boiled down, as worries do, to money or the lack of it.

To start with, there was James. Luckily he'd finally disposed of the *fiancée* he had brought back with him from India, a nice enough but very dominating girl and quite unsuitable. But women, Richard felt, would always be a problem for that son of his—as for all the Southwolds. There'd been all that trouble with the pretty under-housemaid, Sarah. Luckily for everyone she had lost the baby, but it just went to show how irresponsible he was where women were concerned. Perhaps it was as well that he was now all set to leave the army. He'd have to buckle down, particularly with the job he'd been promised in the City. Jardines were an excellent firm. Richard knew several of the directors personally (otherwise James would never have been accepted), and there were splendid prospects if he would only realise his salad days were over and that there was nothing in the least "degrading"—as he had put it—in working for your living.

But before James could leave the army there were his debts to pay, over a thousand pounds of them. Marjorie had promised that they would be paid, but as Richard told her, there simply wasn't that much money in the bank. Normally they lived quite comfortably, but they had never saved, and there had been a run of unexpected expenses over the past twelve months. Elizabeth's marriage and the little house she had at Greenwich had been covered by some shares that Marjorie sold. Similarly, the Rolls they bought was paid for by a legacy from Marjorie's Great-Aunt Flo. But the trouble with a car like that—as he had argued at the time Thomas the chauffeur was bullying them to buy it—was that it gave everybody the idea that the Bellamys were far, far richer than they really were.

One extravagance like that led to another, and Richard, as he recognised himself, was hopelessness itself when it came to managing money. Since they had bought the Rolls most of the household bills had mysteriously risen—"Tradesmen charge you what they think you're worth," said Marjorie—but although she had promised to keep an eye on Mrs. Bridges and check every account herself, the bills had gone on rising.

Then the house had had to be repainted (according to the strict terms of the lease this had to happen every seven years) and the electric wiring completed, and while this was being done it was discovered that the timbers in the roof would have to be renewed. Hideous unheralded expense!

Marjorie would normally have paid. In the past she had always kept what she called her "emergency fund" on deposit in the bank. But eighteen months before, the emergency fund had gone to help to settle some of Hugo's debts and pay his fare to Canada. Hugo's life had changed abruptly. Poor intolerable Lilianne had died, and Hugo, taking Martin out of school to go along, had gone out to Alberta to forget his sorrows and find a fortune. When he got there Marjorie had helped him buy a ranch, and just recently he had re-married—to Marion Worsley, a widowed Englishwoman with a teen-age daughter named Georgina. All this cost money, although Hugo wrote that "an English title here is worth its weight in gold."

Whether it was or not, Hugo had made no sign of repaying the Bellamys what he owed, and Richard decided there was no help for it. For the first time in his life he'd have to borrow from the bank.

He dreaded borrowing and some hidden sense of shame kept him from telling Marjorie. "She's got enough to worry abou already," he told himself, chivalry excusing the deception. But in fact it turned out to be a gentlemanly, almost casual operation. Sir Lionel McMasters, a director of Coutts's Bank, was a member of his club, and as a well-known M.P. and former minister who had banked there for over twenty years, he was treated with extreme consideration. The manager, old Mr. Haldane, with his frock coat, pince-nez and gleaming pate, was the model of discretion, so much so that Richard felt as if he were doing the King's personal bankers an extraordinary favour by asking for a loan.

Of course there was no problem of allowing him an overdraft of "up to—shall we say—two thousand pounds, Mr. Bellamy, sir?"

The eyes behind the pince-nez twinkled happily.

Richard, a little overcome, replied that that should be enough. Mr. Haldane beamed as if thanking him for such extraordinary moderation.

"There is just one thing, Mr. Bellamy, though," he added almost as an afterthought.

"Yes, Mr. Haldane?"

"The slight question of security. Forgive my mentioning it, but almost anything will do—shares, valuables, deeds to your property. The bank, you understand, needs something."

Embarrassed now, Richard did his best to explain his somewhat strange position, with almost everything he possessed being in his wife's name. The manager's benevolence seemed unaffected.

"But there's your father-in-law, of course, sir. Lord Southwold. He is—forgive my saying it, but facts are facts—extremely old and—shall we say—infirm."

Richard nodded.

"And I take it that you and the Lady Marjorie are adequately covered in the will?"

Again he nodded.

"On that basis, then, I'm confident the bank can help you on a short-term understanding, Mr. Bellamy."

So James could leave the army, 165 could have its roof repaired, and Elizabeth's divorce could go ahead with Richard confident that he could meet Sir Geoffrey Dillon's thumping fees. But there was another, most unpleasant task for Richard to perform before all the legal niceties could be observed which would allow his daughter to forget the past and begin her life anew.

Dillon had suggested it to him in that cold, noncommittal voice he used when mentioning something of which as a lawyer he could not possibly approve but which all the same his client would ignore at his peril.

"There is this fellow—what's his name, Richard?—Partridge—what we might term your common-law son-in-law." Somewhere behind his spectacles Sir Geoffrey smiled mirthlessly at his own little joke.

"Yes," said Richard, "what about the swine?"

"Somebody should see him."

"Oh, for God's sake, Geoffrey, you're not suggesting . . ."

"It could be more embarrassing if you didn't—a great deal more. If this divorce is to go ahead, we must be absolutely certain about the man. In fact I'll go so far as to say that I'll not handle the case unless I have his solemn undertaking that on no account will he give any countenance to rumours of his relations with your daughter."

"You mean you want me to ask him to keep his mouth shut?"

Sir Geoffrey Dillon nodded.

It was not an easy situation for any man to have to face—especially Richard, who would do almost anything to avoid a scene. How does one face one's publisher, a man of some distinction and a member of one's club, and calmly broach the subject of whether or not he is your grandchild's father? For several days and sleepless nights Richard agonised over the problem. (Stupidly he didn't ask Marjorie, who would undoubtedly have settled Mr. Partridge in a trice.) Instead he let several lunchtimes pass, with boisterous, expansive Henry Partridge actually eating on the far side of the club dining room, before he plucked up courage, strolled across and spoke to the man in a very hollow voice.

"Partridge—there's something important to discuss. Could you spare me a moment when you've finished eating?"

Much as he despised the dreadful fellow, Richard had to give him full marks for the breezy way he replied, "Richard, my dear chap. Certainly! Give me five minutes and I'll join you in the smoking room."

Perhaps that was the answer to the troubling mystery of how his daughter could have allowed the man to touch her? His sheer effrontery and vulgar push. Some women always seemed to find a bounder irresistible, but why Elizabeth?

"Richard, how very very pleasant!" Partridge exclaimed as he came bustling in. He had a large cigar, a bulbous nose, and small and very piercing raisin eyes. "When are you going to let me have another novel? It's about time, my boy."

His familiarity was odious, but once again Richard found it impossible to snub him. "It's not my book I want to talk about. It's my daughter," he replied.

"Ah yes, Elizabeth. A lovely girl. I met her with her husband. Talented young man—a dreadful pity!"

"That's what I wanted to discuss with you. Let's not beat about the bush. I'm told that you and my daughter—that she—that you are the father of her daughter, Lucy."

Partridge eyed him shrewdly and then roared with laughter. "Richard, my dear good fellow! What an accusation! Wherever did you get such an extraordinary idea?"

"Elizabeth told me," said Richard flatly.

"Oh! Oh, I see."

He paused a moment, thoughtfully stubbed out his cigar, then looked at Richard with a faint smile. "Rather a piquant situation. My child, your grandchild—I wouldn't know what that makes us. But what can I do for you? If it's money you want, or if there's any legal nonsense, I admit nothing. Is that clear?"

Richard had to make an effort not to strike the man. Instead he answered grimly, "That's all I want—to make absolutely certain that under no circumstances whatever will you say anything about it. If pressed, even in a court of law, you admit nothing."

"You must be joking. As if I would!"

"Have I your word?" Richard nearly added "as a gentleman" but checked himself.

"That's one thing you can have—for nothing."

Whilst Richard was being plagued by family and money problems he also had his worries as a politician. That autumn was a time of turmoil. The new King's accession earlier that year had brought no easing of the war that raged between the parties over the power of the House of Lords. Richard was inevitably involved. Along with Balfour, Lansdowne, Austen Chamberlain and other leaders of his party he was inclined to favour a plan of compromise that came orginally from the Liberal Lloyd George, and that would have brought agreement between both parties on some limitation of the power of the Lords, along with a measure of Home Rule for Ireland and various social measures such as pensions, better housing for the poor, and improved education. It all seemed very reasonable, and as a reasonable M.P. Richard told Balfour that the plan had his support.

But it was not that easy. When Marjorie heard—as Marjorie inevitably did from one or another of her friends—that Richard was willing to support that rabble-rousing Welshman in his outrageous plan to emasculate the House of Lords (where the Southwolds had held sway since it began), she was indignant.

"I feel that the family has done enough for you across the years to be entitled to your loyal support. What has Lloyd George ever done for you, I'd like to know."

Luckily for Richard the plan was shelved, thanks to the opposition of precisely those old Tory die-hard interests which the Southwolds represented, but the disagreement between himself and Marjorie lay unresolved. Once again Richard felt the ancient tug of double loyalties that had pursued him all his married life. How much longer could he compromise between his conscience and the interests of the Southwolds? The question took on fresh significance that September when he heard that his father-in-law was ill again.

❧ ❧

"They've sent for Hugo," Marjorie said. "Apparently there's not much hope. I feel I should go at once."

She spoke in the clipped, matter-of-fact tones she always used when trying to disguise emotion. He would have volunteered to go with her but as they both knew it would be impossible. Thanks to the stalemate in the Commons over the powers of the Lords there were constant rumours of a fresh election in the air. As one of Balfour's shadow ministers he was needed in Westminster. And there were other matters that needed his attention: there were still complications over James's departure from the army, and now suddenly Elizabeth's divorce was going wrong. Dillon was being more than usually evasive about it all, confirming Richard's original intuition that it would have been best to allow some other lawyer to handle the affair.

"Dillon's such a terrible old woman," he had said to Marjorie. "I'm sure we should have someone who specialises in divorce."

But Marjorie had as usual overruled him and on the usual grounds that Geoffrey Dillon was the Southwolds' lawyer and had the family's interests at heart.

"Besides, just think how upset he'd be if he heard we'd gone to someone else."

But Richard was beginning to wish he had. The case was dragging on and now Elizabeth had heard that somebody called the King's Proctor was threatening to intervene in the proceedings.

"Most unlikely, I am glad to say," was Dillon's bland reply when Richard taxed him with the possibility.

"Luckily I know Sir Ronald Wakeford, the present King's Proctor, personally. We were at college together."

"But why should he want to hold up the divorce?"

"If he believed that there were any—shall we say—irregularities, it would be his duty."

"But that would be dreadful for Elizabeth. She could be stuck with that husband for the remainder of her life."

"Richard, you worry far too much. You tell me you've talked to Partridge, and as I say Sir Ronald is a very old friend. Elizabeth will be all right."

⁂

Like King Charles, Lord Southwold was "an unconscionably long time dying." Marjorie stayed with him throughout the rest of September, and it was not until October that she sent the telegram to Richard: "Come at once."

Richard went that afternoon and was at Salisbury before dark; dusk was falling as the trap carried him beneath the grey, stripped trees towards the sombre bulk of Southwold House. No lights were showing. A cold wind whistled from the Downs and the great house was like some old abandoned ship, obsolete, forgotten at her moorings, destined for the breaker's yard.

Inside, the sense of doom persisted. Old Widgery, half dead himself, pulled back the bolts and let him in. The house smelt damp and cold. The chandeliers had not been lit.

"Where's Lady Marjorie?" Richard asked.

"In with his lordship. I don't know what we would have done without her, Mr. Richard."

Richard knew Lord Southwold's room, one of the small back bedrooms that overlooked the garden and the Downs beyond, but Widgery directed him to one of the grander main apartments at the front of the house. It was here in ancient splendour and a certain dingy dignity that Lord Southwold was dying.

He had told Widgery to have King James's bed brought from the storeroom. Richard had never seen it before, but there it stood in all its sombre majesty, the white-and-crimson hangings and the ostrich plumes drooping mournfully at each corner. It was like a small, macabre theatre, a relic from the times when the nobility still had such things. Richard knew the stories of how earlier Southwolds had died in it—the great fifth Earl, the friend of Marlborough; Henry Southwold, who died bankrupt and insane; and his son Francis, the Prince Regent's friend, who breathed his last in it after his fatal duel with an unknown officer in the Marines. And now Lord Southwold, traditionalist to the last, was using the deathbed of his ancestors for his own demise.

Marjorie was with him. She rose as Richard entered. She looked pale and miserably thin.

"Richard, my dearest Richard," she half sobbed, and held him for a moment before taking him by the hand and leading him to the bedside.

Southwold was already looking like his death mask. There was no hint of ordinary flesh about those hollow cheeks and gothic features. Even in dying he appeared to be a work of art, yet curiously, with death so near at hand, his face looked younger and less troubled than Richard remembered.

"He's been asking for you," Marjorie whispered, and as Richard came up to the bed the eyelids fluttered and the old man looked at him.

"Ah, Richard," he said in a wheezing murmur of a voice, "you're almost one of us. Pity you're not. I'd have liked you for my son. There might have been some hope then, but with Hugo . . ."

A fit of coughing interrupted him, deep, racking coughs that shook the frail bones of his body. He shut his eyes and Richard felt Marjorie's hand tightening in his. But the coughing passed, and when Lord Southwold opened his eyes his voice was clearer than before.

"No point blaming Hugo. It's been my fault. I've been extravagant. I should have been ready to adapt. You'd have adapted, Richard, but it wasn't in my nature. I'm sorry for the way we've treated you, but you've succeeded, Richard. You've done very well. I'm rather proud of you."

Once again Marjorie squeezed his hand as the old man laughed, a faint and ghostly echo of a laugh.

"Just one last thing, dear boy. Once I am dead the priests can do what they like with me. But make sure that they stay away from me while I'm still alive. And don't let anyone believe I died a Christian."

He closed his eyes.

"We'll leave him," Marjorie said. "He'll sleep. The nurse will stay with him. She'll call us when we're needed."

The nurse didn't call them that night. Southwold seemed to be in a coma now, and Marjorie and Richard had to cope with Lady Southwold, who was maudlin drunk at dinner and by turns self-pitying and aggressive.

"It's the end of all of us," she moaned. "The end of everything." Then she shouted for Hugo. "Where is the boy? He should be here to help his mother."

For the tenth time that day Marjorie patiently explained that Hugo was on his way from Canada and would be there any moment now.

"But Hugo *should* be here, beside his mother. It's his duty."

All this over and over, fretfully and sadly, like a child.

Next morning Dr. Cowley told them that Lord Southwold had had a fresh attack at six o'clock and couldn't last much longer. He was unconscious. Only his natural resilience still kept him tenuously attached to life.

All they could do now was wait, so wait they did, Richard and Marjorie and, later in the day, her mother too. The doctor stayed with Lord Southwold and the others maintained their vigil in the room next door.

It was a bare, cold room with a high-raftered ceiling. Small windows near the roof let in the grey light of the autumn day outside. As Richard sat there waiting for the last remaining drops of life to drain from the shrunken body in the great plumed bed next door, he had the feeling that it wasn't just Lord Southwold who was dying. It was everything the Southwolds had believed in. For months now he'd been watching the power of the old nobility slowly eroded in the House of Commons, but here that power was already nearly dead. It was a strange sensation. He could feel disaster in the cold grey air, as if the house was slowly dying round him. It was like being at the last hours of some stricken once-proud animal of enormous age. For here in this house long generations of the Southwolds had been attempting to create a sort of immortality. Their money and their buildings and their power had all been used to keep alive this legendary creature which should have lived forever as fresh generations of the family renewed its strength. But there was only Hugo now.

"When's the boy coming?" Lady Southwold moaned once again. And once more Marjorie did her best to comfort her. She was pathetic in her age and helplessness, a burnt-out ruin of the old virago who had caused Richard so much trouble in the past. It was hard to feel anything but pity for her now. Anyone who saw her today would think that she was grieving for her husband. Perhaps she was.

During that morning more of the family arrived: first Elizabeth, pale and unsmiling and unwell. Richard was glad she'd come. Then came old Great-Aunt Kate, Lord Southwold's remaining sister. She dithered slightly and seemed none too clear why she was there. Finally James arrived. Richard had not believed he would and suddenly felt reassured and grateful for his children. At this moment when all else seemed in collapse and dissolution there were at least the children to provide some continuity. They would inherit nothing of the Southwold lands or wealth, but that was as well. He had suffered quite enough from Southwold in his time to be glad its influence was over. At least his children would be free to live their own lives and to find their own traditions.

Whilst Richard was brooding thus, Lord Southwold's door was opened and plump old Dr. Cowley, reverent and thoughtful as the priest the dying man refused to have, came tiptoeing out.

"He wants to see you all before he goes. He's quite lucid but he's very weak. It won't be long."

They filed in, Richard first, then Marjorie with her mother and Aunt Kate and finally Elizabeth and James. The room was shaded, with the long curtains pulled and a candle burning by the bed. It was colder here than in the room next door, and Richard smelled the sweet, dry smell of death.

Southwold was propped up on his pillows, to all intents and purposes already a corpse. It was absurd, ridiculous, this deathbed scene, yet Richard couldn't help admiring this dominating proud old man.

One hand was lying on the counterpane, looking like a saint's hand carved in ivory. Richard took it, held it a moment; it was already cold. Then it was Marjorie's turn: she kissed her father on his brow. Richard thought he saw him smile, but it was hard to tell in the gloom of the bedroom and beneath the great canopy.

The rest came closer. Elizabeth was sobbing slightly and James's eyes appeared unusually bright. And then the strangest thing of all occurred. Old Lady Southwold uttered a great howl, whether of despair or rage Richard never could decide, and then threw herself upon the body of the dying man. Was it because she realised that he was finally escaping her, or was it some relic of the passion she must once have felt for him?

She looked like one possessed—eyes staring, thin grey hair in all directions—and as she cried his name she clung to him. The force dragged his body up in bed, and Richard glimpsed the narrow rib cage through the nightshirt. For just a moment everyone was mesmerised—then, quite audibly, Lord Southwold uttered one short low moan. The doctor stepped forward and, gripping Lady Southwold firmly by the shoulders, eased her away as she sobbed. Then he was moving Southwold's body back onto the pillows.

"It's all right now, your ladyship," he said. "There's nothing more now to be done."

Then he closed Lord Southwold's eyes.

"His lordship's dead," he said, and at the words a last despairing shriek echoed from the widow.

Thus expired the eleventh Earl of Southwold in the house of his ancestors, full of years and honours, mourned by his widow and surrounded by those who nominally loved him. And with him died the house of Southwold. True there was Hugo, who, in character as ever, arrived half an hour later, bronzed, apologetic and somehow quite irrelevant, although as Richard had to keep telling himself, Hugo was now Lord Southwold.

There should have been some sort of feudal ceremony, a herald to announce, "Southwold is dead! Long live Southwold!" But there was nothing of the sort—only old Dr. Cowley, snuffling with the beginning of a cold, assuring Hugo that his father "hadn't been in any pain when he passed over." Richard wondered but said nothing. Nor did he speak when Mr. Prothero the vicar was allowed in to do his usual business with the dead.

One imagines death will settle things. It rarely does. Richard had thought Lord Southwold's passing would mark the end of the Southwold influence upon his life and on his family, but the reverse occurred. As the dead Earl's son-in-law, Richard now found himself caught up in the flurry of activity the death occasioned. There was the funeral at Southwold, a melancholy, rather touching ceremony with the small church crammed with workers and tenants from the estate come to pay their last respects to "the good old lord." The coffin was carried on a big old-fashioned farm cart drawn by men from the village all in their Sunday best. As the body was committed to its place in the big granite Southwold vault, there was scarcely a dry eye among them all.

Two weeks later there was the full-scale memorial service in Westminster Abbey. Once again Richard had to take his place as one of the chief mourners while the deceased Earl of Southwold was honoured by the nation. Richard had admired him, been maddened and exasperated by him, and at times almost loved him, but he had never thought of him as that aloof, impersonal creature "a great man." But here were the greatest in the land assembled to insist that that was what he had been. The Prime Minister and Lord Lansdowne represented the King. Lord Rosebery, like the dead man a politician and a racing man, was there for the Jockey Club. There were the members of the Cabinet, the opposition, the ambassadors and envoys and generals and M.P.s—respectability incarnate. But as he listened to the Bishop of London give the memorial address, Richard could make no meaningful connection between these studied words of praise and the strange, unpredictable, sad man he remembered. Nor could he make much sense of what the new Lord Southwold would do with his inheritance.

After the service all the family had lunch in Eaton Place. It was a surprisingly light-hearted meal. The pale London sun lit up the dining room, and Mrs. Bridges, on Marjorie's sensible instructions, had done her best to duplicate the sort of luncheon that the late Lord Southwold himself would have approved of—a lobster *mousse,* an excellent *ragout* of veal, *profiteroles* and brandy sauce and cream. Hudson had managed to unearth some of the Château Jubloteau champagne the old man had loved, and as they drank it even the dullest members of the family seemed to imbibe a little of his sparkle. Hugo appeared particularly optimistic. He had put on weight in Canada and it suited him. Suddenly he sounded like a credible successor to his father, talking of taking up residence at Southwold as soon as possible and telling Richard that he now intended to "do my bit in the Lords against the Liberals."

Old Lady Southwold, a little over-rouged but otherwise unusually restrained, said, "Hear, hear, Hugo darling!"

But the real point of interest was Marion, Hugo's new wife. She was a powerful brunette, extremely self-assured and ladylike, and very much aware of her position as the new Lady Southwold. There was no sign of her daughter, young Georgina Worsley; she had been left in Canada along with Martin, now Lord Ashby. Presumably they would be sent for, since Hugo and Marion obviously meant to settle into Southwold at once.

Hugo was telling Richard about the situation. "Of course there are the death duties to be met, and Marion is hoping to modernise the dear old house a bit, aren't you, darling?"

Marion smiled and nodded gracefully. Marjorie was suddenly annoyed and wondered how her mother would react to this. Rather to her surprise, all that the new Dowager Lady Southwold did was nod as well.

"Everything depends on good old Geoffrey Dillon," Hugo continued. "Wise old owl. Man in a million. He's sorting out the details of the estate and everything should be ready for the will to be read by Christmas. But he's hoping to be able to keep the damage down to a minimum, and when we win this next election everything should be all right."

"If we win it," Richard said.

"Oh, my dear old chap, surely there can be no shadow of a doubt."

Hugo's political optimism was misplaced. That November's general election, for all the passion it engendered, settled nothing—except that the minority Liberal government stayed on tenuously in power with the conditional support of eighty-four M.P.s from the Labour Party. For the new Lord Southwold this meant no alleviation of the threat to his estate, and for Richard it was a further period in the obscurity of opposition. True, he was still among the top dozen in his party, but as he tried explaining gloomily to Marjorie, the period of his political prime would pass.

"I should have followed young Winston and crossed over to the Liberals," he said bitterly. "Then I'd not have spent the best years of my life kicking my heels in the opposition."

"But what about your principles?" said Marjorie. "I don't think I could ever have forgiven you if you had followed that young traitor."

Richard had other worries besides this nagging feeling that he was missing the one chance of his life to make his mark in history. (In fact, unknown to Marjorie, Richard had already received a most tempting secret offer from Asquith if he would join them. He was in such broad agreement with the Liberals that only one thing really held him back—his fear of what Marjorie would say.)

First came a discreet inquiry from Coutts's Bank, a note from Mr. Haldane wondering how his affairs were now progressing and when he would be in a position to discharge his overdraft. Happily, he was able to reply that the late Lord Southwold's will would soon be settled, but the next problem that arose could not be brushed aside so easily. This was a note from Geoffrey Dillon deeply regretting to inform him that the King's Proctor *had* seen fit to intervene in Elizabeth's divorce. He had subpoenaed Henry Partridge, who had made a statement.

"So much," thought Richard as he read the beastly letter, "for the appalling publisher's firm promise to say nothing. And so much, too, for Dillion's friendship with the King's Proctor in their youth."

That night at dinner Richard did his best to cushion the unpleasant news, but Marjorie was predictably incensed.

"What earthly reason can the law have in taking all this trouble to maintain a mere mockery of a marriage?" she exclaimed indignantly when Richard told her.

"It's nothing to do with me, dear," he said. "That's the law."

"Then why have you never tried to do anything to change it? As a politician you must have been aware that these things happen."

Like many forceful ladies, Marjorie suddenly became a reformer when the system hurt her personally, but to Richard's surprise his daughter took the news calmly. Since the funeral she had been looking prettier and slimmer. Now she sat playing with her wine glass and barely acknowledging her mother's outburst on her behalf.

"You don't seem terribly concerned," said Richard. Elizabeth shrugged impatiently, as Richard remembered her doing as a schoolgirl when something bored her.

"I don't see that it matters very much. I can't imagine Lawrence marrying again, and I certainly don't intend to."

"What will you do then," James inquired, "remain a sort of married spinster all your days?"

"Good heavens, no," Elizabeth replied. "I'll just have lovers."

Richard smiled, but Marjorie and James were rather shocked.

"To my son and heir, Hugo Francis Villeroy Talbot-Cary, I additionally bequeath the goods, chattels, appurtenances, usufructs and rights as by time and custom heretofore established on the aforesaid property of Southwold House . . ."

Sir Geoffrey Dillon's voice droned on like a priest's at the litany.

Presumably he understood what these lawyers' phrases meant, since he had put them into Lord Southwold's will in the first place. But it was inconceivable that anybody else in that sunless room would understand them—least of all Hugo Francis Villeroy Talbot-Cary, twelfth Earl of Southwold, who was already nodding off to sleep in the big armchair in Dillon's anteroom. His spouse, however, seemed very much awake. Bright-eyed and bird-like, she was following the lawyer's every word and from time to time made notes in a small gold pad with a small gold propelling pencil.

It was an informal gathering for such an interesting event. Most of the family were there, two clerks from Dillon's office, and that was that. The will was very long: with all its amendments and codicils it took the lawyer over half an hour to mumble through it, and it was not until towards the end that Richard began listening more attentively. The various legacies were listed: "To my daughter, Marjorie Elizabeth Helena Talbot-Cary, now Bellamy, the capital sum of ten thousand pounds. Also the interest on . . ." Here Dillon's testamentary voice listed an unlikely batch of shares and bits of family property bequeathed to Marjorie in trust for her children. Both James and Elizabeth also received five thousand pounds immediately. Richard's ears perked up; he expected to hear his own name any moment now. But after continuing the roll call of recipients of the dead Earl's munificence—"to my butler, Henry Widgery, five hundred pounds and my silver coasters, to my game-keeper, Enoch Charnock, three hundred pounds and my black-thorn walking stick"—Sir Geoffrey's voice ground to an abrupt and dusty halt.

Richard was indignant. Nobody else appeared to notice the omission of his name, but there was clearly some mistake. There had been the codicil Lord Southwold added to his will eight years earlier, leaving the lease of 165 to him. Why had it not been mentioned?

"Embarrassing," said Dillon in a voice that made it plain that the embarrassment lay with Richard, not with him.

"But I see nothing in the least embarrassing," said Richard, struggling, as he often did with Dillon, to keep his temper. "Lord Southwold told me he was leaving the lease of 165 to me. You were present and you made the codicil. So I repeat my question. Why was the codicil omitted from the will?"

Sir Geoffrey sucked his teeth before replying, a habit that infuriated Richard further still.

"We must distinguish here between the intention and the effect. Lord Southwold certainly did tell you he intended leaving you the house. I confirm that unreservedly. But I persuaded him that it was only prudent to make this a discretionary bequest."

"A what?" said Richard.

"A discretionary bequest; that is to say that the bequest depends upon the approval of the executor."

"But, Geoffrey, *you* are the executor."

Dillon nodded, smiling his faint Samurai smile. "And unfortunately I find myself unable to approve the bequest. Not on any personal grounds, of course, but simply because it isn't possible."

"And why not, Geoffrey?" Richard asked grimly.

"Simply because there's not the money. My first loyalty, my only loyalty, is to the Southwold family and to the earls of Southwold. The estate, as you must know, is heavily in debt. On top of that there are the huge death duties to be met."

"And on top of that," said Richard, "there are Hugo's long-standing debts to be paid. That's what you're saying, isn't it?"

Once again Sir Geoffrey Dillon nodded and smiled. "The rights and wrongs of this are immaterial," he said. "All that concerns me is to find sufficient money to insure that the present earl shall live as his ancestors did before him. Assets must be sold and sacrifices made. I am afraid that these include the valuable lease to 165 Eaton Place."

"But this is gross dishonesty. You know as well as I do that Lord Southwold left that house to me!"

"Dishonesty? That's a strong word to use against a lawyer, Richard. I suggest that you repeat it in a court of law."

But how could he? Dillon knew as well as anyone that he could not. Richard possessed no money for a long legal battle, and even if he had, how could he ever fight a case like that? The gutter press would love it—and the lawyers. Just think of the dirt that would come up in court, the skeletons from all those cupboards! Think of the questions learned counsel would undoubtedly put: "And is it true, Mr. Bellamy, that throughout the twenty-five years of your marriage you have been totally supported from the bounty of the Southwolds? Don't you consider that enough, Mr. Bellamy?" No, it was obviously impossible.

But the fact was that without the house the Bellamys were facing something close to disaster. Marjorie still had her income; that was mercifully tied up in equities and nobody could touch them. But there was Richard's overdraft to be repaid and there was not the faintest possibility of discovering sufficient money to buy 165 from the estate. He had been tricked and cheated—and to make it worse there was not a thing that he could do about it. He also had to break the news to Marjorie.

Remorse, that horrible affliction of the middle-aged, was once again pursuing Richard Bellamy. Had he been tougher, firmer, more far-sighted, he would never have let himself be caught in this degrading situation. He could see his mistakes all too clearly now. Throughout his married life he had allowed the Southwold influence to overshadow him. He had been weak and idle and complacent. Instead of standing on his own two feet he had allowed the Southwolds to support him, and now that the show-down had arrived he was seeing the results—failure as a politician, failure as a father, and now failure as a husband too. For what sort of husband was he to allow a thing like this to happen—and then to be too frightened to break the news to Marjorie?

What a wrench they'd find it, leaving Eaton Place! Once more he realised how much he loved the house. It had become as much a part of him as the shell is to a snail. He and Marjorie could change, of course—they'd have to—but how much he'd miss the comfort and dignity of the place. A quarter of a century they'd lived there now, and the house held his memories, his books, his few possessions. It was the background to all the happiness he could remember. It was the centre of his universe.

Ah well. He climbed the stairs in search of Marjorie. If he had to face reality, the sooner now the better, but she was nowhere to be seen. He rang the bell in the drawing room and Hudson answered. No, Lady Marjorie was taking tea with Lady Prudence Fairfax, but Miss Elizabeth was in her room. Did he wish to see her? Richard nodded.

Once again Richard was impressed by the way his daughter's looks had recently improved. Mercifully she had finally recovered from the birth of Lucy, and he was delighted at her calmness over the trouble with the absurd divorce. But the best thing of all about her was her honesty. Maddening she might be—what young lady wasn't?—but he could always talk to her and always know that she would listen (much more than Marjorie, who was more a talker than a listener). They were also so alike that she understood his moods and often seemed to know what he was thinking of before he spoke. She did so now.

"What is it, Father? Money?"

Elizabeth was the last person he had intended talking to about his troubles, but almost automatically he found himself nodding, and before long he was telling her the whole depressing story. She was outraged, especially at Dillon, whom she hated. But she was also very practical.

"Father," she said, "will you let me help you?"

"Of course, my dear, but how?"

"I don't know if I can, but I have a friend who's very rich and always saying that he wants to help me. I think I'll try him."

"What friend?" Richard asked suspiciously.

"A man called Karekin. He's a financier and he's very fond of me."

"You mean that terrible Armenian? Elizabeth, I positively forbid you to do anything of the sort!"

"Don't be silly, Father. He amuses me, and don't forget that according to the law I'm a most unrespectable married woman. It might work and it will do no harm. But in the meantime take my advice Say nothing at all to mother."

Elizabeth's relationship with Karekin was far from innocent, but they were not in love, and Elizabeth had told the truth when she said that he amused her. Indeed, they amused each other in a sophisticated sort of way. After her previous disasters with men, Elizabeth had decided she would never fall in love again. This intrigued Karekin, who had never met a pretty and intelligent young English girl of such good family who was willing, even eager, to sleep with him but who wanted absolutely nothing else—no love, nor fidelity, nor even marriage. This was why he always tried to tempt her with offers of extravagent presents, which she always refused. And this was why he cheerfully agreed when she finally did ask him one big favour—to buy 165 and present it to her parents. For Karekin, unlike wealthy

Anglo-Saxons, treated wealth as the unreal substance it is. If it enabled him to make his strange young mistress happy, that was simply as it should be.

Richard, of course, felt very different. At first he totally refused to accept what he nearly called Elizabeth's "wages of sin." That he didn't call them that was due to a certain vein of—call it common sense or call it opportunism. Either way, it finally permitted him to calm his conscience and somewhat grudgingly accept the offer—although he never liked to dwell on the way 165 had finally been saved for him and for the family, and his sense of delicacy made him insist that Marjorie should not be told a word of what had happened. Rather than that, he asked that the lease simply be continued as it had been before Lord Southwold died—in Marjorie's name. That way the whole distressing business could be quietly forgotten.

1912

14. *Death by Drowning*

"My God, how terrible! How simply terrible!" Richard exclaimed. "And poor dear Cressida. What an appalling thing!"

Marjorie peered up at Richard from the toast and marmalade. She was looking rather drawn these days.

"Cressida who?" she asked a little sharply. "And what's so terrible?"

Richard slowly lowered the barrier of that morning's *Times* and, peering with some solemnity over the lenses of his spectacles, spoke in his bringer-of-bad-tidings voice.

"Boy Hartington's been killed."

"How ghastly, Richard. How?"

"In one of those infernal airplanes at Farnborough. Only this time last week I was talking to him in the House. He was so full of energy and life and now this happens! You really must inquire if there is anything we can do for Cressida."

"Of course," said Marjorie. "I'll write to her at once. Perhaps she'd like to come and stay."

For Richard there was something ominous about Boy Hartington's death. Tall, serious, good-looking, he had always seemed to tread a golden pathway through the world of politics and high society. Richard had rather envied the charmed life he seemed to lead. Heir to the wealthy Viscount Lindfield, he had been something of a poet and a connoisseur of art; he was also a traveller, a wit, a discreet womaniser and an accomplished sportsman. Even his nickname hinted at the atmosphere of effortless perpetual youth surrounding him. If anybody summed up the easy, pleasure-loving world that still existed in that second bright decade of the changing century, it was the Honourable Richard Hartington. And now, with no rhyme or reason, he had been destroyed by one of these so-called machines of the future. If this was what the future would be like, what hope was there for anyone?

"What d'you think Cressida will do?" he asked Marjorie.

"I'm sure she will take it very well. She's young and pretty and she's fairly scatterbrained. I can't imagine that she'll pine for long. Besides, there are no children. She'll find somebody."

Richard nodded—and thought to himself how heartless women were in the face of tragedy.

In point of fact, with Marjorie the exact opposite was true. Just lately there had been too much tragedy and suffering in her life: if she appeared callous in her reaction to poor Hartington it was the sort of self-defence that outwardly impassive and controlled aristocrats like Marjorie frequently employ to hide their feelings. Nothing had gone right for her since her father died.

First there had been the news of Charles Hammond's death. That had required all her self-control to keep from breaking down. The affair, of course, had ended several years before, but they had kept in touch and he had remained a sort of secret, unattainable dream. Nothing had thrilled her more than when she heard that he had won his V.C. fighting on the Khyber Pass, and when the news came through that Major Hammond, V.C., had been killed in an ambush on the North-West Frontier, something had died within her. She told nobody, not even Prudence, but she accepted that this spelled the end of love and passion in her life. She "loved" Richard still, of course. She was fond of him and used to him and she depended on him. All these things she admitted for she was always honest where emotions were concerned. But this was not the sort of love that she had felt for Charles, and without that she often wondered if her life was really worth living.

One of the consolations that had kept her going had been her family, and in particular her granddaughter, little Lucy Kirbridge. But once again nothing had gone quite right within the family. James, since he left the army, had become impossible. He was moody and unsettled, and there had been little real affection between them for some time. It seemed that he blamed everyone for the fact that he was having to "slave" in a City office for a living when with a little luck he might have owned his beloved Southwold. What James needed, she and Richard both agreed, was a good woman he could marry, but he seemed caught in an insoluble marital dilemma: those who were suitable weren't pretty, and those who were pretty just weren't suitable. From the way things were going James seemed all set to be a bachelor for life.

Why had both the children got in such dreadful muddles over sex? She often asked herself that but it was not a question she could answer. Nor could she discuss it with Richard, who got far too worked up over it all. But she suspected in her heart of hearts that it had something obscurely to do with the way she had married outside her class. Her mother had always told her this would happen. She had pooh-poohed the idea at the time, but perhaps this really had caused the children those frustrations and uncertainties that had made their lives so difficult. When she was depressed she told herself that her life had been a terrible mistake from the moment she married.

The truth was that her passionate and dominating nature needed *something* to keep it occupied, and that now she had less and less to do, especially since Elizabeth and Lucy had left for America. Marjorie could sympathise with her daughter and with the reasons that had made her go, but she missed her dreadfully. During the months that followed the breakup of the marriage Elizabeth had confided in her a lot, and for the first time in years Marjorie had felt close to her. Unlike Richard, she could understand Elizabeth's affair with Karekin. As Elizabeth put it, she had had enough of "love" with Kirbridge. He had loved her—but that was all he ever did. One could have too much of undiluted love. It had left her longing for a man who simply wanted her without the muddle and responsibility of love, and in Karekin she had found him. But when the affair ended —as it was bound to—she had felt increasingly oppressed in England. There were too many memories, and although she attempted to brazen out the fiasco of the divorce, she was miserable about the wretched business. As she told her mother, she felt neither one thing nor the other. Since the King's Proctor blocked her divorce, she was a married woman who hadn't got a marriage, and at twenty-four she was not prepared to spend the remainder of her life "either in chastity or in immorality."

It was to avoid this that she finally decided she would have to go off to America for a divorce at Reno. In Reno there was no King's Proctor to insist on keeping young women miserably married to husbands who would not make love to them. But afterwards what Marjorie feared had happened. Elizabeth had fallen for the very New York lawyer who had won her the divorce and had promptly married him. This meant that henceforth she must live in exile, for if she entered England she would be a bigamist.

This was no hardship for Elizabeth. She had Lucy with her, and a husband who adored her, and an apartment overlooking Central Park. But Marjorie was at an age when she needed grandchildren around her, and she became dependent on her weekly letter from New York.

Marjorie had had other setbacks too, most of them associated with the decline of the Southwolds. For a few months after her father died it had looked as if the new Lord Southwold, helped by the unscrupulous loyalty of Geoffrey Dillon, would somehow manage to survive in all the ancestral splendours of his inheritance. Marion *had* started to refurbish Southwold House. Martin and Georgina had been brought over and put into boarding schools. The Grosvenor Square establishment was sold; so were Lord Southwold's horses and his estates in Scotland. Most of the library and the Southwold Rubens went to America.

If it had been only a question of meeting Hugo's debts, all would have been well. Dillon, however much one loathed the man, was a most skilled financial juggler. But not even his sleight of hand could cope with the double disaster of the death duties followed by old Lady Southwold's death.

Marjorie had watched her mother's sad decline knowing quite well that there was nothing she could do about it. The drinking had got worse and her husband's death had finished her. For several months she had been kept, barely human now, in an institution outside Brentford; and then, quite suddenly, she had died. Only then was it discovered how much of the Southwold property was in her name. It was left to Hugo, but in effect it meant that the estate was loaded with two sets of death duties. Not even Dillon's shifty genius could cope with that, and at this very moment Southwold was up for sale. Hugo appeared quite unaffected and talked blithely of "cutting my losses and cashing in on progress." Marjorie suspected this would mean that when he had sold up everything he and Marion would be off again for Canada or the U.S.A.

Materially, thank God, this would not affect her, for her money and the lease of 165 were established as her own, but how she hated this disruption of her past! Emotionally she had depended on the firm rock of Southwold for so much—for her strong sense of continuity, for the belief that her own privileged and private world would never change. Now suddenly the rock had vanished.

All this had taken physical toll of her. If one compared her with the portrait Guthrie Scone had painted of her barely eight years earlier, one would see depressing signs of change. She was still beautiful: the bone formation of her face would guarantee her beauty to the day she died. But something had gone—the boldness of her gaze, the strength and resolution of her chin, the sense of life.

Richard, on the other hand, had been reacting differently to change. Had Scone painted him (it is a thousand pities he did not) one would have noticed something very different over the past eight years. True, he had aged, but now in his middle fifties he looked tougher, more assured than in the past. He was also better-looking. Age, by maturing him, had subtly improved him.

All this reflected, as looks do, the way life had treated him. What had been so disastrous for Marjorie had on the whole been good for him. Lord Southwold's death combined with the shock of Hugo's perfidy had finally released him from his bondage to the family. Once he had learned the bitter lesson that the Southwolds could no longer be relied on, he began standing on his own feet at last. Helped by his old friend Dangerfield (now a distinguished figure in the City), he had accepted two directorships, one in Dangerfield's own merchant bank and the other with a big firm of shipbuilders in which his one-time connections with the Admiralty stood him in good stead. This meant that for the first time since his marriage he was becoming independent. His writing too was flourishing. He had long ago got over the failure of his novel and had accepted the suggestion of the Southwold family to write Lord Southwold's life, a task that had absorbed him for the last twelve months and was now all but finished.

Finally, Richard's curiously erratic political career had recently improved and he had come to terms with the frustrations of being out of office. The heady period when he had felt himself so close to real power was over, and he was more philosophical about the way his hopes had vanished, for a while at least. It was a gamble, he accepted that, and if the turn of fortune brought him back to power he would enjoy it. If the Conservatives did win the next election Balfour would have to give him something, but that was not the point. For Richard recognised that there were more important things at stake than these games of political musical chairs. War was coming: it was in the air and it was here that he could make his contribution. Much of his time and energy now went to the inter-party committee on defence. It made enormous inroads on his time, which also meant that he had less to spend with Marjorie or in missing Lucy and Elizabeth, but it also meant that he had now become one of the leading defence experts in the House. It was in this capacity that he had worked so closely with Boy Hartington until his death. This made him particularly concerned about his widow.

Marjorie was right about that lady's powers of recovery. At the funeral she had appeared pathetic—frail, grieving, with her small white face tragic beneath a small black hat. Richard made a short and much appreciated address (on the theme of "those whom the Gods love . . ."), and when Boy's extremely lengthy coffin was finally consigned to the flinty Sussex earth, Richard's was not the only heart that was touched by slender Cressida's bravery and grief. How could any woman recover from such a shattering disaster?

But she had. Perhaps, as Richard gallantly maintained to Marjorie, it was a further instance of the dear girl's courage.

"Most women," he said, "would have let themselves go entirely," but not Cressida. Mourning became her—and her small, trim figure. When she arrived a few weeks later to spend a weekend with the Bellamys at 165, her grief was as plain to see as ever. Any reference to Boy would bring a bravely stifled tear to those blue eyes. As Richard said again, "Boy would be proud to see the way she's bearing up." Marjorie said nothing.

A few days later Richard suggested they invite her up to Scotland, where the Bellamys were to spend a holiday outside Perth. As he explained to Marjorie, he would be tied to London with the defence committee for part of the time, and Cressida would be company for her.

Marjorie had a favourite motto about lame ducks: "If you see one, run over it." But in this case she considered the thought unworthy; and she wondered too if perhaps she wasn't being slightly jealous of a younger woman. So—somewhat gracelessly, Richard felt—she agreed to write inviting her, and Cressida accepted with alacrity.

Marjorie and Richard would have agreed that their Scottish holiday that year was not the most successful they had had. Where they would have differed was on the cause. For Richard the real trouble was that neither of the children nor the precious baby Lucy had been there, and that Marjorie, for some inexplicable reason, had been difficult, so difficult that one might have thought she was going through the "change" a second time. (He shuddered at the thought.)

For Marjorie there was no such mystery. The cause of the fiasco was quite simple—Cressida. Of course one had to make allowances, but when one had done all that, and more, the plain fact was: Cressida was hell! What other woman, as she asked Prudence when the holiday was over, would have put up with that coy, shameless, sanctimonious little hussy for so long? The way she had thrown herself at Richard! The way she even looked at him! And he, poor silly man, refused to understand what she was up to. (Or so, at any rate, he said.)

She had monopolised him totally—and flattered him and played up to him, as pretty women always could with Richard. (That new secretary, Hazel, did the same, but not, thank God, so blatantly!) Rather than fight or make a scene, which would have been too shaming, Marjorie had simply allowed them to get on with it. And that, as she explained to Prudence, was why she had pleaded a sprained ankle and allowed the two of them to go off together to the Braemar Games. And that, in turn, was how that unfortunate photograph of Richard, standing arm in arm with the widow of the Honourable Richard Hartington, M.P., had found its way into the pages of the *Daily Mail.*

Marjorie's fears were quite absurd, but Richard, it must be admitted, was more than a little disingenuous about his feelings for the Widow Hartington. Had anyone accused him of wanting an affair with that desirable young woman he would have been quite horrified. When he had calmed down he would have said that he adored his wife, that he would willingly lay down his life for her, and that he had never thought of another woman since he married her.

All this was true, but what was happening was subtler than that. During those weeks in Scotland he had been, quite unconsciously, enjoying what amounted to a flirtation with Cressida. Since Marjorie was there, and since his motives were so very worthy, he had felt quite justified in everything he'd done. There had not been the faintest impropriety—and yet he'd gone beyond the joint of prudence. A man with fewer principles, or with more experience of women, would have been more careful. But Richard was so conscious of his good intentions that he inevitably became involved—and inevitably enjoyed it.

Gossip took over then, as gossip does. After the picture in the *Mail* it might have rapidly subsided. It was thanks to Prudence that it didn't. Partly from sympathy with Marjorie, partly from jealousy, she was incensed at Richard Bellamy and never paused to offer him the benefit of the doubt. From her the news soon spread in ripples over the limpid surface of Belgravia. It was disgraceful, quite disgraceful! Richard Bellamy, *the* Richard Bellamy, was having a walk-out with Cressida Hartington, and barely three months after her poor husband died.

Richard, of course, was quite oblivious of what was being said, and even when Prudence cut him dead in Belgrave Square he failed to realise the truth. But if his wife's friends were shocked, his own male acquaintances were frankly envious. For some time now he'd been regarded in the House as rather a bore, "decent but deadly," as Lloyd George somewhat tartly called him after a late night sitting on the Pensions Bill. But it is quite extraordinary how the merest hint of sexual indiscretion can liven up a politician's reputation. (It is also quite surprising what a field for gossip is provided by the Mother of Parliaments.) Suddenly Richard found himself an object of attention. Members who had previously ignored him now came in especially to listen when he spoke. There was high interest in the smoking room when he entered. Reporters in the gallery took out their notebooks whenever he appeared.

Richard was still supremely unaware of what was going on, but he was quietly flattered by this unaccustomed air of deference around him. Marjorie too became a person of fresh interest. "Wronged" wives possess a morbid fascination in the eyes of other wives, and during this period Marjorie received more invitations, visits, confidential sessions with old friends and mere acquaintances than she had had for years. None of her friends had shown such interest since her affair with Captain Hammond.

And, as usual, the one group that was always several steps ahead of public gossip was that permanent and unacknowledged audience who saw almost everything—the servants. Within a week of Mrs. Hartington's *début* inside 165, that embattled student of society and morals Mrs. Bridges was already muttering dire warnings on the subject.

"Trouble with that one, Mr. 'Udson, mark my words," she said, and her suspicions seemed abundantly confirmed when Mrs. Hartington left half her *veau hongrois* and refused Mrs. Bridges' specialty, the rainbow pudding. Hudson, as usual with a pretty face, was chivalrously inclined to give the lady the benefit of the doubt.

"I'm sure nothing untoward can possibly occur, Mrs. Bridges," he replied. "It's not as if Captain James were actually in need of female company now that Miss Hazel's here."

"It's not Mr. James I'm worried for," said Mrs. Bridges darkly. "Its Mr. *Richard* Bellamy."

In the light of all that happened later it is ironic that in fact this whole inflated piece of nonsense was already dying down. Marjorie had sensibly decided—after several strategic planning sessions with a sympathetic Prudence—to do nothing and say nothing "and let the squalid little business die its own death as it's bound to, dear." For, as Prudence counselled, "They've not a thing in common. She's just a pretty bit of fluff, and he, whatever else you might say about him, really cares about you and the family, to say nothing of his precious political reputation."

Richard was seeing less of Cressida, too. He still felt a certain sense of duty to the lady. He would give her lunch, listen to her problems, give her avuncular advice, and frequently invite her back to 165. When she came there to dinner Marjorie would take pains to be scrupulously polite, and Mrs. Bridges would tell Hudson what she thought of Mr. Bellamy bringing his mistress to the house in this shameless manner.

But by now Richard was finding pretty Cressida distinctly boring, and with so much happening that autumn he had little time for her. His book on Lord Southwold, much as he had enjoyed writing it, was difficult to finish and considerably overdue. (Hazel was now engaged full time completing the research and typing the manuscript.) In November there were two full-scale debates on the naval programme and defence, in both of which Richard found that he was leading for the opposition. Then, that Christmas, much of his time and feelings became taken up with Southwold. Hugo had managed to sell the place at last, to an American biscuit manufacturer with a pretentious English wife, and Hugo and Marjorie had agreed that as many of the family as possible should gather there for one last Christmas. Richard at first refused to go. His feud with Hugo had been rumbling on since old Lord Southwold died. But Marjorie, as usual in her family, played the peacemaker and Richard, as usual, finally agreed. But it was a melancholy occasion, despite Hugo's somewhat frantic efforts to enliven things with lavish presents (he could finally afford them) and splendid food. Richard, as he wrote to Elizabeth a few days later, had never eaten so well or drunk so much at Southwold, even when her grandfather was in his prime.

But what was most depressing—certainly for Richard—was the feeling that the new Lord Southwold didn't care about the loss of Southwold, and that his spindly heir, young Martin Talbot-Cary, cared even less. Marjorie seemed slightly numbed by what was going on As she told Richard later, she could not believe that the great house would soon be lost forever. James was affected too. On Christmas Eve he got very drunk and nearly caused a scene by telling his uncle what he thought of him for letting Southwold go. It was left to Richard to step in and stop a brawl. And it was left to Richard, too, to mourn the sale of the house.

How he had loathed the Southwolds in his time! How he had secretly despised them for their arrogance and privilege and wealth! But now that their power was over, and the great house gone, he could feel nothing but a sense of loss.

It was a bitter twist of fate that at this point, when Marjorie and Richard were being drawn together by the loss of Southwold, there should have been a fresh misunderstanding over Cressida. It was also ironic, in its way, that the damage should have been done by Prudence, but it is a fact of life that the suspicion of male unfaithfulness can bring out the harpy in the nicest women.

It was the purest chance that Richard should have met Cressida one January afternoon in Bond Street and shared a cab with her back to her house in Wilton Crescent. It was also chance that Cressida asked him in to see some letters she had promised him from her former father-in-law to old Lord Southwold. And it was chance that Prudence, of all people, was walking past just as they arrived and felt impelled to break the news to Marjorie as soon as possible.

The two women had a long and serious discussion about what was to be done. Prudence, with memories of Major Fairfax, was all in favour now of "having it out with Richard, once and for all." Marjorie, to her credit, was inclined to give her husband the benefit of any doubt that remained. "Besides," she said, "I think I'd like to keep my dignity," which Prudence finally agreed was wise. But then she added, "You really must begin to think about yourself a bit, my dear. With all this worry I can see you heading for a real collapse. Why don't you take a little holiday? It might bring Richard to his senses if he had to do without you for a while."

Fate seems to work so often through coincidence that it is hard not to detect a certain pattern in the history of families. This was certainly the case now with the Bellamys. On the very day that Prudence called, and with her words about a holiday still in Marjorie's ears, two other events occurred that settled everything. The first was the arrival of a letter from Elizabeth. She was missing both her parents, Lucy was missing her grandmama especially, and Elizabeth's husband was suggesting that it was high time both her parents came over to New York. There was plenty of room in the apartment, and it would be so wonderful to be together here in New York in the spring. "Promise that you'll come!" she ended.

The second fateful happening was that Hugo called—a very spry and very optimistic Hugo, now that the sale of Southwold had restored his credit and made him, temporarily at least, quite rich. He and Marion were planning to return to Canada with Martin.

"Nothing to stay here for now," he said.

"When do you plan to go?" Marjorie asked thoughtfully.

"Early in April. I've just been round to book our passage on the new White Star liner, the *Titanic*. By all accounts she sounds a lovely ship. Her maiden voyage should be something to remember."

For Richard the new year brought fresh activity—late night sittings in the House, with Asquith and Lloyd George and Churchill thumping the despatch box, hours of committee work on the new naval programme, and then, on top of all of this, the final revisions on his book. He was both excited and exhausted. This made him slightly baffled and upset when Marjorie suddenly announced that she wanted to sail to New York. He understood that she was missing Elizabeth; so was he. But why should she want to travel on her own? Later, when he discovered that she had booked on the *Titanic* along with Marion and Hugo, he was considerably put out. But since Marjorie had been acting very strangely with him lately, he said nothing.

As February came and went, Marjorie's imminent departure hung between them. She refused to talk about it (feeling, as Prudence said, that this would teach the man a lesson). He in turn did what most husbands would do in the circumstances: he sulked and tended to stay even later at Westminster than he need have.

March was almost over before he finally found out the cause of all the trouble. Then, once more, chance and Prudence Fairfax intervened.

Richard encountered her at a small reception held for some naval charity at the House. She was still very cool. When he said that he simply couldn't understand why Marjorie had to go off to America alone, she replied tartly, "Well, Richard, can you really blame her?"

He asked her what on earth she meant and she explained. Richard was genuinely amazed. Never for a moment had he suspected what the trouble was about.

"But it's outrageous!" he exclaimed to Prudence. Prudence looked as if she wasn't certain whether to believe him.

"All that I did was try to help poor Cressida," he added pompously.

Prudence still looked quizzical.

"I must do something straight away to put things right with Marjorie," he exclaimed.

"I think you should," she said.

Richard did his best, returning home with flowers and a locket bought from Cartier. Had it been anyone but Richard, such extravagance might have convinced Marjorie of his guilt, but she knew him well enough by now to know when he was lying.

"So you really thought I'd been unfaithful, and with Cressida! How could you possibly imagine . . .?"

"All too well, my dearest," Marjorie replied. "She is a very pretty woman and you would still be quite a catch."

"Nonsense, Marjorie," he said, but he was secretly flattered at the thought of all the trouble he had caused.

This was nothing, though, to the relief they both felt. Their troubles and misunderstandings seemed unimportant now, and suddenly they were immensely happy. It seemed to Marjorie that she had recovered the excitement and the joy of love which she had given up for good. It was much later that night, when they were both almost asleep, that a thought struck her.

"How dreadful, darling," she said suddenly. "Next Thursday I'm supposed to be leaving you for America. I'll cancel it tomorrow."

"No, don't do that," he said. "The voyage will do you good. You'll be in the lap of luxury. And think how disappointed Lucy and Elizabeth would be."

"I know what, then" she replied. "Why don't you come as well?"

He paused before replying. It was immensely tempting. He had just rediscovered how warm and passionate his wife could be. Four entire days and nights at sea with her, and then New York . . . He remembered Parliament. He had his duties there. It would be irresponsible to think of going.

He kissed her tenderly. "I'll be over the week after," he whispered. "Then we can all be together in New York and the two of us can come back at the beginning of May."

"You promise?" she said anxiously.

"Promise," he replied.

Those last few days together were days of special tenderness. After the months of coldness and suspicion it seemed as if they'd never been so close. Now that Marjorie was going she seemed very precious, and though Richard told himself that they'd be parted for little more than a fortnight there seemed a terrible finality about her journey. He found himself worrying about her, and as the date of her departure loomed he began dreading it.

She was leaving on the ninth of April. On the eighth he managed to escape from Parliament. They rose late, lunched together, and spent the afternoon shopping for the last few things she needed. As a final treat he took her out for dinner at the Ritz. Then he noticed that she was wearing the gold locket he had given her.

"What do you keep inside it?" he asked thoughtfully. She looked at him and paused before replying.

"Only a picture," she said finally.

"What of?" he asked.

"The man I love. Would you like to see?"

He nodded and she opened it. Inside there was a faded photograph. It had been taken of him on their wedding day.

"You really love him?" he asked gently.

"The only one I ever have," she said.

Richard and James travelled to Southampton to see Marjorie off. Now that she was going all Richard's sadness of the past few days had lifted. Marjorie was bright-eyed, excited at the prospect of the voyage. She wore a new fur coat that he had bought her, and they all chatted happily as the train steamed through the gentle Hampshire landscape: messages from Jumbo to Elizabeth, last-minute presents James had bought for his goddaughter, little Lucy, speculation about Elizabeth's husband.

"Wish I was coming with you, Mother," James said enviously. "I could just do with a week or two away from the City. Might even find myself a job in little old New York."

Hugo and Marion were already at Southampton, Hugo extremely grand in travelling cape and new moustache, Marion flushed and angry because of some trunk that had been left behind, Martin very pale.

Now that the time had come to part, Richard and Marjorie both found themselves inhibited by the presence of so many other people. Also, they'd never had to say a real goodbye before. If it had not been for Marion, Marjorie—who felt like clutching Richard—would undoubtedly have cried, but she would not display her emotions to her sister-in-law. So she made the parting brief. A short embrace, a whispered "See you in a fortnight, darling," and she was gone.

"We'll look after her, old boy, fear not!" Hugo shouted from the gangplank.

In later years Richard always maintained that there *was* something odd about the departure of the *Titanic* on her maiden voyage. He felt uneasy again as he stood waiting on the quay for the great ship to sail. James felt it too. They heard a grey-haired little old lady anxiously asking one of the officials if the ship was absolutely White Star safe.

"God himself couldn't sink the *Titanic,* ma'am," he answered.

❧ ☙

For Richard the next two days dragged as he'd never known days to drag before. Luckily he was busy. The naval estimates were due, and Balfour had demanded a precise résumé of the opposition's attitude to them. This kept him occupied until after midnight. Even so, he kept feeling uneasy about Marjorie. For some reason the words of the woman on the quayside troubled him, and so did the official's reply. One shouldn't tempt fate with remarks like that. As he found it hard to sleep, he wrote Marjorie every night. This was something he hadn't done since just before their marriage, but for some reason he felt impelled to tell her of his love for her and to try again to explain all the cruel misunderstandings that had dogged them for the past six months. Things would be better in the future; this he promised her. Just two weeks and they would be together. Each night he wrote this as if needing to convince himself that it was true.

❧ ☙

It was a Tuesday afternoon when Richard heard the news of the disaster. The unsinkable *Titanic,* travelling full speed ahead, had struck an iceberg somewhere off the Newfoundland coast. At first this was all there was—no further news about the ship, no certainty of whether she was afloat or not, no hint about survivors. And at first the news produced no great alarm. Everyone knew how vast, how strong, how powerful the great new liner was. God himself—let alone a mere iceberg in the North Atlantic—couldn't sink her.

Richard was in the Commons when the news came through. In some strange way he had expected it. He also knew with iron certainty that there was no hope, not for him at any rate. As he left the Palace of Westminster and hurried through the April afternoon to buy a paper with the latest news, he knew quite well that he would not see Marjorie again.

It was this certainty of his that made the wait so dreadful. Everyone else at 165—even James and that natural pessimist Angus Hudson—managed to keep themselves buoyed up with hopeful stories of survivors. A Swedish ship had picked up several hundred from the lifeboats. All the rest must certainly be safe. The Atlantic was a busy thoroughfare of ships, and it was impossible, quite, utterly impossible. that a company like White Star, with a ship like the *Titanic,* could let a single human being drown.

Hudson, who read these optimistic theories in the newspapers, used them to keep the servants' hopes alive. James did his best to do the same thing for his father—but it was useless. Richard said nothing, but he showed no interest in the newspaper reports nor in the news that started coming through by radio from White Star in New York. Most of the day he stayed immured in his study, and that night he could not sleep. Towards dawn he rose, dressed and, without bothering to shave or eat, left the house. He couldn't bear to be inside 165 any longer. The whole house was redolent of Marjorie—her scent, her taste, her very presence.

All Richard could think of was to walk, and he found himself automatically making his way towards Westminster, scene of his efforts and ambitions for so long. There was something strangely consoling in the great slumbering building. Dawn was coming up across the river. Big Ben boomed out the quarters of another day. Somewhere downstream a tug was hooting.

He noticed that he was cold (in his haste to leave the house he hadn't bothered with an overcoat) and in a way this pleased him. The poor wretches in the lifeboats must have been cold as well. He crossed the road and passed beneath the angry horses pulling bronze Boadicea's ample chariot. Apart from Boadicea no one was about, and he headed east along that stretch of the Embankment with St. Paul's rising in the distance from the river mist.

He thought of Marjorie. Suddenly it was as if she were walking beside him. His loneliness was over. He remembered how they had walked together through the city in that first autumn of their marriage. He saw her face, heard her voice, and knew that she was with him. It was quite simple, and there was no point in grieving. Marjorie had lived her life. It was complete and they had loved each other at the end. That, he knew now, was all that mattered.

1912-14

15. *Time Runs Out*

RICHARD LET HIMSELF INTO 165 WITH HIS LATCH KEY. IN THE COLD early-morning light the house seemed alien and empty. Nobody was up, and as he climbed the stairs and felt a sudden weariness assail him, he had his first bleak intimation of what life without Marjorie would mean—loneliness and old age beginning, emptiness and no one waiting for him in their bedroom when he reached the landing.

"Marjorie," he muttered under his breath. "Marjorie, my dearest!" Then he shook his head as if he couldn't understand why she failed to reply. Alone on the Embankment he had felt able to accept her death. Here in the house it was different.

"Marjorie," he called again, louder this time.

"Sir," said a voice behind him, "I'm most relieved that you've returned. We were all worried. Might I suggest that you wait in your study while I fetch you something?"

Hudson *had* heard his entry and was standing just behind him in his shirt-sleeves and black early-morning waistcoat. At the sight of his familiar, loyal, anxious face, Richard finally broke down.

For the rest of his life Richard was to be grateful to Hudson for the way he handled this dreadful moment when all of Richard's grief struck home. Hudson's training had instilled in him the firm belief that the passions and emotions of his betters were none of his business: a lesser man than Hudson would have found himself embarrassed and incapable in such a situation. But Hudson did not just respect his master. Over the years he had grown to love him, and it was this that now enabled him to forget just for a moment the taboos against "undue familiarity" and to give the help and comfort that were needed. Somehow he led Richard to his study and persuaded him into the easy chair beside the fire. He did nothing to try to check the tears that streamed down Richard's face.

"Is there no hope then, sir?" asked Hudson softly.

Mutely Richard shook his head. Hudson placed his hand upon his shoulder.

"There, sir," he said. "It's best not to try holding back the tears."

Richard could not eat, but Hudson managed to produce a flask of whisky and make Richard drink. And then, since he knew that it was bad for people in extreme unhappiness to drink alone, Hudson drank with his master. He sat with Richard for some time, and his presence was calming, but Richard still felt overwhelmed by his appalling sense of loss. He had never had to face bereavement of this sort before, and he was frightened at the pain his grief was causing him.

"Tell me, Hudson," he said finally," how does one go on, just how does one?"

Hudson replied sternly and a shade impatiently, since he knew that pity was the last thing Richard needed: "Och, sir. You go on because you have to, because everyone depends on you, and because that's how her ladyship herself would have behaved if it had been you who had gone."

❧ ☙

Hudson was a tower of strength for others besides Richard. The news of the disaster had resulted in a sort of numbed despair among the servants. True, there had been no close affection between any of them and Marjorie, but she had been the central pillar of their lives. For twenty-eight years she had reigned absolutely over their world. With her unbending sense of order she had guaranteed the continuity of everything they knew, and in a strange way they had largely lived their lives through her, enjoying her enjoyments and taking pleasure in her pleasures.

Hudson understood all this and with a sort of genius he managed to preserve their dwindling morale. He made no reference to the master's certainty that her ladyship had perished.

"No news is good news, Mrs. Bridges," he said philosophically. "There's bound to be confusion after a great sea disaster of this kind. We must just hope and trust in God. And in the meantime, Rose—and this applies to everyone—I know you're worried. All of us are. But try and keep your feelings to yourselves. The master and Mr. James are the ones with most to bear. Do all you can to keep their spirits up."

Thanks in the main to Hudson's firmness and example, 165 did manage to maintain at least a semblance of calm throughout the uncertainty and horror of the next few days. There were no further outward demonstrations of despair from Richard. (Some of the more sentimental servants such as Rose even wondered how he could seem so heartless and unfeeling when poor Lady Marjorie . . . On the other hand, the stoic Hudson was immensely proud of him.)

Another source of order and stability was provided now by Richard's secretary, Hazel Forrest. Richard, despite his show of calm, was quite incapable of coping with the countless queries and decisions that the crisis suddenly threw up. There were reporters to be dealt with, anxious friends to fend off politely, and the complex running of the house needed somebody to take the place of Lady Marjorie. Self-effacing and efficient, the pale Miss Forrest managed wonderfully. It would have been all too easy for a mere outsider to have put Mrs. Bridges' sensitive nose cruelly out of joint, but that embattled lady followed Miss Forrest's culinary suggestions now without a murmur. The other servants respected her quite automatically. "A fine young woman, that, Mrs. Bridges," Hudson said feelingly. "I can't think how we would all be managing now without her." And Mrs. Bridges staunchly agreed.

It was Thursday evening, April 18, when Hazel Forrest entered Richard's study with a telegram. He knew what it contained before he opened it. He was even relieved that the dreadful period of waiting was over. He was impassive as he slid his ivory paper knife into the envelope and cut the paper, and he showed no sign of emotion as he read the contents.

"So, it's official," he said finally. He sighed wearily, then, realising that his secretary was still standing there, he handed her the telegram to read. It was from the London office of the White Star Line and there was something horribly impersonal about the wording.

"Deeply regret," she read. "Lady Marjorie Bellamy missing stop must be presumed drowned." It was signed "White Star Line."

"I'm sorry," she said limply, suddenly all too conscious of the fact that anything she said would sound inadequate. But she did feel sorry—sorrier than she could possibly admit—for Richard Bellamy. During the nine months she had worked with him on his immense biography of Southwold she felt that she had got to know him, and she had felt sorry for him even then. He was so different from the people round him—so much softer and more vulnerable, and so much more intelligent. Now, with his lined face and his brave attempt to cope with this senseless tragedy, he seemed more in need of help than ever.

"Is there anything that I can do?" she said, trying to convey something of the protectiveness she felt for him.

"My dear Miss Forrest," said Richard, unaware of the emotions he was rousing in that passionate young woman, "you have already done so much. I would be more grateful than I can tell you if you could stay on for these next few weeks at least. We really need you."

"But, Father!" James shouted. "How can my mother possibly be dead? I don't believe it and I won't believe it. There must be more survivors. A ship like the *Titanic* doesn't just disappear."

Richard stared gloomily out the window at the rain and yellow gas-light in the street. His son's reaction was exactly as he had expected, the same blank refusal to accept the bitter facts of life that he had shown as a boy.

"James, my dear James," he said gently. "We must not deceive ourselves. It is more than three days now since the *Titanic* sank. No lifeboat can survive three days in the North Atlantic at this time of year. There is a very slender chance that she has been picked up by some unknown vessel and will still be brought to safety, but . . ."

"There you are then. If there is a chance, why are you so anxious to believe her dead? Why, Father? So that you can now go off and marry that Hartington woman?"

"How dare you!" Richard cried, but now that James had found an outlet for his anger there was no stopping him.

"Now, Father, don't pretend this doesn't suit you. Don't try to play the tragic widower to me."

Richard tried to interrupt but there was now no stopping James's flow of frantic bitterness.

"I know why you sent her to America—don't think I didn't realise what you were up to. I only hope you're satisfied. You sent her to her death."

There was silence then as both men realised that something had been said that could never be forgotten or forgiven.

"I'm sorry, Father," James said finally in a low voice. He rose and made as if to come towards Richard.

"I'm sorry," he repeated. "I should not have said it. I apologise."

But Richard shook his head and left the room.

And so the bereavement, which could have brought Richard and his son together, drove them still further and more bitterly apart. James's words seemed to run like poison through the house. Edward, the new footman, had overheard his outburst, and before the day was out a suitably embellished version of the whole affair was being debated in the servants' hall. Rose and Mrs. Bridges were predictably on James's side. "What with 'is poor dear mother dead it's only natural for 'im to defend 'er memory," said Mrs. Bridges staunchly. Rose nodded vehemently and said that she admired Mr. James for what he'd done. But Mr. Hudson said that he was shocked that any son should speak thus to his father—particularly when, as in the present case, there was not a scrap of evidence to back his monstrous allegations.

As for the cause of all the trouble, he kept resolutely to his room, just as he had when he disgraced himself as a small boy. When Rose knocked gently on his door and asked if there was anything he wanted, there was only a muffled "Go away!" from behind the door; and next morning his breakfast tray was left untouched outside his room. Just before mid-day Hudson considered it his duty to inform the master that Mr. James had still not appeared.

"Do you think he's ill?" asked Richard.

"No, sir. But I think that Mr. James might have a considerable head-ache by this evening, to judge by the bottles that he's left outside his door."

But Richard found himself with more important matters than his son's drunken sulking—especially with Geoffrey Dillon due for lunch. Richard would have prefered to see almost anyone but that desiccated lawyer at a time like this, but there was no avoiding it. And since he had to see him, he preferred to do so when backed up by Mrs. Bridges' cooking.

Sir Geoffrey was, as usual, early, and, as usual, Richard was intensely uncomfortable in his presence.

The lawyer made an attempt at sympathy. "My dear Richard," he began as Richard greeted him. "How can I possibly express my sense of shock at this most dreadful loss? My profound condolences." As he said this he took Richard's hand between both of his, a gesture Richard hated, especially from Sir Geoffrey. His hands were smooth and rather cold, and as Richard met his gaze the lenses of Sir Geoffrey's spectacles gave his eyes a look of magnified superiority. Disaster was undoubtedly Sir Geoffrey's element. But Richard felt that, just for once, even Sir Geoffrey Dillon had been shaken by events beyond his lawyerly control.

"Who could have dreamt of this?" Dillon said a trifle querulously, as if fate or whatever legal godhead he worshipped had no right to have behaved so irresponsibly. "At one blow, a million-to-one catastrophe, a great name like the Southwolds is extinguished. Utterly!" He shook his head and for a moment seemed at a loss for words.

"So there's no news of Hugo—nor of Marion?" said Richard.

"Nothing," said Dillon. "Not a word. The White Star people informed me officially last night that Lord and Lady Southwold and their son, along with Lady Marjorie, must be presumed lost."

"Poor, silly Hugo," said Richard slowly. "Who would have thought that he of all people would have been the last Earl of Southwold? And after all those plans of his for recovering his fortunes out in Canada."

"They might have worked," said Dillon as he sipped his sherry.

"But as they haven't, I suppose that all he's left behind him is the usual pile of debts."

Dillon nodded. "That, Richard, is one of the matters that I wanted to discuss."

"Surely a little premature," said Richard.

"In the circumstances, I hardly think so. An event like this raises a lot of problems—particularly for you. I felt that in simple fairness I should make the whole position clear as soon as possible."

"Of course, Geoffrey. But, as I'm sure you will appreciate, I've had a lot of problems of my own to face over the last few days. Let's just leave them for a while, until lunch is on the table."

Although 165 was now in mourning, this did not affect the standard of the food. As Mrs. Bridges had put it to Hazel Forrest when they were discussing that day's menu, " 'Er ladyship would have wanted 'er lawyer to be properly fed, even at a time like this." So at twelve forty-five Sir Geoffrey and his host sat down to a smoked haddock *soufflé* followed by spring lamb and a delicious salad. The Niersteiner was precisely chilled, the service as discreet and courteous as ever.

Richard was grateful. Dealing with Geoffrey Dillon was an ordeal at the best of times, but there was something reassuring now in being able to show him that the routine of life at Eaton Place would continue—at whatever cost. Marjorie had established certain standards: one way of remembering her was to make sure they continued.

Even Sir Geoffrey Dillon—hardly the most sensitive of mortals—seemed to appreciate this. It was as if Marjorie was still making her presence felt, for when he finally began explaining how the disaster would affect the whole future of the inhabitants of 165, he did so with an unaccustomed diffidence.

"Of course, Richard, it will take some while for us to sort out the estate. The details will inevitably be complicated and the whole sad business could spin out for months. But as I've said already, I hardly think that there'll be much to play about with by the time Hugo's debts are settled. With Southwold House already sold, and most of the other property as well, the only substantial assets are the ranch and land that Hugo—that is to say, Lord Southwold—bought in Canada. I have no way of knowing what they would be worth, but I hardly think that the amount will cover what is needed."

"The debts are that big?"

"Unbelievable. And as well as all the creditors there is the child Georgina to be taken care of."

"Marion's daughter. Poor thing, how's she taking it?"

"Not well at all. As you know, her father was killed when she was quite young and the Southwolds were the only family she had."

"Can't you trace her father's people, or her mother's? In the circumstances they'd have to do something."

"My agents have tried without success. Apparently Marion and her daughter were quite alone in the world when they went out to Canada, and the father's estate was infinitesimal. I only hope I can salvage something from the Southwold *debâcle* to complete her education. But that's not your worry, Richard."

"What is, then?"

Dillon carefully placed his knife and fork in the exact centre of his plate before looking up at Richard and replying,

"Simply this. While Lady Marjorie was alive, the two of you were in receipt of a joint income in the region of eight thousand pounds a year, the interest on several capital sums held in trust for Lady Marjorie. This income naturally ceases on her death, and I am afraid that it is my duty to inform you now to this effect."

"I see," said Richard. "You don't exactly beat about the bush, do you, Geoffrey? Barely a week ago I was waving off my wife on holiday. Now you're telling me that I'm not only wifeless but penniless. Thank you very much."

"Richard, I'm not enjoying this, but facts unfortunately are facts. Surely you must have savings and some capital of your own?"

"Geoffrey, you know quite well I haven't. As you'd probably put it with your usual delicacy, I've been living off my wife for years. And as I'm sure you also will remember, the lease of this house was, at my insistence, put in my wife's name too."

Sir Geoffrey sucked his teeth impatiently. "Well, Richard, with a little common sense it should be possible to work something out. Under the terms of Lady Marjorie's will, the lease on this house will pass to James, and since as one of her heirs he also gets half of the capital she had in trust, the two of you can obviously continue as you were."

"Not if my son has anything to do with it," said Richard bitterly.

It was typical of Richard Bellamy not to have foreseen what Geoffrey Dillon had to tell him. He had always been content to let the future take care of itself. At periods of crisis he had felt angry, even bitter, at the servile status which throughout his marriage had been the price of his dependence on the Southwold bounty. But the anger and bitterness had never lasted long enough to make him change things. At heart he had a most complacent, optimistic nature. As long as things went well he never thought it worth while questioning the basis of his comfort and good fortune; and, to be fair to him, what could he possibly have done? Renounce the pleasant life of 165? He had no other. Insist on some more clear-cut situation for himself? It would have seemed most churlish in the circumstances, and with Sir Geoffrey Dillon there to guard the Southwold interests, it is hard to see what chance he would have had of that. Instead the little world of Eaton Place had subtly conspired with him to bring about what seemed to be his present downfall. Hudson's loyalty and Marjorie's love had always made it seem as if he really was the master of the house—and for twenty-eight well-fed and contented years Richard had behaved as if he was. Now that a trick of fate had robbed him of his wife, his world—which in effect *was* 165—was suddenly revealed to him as the flimsy edifice it was.

He was intelligent enough to see this very clearly now, and the truth did little to console him. Losing Marjorie had been bad enough; now he was swiftly losing his self-respect as well.

Hazel was waiting for him in his study when he returned from seeing Sir Geoffrey off. She knew him well enough by now to recognise his moods. Instead of looking at the pile of letters she had typed for him, he swung his chair round and gazed mournfully through the window at the street beyond. Cool and competent as ever, with her graceful neck and spotless blouse, she said nothing—which was wise. Even when he groaned and muttered, "Oh, my God!" she merely raised an eyebrow—and kept silent.

It must have been this show of calm that finally encouraged Richard to confide in her. It seemed an age—a whole eternity—since he had known the luxury of talking freely to a sympathetic woman.

"Hazel," he began (during the last few days he had begun to call her by her first name without realising it), "I am afraid that you will soon have to start looking round for fresh employment. I was hoping, as you know, to be able to employ you permanently here, but circumstances make this quite impossible. I'm very sorry."

Hazel Forrest opened her large grey eyes a little wider, but she still said nothing. Richard's words had not come as a complete surprise.

"You see," Richard continued, "my wife's death has made it hopeless for this household to continue and I must face realities. James, my son, is now the owner of this house. He and Elizabeth will also inherit most of the money that was held in Marjorie's name. As you must have realised by now, James and I don't get on together well enough to make this sort of situation tolerable."

"So what will happen?" Miss Forrest managed to make the question sound almost casual.

"As far as James is concerned, I've no idea, although I can't imagine what a bachelor like him would do with an establishment like this. As for myself, I daresay I'll manage."

At this Miss Forrest gave him a look of quite extraordinary concern.

"But that's terrible," she said. "You mean you're losing everything—your home, your livelihood—and what about your political career?"

Until this moment, Richard hadn't given much concrete thought to the future, but Hazel Forrest's show of sympathy made his situation seem suddenly desperate.

"I'll have to give up politics," he said. "And probably about time too. I daresay I can find myself a job. Something or other in the City. It should be quite a challenge."

"And what about the books you want to write and all the other things you'd planned to do?" Miss Forrest sounded outraged now.

"They were just dreams," said Richard, smiling what he imagined was a brave and realistic smile. "Just self-indulgent dreams. At my age a man should really have got over things like that."

That evening James appeared for dinner—a subdued and very white-faced James, with bloodshot eyes and precious little appetite. Richard made no attempt at conversation. Since his talk to Hazel Forrest he had been brooding on his future and realising with grim satisfaction that it was indeed as bleak as he had said. So it was his turn to be bitter with his son, although poor James, to do him justice, had no idea of his present offence. In his misery about his mother's death he had not given the fact that legally he, and not his father, was the master of 165 a moment's thought, nor did he know about his new inheritance.

But, as usual, there was one group who were all too well aware of what was happening. Sir Geoffrey's visit had aroused considerable speculation below stairs, and this, coupled with the strained relations between James and Richard, had caused much anxiety. This was severely practical, for all the servants, even that paragon of loyalty

Angus Hudson, knew that with Lady Marjorie gone, their livelihood and security hung in the balance.

Edward, the under-footman and one of life's natural pessimists, voiced all their fears.

"Better start looking round for a new appointment, Mrs. B," he shouted cheerfully to Mrs. Bridges that evening after dinner. He enjoyed baiting her, but now for once he was quite serious.

"New appointment? What d'yer mean, you daft young idiot?" she retorted. She was already most put out to see how little of the stuffed leg of veal the two gentlemen upstairs had eaten. Edward's jokes—if that was what they were—were not required as well.

"Well, stands to reason, Mrs. B. With Miss Elizabeth now in America and poor Lady Marjorie no more, the master and young Mr. James won't want this great white elephant of a place for long."

"Edward," Hudson said indignantly, "*no* house in Eaton Place, and least of all number 165, can possibly be termed a white elephant. I think you should learn to mind your language."

"All right then, Mr. Hudson. But you saw the two of them tonight. At daggers drawn they was. Don't try telling me that they intend to go on living happily together just as if nothin's happened. I think we lost more than we expected when 'er ladyship was drowned."

Hudson looked thoughtful and for once seemed at a loss for a reply. It was Mrs. Bridges who finally voiced everyone's opinion.

"Things here won't be right," she said, "until there's a lady in the house again."

For what seemed an age the atmosphere of gloom continued, with James and Richard doing their best to avoid each other. This was not very difficult, as James had to spend his days in the hated office in the City, and his father tended more and more to stay late in the House of Commons and dine in his club. There was no dearth of sympathetic friends for Richard, female ones included. Prudence had been particularly insistent in her attempts to mother him—"As poor Marjorie's oldest friend I feel I have a definite responsibility"—but Richard sensed the predatory female, ducked, and managed to avoid her. He did the same with Cressida, who sent a gushing note of sympathy in violet-coloured ink: he penned a pointedly unchivalrous reply. Indeed, he found that the only woman he could tolerate was Hazel Forrest.

They had a very businesslike relationship. There was still no undue familiarity, still less on either side any hint of the beginning of romance. (Miss Forrest's Wimbledon background, her middle-class morality, and her secretary's training utterly forbade this.) And yet the two of them did have a most extraordinary understanding for each other, and as often happens in such cases, there was an element of self-deception in the way they both pretended to be physically indifferent to each other. Hazel's red hair was the same shade as Marjorie's, and whilst she lacked the older woman's classic beauty, she had the sort of haunting Pre-Raphaelite looks that certainly appealed to Richard. Given time for him to get over Marjorie's death, one would have thought it more or less inevitable for him to fall in love with her. Similarly on her side there was much in Richard to attract her. She always had felt drawn to older men. Since childhood she had always sided with her henpecked, ineffectual father. (Mrs. Forrest was a horror.) And when she told Richard, in a moment of rare candour, that her months of work with him had been among the happiest in her life, she had not exaggerated, for life had not been very kind to Hazel Forrest.

When Richard asked her why she had been so happy, she had seemed curiously embarrassed.

"I just love this house, and I'm grateful for the way you've treated me as a normal human being," she replied. But there was more to it than that.

☙ ❧

Three weeks after the *Titanic* sank, a small memorial service was held for Marjorie and for Marion and Hugo in the parish church at Southwold. This took the place of a funeral, but it was still a melancholy occasion. The absence of coffins seemed to emphasise the absolute finality with which the three of them had disappeared; the age and sparseness of the congregation underlined the way in which the once grand house of Southwold had already been forgotten. There were a few familiar faces from the past. Old Widgery, the Southwolds' butler, was miraculously still alive—a quivery old gentleman with thin white hair and rheumy eyes—and some of the older villagers such as the Tranters from the Post Office and the Gosdens from the Southwold stores were there in force. But most of the mourners were from London, with Hudson looking like the rock of ages, and Rose and Mrs. Bridges, side by side in sober black, snuffling audibly throughout the service. Richard found himself seated next to Geoffrey Dillon, which made it hard for him to think of Marjorie—or of anything except how heartily he disliked the man and the unpleasant facts he represented. As Richard tried to pray, he saw the loss of the *Titanic* as something more than an ordinary disaster. It had become the shipwreck of the world he knew, a great symbolic cataclysm in which affection, happiness, the comfortable, ordered world he loved had foundered utterly. Suddenly he had a vision of the vengeful God of the Old Testament smiting the godless nations of the world as he had heard his father solemnly predicting in his sermons when he was a boy. "The wrath of God!" his father had thundered. "There will be none who shall escape His dreadful anger." Was the disaster only just beginning? As Richard got to his feet he found that he was trembling.

James had insisted on travelling separately to the service. The shock of his mother's death was bad enough. He did not want it made worse by the tension he and his father now felt in each other's company. So he drove down to Southwold by himself—Richard had come earlier in the Rolls—and slipped into the church just as the service was beginning. Hazel was sitting alone, halfway down the church. Almost without thinking James took his place beside her. Throughout the service, which he found sadder and even more pointless than he had expected, James was uncomfortably aware of his neighbour's presence. She was wearing a small black hat which showed off her appealing profile to perfection. Her scent was lilies of the valley, a powerful and most disturbing fragrance that James could not ignore, even as he attempted to compose his mind on other things. When the service ended he was anxious to escape ahead of his father, but something made him ask Miss Forrest if she would care for a lift back to town. He was surprised when she accepted.

They were both rather wary of each other. When Hazel first arrived at 165, James had made the inevitable pass at her. She had seemed flattered at the time, admired his looks and enjoyed going out with him—but that was all. And that had emphatically not been enough in those days for young James Bellamy. When she had made it plain to him, for whatever stupid reasons of her own, that she was not becoming James's mistress, he had made it just as plain that that was that. During the months that followed, while she was working regularly at 165 on Richard's book, James never seemed to let slip any opportunity to mock her.

"Found any skeletons in the Southwold cupboards lately, Hazel?" he would ask her, and she would answer icily that that was not the purpose of the book.

"Oh, but it should be," he would mutter. "Sex and the Southwolds. Ghastly revelations. Father could make it a best-seller if you'd only let him."

But as they drove to London all of this seemed forgotten, and James was surprised to see a new and unsuspected Hazel, eyes sparkling, red hair flying in the wind as he drove his little tourer at an exciting sixty miles an hour up the main road to Reading. It was a bright spring day. There were lambs in the fields and everywhere the trees were bursting into leaf. After the gloom of Southwold, life was suddenly emerging from the winter shadows. He had intended driving straight to London but suddenly found himself suggesting that they have lunch together. Hazel accepted. Both were ravenously hungry, and they had beer and cutlets in an old coaching inn near Reading. James had never thought of Hazel as the sort of girl who'd drink a pint of bitter.

Richard was unreasonably upset when he discovered that his secretary had returned to London with his son. James's behaviour, slipping off like that without a word, had been disgusting too, especially as it left him no alternative to offering Geoffrey Dillon a lift back to London in the Rolls.

Richard was even more upset during the days that followed when he discovered just how much attention James was paying to Hazel. He tried to tell himself that he was simply worried for Miss Forrest's own well-being, although he must have realised that this was not by any means his only motive. It is a curious and most uncomfortable sensation for a grown man to discover that he is jealous of his son, doubly so in Richard's case, since he had always taken his *rapport* with Hazel so much for granted, and Richard had never been very honest with himself where his emotions were concerned.

The signs, however, were quite unmistakeable. Hazel suddenly looked happier than he had ever seen her—bright-eyed and even with a touch of colour in those cool pale cheeks—but she was so preoccupied that all their former understanding seemed to have vanished. When he attempted to discuss with her his plans for leaving Eaton Place, she seemed impatient with the whole idea.

"Sir Geoffrey Dillon seems to think that the sooner I make my plans and go, the better. Things may not be so bad as I had feared at first, and I was hoping that you'd still be able to work for me once I find an office," he had said, only to get a very cool reply.

"Isn't it," she said," a little premature to think so far ahead?'

James too had changed dramatically. Gone were the accusing looks, the gloomy lifelessness which Richard had so recently endured from his son. Instead Richard would come in to breakfast to be greeted by a cheery "Morning, Father! Lovely day" and the sight of James behind the morning's *Times* having already eaten porridge, kidneys, bacon, eggs, and toast and marmalade. It had been years since Richard had last seen him do this, but he was not as pleased as some fond fathers might have been. James's appetite made him feel his age. Besides, he liked to read the *Times* in peace before anybody else dismembered it.

Hazel had been quick to notice the apparent transformation in James Bellamy. He was no longer the brash, impatient, would-be seducer of the previous summer. He seemed much kinder and more serious. Even his voice had softened—or so it seemed to her—and when he asked her out to dinner she accepted, though with a little hesitation.

"Please, Hazel," he said imploringly. "Please!" And when she finally said yes, she had the feeling she was granting him some special favour. Previously he had always taken her to smart restaurants like Romano's or the Café Royal, places where she had felt acutely conscious of her lack of *chic* and of James's smart friends who seemed always there. But tonight he chose a different sort of restaurant, a small place in Soho run by an ancient Belgian with an enormous belly and a great moustache. It had grimy walls and faded prints of old Napoleonic battles, gas jets lit the room, and there were red-checked tablecloths and glass partitions dividing off each table from the next.

The food was quite delicious—*moules* cooked with garlic and a thick cream sauce, a *cassoulet* with chunks of pork and lamb and goose and sausage, fresh green beans cooked in butter. They had a bottle of good burgundy, and as they ate, a wonderful contentment seemed to unite them.

"Better than Mrs. Bridges," James remarked, laughing.

"Different," said Hazel tactfully. "I didn't know that restaurants like this existed, but then there's an awful lot that I don't know."

"Perhaps you'd let me show you," he said wistfully.

"Perhaps," she said.

He smiled at her. His face had relaxed and he looked very young and rather vulnerable. She felt his charm and was on her guard at once.

"Dearest Hazel," he said gently, "why have you always been so unattainable?"

"Have I?" she said, drawing back and watching him through those cool grey eyes. "I suppose it all depends upon what you want to attain."

He shrugged but his smile deepened. "What are you afraid of?" he persisted.

"Do you really want to know?"

He nodded.

"Of being used. As a mere lady secretary from a very ordinary suburban home, I'm not quite like the smart, rich lady friends you're used to."

"You're far more beautiful."

"That's not the point. When you flirt with one of them you flirt as equals. I'm not so fortunate. I've got much more to lose."

"What, for instance?"

She smiled as she realised how pompous she was sounding, but this didn't stop her from continuing.

"My self-respect—and frankly, my respectability."

He began laughing now, and this made her angry.

"Oh, I know that all of you treat the idea of respectability as something very middle-class and boring. I agree. It is boring, horribly boring, but if your livelihood depends on it, as mine does, you just can't ignore it."

"Not even if I told you I was in love with you?"
"Not even then, Mr. Bellamy, sir."

Hazel Forrest's firmness in no way deterred James Bellamy. Rather the reverse. He had been half serious when he spoke of being in love with her. He had often been in love. He was theoretically in love with the vacuous and glamorous Lady Diana Russell at that very moment (just as the vacuous Diana was theoretically unofficially engaged to James's best friend, "Bunny," the young Marquis of Newbury). But since his evening out with Hazel, James had realised that love in her terms meant something different from the captivating pastime that he and his friends and mistresses considered it.

This gave Hazel a distinct air of difference from all the other young women he knew. Her very ordinariness became a source of mystery. She roused his curiosity. With her, the whole idea of love was elevated into something James had never known before—a serious, all-absorbing malady which automatically suggested such ideas as constancy, fidelity, and even marriage.

Normally such thoughts would probably have been enough to cure James at once, but his mother's death had affected him even more deeply than he realised. He was missing her. He was in a serious and somewhat soulful state himself, and the nun-like image of his father's secretary began to obsess him.

That weekend he had been invited to a party with young Lord Randolph, "Randy" Bloodenough, at Staines. He had not been out to a party since his mother died, and he went now only with the idea of forgetting Hazel. Predictably, it did not work. Lord Randolph seemed a drunken boor; Diana irritated him; and to complete a disastrous weekend, he lost sixty pounds which he could ill afford at *chemin-de-fer*. By Sunday afternoon the whole smart world of fun and games which he had previously enjoyed appeared a hollow sham. He had no place in it, and there was suddenly only one person who could put his world to rights. Then and there he decided he must see her.

The Forrests lived in Wimbledon Park, not far from the railway station, and despite the evening fog that blanketed the bottom of the hill, James had no difficulty finding their house. It was in the middle of a terrace and had a large bow-window and a green front door. When he saw it James remembered what Hazel had said about respectability. The privet hedge was neatly cut, the brass door knocker gleamed. Warily he rang the bell. A small man with a large bald head answered the door, and when James, with a certain air of cool authority, asked if Miss Forrest was at home, the small man answered worriedly that no, she was not. She and her mother, Mrs. Forrest, that is to say, had just gone to church for evensong.

"So you are Mr. Forrest," James said amiably.

"That is so," said Mr. Forrest, peering up at James, "and who, sir, are you?"

James introduced himself and added that he would be grateful for a brief discussion. With deference—and considerable suspicion—Mr. Forrest asked him in.

When James got back to Eaton Place it was to find that they had a visitor. A tall, somewhat spotty schoolgirl with plaits and a stammer was sitting with his father on the sofa. Richard, who had been valiantly trying to make her feel at home since lunchtime, was patently relieved that James had finally arrived.

"James," he said solemnly, "this is Georgina."

James looked puzzled but shook hands.

"Georgina Worsley," added Richard. "Your late Aunt Marion's daughter."

"Good heavens!" James exclaimed. "*That* Georgina! The last time I saw you, you were a child. Now you are practically, well, a fully grown young lady"

"N-not quite, Uncle J-James. I only w-wish I was."

"Nonsense. Ladies grow old far too quickly, don't they, Father? There's not a lady in London who wouldn't swap ages with you if she had a chance. And by the way, no more of this Uncle James, if you please. We're cousins if we're anything, so you'll call me James and I'll call you Georgina. Any more Uncle James and I'll call you Aunt Georgina in return."

The girl laughed and nodded awkwardly.

"Sit down," said James," and tell me what you've been up to since you got out of that pram of yours."

"Well, I've been staying with Sir Ge-Geoffrey Dillon and his wife since the a-a-accident."

"Poor you," said James.

"Sir Geoffrey came today for luncheon," Richard said tactfully. "At my suggestion he brought Georgina, since she is really one of the family, and I thought that she would probably enjoy a few days here before she goes back to school. Hazel can look after her during the day, and it would do us good to have a young face in the house again, wouldn't it, James."

"I should just say so," James replied.

James was very good with people younger than himself, and already Georgina's shyness—and her stammer—had begun to disappear. Dinner, which Richard had been dreading, turned out to be the happiest meal that anyone had had at 165 since Marjorie died. James told Georgina stories about Southwold in the old days. Richard joined in. And finally Georgina too began to talk about the past—about living with Marion, Hugo and Martin out in Canada, about her boarding school, which she detested, and also about Hugo and her mother. She talked quite freely, just as if all of them were still alive, and it was obvious how much she had loved them.

As she went off to bed, she thanked James and Richard very earnestly and politely. Her stammer had suddenly returned.

"H-Hugo was right," she said. "He always used to tell me how wonderful the Bellamy family was—and how fond he was of James. G-Goodnight."

"Well, Father!" James exclaimed when Rose had conducted the girl safely out of earshot, "Poor, lonely, ugly little thing!"

"But not stupid," said Richard sagely. "Takes after her mother in one thing. She quite clearly knows how to flatter young men when she wants to. You must look out."

"Oh, come, Father. Don't be cynical. It doesn't suit you. She's so pathetic. How would you like to be orphaned at that age and then have to spend all your time with the Dillons?"

"Very kind of Geoffrey. I never knew he had it in him."

"But it's just not right. We're the girl's only relatives. *We* should be doing something for her."

"Such as what?"

"Such as giving her a home, at least during her holidays from school. Good Lord, Father, there's this great mausoleum of a house and only the two of us to share it. It needs living in. Just think, she could have Elizabeth's bedroom and Rose could easily look after her."

Normally his son's enthusiasm would have delighted Richard, but tonight he was pensive. He shrugged his shoulders and stared at the fire.

"Well," he said finally, "it's your decision. If that's what you want, I suppose there'll be no problem."

"My decision?" James replied. "What do you mean?"

"Just this," said Richard. "Geoffrey Dillon didn't come here today simply to bring Georgina, extremely amiable though that was of him. He really came here hoping to see you."

"What on earth for?"

"James, it seems that he has all but finished sorting out the details of your mother's will—along with the business of your Uncle Hugo's debts."

"And so?"

"And so I must congratulate you on being, if not rich, at any rate quite wealthy."

"But, Father, how?"

"Well, as you know, there were certain sums of capital bequeathed in trust by your grandfather. Your mother and I received the interest on the money but that naturally ceases at her death. Under the terms of your grandfather's will, and your mother's, the capital is now divided equally between you and Elizabeth."

From the puzzled look on James's face, it was clear that he was not sure how much he should rejoice.

"So how much is there?"

"Far more than any of us expected. That is one thing at least that you must thank Sir Geoffrey for. He very wisely put the money into foreign stock, Canadian Railways and South African gold mines. There's something to the tune of a quarter of a million to be shared between you and Elizabeth. You also get what remains on the lease of this house."

"Good God!" said James. For a while the two of them sat silently looking at each other. James still slightly dazed and Richard's face set in a mask of gloom.

"And what about you, then, Father?" James asked at last.

"Oh, I'll be all right," said Richard, shaking his head in manly fashion as if to show that *his* future barely mattered. "I'll move into chambers somewhere and I'll have to start earning myself a living. It's about time."

"You'll *what?*" James shouted. "I've never heard of such a thing.

There's this house and then there's more than enough money for the two of us. This is your home, Father. I wouldn't dream of letting you do any such thing."

"James, my dear boy," said Richard gently, "believe me, I've given this whole subject a great deal of thought, and you won't make me change my mind. You and I—as we've seen just recently—are very different people. We're very fond of one another—at any rate I hope we are—but if we go on living in each other's pockets, particularly now that you're the master of the house, it just won't work. There will be more rows, much more bitterness. Believe me, James, it simply wouldn't work."

James would have argued further, but something in his father's manner told him it would do no good.

☙ ❧

James had his work cut out persuading Hazel to dine with him again. She had been busy helping Richard pack and also looking after young Georgina. (The girl had taken to her almost too enthusiastically and seemed to follow her around.) Hazel had also been having quite a time trying to console and reassure the staff, now that the rumours of Richard's leaving had been more or less confirmed. Some, like Hudson, still refused to believe that he would go.

"The master would tell me if that was his intention," he said calmly. "As he hasn't seen fit to do so, I refuse to give credence to a lot of tittle-tattle." But others, in particular Mrs. Bridges, were in a state of near-panic at the thought that the Bellamys would now inevitably leave. Despite everything that Hazel could do or say, the standard of the cooking fell, and everyone's morale and temper slumped in sympathy.

Because of all this, it was a somewhat preoccupied Hazel who sat down with James one evening in the little Soho restaurant and told the fat old Belgian proprietor that she was sorry, but her appetite had gone, and she would like something just a little lighter than his delicious *cassoulet*.

The great moustache looked disappointed. "Some onion soup, *oeufs mayonnaise,* some delicious asparagus?" Finally she settled for asparagus and *omelette fines herbes*. James, however, who was in an expansive mood, chose the soup and a mammoth plateful of boiled salt beef and fresh spring vegetables.

For a while they chatted about Georgina, Hazel explaining just how much she liked the girl. But as they talked there seemed none of the closeness they had had on the previous occasion. James did his best—and when he set out to be high-spirited it took a lot to resist him—but Hazel managed it. Finally he asked her what the matter was.

"It's very stupid of me, I suppose, but I happen to be upset at the idea of the Bellamys leaving Eaton Place. I've been very happy there. I'm sad to think it's over."

"Is that all?" he asked.

"I'm sorry for your father too. After half a lifetime there it seems hard."

"And any other reasons?" he continued.

"Well, and the servants. It's their home too. Where will they go?"

"Just leave the servants out of it for a moment. Is there absolutely nothing else that you'd regret if you never did see Eaton Place again?"

He stared very hard at her, pulling a mournful face to make her laugh. Finally, half-heartedly, she did.

"And you, you wretched inquisitive man. Yes, I suppose that I'd miss you as well."

He beamed delightedly. "That settles it," he said.

"Settles what? I can't see that it settles anything."

He roared with laughter and took her hands in his. "You've no alternative, my darling lovely Hazel," he said happily.

"What do you mean I've no alternative?" She frowned and even then he thought how beautiful she was.

"You'll have to marry me."

"Oh, James. Dear James," she said. "I wish, I *wish* I could."

"It'll solve everything. I've enough money now to run the house and keep all the servants just as they've always been. You're the only one who'll ever persuade father to stay, and we can adopt Georgina. You must say yes."

But by now the great grey eyes had filled with tears, and she shook her head.

"I can't," she said. "I can't."

"And why not?" he asked very gently.

"Because. Because I can't."

She stared at him in silence as her tears fell on her omelette.

"If I told you that I knew the reason, would it make any difference?" he said softly.

"Oh, but you couldn't know," she replied rapidly. "If you did know you wouldn't be here."

"Hazel, darling. Just because you've already had one wretched marriage, it doesn't mean . . ."

"How do you know? Who told you?" she said desperately.

"A good friend of yours. Your father. I told him that it only made me love you that much more. He gave us his blessing. Hazel darling . . ."

"Yes?" she said in a small, defeated voice.

"As so many other people's happiness depends on ours, I really think you must agree to marry me."

She nodded.

"Very well," she said.

The news took some hours to filter through at 165.

The perceptive Edward was the first one to suspect the truth. "Know what, Mrs. Bridges? Something's up," he exclaimed cheerfully next morning. "Mr. James singin' in his bath. Hasn't done that since I've been here. P'raps she's gone and accepted him."

"What nonsense you do talk, young Edward!" she replied, wiping her hands impatiently on her apron. "Things like that just don't happen any more."

But it was soon quite obvious to everybody that they did. Even Hudson noticed James's extraordinary good humour before he departed for the City, and that very evening the news became official. The only one in Eaton Place who *was* surprised by then was Richard. When James and Hazel burst in on him in his study, the poor man was distinctly overwhelmed.

"But . . ." he said, taking off his spectacles and rising from his chair. "But aren't you being rather hasty? I had no idea. James, Hazel—I mean . . ."

"Now, Father," James said laughingly, "don't be so boring. We're not exactly children and we've known each other practically a year."

Hazel was smiling too; face flushed, eyes alight, she looked radiantly happy. The sight of her like this pierced Richard's heart, but he knew what was expected of him.

"James, my dear fellow, I'm extremely glad. And Hazel, dearest Hazel." As Richard went to kiss her, emotion caught him, and his eyes began to fill with tears. "I'm so very happy," he said manfully. "I only wish that James's mother could be here to share it all."

That night the celebrations, both below stairs and above were as heartfelt as it was possible for them to be. For James's exuberant good nature carried everything before it, and he made it clear that his marriage also meant a total reprieve for everyone at 165.

"So things will go on here just as they always have?" asked Mrs. Bridges unbelievingly when James brought Hazel down to tell the servants his good tidings.

"Just as they always have, Mrs. Bridges."

"God bless you both!" she said, a sentiment which Hudson echoed later in the evening when he proposed the young couple's health before the other servants in a brimming glassful of the master's Krug.

For Richard, too, the idea of continuity was undoubtedly appealing—although that night at dinner when James began his optimistic planning for the future, Richard's self-respect compelled him to say, "No, James, the two of you young things won't want me here. You've your own lives to lead. The house is yours. Much the best thing would be for me to stick to my intention and move out."

But James, for some reason, seemed determined now that everything should stay the same as when his mother was alive; the same routines, the same traditions, the same safe, comfortable world that he had known as a boy.

"Father, you're staying. No further arguments. Hazel and I both insist on that, don't we, darling?"

Hazel nodded. She was learning fast that with her *fiancé* in his present mood, there was no point at all in disagreeing with him.

"And, Georgina," said Richard, turning to address the tongue-tied schoolgirl sitting opposite, "from now on you're one of us. Is that clear?"

She blushed and stammered out her thanks.

"Excellent," said James in his best crisp army manner. "Then I would like to propose a toast. The family!"

They all stood and, in the same distinguished wine as the servants had just enjoyed downstairs, drank to the well-being of the Bellamys.

Because the house was still officially in mourning, the wedding could not take place as quickly as James wanted. But the delay, frustrating though it was to anyone of his headlong temperament, enabled certain things to be worked out and helped everybody acclimatise to what was happening. Richard, for instance, was able to meet the Forrests at his leisure and to turn what might have been an uncomfortable occasion into a fairly painless one. At the small luncheon that he gave for them at 165, Hazel's mother—an emphatic, rather handsome woman with a feather boa—insisted on recounting all the sad details of her daughter's first disastrous marriage: the terrible brutality of her Irish husband, the unspeakable things he did to her, and the way she and Mr. Forrest had been able to make sure that she divorced the brute for cruelty without the faintest slur to her good name. Mr. Forrest kept quiet through this sad recital, but when his wife paused for breath he said firmly, "I think that's enough, Mother. I'm sure Mr. Bellamy has heard all this before. It's best forgotten." Richard hurriedly agreed before the overwhelming Mrs. Forrest could take over again.

More important, he and James came to an understanding, of sorts, about the future. James would provide the money for the household out of the income from his inherited investments and Hazel would manage things more or less as Lady Marjorie had done. Richard, despite his firm remarks about refusing to live on James's money, continued to be the figurehead at 165 just as he always had. The adoption of Georgina, which occurred that summer, showed how little things had changed. James and Richard discussed it with Sir Geoffrey Dillon, who was very much in favour of the move.

"We would like to have her legally a member of the family," James explained. "I was fond of my Uncle Hugo, and this is one thing that I can do for his memory. I gather there's no money coming to her from the estate, so I'll provide for her, at least until she's twenty-one."

"Extremely generous," murmured Sir Geoffrey, "and an extremely fortunate young lady, if I may say so."

But when it came to settling who was to be ultimately responsible for her, everyone agreed that it must be Richard. He was secretly quite flattered and announced the news to her that night with great solemnity.

"I hope you realise, young woman, that you're to become my legal ward."

"Really, Uncle Richard? How v-very exciting. What does it mean?"

"That I can beat you and chastise you when you need it. That you obey me absolutely, and that in my old age you look after me with loving care."

"That sounds a very good arrangement," she replied a trifle archly.

And so in fact it was, for during those weeks before the marriage Richard found himself alone a lot. James was tied up with fresh responsibilities at Jardines and Hazel was busily preparing for the wedding. Richard and Georgina now became firm friends.

In some ways the girl was like Elizabeth. She was not so clever and she lacked Elizabeth's fanatical devotion to lost causes, but she was affectionate and warm and lively. Richard enjoyed spoiling her. Sometimes he'd invite her to the House; he found it a marvellous relief from the sterile battles with the Liberals to watch her demolishing a mound of strawberries and clotted cream as they sat together on the Terrace with the Thames beneath them and she prattled on about the latest crisis in the marriage preparations.

"Uncle Richard, why are they getting married from Eaton Place?" she'd ask, and Richard would tactfully explain that the Forrests' house was just not big enough and that Eaton Place was more convenient for guests than Wimbledon.

"And doesn't Hazel mind?"

"Why should she mind? It will be her home, so what difference does it make?"

"All the same, I'd mind, *dreadfully,*" said Georgina.

⁂

Richard was quite right. Hazel didn't mind at all. She was in love with James and what mattered was to survive the boring weeks until her wedding and then live happily ever after. There was something very touching and appealing now about the pair of them. Love suited Hazel. She bloomed, and for those early months of summer she became what she had never really been before—a beauty. James had changed too. His prickliness and discontent and moodiness had gone. He was gentle with his *fiancée,* and the two of them made such a happy pair that there was hardly any of the snobby gossip from Belgravia that might have been expected. Just the same, James very wisely kept his bride-to-be well out of range of the smart set he used to know—and particularly of that arch-bitch, Diana Russell.

The wedding took place in July, and it went off exactly as smart weddings invariably do (the pattern of these tribal celebrations doesn't, after all, permit a great deal of variety). It was perhaps a little smaller than it might have been had James been marrying someone from his own stratum of society. Nor were there any of the grander names that might have been expected on the guest list of a tip-top Society affair. But nobody disgraced himself. The Forrests and their few presentable relatives were safely swamped by Bellamys and James's sober friends from Jardines. At the reception, Prudence stood in for Marjorie. Richard drank too much and became distinctly sentimental. As the young couple were driven off to Victoria by Edward in the Rolls—they were to honeymoon in the South of France—it seemed impossible for life to go wrong for them. They had love, youth, good looks and money on their side. If any newly married couple seemed guaranteed a lifetime's happiness, it was James Bellamy and his bride.

In later years Richard would often ask himself just what went wrong and how much, if at all, he was to blame for what occurred. He had had his doubts from the start, but in the circumstances what could be have said? And for that matter, when had saying anything to anyone in love done any good? But it was a most depressing business, for him particularly, being half in love with Hazel on his own account and also feeling both sorry and responsible for his handsome, self-destructive son.

At least they had a year or so of some happiness together, and Richard's uneasy status as head of the household seemed to work. There were times, of course, when he required all his reserves of tact to avoid rows with James. For James was very much a Southwold—impulsive, arrogant, and none too sensitive of other people's feelings. But Hudson did a great deal to ensure that the prestige of "the master" was maintained at 165. The household went on very much as when Marjorie was still alive, as Richard and James both wished, and Hazel too turned out to be an excellent manager. Like Richard she was essentially a tactful person. She got on well with Hudson, played along with Mrs. Bridges' oddities, and acted as part mother, part elder sister to Georgina.

The first Christmas the newlyweds spent together in Eaton Place passed off splendidly, thanks in the main to Hazel, who had arranged it all with considerable flair. What might have been a time of gloomy memories turned out to be a great success. It was Hazel who had the huge tree put in the drawing room, carefully selected presents for the servants, planned the candles and the holly and the other decorations. Even with Marjorie the house had never looked more beautiful.

To complete the party, Georgina arrived home from hated boarding school on Christmas Eve. At first Richard hardly recognised her. Gone were the spots, the stammer and the pigtails; gone too the shyness and uncertainty he remembered.

"Georgina, my dear, you're beautiful," he said with involuntary admiration when he saw her.

"Thank you, Uncle Richard," she replied demurely.

Hazel's efficiency, her tact, her essential kindness were enough to make the household happy—but apparently not James, her husband. Slowly Richard noticed that James was tiring of her. He was becoming difficult and restless again. Part of the trouble was quite simply that he was still frustrated by his job and missed the old easy, carefree life of the army. Also the fact was that James had married Hazel when he had needed the sort of quiet support that she offered after the shock of Marjorie's death. Now that the shock was wearing off, so was his need for her. So their squabbles increased, with James shouting and Hazel sulking in response.

Richard had the sense to try to keep aloof from their troubles. He dined out more and more, surprised and flattered to discover how much in demand he was. He had a curiously platonic relationship with Prudence now. They would talk, dine, go out to the theatre together, but that was all. Richard knew quite well that she was eager for the relationship to go much further, but he had no wish to hurt the lady's feelings, still less to end up married. Just at the moment he was seeing quite enough of marriage at home, as James increasingly resumed the social life he had enjoyed before he married Hazel.

At first she gamely tried to join in, but these were not the sort of people she was used to, nor was this a world she understood. She was too serious and prim to fit in with the crowd of scatterbrained young socialites that James enjoyed. She disapproved of drinking, hated gambling, and there was one hideous weekend when she went off with James to hunt at Lord Newbury's estate. She had never hunted in her life. Her horse bolted, and James, being James, was typically far more concerned at the frightful loss of face than by the fact that Hazel herself had come within an ace of being killed. He was repentant afterwards, of course. He always was. But Richard, who for once did castigate his son, began to realise how deep a rift there was between them.

Throughout that year incidents kept occurring that shook the thin foundations of their marriage.

One night at Londonderry House Hazel thought Margot Asquith was the cloakroom lady and gave her sixpence and her evening coat. Instead of laughing, as Lady Asquith did, James was furious and made the scandal worse by insisting that he and Hazel leave. At another smart reception during the summer Hazel was introduced to Mrs. Keppel, and in making conversation asked that lady if all the stories that one heard about his late majesty and his lady friends were true. A few days later James distinctly heard two members of his club laughing about the *gaffe* behind his back.

"For God's sake, Hazel," he stormed at her that night, "I'll be forced to leave the club if you go on like this."

"But how should *I* know she was King Edward's mistress?" she wailed tearfully.

"There are some things *everybody* knows," he retorted.

Even then, sorry though he was for Hazel, Richard kept scrupulously apart from what was going on. He had matters of his own to attend to now. There was a brief fling that autumn with an Austrian countess; it meant little, lasted a mere fortnight, but did quite a lot to show him that he could still enjoy a pretty woman. Politics too began to take up more time than they had for many months. Richard had obviously lost out the year before when his old chief, Balfour, was replaced by Bonar Law at the head of the Conservatives. Once again he had been tempted to cross over to the Liberals and once again the old loyalty to the Southwold interests restrained him. Instead he had merely withdrawn somewhat from active politics.

Now all this was changing. In the autumn of 1913 the Prime Minister designated him as one of the Conservatives on a newly formed committee of defence. Richard accepted with alacrity and found himself with a brand-new role to play in Parliament. Once more he became one of his party's leading spokesmen on defence, and once more he found himself close to his old love, the Board of Admiralty, where Lord Randolph's son, young Winston Churchill, was now in charge. Richard admired his zest for politics, though not his apparent relish for a full-scale war.

During the debates in Parliament that winter Richard made it plain that he at any rate still passionately believed in peace, despite the dreadnought programme that was now in progress. But in the new year Richard's belief began to change. The more he learned of German preparations, the more convinced he became that war was looming. Even more of his time was spent away from home, as he travelled, talked to generals, and tried to warn the leaders of his party of the real threat of German armaments.

During Parliament's Easter recess of 1914 his work brought Richard an unexpected bonus when he and the Liberal Lord Ivor Dennison were sent on a fact-finding mission to the United States. They had a crowded programme, visiting dockyards and munition works and sailing with the North Atlantic fleet on spring manoeuvres.

They also had to go to Washington, which Richard wrote had "too much marble, too much bourbon whisky, and far too many politicians." Nevertheless, he managed to squeeze in a few days in New York and have his first reunion with his daughter since her marriage.

It was an uneasy meeting at first, for on the surface both of them had changed a great deal. Elizabeth was shocked at how much her father had aged since her mother's death: he was not only greyer and more lined than she remembered him, but more tired as well. Much of his old exuberance seemed to have gone. At the same time, Richard's first reaction was that this sleek, self-confident young matron with the beginnings of a New York intonation in her speech could not possibly be his daughter. There seemed no trace of the wild young woman he had loved, and who had caused him so much trouble, nor of the desperate girl who had once seemed scarred for life by a disastrous marriage and headlong love affairs. Everything round her breathed contentment now—the opulent apartment with its views of Central Park, the casual talk about the holiday they planned to take in Maine, her new and very solid-looking husband, Dana Wallace. She seemed to keep him firmly in his place and did almost all the talking, so much so that Richard felt that stolid Mr. Wallace was thoroughly in awe of Mrs. Wallace. He felt rather the same himself.

But not for long. After half an hour or so the old Elizabeth began to break through. She was eager for news of the family, anxious about James, curious about Hazel. She wanted to discuss the rumours that a European war was coming.

"And what are *you* doing to avoid it, Father?" she blurted out.

Richard shrugged and replied that the only thing that anyone could do was to make sure Britain was prepared.

"But how can you talk like that, you of all people?" Her anger and impatience were the same as she had always shown when she argued with him, and, as always, she had the uncanny knack of saying what he half believed himself. But now she had more than Richard to contend with.

"Elizabeth," her husband said, in his quiet and most reasonable courtroom voice. "Just be sensible. Your father doesn't want a war. None of us does. But with a warlike maniac like the German Kaiser arming his country to the teeth, just what else do you do?"

"Oh, I don't know," Elizabeth replied, frowning in the same way she always had when beaten in an argument. "But it must be possible to do something other than just go on arming all the time yourself and bleating that war's inevitable."

"Nobody's saying war's inevitable," said Richard though in his heart of hearts he was sure now that it was.

It settled nothing, of course, but the brief exchange showed Richard that in Mr. Dana Wallace, Elizabeth, thank God, had more than met her match. And after this the four days in New York passed all too quickly. Lucy, his granddaughter, now nearly five and mercifully looking exactly like her mother, was thrilled to see him, and for those four days Richard enjoyed the unaccustomed luxury of playing the doting grandfather. He took her to the zoo and Coney Island, and all four of them spent a golden afternoon aboard the pleasure boat that chugged and puffed its way around Manhattan Island.

Following as it did the anxieties and nightmarish imaginations of the past few months, this was the happiest day that Richard could remember. He knew that one member of his family, at least, had managed to survive and make a genuine success of life. As he looked at the newly matronly Elizabeth with her substantial husband and her dark-haired daughter, he felt a sudden surge of gratitude for America. Whatever horrors Europe had in store, Elizabeth and Lucy would be safe and happy here. But how he dreaded going back to England!

Two days later, when he sailed aboard the *Mauritania,* Elizabeth's farewell to him was, "Promise to be happy, Father!"

But there was not much happiness at Eaton Place when he returned there at the end of April. It was a glorious springtime. Outside in the park the chestnuts were coming into leaf, the lilac was in bloom. After the grey of winter London appeared reborn in all its style and splendour. Belgravia's long, cream-painted terraces and squares were like the centre of some northern capital, gleaming and sparkling in the pale spring sunlight. But 165 appeared a house of shadows. Richard's first night back there was no sign of James at dinner. Hudson was subdued, Edward distinctly surly, dinner was cold and nearly inedible. As for Hazel, Richard was shocked at what he saw. She seemed to have aged ten years in a few weeks. Her figure looked shapeless and her face was grey. As Richard held her and kissed her on the cheek he felt her trembling.

"Thank God you're back," she said.

He did his best throughout the meal to act as if everything was normal, even when Hazel said she didn't know when James was coming home.

"Oh, so he didn't get my telegram," he said.

"Of course he did," she replied.

"The same old James," he said and did his best to laugh it off. Edward was listening hard to every syllable. Whatever had gone wrong, there was no point in broadcasting it to the servants. They would learn soon enough.

"Yes," she replied. "The same old James. He doesn't change."

Most of the meal passed in silence. When he asked Hudson why his favourite claret, the Longueville '98, wasn't on the table, Hudson replied that Mr. James hadn't seen fit to reorder it. Richard nearly asked him why the devil he hadn't seen to it himself—but bit his tongue. Not until that penitential meal was over and he and Hazel were alone together in the drawing room did he burst out, "My dear girl, what on earth has been going on?"

"Nothing," she replied, shaking her head with painful emphasis. "Nothing at all!"

"Hazel, my dear. We know each other well enough. I beg you to tell me, whatever it is. Just what has happened?"

"I'm pregnant," she replied.

"But, Hazel, my dear, that's marvellous!" He went to kiss her but she pushed him wearily away.

"It isn't marvellous at all," she said. "It's horrible."

"Hazel," he reproved her. "It's only natural you should get depressed occasionally. I remember Marjorie was just the same when she was having James. It's all that morning sickness and, er, all the other things. You must see Dr. Bingley first thing in the morning."

"No" she said flatly, "it's not morning sickness, nor anything the doctor can do much about."

"What is it then?" said Richard, genuinely puzzled.

"I don't want it. I don't want to have the baby of a man that I despise." She spoke in a voice so calm and yet so helpless that it left nothing further to be said.

Richard tried to make her talk, but all she would add was, "I don't know what to do, and I don't much care."

He took her hand and they sat in silence for a while. Then she went off to bed.

Richard decided he must wait up for James, however late he came in. He tried reading in the library but nodded off. The small gilt library clock was striking three when he was wakened by a noise from downstairs. He stumbled to his feet and opened the door.

"James, is that you?" he whispered loudly.

"Whozat?" came a slurred voice from the dimness of the hall.

"It's Father. I'm here, James. Got back this afternoon. How are you, my boy?"

"Oh!" said the voice. A hiccough followed and then James came swaying up the stairs, his tie askew, an idiotic grin on his face.

"How d'you do, Father? Welcome back to the lion's den."

Richard had always had a puritanical dislike of drunks, but he managed to restrain his temper and somehow got James safely seated in the library.

"What on earth's been going on while I've been away?" he asked firmly.

His son grinned owlishly and put his fingers to his lips. "Shh, Father. You'll wake the servants. Old Hudson will be cross."

"James, pull yourself together. I must know what has happened."

"Oh, I see, Father," said James mysteriously. "Little Hazel has been sobbing on your shoulder, telling you all her troubles. But then she always was very fond of you, wasn't she, Father? You can't fool me."

"James, don't talk such utter rubbish. I want the truth."

"All very simple really. My wife doesn't want to have to bear any child. Have you ever heard of such a thing before? Doesn't want my baby, Father."

James was becoming maudlin now but Richard persisted. "Why not? She must have a reason."

"Jealousy," said James in a dramatic voice. "Sheer unadulterated jealousy. If I had known just now how jealous little Hazel was I'd not have married her."

"That's neither here nor there. You are married to her and she is having your child. Why is she so upset?"

"I tell you, Father. Jealousy. A little romp I had with old Diana. Such a good sport, Diana. She's who I should have married. Game for anything."

"You mean that having made Hazel pregnant, you then started an affair with Diana Newbury?"

James grinned knowingly. "That's it, Father. Hot stuff, Diana. Poor old Hazel never was particularly keen on it, you know. That's why I still can't really understand why she got so worked up about it when she found out."

For a moment Richard stared at him, silent with disbelief. Then he said, as calmly as he could, "Get to bed, James. You're drunk and you disgust me."

Richard was so tired that night that he fell asleep as soon as he got to bed, and next morning he over-slept, so he was spared James at breakfast. But strange to say, Richard's return to 165 did make a difference in the atmosphere that day.

"Glad you're back, sir." said Hudson. "More like old times again." Richard had brought him back some interesting American cigars, but he knew that wasn't what Hudson meant, and with Hudson happier, the entire house seemed suddenly to revive.

Richard had a fairly crowded day, which included a long visit to the Admiralty, where the First Lord was eager to hear what Richard thought of the U.S. Atlantic Fleet, and to the Foreign Office, where Lord Curzon seemed delighted with his report on the state of American sentiment for Britain.

"Excellent to know that we will have some friends on the other side of the Atlantic, Bellamy," said Lord Curzon in that superior way he had, "but I am sanguine that this talk of war is much exaggerated."

Because of his official business, Richard had no chance of talking privately to Hazel during the day, but that night at dinner he saw that she had made an effort. She looked healthier and prettier, and Richard was relieved to see that Mrs. Bridges had more than made amends for the fiasco of the night before. James was a shade too hearty to be true—and this made Hazel nervous—but they were now at least making an attempt to keep up appearances, and that was something. Richard wondered just how much of their conversation of the night before James could remember.

To start with, Richard did most of the talking—which meant America and all the news of Lucy and Elizabeth.

Then in his boyish way James suddenly announced, "Hazel! Great news for you!"

"Oh?" she said, trying hard to sound excited but fooling no one. "And what could that be, James?"

"My years of serfdom have finally paid off. The managing director actually took me out to lunch today. Said various nice things about me, then said he wanted me to take charge of—guess what?"

Hazel and Richard shook their heads.

"The Bombay office. And a directorship as well. India again. Don't you think that's unbelievable?"

"Unbelievable," said Hazel nervously. "When?"

"Not for about a year. They say that they need time to groom me for the part. It's a splendid opportunity."

"Congratulations, James!" said Richard, although he was already wondering what would happen to 165.

"Yes, congratulations," Hazel echoed.

"You don't sound particularly enthusiastic," James replied.

"Of course I am," she answered quickly. "How long will you be gone?"

"Two years at least. But good heavens, Hazel, you don't honestly believe I'd leave you here. You'll come too, and the baby. Naturally. You'll love it there. The wife of the head of Jardines in Bombay really counts for something, I can tell you. Fine house, a carriage, all the servants you want . . ." His voice trailed off, for Hazel was emphatically shaking her head.

"What d'you mean, Hazel?" he asked, harshly now.

"I'm sorry—but I couldn't. It's no use pretending. I couldn't, I couldn't face it."

"And if I decide to go alone?'
"It will be your decision."
"You realise what this will mean for us?" he said slowly.
Hazel nodded.

Richard did his best to smooth things over during the weeks that followed. How much good he did is anybody's guess. Certainly he talked a lot—to Hazel and to James—preaching the virtues of such qualities as common sense and tolerance and seeing the other person's point of view.

To Hazel he spoke of the way her pregnancy had obviously upset her. James was an immature and irresponsible young fool. Of course he was. But at heart he wasn't really bad, and once they had the baby everything would seem quite different. That much he could promise her quite definitely. And to James he spoke about the way he'd hurt her female pride by his infidelity with Diana. He must realise how badly he'd behaved, and that Hazel's attitude to India was understandable. It was her way of getting her revenge. Once the baby came, things would seem quite different. That much he promised *him* quite definitely.

With all these promises and all this good advice—and because both James and Hazel in their very different ways both loved him and respected him—Richard succeeded in persuading them to avoid an open break. Indeed, the two of them did actually show signs of re-establishing a little of their old affection for each other, especially now that Hazel was becoming very large and touchingly ungainly with her child. James, for the first time, seemed excited by the prospect of becoming a proud father. Yes, everything could still have worked out happily, but for the heat that summer and the arrival of Georgina.

The two arrived at Eaton Place almost simultaneously. Right at the beginning of that blazing hot July, there was suddenly Georgina home from school, but a transformed Georgina, *svelte,* golden-skinned, bright-eyed—a raving beauty. Almost inevitably her presence upset the precarious equilibrium of 165.

Already it was showing signs of faltering. For several weeks now Richard had been having arguments with James about the imminence of war. James pooh-poohed the possibility. He knew Von Bolenstein, the Kaiser's military attaché: "Capital fellow and a splendid shot.

Might almost be an Englishman. He has assured me as a gentleman that all this talk of war is sheerest nonsense."

Richard replied that the Kaiser was no gentleman, and that now that he had finished widening the Kiel Canal so that his battleships could sail unhindered to the North Sea, everything was ready for a war.

"It'll be August, mark my words," Richard said soberly. "That's when the latest German conscripts will be in the regiments. That's when it will start."

"But, Father," James would say: "Von Bolenstein assures me that the Germans' natural enemy is Russia. If there's to be a war it will be in the East."

Hazel was showing signs of irritation too. The heat, the talk of war, increased her depression.

"Is India as hot as this?" she asked wearily. And with his usual lack of tact he replied, "Oh, this is nothing to Bombay when it gets really warm. But you'll get used to it. Surprising how one does."

Georgina, on the other hand, revelled in the heat. She spent these baking summer days riding or on the river with her friends until she looked like an Indian herself. Soon it was obvious that James could not keep his eyes off her. He should have realised, of course, the dangerous game that he was playing, but when Richard tried to warn him he replied furiously, "Father, you must be mad! You're like some prurient old spinster. Of course Georgina's pretty. Damned pretty. But if you think I'd ever touch her! To me she's just a—just a—well, a sister."

"But she's not your sister, James," Richard said reasonably. "She's a very beautiful and susceptible young girl. Of course you'd not do anything, but that's not the point."

"What is the point then, Father? Let's get this dirty-minded business straight."

"Simply that I'm worried about Hazel. In her present state she's quite likely to misunderstand things. Believe me, James, pregnant women do. She's not unusual in this. And she naturally feels vulnerable and at a disadvantage with a girl as pretty as Georgina. Just be careful, James. I don't want Hazel hurt."

"Anyone would think that's all that matters."

"For these next few weeks I rather think it is."

But Richard's warning did no good, with Georgina seeming to

become prettier every day and James now apparently incapable of not playing up to her. Barely a week had passed after Richard's warning before the trouble he had feared occurred. Georgina had been invited to a party at the Allministers' in Grosvenor Square. Edward was having trouble with the Rolls so James quite casually volunteered to collect her in his *coupé*. Richard was old-fashioned about not having his ward brought home by young men in taxi cabs, and without thinking instantly agreed. Hazel said nothing.

James was supposed to pick Georgina up at midnight, but the party went on longer. James stayed himself, and the upshot was that he and Georgina, both in highest party spirits, arrived back at Eaton Place at two in the morning. Hazel was up and waiting for them. James tried to laugh it off.

"Ah, Hazel. Just what d'you think you're doing up at this time of night?"

Georgina, a little bit tipsy, giggled. At that, Hazel, quivering with fury, raised her hand to strike the girl, but James caught her arm and held her.

"Hazel! For God's sake, Hazel! What on earth . . . ?"

"Just tell that simpering young slut of yours to keep away from you," she panted. Her splendid hair had come undone, her eyes were bright with fury. Georgina backed away and began to cry. At this James's own quick temper flared up dangerously.

"I've had enough!" he shouted. "First Father and now you. You don't seem capable of seeing two people of different sexes without thinking of them in bed together."

Whilst he was saying this Hazel was struggling to free herself and James, enraged, began shaking her.

"Just let me go," she muttered.

"Not until you come to your senses and apologise to Georgina for what you've said!" he shouted.

"Never!" she shouted back. "Never, never, never!"

Luckily at this point the landing light went on.

"James. Would you mind explaining what is happening? You must have woken the whole household with your noise."

It was Richard in his dressing gown, a very angry Richard whose appearance brought a touch of sanity to the proceedings.

"Hazel and I were having a slight discussion, Father," James said sheepishly. "I'm sorry if we woke you."

"And so you should be. And as for Hazel, what you think you're doing keeping her up at this time of the night I hesitate to think. Get her to bed at once. You too, Georgina. And not another squeak from any of you. James, we'll discuss this in the morning."

Discuss it they did, at great length. And at the end of it a sort of understanding was patched up. Hazel apologised to Georgina and James to Hazel. But apologies were not enough to save the baby. Hazel did her best to persuade everyone that she had strained herself dragging an old trunk from the attic, but clearly it was the shock of that ferocious argument that brought on her bleeding the next afternoon. The doctor tried to save the child, but as he told Richard, Hazel seemed to have no will at all to bear it.

"Perhaps it's just as well," Richard said sadly. "I can't think it would have had much of a life between two parents who detested one another."

But "detested" was too strong a word after all. Now, at this point of absolute despair, some strange residue of love appeared to reassert itself. Hazel wanted only James to be with her, and he was far more tender than he had been since they were courting.

"What went wrong with us?" she asked a few days after the catastrophe.

He looked at her and smiled. "I think we were both a little immature, but we can start again. At least we're young enough for that."

"And there's India too," she said. "If you still want me. I quite like the idea of getting away from Eaton Place."

He laughed gently then and shook his head.

"No, somehow I don't think that we'll be getting out to India. Not yet awhile, at any rate. It looks as if Father could be right. The Kaiser's troops are mobilising as he said they would, and just this morning I got a note from the War Office to hold myself in readiness."

"For what?" she asked.

"For war." He smiled and kissed her softly on the cheek. "It looks as though we'll need each other," he said gently.

"Oh, James, my love, I'm so afraid," she said.

1914-18

16. *A House at War*

SHORTLY AFTER TEN A.M. ON THE FOURTH OF AUGUST, 1914, AN ALL BUT fatal blow was struck against that prosperous and peaceful world of which Eaton Place was so privileged a part. His Majesty King George the Fifth, attended by two courtiers and a solitary minister of state, issued a royal proclamation against his German cousin in Berlin. Within the hour the Empire had entered the cruellest war in human history.

But, strange to say, that night at 165 there seemed no trace of apprehension in the air. Rather the reverse. Mrs. Bridges had excelled herself. In keeping with the weather she had served ice-cold cucumber soup, superbly poached cold salmon—sent down the day before from Speyside by Sir Geoffrey Dillon—and a delicious summer pudding. At Hudson's suggestion they drank a fragrant Lafaurie-Peyraguey. (Richard had wanted to taste some Schloss Johannisberg, but, as Hudson rightly pointed out, it was hardly fitting to consume a Rhine wine at a time like this.) Faced with such splendid food, and with all the windows open to a warm summer evening, it was hard for the Bellamys to avoid a certain sense of celebration. Everyone seemed to consider this an occasion to remember, but an occasion of adventure rather than one of doom.

James was in uniform, and although it was all but five years since he last put it on, it fitted perfectly.

"Not bad, eh, Hudson?" he had said as he tried it on before the long glass in his dressing room. "No sign yet of middle-age spread?"

"Indeed no, sir. A perfect fit. What does it feel like to be wearing it again?"

"Wonderful, Hudson. I feel ten years younger."

And so he looked as he sat opposite Richard at dinner.

"You know what, Father?" he said as he drained his glass. "The sergeant-major at Knightsbridge this afternoon actually remembered me. Chap called Wilkins. Used to be a corporal in my day. As he saluted he said, 'Glad to have you back, sir'! Pretty good, eh, remembering like that? Makes one feel at home."

"Did anybody say how long before you go?" asked Hazel brightly. She and her husband had discussed it all quite sensibly and had concluded that after the nightmare of the last ten weeks some sort of change was what they needed. With James so plainly thrilled to be back with his beloved regiment, she was determined she would do her best not to discourage him.

"Oh, nobody will let on. All this security, you know. Keep the Kaiser guessing. But it can't be long. Off to help little Belgium, I suppose. It ought to be an interesting scrap, then home for Christmas."

"You think that it will take that long?" asked Prudence. (Tiresome though Richard found her these days, she *was* James's godmother, and he had felt it appropriate to ask her round for what might well be James's last night at home for quite some time.)

James put on an old campaigner's look before replying, "Well, Aunt Pru, it all depends upon the French. Kitchener says—and I agree with him—that the present British army is the finest in the world, bar none. Thanks to Brother Boer, we've had a chance to learn our lessons in South Africa, so there's no reason why we shouldn't hamstring the German army out in Flanders and then sweep our way along the Rhine. No excuse if we're not in Berlin by the autumn."

"Exactly what a general friend of mine was saying just this afternoon," said Prudence. "Thank God for Kitchener! Don't you agree, Richard?"

"I'm more inclined to say 'Thank God for the Royal Navy!' " Richard replied, smiling at James. "And I can't say I feel too happy fighting a European war under this present lot of Liberals. Asquith's a drunk, Grey's a nonentity. Only young Winston seems to have the faintest idea of what it's all about, and he's too reckless."

Prudence was up in arms at once. "Richard, how could you start preaching party politics at such a time? Everybody knows that Kitchener's a genius."

"Let's hope so," Richard said, still smiling and filling James's glass.

"And that our brave lads are off to fight for everything that you and I believe in, Richard—"

Richard raised an eyebrow. "Everything? Prudence, come now."

"Well, everything that matters. I think it's very wrong of you to talk like that. Especially in front of James."

James laughed at this. "Come now, Aunt Pru. Surely I'm old enough to take anything that Father says with a hefty pinch of salt. And anyhow, perhaps he's right. I'm none too keen on any of this present gang of politicians myself. All I know is that, man for man, there's no one in the world to beat the British Tommy, and that I'm proud to be going into battle with him."

"You know," Georgina said, "this afternoon there were crowds outside Buckingham Palace, and they were cheering all the ministers as they drove out through the gates. I saw them. It was really quite exciting."

"There, you see, Richard?" Prudence said. "Not everybody thinks like you."

Two days later, Captain Bellamy of the Royal Life Guards left for France. Hazel was still trying to be sensible, but once his bags were packed and his military trunk was standing in the hall, her painfully maintained façade of calm and common sense collapsed. She was still far from strong after the miscarriage, so he refused to let her see him off from Waterloo. Instead they said their farewells in the privacy of her own sitting room. As he strode in, resplendent in his polished brass and gleaming leather, it was a different James Bellamy from the unsatisfactory husband she had been fighting against for so many months. She knew all his faults—none better—but when she saw him standing there and knew that he was leaving, she felt her heart turn over with unhappiness.

"Oh, James, my dearest James," she cried and clung to him. "However will I manage when you've gone?"

"Now, now," he said, lifting her face and slowly stroking back her hair. "You know quite well that you'll be better off without me—for just a while at least."

"I won't," she sobbed. "I won't, I won't."

"Oh, yes, you will. After the way I've treated you. I apologise, my love. I'm truly sorry. When I return, things will be very different."

"I don't care what you do, my darling James. Only promise you'll come back."

"Oh, I'll be back all right. No one gets rid of me as easily as that. And, Hazel—"

Her tears had stopped, but she was gazing up at him with a small, worried frown.

"Yes?" she whispered.

"When I do come back, we'll start again. You understand. No more failures, no more sadnesses."

She nodded mutely, then burst out, "Oh, James, I wish I hadn't lost the baby!"

Richard had said that he would be taking James to Waterloo in the Rolls.

"Off to the war in style, eh, Father?" he replied. "I only hope the return journey will be as comfortable."

After his emotional farewell to Hazel, James found that he was dreading any further scenes, but fortunately there were none as they left the house. Georgina's eyes were very bright, but she knew how much James detested tearful women and she managed to make him promise to write regularly without disgracing herself by crying.

"Make sure you wrap up warm of nights and always have a good cooked breakfast," shouted Mrs. Bridges.

"God's speed, and you can count on all of us to keep the home fires burning, sir," cried Hudson, as the stately car drew off with Edward at the wheel. For James it was suddenly like going back to school with Father—except that now he was some sort of hero, which he had never been when he went off to Eton.

When they reached Waterloo their farewells were of necessity quite brief. Most of the regiment was already drawn up by the platform, the troop train in, the men at ease but waiting to be off. James was suddenly very much the regular officer as he stepped from the car and shook hands with Richard.

"Goodbye, old boy, take care," said Richard.

"'Bye, Father. Look after Hazel for me while I'm gone."

Richard nodded briskly. Already N.C.O.s were bawling out places for the train. A porter was helping Edward with the Captain's baggage. James, poker-faced, saluted, then strode hurriedly away. Richard took one last look at the tall young officer marching off, very erect, down the long platform: as the Rolls drew away, he found himself wondering if he would ever see him again.

For the next few weeks the story of James's life was the story of the "contemptible little British Army" that fills the pages of the wartime history books: arrival that same afternoon at Calais, two days at base camp with his men, entrainment on to Amiens, then up to Maubeuge on the Belgian frontier; and there they waited, none too certain when or how the enemy would come, but thoroughly determined to defeat him when he did.

James was extremely busy. As a Sandhurst-trained officer, he was placed second in command of a squadron of eighty-seven men, all of them regulars and some of them wearing the red-and-orange ribbon of the South Africa campaign. From the beginning James was popular. He knew his job, took good care of his men, and at this stage was still so delighted to be suddenly transported from his office in the City that his high spirits quite charmed everyone. He was quartered, along with four other officers, in a deserted farmhouse by a river; his first night there he wrote a letter to Hazel. As letters go, it was short and uninformative to a degree, partly because all mail was censored and partly because he'd had barely six hours' sleep during the previous seventy-two, but when it arrived at Eaton Place some four days later it brought more happiness than the highest flights of literature. It had no date and no address and was scrawled in pencil on a page torn from a field service pad:

My Dearest Hazel,

I am fine but missing you—and hope you are the same. Everyone here in very best of spirits. A finer bunch of chaps it would be hard to find. Will soon be putting the Boche back where he belongs, then home for Christmas. My love to Father and tell Mrs. Bridges I could do with some of her baked jam roll.

Your loving husband,
James

Even while James was writing this, the grey-clad troops of von Kluck's First Army were advancing almost unopposed through the flat green countryside of south-west Belgium, and swinging down the coast in a attempt to outflank the whole Allied line. The French army, under Joffre, were on the British right; and even now were wisely getting ready to fall back on their main defence positions on the river Marne. But James, of course, knew none of this—and for that matter, the British general in command, Sir John Denton Pinkstone French, a cavalryman with a red face and an optimistic nature, was equally ignorant. His strategy was one that James endorsed: "to find the enemy then hit him for six." And in that third, still sunny week of August, Captain James Bellamy and some six thousand other British regulars began to carry out their general's somewhat sporting orders.

James and his squadron were moving up towards the little town of Mons when he heard the first straggling bursts of rifle fire ahead of him. As he told Richard later, "My first thought was that some of our chaps were trying out a spot of target practice, especially when it stopped as suddenly as it started." Then, in the lull that afternoon, the rumours started trickling back. It seemed that an advance patrol had fired on a troop of German cavalry. Several of the Germans had been captured and from them somewhat startled intelligence officers began to learn the truth. The British had blundered straight into the path of von Kluck's advancing army. They were outnumbered three to one. Two days later James and his squadron of Guardsmen found themselves in the very thick of the Battle of Mons.

❧ ☙

It is ironic that while this was going on the war's ill wind was blowing Richard a modicum of good. He was emphatically the master once again at 165, and his life there was no longer plagued with worries about James and Hazel's marriage. Indeed, after the shocks of her miscarriage and James's departure Hazel had pulled herself together almost as a patriotic duty. Richard's tenure of the house was all but guaranteed as well, at least as long as the hostilities persisted. While the war lasted there was no chance at all of James and Hazel going off to India and so closing down the house in Eaton Place. Instead, Richard and the entire household felt it their bounden duty to keep the house functioning as cheerfully as possible for James's sake. And this, with some efficiency, they did.

"Hudson, I feel we should keep back the last six bottles of the Krug '98 for Christmas when Captain James returns," said Richard, and Hudson fully agreed.

Hazel, in her turn, took more trouble than she had for some time in making sure that everything at 165 was kept immaculate; again for James, whose sepia-coloured photograph surveyed the drawing room from a heavy silver frame.

His name was invoked again by Hazel when she suggested that 165 should "do its bit" by taking in eight war refugees from Belgium. Only when she said, "James would expect it of us," did Richard finally agree (and very much regretted it, although the unhappy Belgians did not stay for long).

Georgina was the only one at 165 who could complain that autumn that the war had caused her hardship. After her time at boarding school she had been looking forward to a year "finishing" in Switzerland. This was impossible now, and a rebellious Georgina had to make do with a finishing school at Queen Anne's Gate. But once again the war was the ideal excuse. "How can you possibly complain, Georgina," Richard said, "when you just think what James is having to endure?"

Needless to say, the servants all believed they had an almost sacred duty now to work as hard and conscientiously as possible "to do our bit for Captain James while he is fighting over there," as Mrs. Bridges put it somewhat fulsomely to Rose. Rose, who since the departure of her under-housemaid was doing almost twice as much work (of course, for no extra pay), wearily agreed. And when Edward mentioned fairly casually to Hudson that it was several years since any of the staff had had a rise, he almost brought the wrath of God about his ears.

"I should have thought it was our privilege as servants, Edward, to have this chance to bear some small self-sacrifice without complaint." Edward retired, squashed, and every night before they ate, the servants, led by Hudson, prayed that the God of Battles would simultaneously "smite the enemy, protect Captain James, and help us do our duty."

So, thanks to Hudson, God, and patriotism, Richard could face that first autumn of the war with 165 running more smoothly than it had since Marjorie died. But he was far from happy. Part of the trouble was undoubtedly the absence of a woman from his life. True there was Hazel, but since James had left she kept herself uncomfortably aloof. It was her patriotic duty now to be in love with the departed hero, so there was nothing like the closeness there had been before; and Richard, an uxorious man, needed a warm, sympathetic woman to come home to.

Another source of real frustration was his feeling that at this crisis in his nation's history he, Richard Bellamy, M.P., ought to be doing something. He wasn't all too certain what. That in itself was one of his problems. At fifty-seven he was too old to fight, but he applied to his old crony, Admiral Hall, to see if he could be of any use to Naval Intelligence. They lunched together at the admiral's club, and although the pink-faced little man with the great eyebrows was now one of the busiest and certainly the most important men in Whitehall, he hadn't lost his quirky sense of humour.

"Work for *me,* Richard? Oh, that's a good one! Very good indeed."

"But why not, Adam? I'm quite serious."

The sharp little sailor screwed up his eyes and nodded. "Just ask yourself, Richard, what could you do?"

"Well, anything you asked me to. I'm not exactly ignorant of naval matters."

"No, you're not. But you're a politician, Richard my friend. The sort of chaps I need are specialists—coding experts, navigation men, gunnery officers."

"I could learn."

The admiral shook his cropped grey head. "We haven't time to teach you, I'm afraid." Then, seeing how crestfallen Richard looked, he added kindly, "Richard, my dear old thing, you must be realistic. War is a job for young men and for specialists. Your specialty's politics. That's where you belong and nowhere else. Just stick to that."

Easier said than done. With war, the game of politics had ceased. Churchill, like some old-style buccaneer, was running the war at sea now from the Admiralty, whilst the great Kitchener, moustache and all, was the invulnerable war lord with direct responsibility to Asquith for the campaign in France. Opposition M.P.s—even when as well informed as Richard Bellamy—were not required.

But, as we know, it is the nature of political animals to long for power. Richard was no exception. He disliked Asquith, mistrusted what he called "that gang of mediocrities around him," and as the war began in earnest, Richard, along with several of his front-bench opposition colleagues in the House, began to plan in earnest to dislodge him.

❧ ❧

Like every soldier, James had had secret nightmares over how he would behave in the thick of battle. Would he disgrace his comrades? Would his nerve fail him at some crucial time? He need not have worried. From that first moment when he heard the gunfire crackling across the morning air of Mons, he recognised that he was in his rightful element at last. He was a soldier. This was something he had trained for, and it was just as well he had, for Mons was a terrifying baptism of fire for anyone

At first James's squadron was in reserve, so that during the first days fighting rumbled on in front of them with nothing but the gunfire and the smoke of battle and the long lines of wounded to give much hint of what was happening. At this stage, everybody's optimism was such that the main feeling in the squadron was fear that the fighting would be over before they had their chance for what their commander called "a good hard crack at Fritz."

James felt this more than anyone, but his colonel, a slow-spoken giant of a man who had ridden at Omdurman in '98, counselled patience.

"Jerry'll be out there for quite some time yet. Your chance will come soon enough, young Bellamy."

"But surely, sir, our cavalry will soon be breaking through and we will simply have to follow up and guard the prisoners. This is the offensive General French has planned for."

"You think so?" said the colonel drily, stroking his thin moustache. "I've an idea that our general's been a shade too hopeful this time, Bellamy."

"What do you mean, sir?"

The colonel shrugged his massive shoulders. "From the sound of things, I'd say the opposition's far stronger than he'd reckoned. It doesn't sound to me as if we've made our precious breakthrough. More like it someone's breaking us."

And so it proved. All afternoon the sound of firing steadily increased. Far away on the right the town was burning and a thick pall of smoke was drifting back towards the British lines. To start with all the firing seemed to come from rifles and machine-guns, but just before dusk artillery joined in—German artillery.

James and his squadron moved up soon after midnight. Morale was high, for there was still the firm belief that this was the start of the offensive that would bring them home by Christmas. But in their orders there was no mention of an advance, only of digging in and holding their section of the line. When dawn came James saw a scene of carnage—the shattered and abandoned town, dead British soldiers lying where they had fallen the day before, and out ahead of them the enemy.

Before the sun was up the enemy artillery had started again. The shells were falling half a mile ahead of them, and James and his men were waiting for the promised British field artillery to answer back. It never did. But just before eight o'clock the first grey wave of German infantry appeared, and hell broke loose. This was the chance the well-trained British infantry had waited for. Each marksman worked like an automaton—indeed, the British rate of rifle-fire was such that the Germans thought that they were up against machine-guns—and by eight-twenty the first enemy attack had failed. But throughout that morning the attacks renewed—again and yet again—and with each attack the British lines were thinned and fresh men scurried in to take the dead men's places.

"Still no news of James?" asked Geoffrey Dillon.

Richard shook his head.

"Ah well," said Dillon, making his best attempt at human sympathy, "no news is good news, I suppose."

Richard nodded. "I suppose so," he said wretchedly. "Of course one reads those ghastly casualty reports each day. Over twelve hundred dead already and the retreat still going on. Just tell me, Geoffrey, what does our blithering British high command think it's up to? Throwing away our finest troops like this—not even knowing that von Kluck was there—and all to no earthly purpose!"

"Extraordinarily heroic, though, Richard. Six regiments holding up a German army corps for three whole days and giving our gallant allies time to scuttle back in safety to the Marne."

"Exactly, Geoffrey. The usual British story, sheer incompetence at the top and heroism from the men who do the fighting. You know, if any harm has come to James, I'll not rest until Sir John French has been court-martialled for wantonly hazarding the lives of the troops in his command. As for Asquith . . ."

"Yes, Richard. What about Asquith?"

"The sooner he's out and we've a government that really knows how to fight this wretched war, the better."

"Absolutely, Richard. On that I think that we're agreed."

But James was safe. In mid-September Hazel heard from him. After Mons he and his regiment had fought their way back south towards the Allied lines. It was a heroic retreat but one thing it destroyed forever was the British dream of "Home for Christmas." As autumn turned to winter British troops were starting to dig in for what looked like being a long, hard-fought war. Mile on mile of barbed wire was going up through northern France, and James and his company advanced into Flanders and dug in before the little town of Ypres. Throughout October and November James somehow managed to survive the six weeks' slaughter that was later known as the First Battle of Ypres. Tired, battle-stained, and half frozen, he spent that Christmas in the trenches. Instead of Mrs. Bridges' cooking and his father's best champagne, he dined off bully beef washed down with army tea and capped with a special Christmas tot of army rum. That was the one day when the barrage ceased, and on Christmas night he heard the British and the German troops singing their Christmas carols back and forth across the silent wastes of no man's land.

It would have pleased him had he known that at that moment, in far-off Belgravia, as his wife, his father, Georgina, Prudence Fairfax, and the Dillons settled to *their* Christmas dinner, he was foremost in their thoughts.

"And what's the latest news of James?" Prudence asked before her lips had even touched her turkey.

"Oh, he seems wonderful," Hazel replied. "I heard from him for Christmas and he seemed in the very best of spirits."

She didn't add that she was worried by the recent change in his letters. They were no longer full of all the optimistic chat of the first few weeks of war. Instead they now all seemed much the same; he was missing her, he loved her, he was "managing all right," his men were "the finest bunch of warriors a man could wish to serve with."

"Pity he didn't land a spot of Christmas leave," said Dillon tactlessly.

"Oh, but he did," said Hazel quickly. "He turned it down, though, because he said his duty was to stay with his men. One of the other officers with a family came instead."

"How very wonderful your husband is, my dear," said Lady Dillon. "You must be so very proud of him."

A big, fat, gushing woman with a heart of gold, Lady Dillon was as different from her husband as one human being can be from another. Hazel and Georgina liked her, which was as well, since the Dillons had been increasingly making their presence felt at Eaton Place and a strange friendship seemed to have developed between the two archenemies, Richard and Sir Geoffrey. This was the first time that the Dillons had shared such a family affair; and with dinner over, as the two men sipped their port before they joined the ladies, they had quite clearly reached a state of mutual understanding.

"Come now, Geoffrey," Richard was saying. "You know more about the inner workings of the Party than any man alive. What's going on?"

Dillon smiled with bland self-satisfaction. "Richard, you flatter me," he said.

"Not flattery at all. You know it's true. But that's not the point. The time has obviously come to act. We can't allow this muddle and this slaughter to go on. We're paying for Asquith and Kitchener and the whole gang of them in young men's lives. Perhaps I feel all this as strongly as I do because of James, but the time has clearly come to get a coalition of the best brains in the country to run this war. There's no other way."

Dillon drained his port appreciatively. "I quite agree, and so do a lot of others. But as you realise there are difficulties."

"You mean because Bonar Law, our gallant leader of the opposition, is too spineless to speak out."

Dillon smiled and peered over his spectacles at Richard. "Bonar's a wise old owl. He knows how easy it would be for opinion to turn against us, so he bides his time."

"Meanwhile thousands of men are getting slaughtered every day because of conceited generals and drunken politicians."

"Strong words, Richard."

"I mean every one of them."

There was a brief silence, broken only by the sound of Geoffrey Dillon snipping the end off his cigar. "If you are really serious, there is one thing you *could* do," he said slowly.

"Anything, Geoffrey, if it would sink this government."

"Write for Northcliffe."

"You must be mad."

"I'm utterly in earnest. How else can we get the facts across? You'll never get the chance to tell the truth in Parliament, but Northcliffe's the sworn enemy of Asquith. Just state your case, and you could get that coalition quicker than you think."

"Geoffrey," said Richard cannily, "I think you know a good deal more than you're letting on."

"I generally do," said Dillon. "But there's one thing that I'm quite sure of. You are the one man who could do this properly. You're not a cheap journalist from the gutter press. You're an ex-minister who's specialised in matters of defence. You know the facts and feel powerfully about them. Think it over, Richard. This could be the most important thing you've ever done."

Richard pondered. "I'll think about it," he said finally. "But from the start, there's one absolute condition I must insist on. My name must not appear. For James's sake, if for none other."

Dillon nodded. "Pity, Richard, but I understand. Now shall we join the ladies?"

That spring saw two offensives. In France, the British General Staff began to pour its new reserves of men into the two-mile-wide death trap that formed the gruesome setting for the so-called Second Battle of Ypres. And in London, Alfred Harmsworth, Baron Northcliffe, proprietor of the *Times* and the *Daily Mail* and probably the most influential newspaperman in history, began his offensive against the Asquith government. Both battles raged with great ferocity.

At Ypres, James Bellamy, still a mere captain, but because of losses now in command of a squadron, fought with desperate gallantry. In the abortive storming of the ridge, his was the one original squadron which reached and held its full objective. They stayed there two days and nights against the full power of the German army. When they were ordered to retreat before a German poison gas attack, James led back the remains of his squadron. There were nine of them. In divisional despatches James was recommended for the Victoria Cross.

In London, Richard Bellamy had launched his attack upon the government in the *Daily Mail,* but his timing was a good deal better than the British General Staff's. He had prepared his articles with skill and his facts were virtually unanswerable. He exposed the muddles in the High Command, the shortages of ammunition, and the defects in the Allied strategy just at the moment when the scandal of the lack of shells at Ypres was breaking. The evident authority with which he wrote undoubtedly increased the popular demand for a new coalition government to pursue the war with skill and vigour. Not unnaturally, Richard hoped that he would find his place within it.

It was the end of April when James came home on leave. He was exhausted, very much on edge, and still suffering from the effects of German poison gas. But no one at Eaton Place really appreciated this. They saw a moody, sullen, bitter man in place of the high-spirited young officer who had gone off to war just eight months earlier, and they wondered miserably what had happened.

Hazel inevitably bore the brunt and there was little she could do for him. Suddenly he seemed to have no hope, no aim in life, and no desire for anything—not even love. His one obsession now was with the Front and with his comrades who were in the fighting. His second night at home he awoke shouting that the Boches were coming. She did her best to calm him.

"Darling, you're back in London. You're away from it," she said. But he would not be comforted.

"You don't understand," he said. "There's no escape. When you have seen what I have it's with you night and day."

Then he began to shake. She held him until he slipped off into troubled sleep.

Richard never discovered how his name got out as the author of the Northcliffe articles. He always suspected Geoffrey Dillon; there was no proof, but it would have been in character. At any rate, by the time the damage had been done it scarcely mattered.

Certainly the rumours were around Westminster by the time James came home on leave, and as a result the name Bellamy was not the best loved among the senior officials in the War Office. It was one of these, an elderly, officious man, who noticed that a Captain Bellamy was being recommended for a V.C. He stopped it just in time.

"Thank God I spotted it," he said to another senior official. "The

Minister would never have forgiven us if we'd gone and made a hero of that Bellamy fellow's son."

The other senior official nodded. "Good for you," he said. "But what are we going to do with him?"

"Young Bellamy? Oh, shove him somewhere on the staff where we can keep an eye on him. One must be careful."

And so it was that just a few days later, still in the middle of his leave, a very puzzled James was summoned to appear before his colonel commandant at Knightsbridge Barracks, to receive the most scathing lecture of his life. Word had got round, the colonel said, that whilst on leave James had been spreading rumours prejudicial to the interests of the service. He had been making criticisms of his senior officers and of the supply of ammunition at the front. There was a possibility that these remarks had been picked up by the yellow press.

Angrily James attempted to ask who was accusing him and what the charges were, but the colonel brushed aside his interjections.

"No one's accusing you of anything, Captain Bellamy. It's just that, as you should be aware, there are some things that officers in this regiment do and some things that—er—they don't. I feel you have disgraced your comrades and yourself. You are no longer one of us, and I have recommended your secondment to the staff."

There was no argument or chance of an appeal, nothing for James to do except salute, turn on his heel, and march off in the cold wind, an outcast from the regiment he loved.

When he had gone, the colonel commandment looked over at his adjutant.

"Dashed hard on a fellow having a politician for a father," he said wearily.

But things weren't all that promising for Richard either. The changes he had campaigned for all came to pass within a month—a coalition government, a Ministry of Munitions under Lloyd George, Bonar Law and Balfour both back in the government. But what about himself? He had been hoping for the Admiralty or the Secretaryship of State for War. He had the knowledge and ability and he had done more than most to bring the coalition into being. But once again he learned the saddest lesson: there is no gratitude in politics. When he was finally fobbed off with one of the most modest offices of state the government could offer, he accepted with bad grace—but he accepted. Better to be First Civil Lord at the Admiralty than a mere backbencher: better almost anything than that. Years later, in an unguarded moment, Balfour told him what went wrong.

"You know what ruined your career," the great man said. "Writing those wretched articles for Northcliffe. When Bonar Law found out he said he simply couldn't trust you any more."

Almost inevitably the long middle months of war became a time of discontent at 165. Now for the first time food was getting scarce. Edward joined the infantry, Rose became a "Clippie" on the buses, and even Hudson felt that loyalty to King and Country outweighed his duty to the Bellamys. Luckily the recruiting board rejected him when he tried to volunteer to join the army, but he was finally enrolled as a special constable. As he explained to Richard, "Humble although it is, it does permit me to make my contribution to the waging of this war."

"Quite so," said Richard. "Most commendable. But are you sure that you'll be able to combine your duties as a constable with your work within the house?"

"I trust I will, sir, but if I do fall short in any small particular I hope that due allowance will be made."

This was not like Hudson, but in the circumstances there was not much that Richard could say in reply. And similarly when Mrs. Bridges' cooking showed the hideous effects of wartime recipes, Richard could only munch and bear it. Certainly the air of loyalty and optimism with which the united household had begun the war had gone; and the frustrations of the two male Bellamys started to spread fresh dissatisfactions in their wake.

James was by far the worst. Those very qualities that made him a first-rate fighting soldier almost entirely disqualified him as a successful staff officer. For several months he had an office in Whitehall and found himself shuttling between senior officers, War Office clerks, and government committees.

"It's just like being back in the confounded City," he would moan to Hazel. "Only worse. Far worse. You can have no idea of the sheer unadulterated pettiness of the military mind. The higher you go the smaller and sillier they seem. Do you know how I've spent the past three afternoons?"

Hazel shook her head.

"Working together with a general, a brigadier, a major, and three geniuses from the War Office amending the official army form sent out to battalions to check the supply of ink."

Hazel laughed.

"Nothing at all to laugh about," said James. "Wait till you see the headline in the *Evening News*—'Staff Officer Goes Berserk with Boredom in Whitehall'—then realise it's me."

"I'd rather that, my love, than have you back at the Front."

"Oh, Hazel, for God's sake! Is that the only thing you can think about?"

She nodded. "It probably seems ridiculous to you, but I thank God every night for those two red staff officer's tabs on your lapels."

"You *what?*"

"I'd rather almost anything, my love, than have you dead in France."

This reply infuriated James almost beyond endurance, but for his wife its logic seemed so obvious that she found it hard to understand his anger.

Richard was enjoying his work more than James. Disappointed though he was with his appointment, at least it gave him that strange something which is the breath of life itself to every politician, the sense of being even marginally within that magic circle where the power lies and the decisions happen. Also, not realising the extent to which his involvement with Lord Northcliffe had upset the inner caucus of his party, he still had hopes of real advancement.

He was kept very busy, working between the House of Commons and the Admiralty, where he now had an office of his own. Most of his work went on behind the scenes—chairing committees, doing liaison work between the War Cabinet and service chiefs, answering recalcitrant M.P.s. He was the epitome of the sort of tactful, hard-working politician of the second rank that all administrations ultimately need to get their business done. This was the trouble. He was kept so busy that he failed to see the situation that was developing at Eaton Place.

Young girls are dangerous creatures, especially to discontented men of thirty-two, and even more so when they live beneath the same roof. Hazel saw the danger but was far too proud to act the jealous wife. Richard should have realised it too, for at this stage Georgina was a very obvious young lady, and she made no attempt to hide her infatuation. As for its object, he was amused and rather flattered by it all. It made a change from ink returns and Whitehall brigadiers, and for some while he pretended to himself that Georgina was no more than a pretty schoolgirl with engaging dimples.

Since his return from France, James's relations with Hazel had been growing worse. All their peacetime problems seemed to have been magnified by war. When they were apart they loved each other. Indeed, it was this love of theirs that caused the trouble—her dread of his return to the fighting, his guilt about the pain he caused her. No, without love they would both have been far better off. But as they were in love they tortured one another, torture which increased steadily after the dreadful summer months of 1915, when James's own request to be seconded back to his regiment was finally turned down.

Much of the trouble was his health. At Ypres his nerves had been shot to pieces and not even the army doctors would commit themselves on the long-term effect the German gas would have on him. But he seemed strong and healthy. Only in bed when his nightmares started did Hazel glimpse the damage he had undergone. Then the next day he'd always turn on her as if he hated her for witnessing the dreadful fears that stalked their nights together.

It was her attempts at patient understanding that annoyed him most.

"You're just like some bloody nanny," he would rage at her. "Whatever I do or say you just smile sweetly and say, 'Yes, dear, no, dear, three bags full, dear.' Can't you realise, Hazel, that I'm sick to death of being 'understood'?"

Young Georgina didn't "understand" at all; and this began to be her chief attraction. She could see him as he longed to see himself, as he appeared to be on that well-groomed, carefree surface. For her he was romantic, handsome, worldly-wise and brave, and it was an extraordinary relief to play the part that she expected. She even remem[illegible]bered the old nickname which Uncle Hugo used to call him. A[illegible] was Jumbo, not the war-torn Captain Bellamy, who began to r[illegible] to her flirtation.

That autumn James did return to France; not as he wanted to, in the front lines with his regiment, but very much the privileged staff officer attached to Corps Headquarters in the rear. It remained a job he loathed. Indeed, it was almost worse than being in Whitehall to be so close to his ex-comrades and to prepare the orders that would send them into battle.

"You have already done more than your share of fighting," his father wrote in one of his letters soon after he arrived. "On no account must you feel the slightest guilt at being with the staff." But, being James, he did. He never could forget what he had called the staff officers when he was at the Front. They were always referred to as "the Yellow Brigade."

As well as the letters from his father, he heard almost every day from faithful Hazel, earnest, cheerful letters written in her neat secretary's hand. But the letters he most enjoyed receiving where those beginning "Darling Jumbo."

The second Christmas of the war found him at home in Eaton Place, but it turned out to be a most uneasy gathering. Richard was tired and Hazel very tense, but the real cause of tension now was James. On Christmas Day he was so drunk that he could barely sit through dinner. Richard tried not to notice—even when his son dropped a decanter and swore at Hudson—but finally James turned on the defenceless Hazel.

"Father," he said softly, "d'you know what my wife does every night before she goes to bed? She prays to God to keep me on the staff. Touching, isn't it?"

Richard glanced across at Hazel. She was near to tears by now.

"James, that's quite enough," he said.

"No, but seriously, it's very interesting, Father. It proves that God exists—something I'd begun to doubt after some of the things I've been seeing out in France. But what d'you think that God will do if I start praying too and ask him to send me back to the regiment? Who will he plump for, me or Hazel?"

"Oh, James, do *stop* it!" Hazel cried. "Even on Christmas Day!" But James grinned back at her.

"That's all you ever say these days—'Stop it! Stop it!' But I was simply starting a little theological discussion. Most appropriate to Christmas."

"And I think we should change the subject," said Richard sharply.

Throughout this long unhappy meal the one person who seemed blissfully untouched by what was happening was Georgina. Eyes bright with adoration of her wartime hero, she made a cruel contrast to the distracted-looking Hazel. Unused to the champagne, the girl was giggling at James's silliest remarks. He played up to her, and, dinner over, joined her in a game of poker for forfeits. There was a good deal of hilarity. Hazel went off to bed and Richard soon went up too.

But Hazel could not sleep. For a long time she heard the faint noise of laughter from downstairs, but when this died away there was still no sign of James. Finally there were footsteps on the stairs, then a rustling from across the passage.

"Georgina," she heard her husband saying in a heavy whisper, "it's Jumbo."

A door squeaked. Then came silence.

⁂

Hazel was too sensible to blame Georgina. Try as she might, she could still regard her only as a child; but James was different, and that night something in her love for him expired for good. Next day she confronted him with what he'd done. He confessed at once, was contrite in his former boyish way, and begged her to forgive him. She felt so weary, so past caring that she did. "But why, tell me why you did it," she asked sadly.

"Well, she's a very pretty girl and I suppose I'd had too much to drink."

"But Georgina of all people! And here in your own home! James, I just cannot understand you any more."

He looked so bleak and hopeless that she found herself beginning to feel sorry for him.

"It's all this filthy war," he said bitterly. "You've no idea how much I've grown to despise myself during these last few months. That dreadful staff job. For somebody like me you know it's living hell."

"One thing's quite certain," she replied. "Neither of us can go on like this. Something must be done."

⁂

There were always two quite separate schools of thought about what Hazel did. Some, like Richard, felt that she showed the greatest love and understanding that a woman could when she went personally to plead with her husband's colonel to take him back into active service. The colonel must have felt so too. Otherwise it is inconceivable that he would have acted as he did, for within two weeks a posting order had come through seconding Captain Bellamy from the general staff to the command of a newly formed machine-gun company with the Life Guards. Thanks entirely to Hazel's pleading he had got what he wanted.

On the other hand, Georgina was outraged at Hazel's intervention.

"How could you have done it, Hazel?" she stormed on at her. "You of all people. Was it because of me, because I loved him?"

"Don't be ridiculous, Georgina. You're far too young to understand these things," Hazel replied.

"You were just jealous, Hazel," wailed Georgina. "I know. You wanted your revenge on both of us. If anything should happen to him . . ."

"Georgina," Hazel snapped with icy self-control, "please stop behaving like a shop-girl!"

The upset between Hazel and Georgina was only one of the crosses Richard had to bear in the bleak third year of war, but inevitably it made life still more difficult. Inevitably too it helped fuel the gossip about the whys and wherefores of his son's return to active service. Prudence was only one of those who picked up half the story and opined most forcefully that "Hazel Bellamy really did behave with quite appalling callousness."

At any other time Richard would have tried to put the record straight. Now he scarcely bothered. James was happy training his new company and getting ready for the "Big Push" planned for that summer on the Somme. Now that the German U-boat war had started, Richard and the British Admiralty had more important things to think about.

In fact, of course, Hazel and Georgina soon made peace, though not before Georgina had rushed off in pique and desperation to become a nurse. Part of the reason she did this was to show Hazel that she emphatically was neither a child nor a shop-girl; part also was that she felt this would be the one sure way she had to get out to France and be near the man she loved. But instead of service overseas, Georgina found herself slaving through that summer in her London hospital.

The house at 165 had now become a mournful place. Hudson's patriotism tended to be irritating, particularly to Rose, after her *fiancé,* an Australian named Wilmot, was reported missing at the Front.

"I wish to goodness, Mr. 'Udson, that you'd think a bit about them poor men dyin' out there in their thousands when you go sticking pins in your beastly war map of the Western Front."

Hudson's war map was his pride and joy, and he loved talking knowledgeably of strategy and tactics to the servants in the evening when he had had time to absorb the war news from the day's edition of the *Daily Telegraph*. For Rose to have spoken out like this was evidence of how the strains of war were starting to affect even the most level-headed of the inhabitants of 165.

At the same time Mrs. Bridges' cooking seemed to receive its death knell from the wartime shortages. She who had managed to perfect her art in the abundant days of fat King Edward could not adapt to managing with margarine and substitutes for eggs. She herself lost weight, and the dining room became a grimmer and a sadder place.

All this helped to form a mood of resignation in the house. Richard, working harder now than ever in his life, was simply grateful to get through each day. Hazel had sunk into a state of lifeless unconcern about herself, and she seemed unconcerned about James too. She still wrote to him, once a week now, giving him the news of what was happening at home. This salved what conscience she still had about him. As for affection, he was doubtless getting that from young Georgina's letters. And that July, as James and his men were trying out their Lewis guns in the first of the great, disastrous battles of the Somme, Hazel went back to work. As the wife of a serving soldier she had no need to, but she told Richard, "I get bored and morbid sitting round at home all day." She worked as a secretary in the Government Pensions Office in the Horseferry Road. It helped to pass the time.

Although 1916 was a bleak year for Britain, it ended with a certain note of hope at 165. Georgina attained her ambition and went off, a neatly uniformed and fully trained nursing sister, to a base hospital behind the Western Front. Richard had done his best to dissuade her to the last, but she had all her mother's strength of will—and it was undeniable that her departure made life with Hazel that much easier. The news from James was good as well. His charmed existence seemed to be continuing. He had got through the Somme campaign, been mentioned in despatches, and was now officially a major.

Richard was preparing to take Hazel out to dinner at the Ritz to celebrate that news when he received a telegram. His heart missed a beat. At this stage in the war a telegram had come to mean one thing and one thing only, tidings of someone's death in action. And an impassive Hazel watched as Richard's fingers fumbled with the envelope. Almost despite herself she found that she was praying silently, "God, may it not be James. Let him be wounded, captured—anything but that, oh Lord!"

But as he read the yellowish piece of paper, Richard's face changed from deep anxiety to puzzlement to sudden joy. He passed his hand across his brow, blinked, sat down, then said in a small stunned voice, "Good heavens! Who'd have thought it? Bless my soul!"

He handed her the telegram. It was so unexpected that at first, like Richard, she found it difficult to comprehend.

"Am wishing to recommend you for peerage in New Years Honours. Will you accept?" It was signed, "Bonar Law."

"You don't think somebody's trying on some sort of practical joke?" he asked uncertainly. But she took his hand and kissed him firmly on the cheek.

"Congratulations, dear Lord Bellamy." she said. "Of course it's not a joke. If anyone deserves it you do. It will suit you wonderfully."

And so they had a double celebration. It was so long since there had been anything but bad news that they were both a little out of practice. Wartime London, blacked out against the Zeppelin attacks and crammed with troops, was not very festive either. But as he sat with Hazel between the chandeliers and the sand-bagged windows of the Ritz Hotel, enjoying an unbelievably expensive bottle of champagne, Richard felt as if he were reliving a few brief precious moments from some earlier existence.

"You know," he said, "one does forget what it's like to be happy. It's a strange sensation."

"I suppose it will come back," she said, "when the war ends. If it ever ends."

She looked lined and older than her years yet strangely beautiful tonight.

"Oh, it will end now, sooner than you think," he said.

"Will it really, Richard? You know, I've given up thinking about it any more. All I know is that at this moment you and James are happy—so for tonight I'm happy too."

"What about you and James?" he asked.

She smiled enigmatically and stared at the tiny bubbles rising in the champagne.

"That's something else that can begin again when the war's over. I hope. If we survive that long, we'll both have grown up. Perhaps we'll make it work."

"You don't sound very hopeful."

"I don't think about it very much," she said. "If I start thinking it becomes unbearable. No, I think we're like people in limbo. We can only wait and see what happens. Until then . . ."

"But you still love him?" Richard asked quickly.

"James? Oh yes."

"Despite the way he's treated you?"

"Of course. I've not always treated him that well, you know. I lost his baby."

"That wasn't your fault."

"No, but I didn't want it at the time. I often blame myself for that."

There was a silence then, and Richard felt as if the great black cloud of gloom outside was reaching in for them. But Hazel smiled suddenly.

"Pour some more champagne," she said. "It's you we should be talking about tonight, not me. How does it feel to be Lord Bellamy after all these years?"

"I'm not yet. Give me time."

"But it must be wonderful to suddenly win such a prize."

"Well, you know, it's very strange. In one sense of course it's marvellous. I'm a vain, silly fellow and for all manner of unpleasant snobbish reasons I will love being Viscount Bellamy. I only wish Marjorie was alive. I'd have enjoyed telling her that she was Lady Marjorie now because she was my wife, and not because she was the Earl of Southwold's daughter."

"Used that to rankle then?"

He smiled and sipped his wine. "Terribly," he said. "Then there's James," he continued. "It will be good as far as he's concerned. One of these days he'll inherit my title, something that he's got from me, not from the Southwolds. That's nice to know. And for that matter too, my dear, I'm glad that you'll be Lady Bellamy one day because of me."

"Why do you seem so doubtful about it then?" she asked.

"Do I seem doubtful? Oh, Hazel, you must know me very well. Yes, of course I'm doubtful. It really marks the end, you see."

"The end of what?"

"The end of all those dreams I had of climbing to the topmost branches of the tree. This means I'll never really get there now."

"But you'll still remain as First Civil Lord?"

"Oh, yes, for a while at least. For as long as Lloyd George likes the look of me. But now I know that I can get no further."

"Still, you'll be in the House of Lords."

"That elephants' graveyard! Well, I'm nearly sixty. Possibly it's time. Lord Richard Bellamy. Just fancy that!"

Richard's title annoyed him in a way. As he complained to Hazel, "For more than a quarter of a century I sit in the House of Commons, I become a minister, but for the people round me I'm like anybody else. Then because the Party needs my seat, I'm kicked upstairs and what happens? For the first time in my life the post arrives on time, my wine merchant bows to me and calls me 'my lord'—then doubles up my bill. And as for Hudson—"

"He's in seventh heaven. It was the greatest boost you could have given his prestige. Butler to Lord Bellamy," Hazel said grandly.

"And doesn't he just know it! I've increased his salary by a full pound a week. It was made very clear to me that a viscount's butler is worth a minimum of fifty pounds a year more than a mere commoner's."

"Poor Richard."

"Poor Hazel, too. You'll have to face it all one day. It'll serve you right."

But although he grumbled, the time came when Richard was grateful for his title and all the subtle privileges that it implied. This was in the spring of 1917, when James's luck finally deserted him and he was badly wounded during the bitter Passchendaele offensive.

At first the family all feared him dead. Several days later a patrol discovered him lying in a shell hole, delirious and wounded in the thigh. Then, by one of those extraordinary coincidences that seem to happen only during wars, he was brought back to the very hospital where Georgina was nursing. It was a telegram from her that brought the first news of his safety.

As soon as Richard learned what had happened he was uneasy. It was wonderful, of course, to have his son alive; wonderful as well to hear the news of his recovery. What troubled him was the news that it was Georgina who was nursing him. Not that he mistrusted her skills as a nursing sister. Far from it. But what did worry him was the effect all this would have on James's marriage. It was rickety enough already and Richard had a fair idea of the relationship between Georgina and his son. A month or so now with a convalescent James in continual contact with Georgina as his loving nurse! Whatever chance the marriage still possessed would vanish utterly.

Richard spent several anxious days trying to decide exactly what to do. There seemed to be no way of getting James shifted from the hospital without upsetting Hazel (and she was of course upset enough already). Then somebody suggested the idea of going out to fetch him in a private ambulance. At first the plan seemed crazy, but the more he thought of it the more the whole idea appealed to him. If James and Hazel were to have a chance together it seemed to be the only way. And here his title and position really counted.

Had he still been plain Mr. Bellamy, he would never have so much as got his private ambulance aboard the Dover Ferry, let alone have been permtted to drive unimpeded all the way to the base hospital where James was. Nor as straightforward Mr. Bellamy could he have over-ruled the opposition of the doctors and nurses—to say nothing of a furious Georgina—and brought James safely home to convalesce in Eaton Place. There was in fact no danger now to James in travelling, but regulations being what they were . . . Viscount Bellamy, with lordly arrogance, calmly over-rode them all. The matron finally agreed. The R.A.M.C. brigadier was positively servile. Georgina never quite forgave him.

It was shortly after this, and the war was limping to its close, when Richard met Virginia. By then she was in her late thirties, the lively, pretty, somewhat pushing widow of a Scots naval officer named Hamilton. She was tough, middle-class, and practical—as she had to be to force her way completely unannounced into 165 one afternoon when Richard and Hazel were having tea together.

Outrageous woman! Why on earth should he consent to have anything at all to do with the court-martial that involved this pretty widow's son except, to put it frankly, that she was a *very* pretty widow? Her wretched son, a seventeen-year-old midshipman, had been charged with cowardice before the enemy when he broke down during a torpedo-boat attack on Zeebrugge, on the Belgian coast. It was all most distressing, but as he tried to explain to Hazel after Mrs. Hamilton had left, "Cases like this are two a penny these days. It's rough justice and I know the boy's extremely young, but cowardice is cowardice, and in time of war one has to make examples of such flagrant cases."

"*Pour encourager les autres,* as Voltaire said when we shot poor Admiral Byng."

"Good heavens, Hazel, he won't be shot—simply disgraced and dismissed from the service."

"Couldn't that be as bad?"

"Of course not. Why, you women are all the same. Sheer sentimentality! That won't win the war!"

But sentimentality or not, Richard did help the widow Hamilton by bringing in Sir Geoffrey Dillon to defend her son. And when Sir Geoffrey won the case he was delighted, but again, as he admitted to himself, his delight came more from the service he had done the mother than from the help he had brought to the son.

And in fact Virginia was just the sort of woman that he needed, especially now. For James's return had placed a hideous emotional burden on the whole of 165. Had Richard known how his son would be, he might well have left him to Georgina. As it turned out, the ultimate results could hardly have been worse.

During the first few weeks things had gone comparatively well. Hazel gave up her job and nursed her husband with devotion. His wound was healing slowly, but he was still weak, bed-bound, and apparently grateful to be home. Richard rejoiced to see that the marriage seemed to have survived. But when the weeks dragged on and James's leg still kept him to his bed, a change came over him. The war had damaged more than his body. Nearly four years of fighting had exhausted him and now he was undergoing some sort of breakdown.

For hours on end he would lie stationary in bed, staring at the ceiling. When anyone upset him, he would throw everything—food, books, even plates and crockery—at the wall opposite. Suddenly poor Hazel found she couldn't cope with him alone. A nurse was hired, more to protect him from himself than because of danger from his wounds.

"Shoot them all!" he'd rage. "Shoot all the politicians! Shoot all those safe fat profiteers! Let them have a taste of dying for democracy!"

At other times he would awake from sleep screaming about the rats. When Hazel tried to comfort him he would lie trembling, then lash out at her. "Filthy, black, creeping bastards," he would pant. One night he even tried to strangle her. Richard, who heard the rumpus, managed to pull him off, but next day when he tried to question him about it James refused to speak. Instead he was once more inert, eyes open, staring at the ceiling.

It was after this that Richard insisted that a male nurse sleep in the room at night, and Hazel reluctantly moved into the dressing room next door. James barely seemed to notice. The specialist who saw him, a tall, bald Czech called Professor Seltzer, diagnosed "war exhaustion."

"Haven't we all got that?" said Richard, but Seltzer didn't seem amused.

"What treatment do you advise? Should he be sent somewhere to a clinic or a hospital?"

"Later, perhaps. Just at the moment I would advise against it. Most of his trouble is reaction to his wounds. Give him security and love—and let him cure himself."

They did their best. The servants were particularly understanding, and seemed prepared to overlook James's rages and his rudeness. They heard the news that he had been awarded an M.C., and now that he was a wounded hero they could make allowances. So, in his way, could Richard. After all, he knew James better than anybody else. He had experienced that stormy nature, the sullen moods and the cruel way he had with those who loved him.

Also, by now, Richard had Virginia. After her son Michael, now a sublieutenant and restored to active service, went off to meet a hero's death in a fresh sea-borne raid on Ostend, she relied on Richard increasingly to see her through her period of grief and mourning. Richard, discreet, unpressing but immensely comforting, was exactly the steady father figure that she needed. She in her turn, with her trim figure and uptilted nose, was just the sort of little woman who brings out the protective male in romantic-minded gentlemen of a certain age.

He would send flowers to her hotel, place the Rolls at her disposal when she went shopping, take her to tea at Gunters.

"Richard, you're spoiling me," she would say.

"Well, Virginia, someone must look after you," he would gallantly reply. And Virginia, who was really as capable of looking after herself as any widow in London, would lean dependently upon his arm and smile demurely.

It was certainly no passionate elopement. For Richard, much of the pleasure that he found in Mrs. Hamilton was simply in her conversation. She was so down to earth, so utterly direct and practical, that it was a relief to talk about the tensions and the troubles of his family to her. Also, she never really rivalled Marjorie: Marjorie was so different, so distant now and so regal in his memory, that he could love Virginia without impinging on her world at all.

Prudence always said, of course, that Virginia vamped Richard outrageously, that she had planned to catch him all along, and that she really was a very cunning, common little woman. This was predictable but it wasn't really true. Virginia had never had to play such games with Richard. By the time he proposed to her in the summer of 1918, he had made himself so totally dependent on her that it would have been sadistic to refuse him. Instead she pointed out her disadvantages as the next Lady Bellamy. She had no money, there were two young children, and she came from very lowly stock. Such honesty enchanted Richard.

"Dearest Virginia, you'll bring a breath of life to Eaton Place," he declared.

"It that what you want?" she asked him in her level-headed Scottish way.

"I think that we can make each other very happy," he replied, taking her hand. And since she believed him, she accepted him.

At the age of sixty a brand-new marriage is one of life's little extras that are vouchsafed to few of us. Richard was duly grateful. It was clear now that the war was ending, and quite suddenly his life was filling with hope. The only problem now was James, and even he was gradually recovering. His leg was almost healed, leaving him with a faint but not unattractive limp. As for his breakdown, the worst was over. The periods of rage and lethargy had gone, leaving him irritable and bored—but much more like the pre-war James than he had been for years.

But Richard was worried now for Hazel.

"Poor lost thing," was Virginia's verdict on her after the dinner Richard gave to celebrate his engagement.

"Why d'you say that?" he asked.

"She seems so beaten, so depressed and lifeless with the strain of coping with him. Does he have to be so cruel to her?"

"He's always been hard on her. Something about her seems to invite it."

"Well, he should stop it, or she'll be the one who breaks—not him."

But when he spoke to James they had the usual stormy interview.

"Hazel? Oh, she's all right. Perhaps a touch of flu. There seems to be a lot of it about," James replied airily.

"Well, that could be extremely serious," said Richard. "I'm going to call the doctor."

"Haven't we had enough members of the medical profession in this house lately, Father?"

"For you, James, but you're better now. I think it's time you thought about your wife."

But James refused to listen and it was Richard, on his own authority, who called in Dr. Foley two days later.

Hazel as usual made so little fuss that no one realised how ill she was. The doctor called, found she had a temperature, and ordered her to bed. She ignored him for as long as possible and it was Rose who saw her tottering unsteadily around the house and finally persuaded her to do as she was told.

"Come along now, Mrs. Bellamy," she said firmly. "You're ill, real ill. I'm getting you to bed and telling the master straight away."

"No, don't do that," she said. "I'll go to bed, but don't go worrying anybody."

But Rose had the sense to tell Virginia. The doctor was re-summoned. This time he looked serious.

"No doubt about it," he said gravely. "Spanish influenza. Not much resistance by the look of it. Warmth, quiet, all the fluids she can drink."

But all that Hazel wanted now was James. She called for him pathetically most of that evening. When he came home at ten o'clock he had been celebrating, and went limping up the stairs to Hazel's room to tell her the good news.

"Hazel. Dear old girl! It looks as if it's over."

She stared uncomprehendingly, her eyes grown large with fever.

"James," she gasped. "My darling, darling James!"

But James had drunk too much to realise quite what was happening.

"Hazel, cheer up," he said. "Cheer up, old thing. Can't have you feeling down at a time like this. I've been all evening at the club. The news is coming in. It's definite. The Boches have asked for peace."

Richard glanced quickly at Virginia, who shook her head.

"James," he said. "James, listen to me. Hazel is very, very ill."

"Nonsense," he said. "Nobody's ill tonight. The war will soon be over. Come on, Father, Virginia. Let's have a song."

"Get him to bed, Richard," said Virginia. "I'll stay with her. When he is sober we can have him back, but now he's only upsetting her."

So Richard did as he was told, then he and Virginia stayed up all that night with Hazel. Most of the time she was in a coma.

Next morning, the eleventh of November, Europe was at peace—and so was Hazel.

1918-29

17. *Exeunt*

WHILE BRITAIN WAS GOING WILD WITH JOY DURING THOSE FIRST THREE days of peace, the Bellamys were burying Hazel. The contrast was so macabre that in years to come Richard discovered that his memory had mercifully blanked out the details. James's bouts of weeping and remorse, the stifled tears of the servants, the last pathetic view of Hazel in her coffin—all these images finally dissolved into a vague, sad memory.

His only vivid memories were of the funeral itself—the way the hearse was jostled by the cheering crowds on Putney Bridge, and then the drunken shouting from the streets outside as they stood bareheaded in the cemetery. This mourning in the midst of rejoicing made the bereavement that much worse. The Forrest family was there—Hazel's mother grim and dignified, the father pale and frightened-looking in a bowler hat. Richard felt embarrassed that he'd never bothered much with them. Throughout the burial he stood beside the little man.

"Well," said Mr. Forrest when it was over.

He sniffed, but there seemed nothing anyone could say. "Well," he repeated in a flat voice. "She was our only one."

That night poor Mr. Forrest had to endure the bitter lamentations of his wife.

"The way they all stood there," she said. "His lordship and our precious son-in-law and that cousin creature in the nurse's uniform. What's her name, Albert?"

"Georgina."

"Exactly. Hard-faced young hussy! All of them just letting our daughter die like that and not a tear from any of them. Oh, Albert Forrest, we never should have let her marry him. You were the one who persuaded me against my better judgement. If it hadn't been for that, our Hazel would have been alive today."

But Mrs. Forrest in her grief was wrong about the Bellamys. Dry-eyed they may have been. Unaffected they were not. Indeed, the misery that night in Eaton Place was every bit as great as in the terraced house in Wimbledon.

Richard had no idea of how to cope with it. He did his best but merely seemed to make things worse. James was immured in his room, refusing to come down to dinner. Richard made the mistake of trying to persuade him.

"James, my dear old chap," he said. "Behaving like this doesn't do Hazel any good. Life must go on. Come down to dinner."

"Dinner!" shouted James. "How can you think of eating at a time like this? We let her die and all you talk about is dinner. You disgust me, Father!"

Georgina too was knee-deep in remorse. "I treated her so *dreadfully,*" she sobbed. "It was disgusting of us both. She was so good and we were so absolutely *awful* to her, Richard."

"There," he said, patting her shoulder in an avuncular, understanding way. "There, there. You know that she'd forgiven you for all that years ago."

"That's not the point. To think of her in that dreadful grave, whilst James and I . . . Richard, how *could* we have done it to her?"

"But you were very young."

"It was no excuse."

"Come and have dinner," he said gently.

"Dinner!" she sobbed. "Oh, Richard, how could you?"

So Richard and Virginia dined alone. It was predictably a gloomy meal, but not for the reasons Richard had expected. Virginia refused to talk about the funeral and seemed angry that James and Georgina had refused to join them.

"But you must understand, Virginia," he said. "They're naturally upset."

"And so are you. For that matter, Richard, so am I. But they have no call to carry on like this."

"But they were very fond of her. James and Hazel had been married eight years—and she was like a mother to Georgina."

"Fiddlesticks!" Virginia replied.

"What did you say, Virginia?" Richard was aghast.

"You heard me perfectly. I said fiddlesticks. You know as well as I do that almost until this time last week James was still treating Hazel quite appallingly. You also know that your precious ward, Georgina, couldn't wait to get back into bed with him. Now that poor Hazel's dead the two of them both wallow in their grief—and you feel sorry for them."

"Virginia, how dare you?"

"How dare I, Richard? I'll tell you how I dare. I dare because it's the truth—and because I love you. I can't stand by and watch that pair indulging in an orgy of self-pity at your expense, Richard Bellamy."

But Richard shook his head. "You're wrong, Virginia. Poor James has had a dreadful battering—his mother dying, then the war, now this. We must be understanding."

"I think I understand him all too well. We all have our sorrows. After Michael died I thought my world was coming to an end—but it didn't. With James you're all so busy being sorry for him that he doesn't have a chance. Let him stand on his own two feet. Stop giving so much sympathy."

"But, Virginia, my dear. That is the least that we can do."

She shook her head. She was no longer the demure Virginia but the embattled widow Hamilton.

"If that is what you really think," she said, "perhaps we should forget about the wedding. I don't think I could bear to see you going on playing the doting nanny to that son of yours—and getting torn to pieces in the process."

Throughout the period of the engagement Virginia had insisted on staying in a modest but respectable hotel in Sloane Street. Richard drove her back in silence. Twice he attempted to take her hand, but she repulsed him—unemotionally but firmly.

"Richard, goodnight," she said and kissed him on the cheek.

"Virginia," he said imploringly.

"I said goodnight, Richard," she replied with the quiet self-control so typical of her.

"When shall I be seeing you?" he asked.

"I think it's time I got back to Scotland to the children," she replied. "I'll write."

"Virginia!" he cried. But instead of answering, Virginia was gone.

Richard was simply not equipped for dealing with a woman like Virginia. There had been all sorts of women in his life—dominating ones like Marjorie, adoring ones like Cressida, daughterly ones like his Elizabeth, and tiresome ones like Pru. After his fashion he had coped with all of them, but with Virginia it was the first time he had ever had to deal with the rarest woman of them all, the one who means exactly what she says.

At first he couldn't quite believe that this was what she was, but when he rang the small hotel next morning she had already left.

"Absurd! How perfectly absurd!" he muttered to himself. "She can't just walk out on me like this. She'll be back. She's bound to be!"

But a small worried voice was already whispering that perhaps she wouldn't.

"How could she behave like that?" he asked himself. "And after everything I've done for her." He became angry at the thought of this, and anger led him to consider what a fool she'd make of him with his children, with his friends. She had been welcomed in his house, treated as a member of the family. Why, the servants were already regarding her as the future Lady Bellamy!

This made him angrier than ever, and by dinner time that night he was in such a state that everyone in 165 was wary of him. It was surprising the effect this change in the normally affable head of the house created. James at a flash seemed cured of his extremes of grief. Georgina too seemed rescued from remorse, as Richard took his place at table with a face of thunder.

"Georgina, I do wish you'd tell Mrs. Bridges that I'm sick to death of ox-tail soup," he snapped at her.

"Of course. I'm sorry," she said nervously, "but I always thought you rather liked it."

"Well, I don't," he said and shoved his plate away.

"No Virginia tonight?" James inquired brightly. "What's she up to? You'll have to keep an eye on that young lady, Father."

Richard glowered at him. "James," he growled, "I'd be pleased if you would mind your own damn business and keep your insinuations to yourself."

The next few days ranked among the most uncomfortable in the whole history of the Bellamys.

Rose gave in her notice after Richard shouted at her and made her drop a tray. Edward was mutinous with Richard, who was threatening to sell the Rolls. Mrs. Bridges hovered perpetually, it seemed, between tears and walking out.

Hudson did his best to keep the peace, but even he had to admit that his lordship's temper was "distinctly edgy." "Now, Mrs. Bridges," he began consolingly, "we must make some allowances for our betters. Lord Bellamy has led a somewhat sheltered life. He has an attitude towards the fair sex which we, as servants, find it difficult to understand. He is a man of elevated sentiments, so naturally he suffers more than we would when he's jilted by a lady such as Mrs. Hamilton."

"Well, Mr. 'Udson, that's as may be," Mrs. Bridges stolidly replied. "I speaks only as I finds, and I must say that I liked 'er. But 'owever badly she's behaved, it never can excuse the things 'e said about my leg of mutton *nor* my caper sauce. In all my years in service I've never 'ad to endure such comments, Mr. 'Udson. An' I don't see why I should."

The grumbling went on upstairs as well, when it became quite evident that Richard's black mood wasn't, as James hopefully suggested to Georgina, "due to something he had for luncheon in the House of Lords." The next day it was worse; the day after, worse still.

"What can we do about it, Jumbo?" asked Georgina.

"Lord alone knows. Old Virginia must have ditched him, but I can't get through to him."

"Well, you'd better think of something. Life here is not worth living. The servants are all on the point of leaving, and every time your father sees me he blows me up for something. Frankly, I'd rather bed and breakfast at the Y.W.C.A."

The crisis deepened and for the first time James became really worried. Always in the past his father had been the one who solved the problems in the house, kept the servants happy, and generally ensured that life continued as it always had. Now, instead, *he* had become a problem on his own account.

At Hudson's discreet suggestion, James had the task of tactfully placating Rose and persuading her to withdraw her notice. It was hard going.

"But I'm not used to being shouted at like that, Major Bellamy," she said, sticking a small, determined chin up in the air.

He replied with all the charm he had, "Rose, you know how much we all rely on you. I'm sure you realise how big a strain these last few weeks have been on all of us. I'm sorry that it happened. Can't you forget it, Rose?"

Reluctantly Rose agreed.

"For your sake, Major Bellamy," she said, but afterwards James fumed at Georgina.

"Damn father, damn Rose and damn the lot of them! Why should I have to go down on my knees to servants in my own home and all because of Father?"

"And things are getting worse," Georgina said. "Most of the time he ignores me now. I even heard him shout at Hudson. Another month of this and we won't have a servant left. For goodness' sake do something, Jumbo!"

⁂

It was Lloyd George who gave them all a breathing space from Richard's evil humour by calling an election with the ending of the war. Now that he was in the Lords, Richard was mercifully free from the worries of the hustings, on his own account at least, but as a former minister he was in some demand from the Party. Candidates needed all the help that they could find, particularly from a Conservative like Richard who had had an active part in winning the war.

"You've become, like me," said Balfour in a voice that Richard wasn't certain he appreciated, "one of the elders of the Tory Party." And as a Party elder he dutifully embarked on a lightning speaking tour of the Midlands. He found it a sobering experience: everywhere he went, immense support for Lloyd George as "the Welsh wizard who won the war for us"; increased backing for the Labour Party from the returning servicemen; an end, or so it seemed to him, of the respectful old-style toryism he had grown up with during his thirty years in politics. In Birmingham a heckler in a cloth cap yelled, "Get back to yer old folks' home, yer lordship!" and everybody laughed, except for Richard.

⁂

The house at Hellensborough wasn't difficult to find. It was a trim grey double-fronted villa facing across the pewter-coloured waters of the Firth of Clyde. After the all-night train from London, and the slow branch line on from Glasgow, James was grateful for the exercise of walking from the station. Although he still had a limp and the doctors still occasionally dug out small bits of shrapnel from his thigh, his wound was really healed and he had been told that he should have "all of the exercise that you can bear."

He rang the bell and a maid with a thatch of carrot-coloured hair answered the door to him.

"Mrs. Hamilton?" he asked.

"Och, she'd be away in Glasgee for the day."

"She's where?" asked James.

"As I was sayin', she's in Glasgee."

"Oh, in Glasgow!" The maid smiled indulgently, rather as people do with backward children.

"And when will she be back?" he asked.

"She dinna say."

So James spent the day in Hellensborough, and an extremely long, cold day it was. He walked beside the Clyde until his leg began to ache. He lunched at a hotel by the railway station. He read the local papers, then had tea. And then, when he returned to the grey villa by the sea, Virginia was there. She didn't seem particularly surprised to see him, nor for that matter was she particularly welcoming.

"I've come from London specially to see you."

"So I see, James," she said. Her drawing room was chintzy, comfortable, rather prim. She was looking rosy-cheeked and far too pert and healthy to be pining.

"And how is everyone in Eaton Place?" she asked brightly. Picking his words with unaccustomed care, James began to tell her.

"Good morning, James, morning, Georgina. Lovely morning, isn't it?"

The two glanced up at Richard in alarm. True, a watery December sun was dribbling through the windows of the breakfast room, but that was no excuse for such unheard-of heartiness from the master of the house at this time of the day. He helped himself to bacon, fried bread, eggs and kidneys and walked, humming cheerfully, towards the table.

"Terrible news about this damned election," said James convivially from the deepest folds of the *Times.*

"Only to be expected," said Richard philosophically. "Lloyd George is bound to win. Taking the long view, probably as well. He'll come unstuck. That sort of bounder always does."

"You can afford to talk like that, now that you're in the Lords," said James. "If you were out there scavenging for votes it'd be rather different."

"Indeed it would," said Richard, tucking his napkin into his collar and smiling with extreme benevolence at James. "One of the few real benefits of privilege and age, to find yourself above such things."

There was silence then, save for the rustling of James's paper and the happy sounds of Richard eating. Georgina got up to go.

"Ah, my dear," said Richard, "would you be good enough to have a word with Mrs. Bridges? Something has obviously been upsetting her lately, I can't think what. But I'm most anxious to have something rather special for dinner tonight. Perhaps some pheasant, or better still, some grouse. I've a surprise for both of you."

Virginia returned that night to Eaton Place as something of a conqueror. If nothing else her month-long absence had proved one thing quite decisively—that 165 simply could not function properly without her. Now, from the moment a radiant Hudson opened the front door to her, the house appeared to be transformed.

"Wonderful to see you back again, if I may say so, madam. And how was Scotland?"

"Well, it's still there, and still as cold as ever, Hudson. You must go back and visit it one day."

"I think not, madam. I'm really quite a cockney now, you know."

Encouraged by Georgina, Mrs. Bridges had excelled herself—delicious lobster *mousse,* grouse cooked to perfection, a *tarte aux pommes* as fine as any in the grandest Paris restaurants. It was the perfect gastronomic setting for an exultant Richard Bellamy.

"James, Georgina," he said finally, "Virginia and I have something we must tell you. I'm sorry to launch it on you both like this, but we've just got married."

"You've *what?*" said James.

"Got married, Virginia and I. This afternoon at four o'clock in the Chelsea Register Office. I do apologise for not inviting you but I simply couldn't risk her changing her mind again."

Virginia laughed. "You make me sound extremely fickle, Richard."

"Oh, but you are, my dear. And quite right, too."

"But why not ask us, Richard?" said Georgina. "After all, James and I are your closest relatives. We're very fond of you. You might have let us be there if only to throw confetti."

"I know," said Richard unrepentantly, "I know, I know. Quite dreadful of us both! And yet, quite honestly, my dear, I seem to have been worrying about the two of you for far too long. Will this upset Georgina? Will James be furious at that? Today, for once, I simply pleased myself. And also, I hope, Virginia."

"Of course," she said. "I'd never realised how easy getting married can be."

"Or how enjoyable," Richard added. "It was the most exciting thing I've done for years."

There was a brief, shocked silence then, and finally James said, "Congratulations, Father. Virginia, I couldn't be more delighted."

He got up from his place and kissed her, a trifle warily perhaps, on the cheek.

Georgina followed.

"So we're forgiven, are we Georgina?" Richard asked.

"Just this once," she said. "But don't do it again, either of you."

"I think we should celebrate our being forgiven then," said Richard. "You know, the year the war broke out I put aside six bottles of extremely good champagne to drink that Christmas when James came home on leave. You never got your leave, James, and the bottles are still there. Perhaps we should try one, so that we can toast Virginia and peace and happiness for all of us."

"And about time," said Virginia.

"Indeed yes!" Richard said and smiled towards his son.

"I gather I've a lot to thank you for," Richard said slowly. The ladies had retired and James and Richard were enjoying a glass of excellent port before rejoining them.

"Don't mention it. How much did she tell you?"

"Enough. I'm very touched that you took my happiness so seriously."
"Pure self-interest, Father. Couldn't have you going on as you were. Life was impossible."
"I'm sorry, James," said Richard, looking nothing of the kind.
"Not at all. But one thing worries me. Have you decided where you'll live?"
Richard shook his head. "Please give us time. We've only just got married."
"I know," said James. "I know. But when I saw Virginia I told her very firmly that I wanted you both to stay here in this house."
"She never told me."
"She didn't, eh? That's bad."
Richard sniffed his port judiciously. "Delicious," he said quietly. "Quite delicious." Then he looked up at James. "I'm very touched that you should want us here," he said. "It's very kind of you. But I'm afraid that it's impossible."
"But, Father, why on earth? I know that legally the place belongs to me, but you know as well as I do that you're the centre of it all. It's your house, really. You'd be lost away from it."
"I'm not certain that I would," he said. "It might be rather nice to have a change. Somewhere smaller, easier to run. Times have changed. Servants are like gold-dust since the war. When Virginia has sold the house in Scotland I think we'll buy a little place in Chelsea, or even on the far side of the Park."
"You mean Bayswater?"
"One could do worse."
"Now, Father, really!" Richard was smiling, James was becoming angry.
"Listen." he said. "There's absolutely no question of you and Virginia setting up home away from Eaton Place. You can state your terms. Servants, expenses, food—I'll pay them all. Virginia's two children can have the old nursery when they're home from school. Virginia can redecorate the house exactly as she wants. Heaven knows it's big enough for all of us."
"But why are you so desperate to keep us?"
"I'll tell you why. Ever since Hazel died I've realised that this house and what it stands for is really all I've got. When I was out in France I used to dream about it every night. All my memories of Mother are here, and of Elizabeth and you. Southwold's gone. Everything worthwhile seems to have vanished with the war. I want this house

to continue as it always has—and that means with you and Virginia at the head of it."

Richard was far more touched by James's speech than he admitted. Also, to be quite honest, Bayswater did not appeal to him. (That was Virginia's idea. After Hellensborough, even Kilburn would have seemed luxurious.) No, for someone who had spent the greater part of his existence yielding to other people's offers of an easy life, the thought of quietly continuing at Eaton Place *was* tempting. Most of the things that made Richard's life agreeable were here—his library, his cellar, the servants. Also, like James, he felt a deep affection for the place. It was a part of him. It was convenient for getting to the House of Lords, and now that the war was over Mrs. Bridges showed signs of recovering her position as the best cook in Belgravia. (Virginia was threatening to bring down her red-headed treasure from the Clyde. Richard's inner man was worried.)

His only difficulty lay in presenting all this to Virginia, and he was quietly pondering that as he and James entered the drawing room. They were greeted by an anxious-looking Georgina and an equally solemn Virginia.

As Virginia poured the coffee she looked suspiciously at Richard, who wondered what the two women had been saying in their absence. Before long Virginia told him.

"Dearest," she said sweetly, "I've been talking to Georgina, who has been telling me several things I never really understood before."

"Really?" said Richard innocently.

"Yes. She says you really love this house and it would be a dreadful wrench for you to leave it. Would it, Richard?"

"Well, in a way. You know a man does get attached to a place like this, and I have lived here for quite a while."

"She also says that she and James are extremely eager for us to live here. Did you know that?"

"James did say something of the sort."

"And that my children could quite easily have the empty bedrooms on the third floor."

Richard nodded. "I had thought of that," he said. "But it's entirely up to you. I couldn't possibly impose this house and all its problems on you."

"Oh, but you wouldn't be." Virginia was smiling now. She was a very pretty woman and clearly not as obstinate as he had thought. He was a lucky man to have her.

"Then we'll stay," he said. "I'm sure that Hudson, at any rate, will be delighted."

"And so am I," said James.

"And I'm absolutely thrilled," Georgina said, smiling mysteriously. As Richard looked across at her he realised that possibly Virginia had met her match.

❧ ❧

And so a new lease of life began at Eaton Place. Richard and Virginia spent their bridal night at the Hyde Park Hotel, leaving next day to honeymoon at Monte Carlo for a surprisingly warm winter fortnight in the sun. They gambled moderately, made love carefully, ate judiciously, and were extremely happy. But it was not until they had been comfortably installed in Eaton Place for several months that Richard's good fortune in his choice of a bride was truly evident.

Perhaps it is unfair to compare her with Hazel as the mistress of the house. Hazel had been unhappy and for much of the time she had had to cope with the miserable conditions of the war. Virginia had nothing similar to worry her, and from the start she brought enormous energy and drive to the running of the house. Several of the servants wondered what had hit them.

Rooms were repainted, accounts were double-checked, several long-standing tradesmen were abruptly changed. Mrs. Bridges had several famous battles with her—and generally lost. (Virginia made it plain that she was not putting up with Mrs. Bridges' well-known habit of agreeing on a menu in the morning and then calmly producing something very different when it came to dinner. Mrs. Bridges, in reply, secretly complained that Lady Bellamy didn't know a tenth as much as Lady Marjorie when it came to the serious facts of *haute cuisine*.)

There was some truth in this, but Virginia's greatest gift was for creating order, and it was this that 165 responded to. So did its inmates, and it was thanks to her that those early years of peace seemed to roll by as effortlessly as they did. She was a tactful woman too, and generally managed to keep a truce among the temperamental members of the family.

Before long Richard was depending on her absolutely. She organised his day for him, helped him with his mail, made sure he had sufficient quiet for his writing, and was a capable if not a scintillating hostess. It was thanks to her that Richard finally achieved a measure of financial independence too, for she was shrewd enough to see that a title was a valuable commodity and it was at her imagination that he became associated with half a dozen prosperous and very respectable companies. Within a year of marrying, Richard was a director of a merchant bank, an insurance company, a construction firm, a wholesale wine company, and a firm that made ball bearings. He was also, on Virginia's advice, a member of the British War Graves Commission, a sombre but prestigious post which involved them both in trips to northern France and in helping to make sure that a million Allied dead were decently buried by a grateful nation. They made these trips together and invariably combined them with a few days in Paris. Virginia was beginning to enjoy good food.

Surprisingly James relied upon Virginia as well. He liked her common sense and liked to call her his mother confessor. She was the only one who could get him out of what were known in the house as "the Major's Black Days," when he was gripped by hideous depression and retired to his bedroom with a whisky bottle. She used to go and drink with him—James said she had the strongest head of any woman he had known—and simply make him talk. He would describe his nightmares and what happened to him in the war. During these bouts he would swing between helpless rage and utter hopelessness.

"What's the use of anything?" he'd shout. "We fought the filthy war and already they're talking of another. Look at the politicians too —war profiteers and criminals, the lot of them! It's a disgusting, filthy world."

"Don't be so damned self-pitying," she'd say. "You might be dead."

"I wish I was," he'd moan. "I often wish I was."

But somehow Virginia seemed to have the knack of helping him recover. Sometimes she'd nag him, sometimes she would simply make him laugh at himself. And certainly it was thanks to her that he took up his job at Jardines again.

"But I hate it," he would say to her. "I hate the beastly City. It's the one place in the world where they succeed in making even money boring."

"Well, you're pretty boring too," she'd say, "so obviously you're suited." He'd scowl at her, but off he'd go—and in fact he did pick up the directorship that had been promised him before the war, although he dodged the chance of going off to India.

Sometimes they'd discuss his women. Like a true mother confessor she was virtually unshockable, and James began to tell her everything:

the girls he slept with and the girls he didn't, those who were married and those who were sufficiently ambitious to want to marry him.

"Well, why don't you?" Virginia asked after he described, with lurid detail, the way some young American tobacco heiress had actually proposed to him.

"What, marry? *Her?* You must be joking, my dear Virginia. I'll never marry anyone."

"But why on earth not, James?" she said. "I've done it twice and really recommend it."

"And I've done it once and it was not a great success."

"The second one is often better than the first."

"Not in my case. The war really did for me, you know. It would be cruelty to inflict myself on any woman now. I realised that after Hazel died. No, stepmother mine, I've found my rut and I propose to stick in it. I love this house. I'm grateful for the way that you and Father humanise the place and I'm not taking any risks. I just intend to go on as a crusty, self-indulgent, increasingly drunken old bachelor—then, like a genuine old soldier, I hope I'll fade away."

"And wouldn't you like to have a son to leave this place to then?"

"A son? Good God, no. He'd probably be like me, or worse. If I'd inherited Southwold I'd agree with you, but I didn't. And all that business of great families and dynasties has had its day. No, if there's anything of all this left when I go, your William can have it. That's if he wants it."

James's hints that he might leave 165 to Virginia's son were nearer to the truth than anyone suspected. Now that he had virtually abandoned any thought of starting his own family, he seemed to be adopting Virginia's two children. He spoiled them, indulged them, showed them conjuring tricks and made them laugh. Part legendary elder brother and part wealthy uncle, he was, in fact, far closer to them both than Richard was. Richard did make strenuous attempts to be friends with them, and to some extent succeeded. They both liked him and obeyed him, but secretly found him most formidable—and very, very old. James, on the other hand, was always at his best with them, showing no sign of misery or gloom. When they came home from boarding school he was the one who always took them out to an enormous tea, then on to the theatre. He would take them off on great excursions in his car (a very rakish Alvis tourer). And when the time came it was James who almost automatically paid William's fees at Eton.

Georgina, on the other hand, was far less involved in the family now. Indeed, she used to worry Richard with her apparent wildness and irresponsibility.

"Unmarried girls are all the same," he'd moan to Virginia. "Deceitful, silly young hussies. Why can't she find herself a husband and just settle down to a decent useful life? The way she's going on, she'll soon be nothing more than a loose woman!"

"Oh, come now, Richard," Virginia would reply, smiling at him in her most indulgent way. "She's not as bad as that. From what you tell me, your Elizabeth was fairly wild at her age and now she's a pillar of respectable New York society."

"Don't compare her to Elizabeth, Virginia! I forbid it. And anyhow, she had ideals. She wasn't like this present empty-headed lot of, of—" He spluttered for the word. "Of footloose pleasure seekers."

"Now, now," she said. "I'm not a public meeting, and you must realise that times have changed from when Elizabeth was growing up. Frankly, I don't blame Georgina for being a pleasure seeker, for a while at least. She lost four good years of youth in the war and she saw the most dreadful horrors in that hospital of hers. If I were in her place I'm not certain that I wouldn't do the same."

"Virginia!" said Richard, quite aghast.

Georgina's situation was more complicated than either Richard or Virginia suspected. She had grown up in love with James. Throughout the war her love had deepened and she had remained faithful to him even when she tried to rouse his jealousy with other bright young officers. For at heart Georgina was a very serious and passionate young lady.

Perhaps it was because of this that Hazel's death affected her so cruelly. She realised how much a year or so later when James took her to a dance and tried to kiss her. Suddenly she was horribly aware of Hazel's presence and all the ancient guilt came flooding back.

"No, Jumbo, no!" she said, and tried as sensibly as possible to prevent the moment from going any further. But James was amorous and slightly drunk, as usual by this time of evening, and he persisted.

"Georgina darling, my little Georgina. Let's enjoy ourselves. You always used to like me kissing you, Georgina. Why not now?"

She had to struggle to release herself, and in her anger said far more than she intended.

"Can't you see that it's obscene?" she blurted.

James stood as if she'd struck him, then slowly backed away.

"Obscene," he muttered to himself. "Yes, I suppose she's right. I am obscene. Trust Georgina for telling me."

After that night his drunkenness got worse, and it was then that Georgina became a "footloose pleasure seeker" in earnest.

Despite Virginia's firm discouragement, politics still involved the family from time to time. With Richard this was probably inevitable. A gregarious man, he knew everybody at Westminster. The world of smoking rooms and government committees was the only outside life he knew well, and he made certain that his new directorships and City interests didn't impinge on it. Balfour remained his closest friend within the party hierarchy. He never did like Bonar Law, although he felt genuinely sorry for the man when cancer of the throat abruptly ended his parliamentary career in 1923. And when this brought up the question of the leadership, he naturally sided with the new man, Baldwin, rather than Lord Curzon. This was partly instinct. He felt that Baldwin was, as he put it to Virginia, "my sort of man." He liked his unpretentiousness, his middle-classness, and his solidity. Also, although he would not have admitted this to anyone, the aristocratic Curzon reminded him unhappily of old Lord Southwold.

As usual, too, Richard's instincts seemed to coincide with his self-interest. His feeling for Baldwin was reciprocated, and it was through him that in 1924 a surprised and utterly delighted Richard Bellamy received a final prize he'd hardly dreamt of. Although he was in the Lords he was appointed Undersecretary at the Foreign Office, with responsibility for the League of Nations.

"It looks as if I've come full circle," he said jokingly to Balfour. "I started as a diplomat, and now it looks as though I'm ending up as one again."

"Well, you see," said Balfour wisely, "it takes some people quite a while to realise the promise of their youth."

The post was perfect for Richard. He was enough of an idealist to believe enthusiastically in this first attempt to achieve cooperation between all the nations of the world, and enough of a cosmopolitan to enjoy his time in Geneva. Virginia was invariably there with him and he would often take the Rolls. During those carefree summers of the twenties they got to know the Riviera and especially the Italian lake country extremely well.

Richard's political success, although admittedly late in life, served in a cruel way to underline James's political failure. It was a great mistake for him to stand for Parliament as he did, especially in a working-class constituency like Barking. And it was still more of a mistake for him to have worn his ideals quite so firmly on his sleeve. But he did feel most strongly that the ex-servicemen he knew were getting extremely shabby treatment from a government that should have known better. The mistake, as Richard tried to tell him at the time, was in thinking that this honest anger would unite a working-class electorate behind him.

James, of course, knew best. He always did when it came to self-destruction. Richard had several rows with him when he attempted to "talk sense" to him. "Don't you understand?" he said. "The working men in Barking must inevitably see you as just one more smart young Tory officer who'll promise them the moon and then do nothing."

"But I *will* do something. If I promise them houses and employment and a decent pension, I'll make sure they get it."

"Why should they believe you?"

"Who else do they believe?"

"And why are you so sure that you'll be able to do what you say? Many other men have tried and not succeeded."

James turned on his father then. "Father, if every politician is as cynical as you, I can understand exactly why this country acts the way it does. If everybody says it's hopeless, we'll get nowhere."

Richard broke off the argument, knowing already just how badly James would be defeated—and even worse, how he would take it. And as usual with his son, Richard was right. When Barking, as expected, sent a Labour man to Westminster, it drove another nail in the coffin that contained James's dwindling reserves of hope and courage and self-confidence.

It was Virginia who understood James best. Even Richard was increasingly inclined to take him, as the world did, at his surface valuation. He now seemed to be, as someone called him, "a middle-aged young bounder on the make," elegant, well dressed and highly enviable. The Alvis had been exchanged for a Lagonda. His shares did well. He tended to be seen in the smartest places with the smartest divorcées. He gambled quite a lot and drank a great deal more. But he had one thing that apparently redeemed him—style. He was a stylish drunk, a stylish businessman, a stylish lover. It seemed to be the thing that mattered.

He no longer confided in Georgina, nor did he see much of her. He had even begun to disapprove of her. She was becoming just a little too outrageous for his taste. "Outrageous men are bearable," he'd say. "Outrageous girls are not." When some poor would-be lover shot himself for her during a party held at Eaton Place, the scandal appeared to prove his point.

"Georgina's being talked about too much. You must do something, Father. Scrapes of this sort are bad for a girl's reputation."

Richard agreed but shrugged his shoulders. Then a few months later there was another scrape. Georgina was involved in the notorious accident in which a Sussex farm hand was knocked off his bicycle and killed by Richard's Rolls.

"For God's sake, Father, think of the family! Think of the damage that this sort of thing causes your name. Put your foot down, Father!"

Once again Richard replied that he agreed, and once again he shrugged his shoulders.

James meanwhile was, as he admitted to Virginia in one of his "confession sessions," "just dabbling with life." Others envied him but he was bored. His brief flirtation with the Fascist Party failed to convince him that they were any more sincere than any of the other politicians that he so despised. His love affairs were tedious. Even his enthusiasm for flying was short-lived. He bought a little biplane, learned to fly, and then found there was nowhere in particular he wished to fly to.

He was complaining about his health these days, too. He felt increasingly lethargic, out of breath, depressed.

"What on earth *is* it, Virginia?" he asked. "You and father are obviously happy. Why can't I be the same? I'm not so very different, am I?"

"Perhaps you expect too much," she said.

"Too much. Good God, I don't want anything. That's half the trouble."

"Perhaps you ought to have a change," she said.

It seemed to work. New York in 1928 was such a thriving, thrusting, life-enhancing place that even James's jaded taste-buds were restored. Elizabeth helped a lot as well. Although it was so long since he had seen her, nothing had really changed. She was the same Elizabeth that he had teased in the nursery and chased across the roof at Southwold.

"James, my precious James," she said. "What an extraordinarily presentable English gentleman you seem to have become."

She was extremely self-assured. Lucy was now a pretty teen-age girl, uncannily like Marjorie as a child, and there were two other children too—Richard, aged ten, and seven-year-old Marjorie Elizabeth.

"It's just like coming home," said James. And home it was for him throughout the months he spent in New York. The apartment was enormous, and Dana Wallace would not hear of James's living anywhere but there. Wallace was a hearty, healthy, solidly successful man now in his middle forties. Since the war, he had moved from his law firm into a firm of Wall Street brokers, and had already made a killing. Shares were booming, life was very, very good.

"Why don't you stay out here and make your fortune?" he asked James.

"Perhaps I might at that," said James.

And so he did. Helped by his brother-in-law he transferred his capital from London to New York, and then invested heavily in railroads and steel-mills, commodities and utilities, chemical firms and shipyards.

"America is working for you now," said Dana Wallace. "You can't go wrong."

But for James there was far more to America than a fortune—important though that was. It spelled a brand-new view of life, an end to the worn-out philosophies of Europe, a chance to start again. He even felt that he had roots here, thanks to Elizabeth and to a long-legged blonde called Regine Dollamore. Her father was a banker. She was twenty-two. For the first time in what seemed like a century to him, James fell in love.

It was a very brief affair, but perfect in its way. Regine seemed quite unlike any other girl he'd known. She was straightforward, clever, and had violet eyes. They spent part of that autumn in Vermont. When he told her he was going back to England, he promised he'd be back and marry her. And so he would have done.

That spring in England everyone saw the change in him and was delighted.

"Well, Virginia," he said on his first night back in Eaton Place, "you were quite right as usual. America has done the trick."

"It certainly would seem so by the look of you," she said. "You look ten years younger. I was getting just a little worried for you, James."

He kissed her lightly on the cheek. "Well, there was no need, was there, dearest stepmother. The prodigal is back, and younger and much richer than he's ever been before. How's Father?"

"Wonderful. Still caught up with his old League of Nations, but it suits him. He's thrilled about Georgina, as we all are."

"Georgina? What's happened to Georgina?"

"Didn't you get our letter? She's engaged. To a duke's son, too. Young Robert Stockbridge, such a nice uncomplicated fellow."

"Good Lord alive! Not Bobby? He's all right, but our Georgina's going to meet her match with her future ma-in-law. The Duchess is a Tartar."

"We know that, but Georgina's quite a strong-willed girl—as you may remember. The Duchess may have met *her* match."

For Richard, that evening of his son's return was one of the happiest he remembered. James was so full of life and confidence. His stories of Elizabeth and of the girl he had met, his sheer excitement about New York, seemed to have cured him for good of all the gloom and bitterness he had carried since the war. Only one thing worried Richard as he spoke to him that night. Money.

"From the way you talk, James, you'd think you'd just discovered it," he said.

"Well, Father, in a way I have. Until you actually see Wall Street for yourself you've no idea of the power of money. Why, if you're smart you can make your fortune almost overnight. It's not like the City. It's exciting. You must get Dana Wallace to invest for you. It would suit you to be a genuine capitalist after all these years."

"No thanks, my boy. I'm quite all right. But one thing puzzles me, you know. With all this money being made, doesn't anybody ever lose?"

"Lose, Father? Why, of course not. That's impossible."

"Why?" Richard asked.

Other people were asking Richard's question—and becoming more and more unhappy with the answer. As the disquiet spread, the market melted like a bowl of jelly on a summer's day. And as the market melted, so did James's happiness. It was as simple and as cruel as that.

There was a lot of drama, naturally—especially in New York—but when the great Wall Street crash hit Eaton Place it did its damage with a sort of studied calm. It was all very English, very stoical, but no less painful for that.

James seemed to take it very well. His training on the Western Front, those dreadful losses he had witnessed with his men, must have accustomed him to the reality of losing. Also he was a gentleman—and gentlemen don't get worked up when their world collapses. All he said that morning when he heard the first news of the Wall Street slide was, "Dashed rum!" And as the day went by and it was made increasingly clear to him that he'd lost everything, he was still very calm.

He was apologetic to Georgina. He had been promising her a splendid wedding, one that would put the Duchess in her place. Now it seemed quite impossible, but she was not to worry. Something would turn up. Father would find a way. He always did.

The only point at which James appeared to falter was when Rose came to ask about her savings, which he had just invested for her. He was sorry, but they had gone as well. Rose said she was sorry too (although the loss spelled out the end of all her dreams of a house, an end to drudgery, a secure old age. She too was very English and a perfect lady.

Richard was the only one who failed to observe the niceties of the occasion, and then he only did it on poor Rose's account.

"How could you have stooped so low as to take money from a servant to invest?" he stormed at James. "Aren't you ashamed? Don't you feel degraded to have robbed the poor girl who trusted you?"

It was no reply for James to say that Rose had begged him to invest the money, that he had acted in good faith, that had the market held, Rose would have been extremely rich. James had broken an accepted code. He had to pay the penalty.

⁂

For the rest of his life Richard reproached himself for speaking as he had to James, but as Virginia kept telling him, it really made no difference. From the moment Wall Street crashed, James, being James, was finished. He had no chance of getting back to the good life in New York. He had no hope of ever seeing his long-legged blonde with violet eyes again. He had no possibility of surviving in a bleak, cold world without those pleasant things that make it bearable.

Money had made him what he was. Lack of it now destroyed him.

So, in a way, it hardly mattered how his end reached him, and as Virginia kept saying afterwards, Richard's words could have played no part in making him take his gun and drive to Henley on that spring afternoon. And when he booked into the hotel, lay on the bed and shot himself, he was just doing what he had seen so many times before in France. He knew what he was up to.

What made it easier for Richard to bear was that he too had really acted like a gentleman. His outburst—such as it was—had been on behalf of Rose, a servant. He had refrained, most scrupulously refrained, from reproaching James in any way for what he had done to them all. For by gambling and going broke, James had effectively banished the Bellamys from Eaton Place for good. It had been Southwold money which had brought them there and kept them there. Now it was gone—and they would go as well.

Georgina had her wedding. Virginia paid for that. And Richard had sufficient income now to live quite comfortably in Wiltshire. He was even able to help Angus Hudson and Mrs. Bridges open their boarding house when they married and went to live in Broadstairs. Rose went with the Bellamys to Wiltshire, where they found a small Queen Anne house with an orchard and a view of rolling country. It was not far from Southwold.